Lissie

Tangled Hearts

Jennifer Lee

Self-Published

Lissie

Eliza Montgomery and Jonathan Stanton have unexpectedly found themselves alone in the world. Getting married seems like a smart business decision, but can they find love? Or will flames from the past steal their hearts away? And what if one of those flames has a darkly burning obsession?

Chapter 1

Eliza looked in the mirror, barely recognizing the pale face reflected back at her. Her dark hair was the same, gently curled around a pale, smooth forehead. Dark brows arched gracefully over eyes that were slightly glassy, round, but underlined with faint shadows. Her normally rosy cheeks were pale, bordering on ashen, and her delicate jaw seemed to stand a little firmer in her face. She forced a smile and pinched her cheeks, hoping to bring some color to her face before it was time. She pinned her mother's brooch at her neck, her fingers remaining on it for a moment. She sighed, but was thankfully interrupted from her musings by a knock at the door. She rose and answered it herself, her low heels silently crossing the plush carpet of the guest room.

The door opened to reveal her godfather, looking dashing in a morning coat. "You look lovely, my dear," he said, taking her elbow and leaning forward to brush a kiss across her cheek. "Are you nervous?"

"Not really," Eliza replied, stepping aside to allow him to enter the room.

Brandon St. John was a tall man, his sandy blond hair touched with gray at the temples. His strong cheekbones and natural smile made him look perpetually happy, and his gray eyes were calm still pools that flashed with keen intelligence. He turned those eyes onto his goddaughter, looking her over with concern.

"You're the image of your mother," he said. The words threatened to bring tears to Eliza's eyes, making her turn toward the window, overlooking the garden below. "I hope with all my heart that you two will find happiness together. You both deserve it. I know your mother isn't here, and you don't have a mother-in-law to fuss after you, so you'll have to settle for me. I'm not so bad, though, hm? And I've brought you something." She could hear the smile in his voice.

Eliza turned back as Brandon brought forward a small wreath of orange blossoms. He stepped forward and settled it gently in her hair. Choking back tears, she took his hand in hers, squeezing it. "You've always been there for me, godfather. I can't thank you enough."

Returning the squeeze, Brandon winked at her. "After today, you'll have to call me 'Uncle'!" he exclaimed with some mild delight.

"Of course...Uncle," Eliza still seemed somewhat hesitant. So many things were changing this day.

"You know that you can always count on me, my dear. I've tried to do what's best for you, and I always will. Your father was one of my dearest friends."

"I know. He loved you so much. I do, as well."

"And I love you as though you were my own. Are you ready?"

"Yes." Eliza took a deep breath, taking his arm as they exited the room together.

Descending the staircase, the doors to the parlor were open. Eliza's mauve silk gown rustled slightly on the stairs, and she could hear feet shuffling in the parlor. The gathered assembly was small. The Methodist minister stood at the end of the room. His wife and Brandon's close friend, Mr. Michael Crowley stood off to the side while the groom, Jonathan Stanton, stood next to the minister looking rather nonplussed. Brandon escorted Eliza to her place, next to Jonathan and in front of the minister, and took a step back to stand next to Michael.

The ceremony was short, but sweet, and at the end of it Eliza Ann Montgomery had officially become Elizabeth Ann Stanton. The bride and the groom did not kiss. The only contact they had during the ceremony was the moment Jonathan placed the delicate gold band on Eliza's slim ring finger. After the fateful words, "man and wife," had been pronounced, there was a quiet round of clapping followed by hugs and smiles from those assembled. The couple was wished congratulations by all in attendance, before the entire company adjourned to the dining room for a late celebratory breakfast.

Jonathan and Eliza sat next to each other, as the couple of honor, but both were kept busy by their dining partners to the opposite sides, the minister's wife seated to Jonathan's left, and Mr. Crowley seated to Eliza's right. They heard snippets of each other's conversations throughout the meal. Jonathan studiously listened to Mrs. Rev. Hollister's gardening adventures, while Eliza was being entertained by Mr. Crowley's tales of his latest inventions. Mr. Crowley was a mechanical engineer, and was fascinated by the possibilities of steam engines. Thus, the newly married couple were introduced gently to the world, without much pomp and circumstance. There was a small bang, though, as Brandon ceremoniously opened a bottle of champagne to offer a toast.

"To the two people whom I love most in the world," he said, raising a glass with a smile, "There is happiness in the world just waiting for you both to find it. And you shall find it together." Glasses clinked around the table as the couple made tentative eye contact with each other. Happiness felt so very far away, for both of them. But they were separately determined to move forward with life as the minister had said, for better or for worse.

A portrait of Jonathan's parents hung on the wall opposite them, amid a small gallery of family portraits, and Eliza glanced up at it. Seeing the younger versions of Edmund and Margaret Stanton brought back memories of her childhood.

She had had a happy childhood, even if she had been a somewhat quiet and sedate child. Her parents, her godfather, and Jonathan's parents had been old friends. Jonathan's mother and her godfather were sister and brother. Edmund, Brandon, and Gregory Montgomery, Eliza's father, had all gone to school together, and been fast friends ever since. Summers often featured their families and other friends gathering for lazy afternoon picnics at the Stanton home, which was north of the city, in the country. The children played in the lush gardens while the adults sipped lemonade and enjoyed the shade of trees and umbrellas closer to the house.

In the evenings, after everyone had gathered together and enjoyed dinner, and the parents of the smallest children were saying their goodbyes, all the children would stay closer to the house, playing or talking quietly amongst themselves. The oldest girls would giggle behind their hands, eyeing the older boys, while the older boys would pretend not to notice, speaking amongst themselves of what they imagined to be manly things. The younger children played board games or giggled at their own silly jokes.

Those sunburnt summer weekends stopped suddenly when Eliza was just 9 years old. Jonathan was 14, and after the awfulness that occurred, he was sent away to boarding school.

She was brought out of her reverie by a light kick under the table. She brought her eyes down from the painting and met Brandon's gaze across the table. He winked at her and smiled before suggesting that the newlyweds might want to get home to enjoy some time alone together, as the meal had ended some time previously.

Eliza blushed, not sure how long she had been musing on the past. But no one else had seemed to notice, thankfully. The wedding had taken place at Brandon's uptown home, being a bright, welcoming place where everyone felt comfortable, and there were not too many reminders for anyone of the recent sorrow. Both Eliza and Jonathan had lost their fathers, a mere month apart from each other, the former to illness, the latter to an unfortunate hunting accident. So, while they would now return to the Stanton house to start their married life together, Brandon had thought that a slightly more neutral wedding location was in order. He truly did love both of them as his own children, so he wanted to do everything he possibly could for them.

In truth, he had wanted to give his goddaughter an elaborate wedding ceremony, with pomp and circumstance, surrounded by flowers and friends. But she had declined anything like that. Being in mourning still, even half mourning, she thought it would be inappropriate to have such a celebration. And, after all, it wasn't as though she and her betrothed were blissfully in love with each other. Marriage suited their needs, and while they didn't despise each other, they frankly just didn't know each other well. That made any more of a production seem farcical and insincere. Therefore, the wedding had been small, though as sweet as Brandon could make it.

More hugs and well wishes followed the couple into a carriage, as they set off toward their home. It wasn't as though they'd never spoken, and it's not that they hadn't agreed to this marriage. They both willingly stood in front of the minister and pledged before God to be together. The problem, at least in part, was that they were both still grieving their losses, and they didn't know how to share that grief with each other. So they sat in silence as they rode through the edges of the city into the countryside. Eliza busied herself studying the fields and houses they passed. This ride was still familiar to her, and she felt unexpected warmth rise in her heart, as happy memories rose in her mind.

While Eliza studied the surroundings, Jonathan took the opportunity to study his bride. Her petite nose was slightly turned up, and her chin in profile was strong, but graceful. The dark curls pinned at her temple were carefully contained, but the soft hair at the nape of her neck suggested a wildness to her locks, curling more wildly, untamed. His wife was beautiful, he thought. He mulled the word "wife" over in his brain. It was foreign, and unexpected. It brought a sense of dread into the pit of his stomach and he swallowed hard.

He had never considered getting married. More than that, he had vowed never to marry. Not after what he had lived through and witnessed as a young man. He didn't want a life that was so complicated, and yet here he was. He was at a bit of a loss.

"Elizabeth," he muttered. She turned her gentle brown eyes toward him.

"Yes?" Her voice was soft. Every part of her seemed delicate and gentle. It made her new husband feel panicked.

He hadn't intended to speak out loud, so he stumbled a little bit. "You have...I mean, that is to say, your things arrived yesterday evening." He paused and cleared his throat. "Your room is in the east wing of the house. It was my mother's favorite room in the whole estate, because of the view from the windows. They look down upon the gardens. I hope you are pleased with it. Of course, if anything is not to your satisfaction, Mrs. Davis will be happy to help you."

Eliza smiled sweetly. "I'm sure everything will be lovely, thank you."

He returned the smile, not knowing what else to say.

"I have some work to attend to once we arrive, so I'm afraid I'll be in my office all afternoon." His tone was somewhat rushed.

"I understand." In truth, Elizabeth didn't understand, entirely. She wasn't at all sure what to expect of her marriage, and she didn't have a good basis for understanding. Her parents had been content in marriage, rather than happy, and she thought that she would accept the same. But she found that the wedding had provided no clarity of feeling. There were too many unknowns for her to feel content. She strove for patience. Experience would lead to understanding. She just had to wait for experience to happen. If her husband had to occupy himself with work today, that was just as well. It would give her the opportunity to familiarize herself with her new home without bearing his scrutiny or judgment, if he were inclined toward either.

Jonathan had turned his face to the window, and Eliza took that as her own opportunity to study his profile. She had to admit to herself that he was a handsome man. But then, he had been a sought-after bachelor ever since his return from school two years ago. His sandy brown hair never seemed to fully behave, and his blue eyes were his mother's gift to him. If his beard weren't so neatly trimmed and kept, he would look both younger and more roguish. He had a pale scar on his cheek, just above the line of his beard, and she wondered idly where that had come from, but as he seemed disinclined toward conversation, she thought it better not to ask. As they neared the Stanton house, her hands grew clammy, and her nerves mounted. She had butterflies in her stomach that hadn't been there before the ceremony.

Chapter 2

Mrs. Davis must have heard the carriage approach, because she was outside to meet them. As the driver slowed, she stepped forward to greet the newlyweds. Always cheerful, Mrs. Davis had been a fixture of the house since Jonathan and Eliza had been children. "Mr. Stanton, Mrs. Stanton, congratulations to you both!" she beamed as the driver helped Eliza down, and Jonathan came around from his side.

"Elizabeth," Jonathan said somewhat stiffly, "Mrs. Davis is our housekeeper. She manages the house and if you need anything she'll be more than happy to help you."

Eliza couldn't help her mounting excitement at seeing a familiar face. "It's so nice to meet you," she said warmly. "Do you happen to remember me, or my family, from many years ago?"

"Of course, ma'am. You are the very image of your mother, God rest her." Naturally, Mrs. Davis, having been at the house for so long, had known Eliza's parents. The housekeeper had been there for every lawn party and bonfire, and she had made special treats for the children. She was ten years older, and a little grayer; the lines around her eyes and mouth were more deeply carved, but they revealed a life of many smiles. "Come inside, come inside! I'll show you to your room. You'll want to freshen up, after the drive."

The bustling older woman shepherded her charges into the house. Her motherly warmth stood in stark contrast to Jonathan's stiffness. Jonathan excused himself before retreating to his office. Mrs. Davis clucked to herself. "That man will work the morning of his own funeral, just wait and see. He works so hard, the poor man."

Eliza listened with one ear as she took in the foyer. It was just as she remembered it. Wide and light, with a chandelier hung from the ceiling. It was the center of the house, which opened like a flower around it. The two women ascended the stair, turning right where it branched halfway up. "Your room is this way, ma'am. It has the best view of the gardens. You can see all the way from the roses to the willow tree. Mr. Stanton thought you would appreciate it."

"That was very thoughtful of him," Eliza said, somewhat absently, as she studied the portraits and artwork in the wide hallway. The floor was dark wood with rugs that ran the length of the hall. The walls were creamy white, but paintings hung with a distinguished air throughout, punctuated here and there by a pedestal with a vase or bust, turning the corridor into an art gallery of sorts. Mrs. Davis opened the second door on the left, which led into a charming room with a four-poster bed in the middle of one wall. A vanity with a wash basin sat next to a chest of drawers straight ahead, and Eliza's trunk sat next to the small stool. A plush loveseat occupied the foot of the bed, and two small sets of shelves flanked a small fireplace with a wooden mantle on the opposite wall. The walls had yellow paper with a pale pink rose print, while the carpet was shades of mint, cream, and rose. There were lacy curtains framing an open window, and even from where she stood, Eliza could see the top of the willow tree through the window. The room was lovely, but the sight of the tree is what caused faint excitement to rise in her stomach. She didn't realize exactly how much happiness she had experienced here when she was younger, but feelings of warmth surrounded her.

The Stanton gardens were famed in the community, featuring walks that meandered through a more structured garden, which boasted roses and topiaries. Off to one side there lay more utilitarian spaces planted with fruits, vegetables, and herbs, but to the other side, under the picturesque

JENNIFER LEE

willow, a little bridge crossed a meandering brook into what felt like a secret, hidden garden, more wild, featuring large rocks and tall grasses, landscaped with a riot of wildflowers and heavily scented plants, meant to attract butterflies and birds. A picturesque gazebo sat in one corner, and beyond it a true labyrinth garden lay, built with box hedges and featuring pockets of other plants throughout. A large, decorative fountain marked its center.

Eliza had fond memories of exploring those gardens with her friends, playing adventure games and princess games, tag and chase. Carefree childhood summers spent playing yard games on the lawn under their mothers' watchful eyes always ended with a bonfire at the start of fall, when school would start again, and nights would begin to get chilly. Jonathan was five years older than Eliza, so while they knew each other, they belonged to different circles of friends. The older children were allowed to go farther afield, into the bit of forest beyond the labyrinth, where wild blackberry brambles grew; there was a small lake there, as well. The smaller children had to stay within shouting distance of the adults, and the maze was the farthest they ever dared to go. She smiled as these sweet memories circled in her mind.

Mrs. Davis surveyed her new mistress with satisfaction, noting that the young lady seemed quite taken with the room. "I've unpacked your clothing into the closet and chest. I didn't know where you'd want to put your other things, which is why the trunk is still in here. There's a small desk in the parlor that Mrs. Margaret had, as well, which you may wish to have use of."

"Thank you, Mrs. Davis. I appreciate all that you've done."

"Of course. I shall leave you to settle in. Mary, our maid, will help you finish unpacking this afternoon. If you need anything at all, I'll be in the kitchen."

Eliza hesitated. "I'm not yet familiar with the house, Mrs. Davis. It's been so many years since I was here, and I never

10

ventured upstairs or to the kitchen as a child."

"Oh! Silly me, getting ahead of myself. Please, let me give you a tour. It's a large house. It would be easy to get lost or turned around in it, if you don't know your way."

"That would be lovely, thank you." Eliza was already feeling overwhelmed and homesick. While she remembered the public spaces of the Stanton house in broad strokes, she had never even had reason to see the second floor from the landing, and it was a large house. Larger than the townhouse she had grown up in, and while it was beautiful and elegant, it felt very foreign.

Exiting the bedroom, Mrs. Davis opened the door they had passed, on the same side. "This is simply a linen closet," she opened the door as she spoke, revealing neatly stacked sheets and blankets on shelves. "The rest of the rooms up here are bedrooms. You're welcome to explore them, but they haven't been in use for many years. Not since the master's parents entertained. The last door leads to the attic stairs. It's drafty up there, and cold in the wintertime. Mostly old furniture, clothes, and some old toys from Mr. Stanton's childhood. We can go up, if you'd like to see it?"

Eliza shook her head. Visiting a drafty attic wasn't an adventure she was up for today.

There was an interior balcony that connected the east and the west wings, that had a view of the foyer and the flight of stairs that led to the ground level. The two ladies crossed it to reach the west wing. Mrs. Davis became slightly more furtive, and she lowered her voice when she spoke, "This is Mr. Stanton's office," she said, gesturing to the first door on the left. Gesturing to the door opposite, "and this is his bedroom. He works long hours into the night; he doesn't care to be disturbed while he's working."

Moving further down the hall, she spoke more normally. Gesturing at the next door on the right, "This is another linen closet. This next room here has traditionally been used as a nursery." She opened the third door to reveal a large, pale blue room with shuttered windows, and sheets draped over furniture disguising most of it, but Eliza recognized a crib and a rocking chair, at least, among the shadowed forms. A simple white fireplace occupied one wall, somehow looking cold and drafty in spite of the warm April weather outside. There were sweet paintings of pastoral scenes and animals on the walls, and she could see how it could be a cheerful room, if light would be let into it.

Closing the door to the nursery and moving to the last door on the left, Mrs. Davis opened it to reveal a cheery sitting room, with berry colored damask wallpaper, a deep green carpet, and pale yellow wainscot. A bronze chandelier hung from the center of the room, and delicate little lamps sat on tables placed between a soft sofa and two wing chairs. A potbellied stove sat in one corner. The artwork hung on the walls was mostly pastoral, with a single portrait of a woman Eliza didn't recognize placed between the two windows, which seemed to overlook the front of the house. "This is lovely!" Eliza exclaimed. The windows of this room were open, letting the afternoon light pour in and bathe the room warmly.

"This was Mrs. Margaret's sitting room. Mr. Stanton doesn't use it, but I aired it out in case you might like to."

"Thank you." Eliza didn't know what else to say. There were several more disused bedrooms that sat at the farthest end of the west wing. One had been Jonathan's childhood room, after he grew out of the nursery. The others hadn't been used since the previous generation of children inhabited the house. This house was so large, she couldn't imagine any family big enough to use all its rooms. Watching as Mrs. Davis retreated and practically tiptoed past her new husband's office door, she wondered if she dared enter the west wing at all, even for the sake of the charming little sitting room.

Back downstairs, Mrs. Davis showed Eliza the kitchen, which was large and bright and clean, quickly showed her the location of the larder and staff quarters, and then led the way to the public rooms that Eliza was somewhat more familiar with. The library was large, with dark wood paneling and shelves stacked with more books than a single person could possibly read, Eliza thought. A grand fireplace with an ornate wooden mantle sat on one wall with a set of decorative irons next to it. There were several clusters of furniture, featuring deep chairs and loveseats, each perfect for reading or quiet conversation among sober people. The parlor sat next to the library, overlooking the front drive. It had mint walls and white wainscot, the wood floor gleaming with freshly polished wax. A densely patterned carpet took up the center of the floor, and genteel furniture was placed in congenial groupings. Spindle backed chairs and striped tufted sofas collided with crocheted doilies in a sweet riot of friendliness. True to what Mrs. Davis had said, a small writing desk sat to one side of a window, with stationery blazoned with a capital S all ready for correspondence to be written.

The dining room was very formal, the long walnut table laid with an ivory linen cloth, overlaid with a long and intricate lace runner. Fresh flowers were set at the center of the table with crystal candlesticks on either side. The room was long enough to require two chandeliers hanging over the table, and sconces were set into the wood paneled walls to provide additional light for evening meals. Old fashioned tapestries hung on either side of the fireplace that was set in the middle of the room. The high-backed wooden chairs had green velveteen seats, and the room exuded warmth in spite of the formality. It was quite different from the white, airy dining room they had eaten breakfast in this morning. This room would be suitable for a scene from a Shakespearean play, one of the darker or more solemn tragedies, Eliza thought to herself.

Beyond the dining room lay the drawing room. The wainscot there matched the dining room's paneling, but the plaster walls above were painted a warm gold. The green carpet with red and yellow patterns looked soft and rich, and this was perhaps the room that felt most familiar to Eliza. Looking around, she couldn't help but remember the last Christmas party she had attended here. There had been a decorated tree in the foyer, but there had been a larger, more elaborate tree here in the drawing room. All the children had gathered in this room, playing games here on this very carpet, while the adults sipped mulled wine and coffee, enjoying the holiday merriment. Eliza remembered the toys and music. She had even been allowed to play the big piano, as she had recently learned a Christmas song. Adult Eliza now turned her eyes toward that same piano. Without really thinking about it, she crossed to it and lifted the lid. She tried one key, but it was badly out of tune. She and Mrs. Davis both winced, the latter saying sadly, "Unfortunately, the piano hasn't been tuned in several years. Mr. Stanton never had a love of learning it." Eliza lowered the lid gingerly and stepped away from the instrument with deep disappointment.

The drawing room opened directly into the garden, just to one side of the rose garden, and from the door, you could see the little bridge under the willow tree, away across the lawn. Mrs. Davis opened the door and gestured as she said, "Surely you remember the gardens."

"Of course! They're still so beautiful. Like Eden." Eliza stepped out onto the back terrace, a semi-circle of brick floor that extended away from the house, toward the rose garden. The kitchen garden was on the other side of the house, closer, naturally, to the kitchen, with its own door directly into the larder.

"You've seen all of the main house, now. There is also a garden house behind the kitchen garden, and there are stables near the lake. And, of course, the carriage house."

Eliza was vaguely shocked. She hadn't realized that the property was so large. Stables? But she acknowledged that her previous associations with it had been in her childhood, and there was no reason for a child to know the extent of it. Knowing how much property there was, though, and being in this house alone, with just her quiet husband and Mrs. Davis, was suddenly a little overwhelming. Was there no other staff? Even her family had had a butler, as well as a maid, a cook, and a housekeeper.

She all of a sudden thought of those people and wondered where they were. Were they still at the house in the city? She hadn't sold it. She hadn't discussed it with Jonathan yet, but she couldn't fathom the thought of selling her childhood home. She had been adamant about it with her godfather, if not her husband, and surely Brandon would have conveyed it to him. And wouldn't it possibly be convenient to have a place in the city? The wedding had happened so quickly, and it had all been arranged by Brandon. Even having her clothes and personal things packed had been an orchestration of her godfather and her maid, Molly. Molly... Eliza's mind jerked to a halt. Where was Molly? Why wasn't she here, with Eliza? Was she still at the house in the city? Or had she been let go, and no one had told Eliza? She started to panic. She felt control of her life and surroundings slipping through her fingers, now that she was married, and she didn't enjoy the feeling at all. Mrs. Davis saw that the young woman was clearly overwhelmed and guided her to a chair.

"Are you unwell, ma'am? Can I get you some water? This is a big change for you, but it will be pleasant, I hope. It's nice and quiet here. Very peaceful," she patted Eliza's shoulder before leaving to get a glass of water. On her return, she encouraged Eliza to return to her room, take some time to rest, and change into a day dress, which may be more comfortable than the mauve silk, with its long sleeves and ruffled chemisette. Eliza sipped the water slowly before following Mrs. Davis back upstairs.

"Mrs. Davis, is there anyone else in the house, who lives here, I mean, besides us and Mr. Stanton?"

"Why yes, of course, Mr. Davis lives here, as well. He tends the gardens and looks after the house. We have small living quarters attached to the garden house. He would normally drive the carriage, but this morning he had a few errands to run, so Mr. Stanton hired the neighbor's driver. Mrs. Smith is the cook." Mrs. Davis checked people off on her fingers, as she spoke. "There's also our maid, Mary, who lives with her parents nearby. She comes most days of the week to help Mrs. Smith and me. It's a large house, and there used to be more staff, but so much of it is shut up, it really doesn't take that much effort to keep it in order. The gardens pose more of a task, and there are two young men who help tend it, under Mr. Davis's direction. It's springtime now, so Mr. Davis has hired an additional one of the local boys to help with the kitchen garden, but he'll only work for us through the early autumn. And Joshua takes care of the horses and the stables, but he has living quarters down there."

"I see," said Eliza. That made a bit more sense to her. She was still worried about her own staff, something she hadn't thought about before this late hour. She thought it best to send her godfather a letter, inquiring as to how he had arranged for her home to be left. She was flushed with embarrassment to not have asked after that earlier, but she had been so lost in grief these last few months, she hadn't thought about much at all. At nineteen, she wasn't new to the world, but she wasn't fully aware of how to manage a household on her own. Her godfather had seen to many of the details for her, in the wake of her mother's death, and then her father's. She would have to ask him what exact arrangements had been made. She considered that she might ask Jonathan, but she pushed that thought to the side. Her husband intimidated her.

Arriving back at her room, Mrs. Davis left her alone to change and rest.

She carefully removed the mauve silk taffeta gown. It was almost a light plum in color, and it rustled smoothly as she laid it on the bed. She removed her kid leather slippers and silk stockings and laid them out carefully. In her petticoat and stays, she sat down on the stool next to her trunk and took out her own stationary. Unable to relax without reaching out to her godfather, she quickly penned a note to him, inquiring about the townhouse and its caretakers. Satisfied with her missive, she changed into a pale blue poplin day dress and left the room to find the housekeeper, who was in the kitchen, peeling potatoes.

"You're looking refreshed, ma'am." Mrs. Davis smiled at her, pleased.

"Thank you, yes. I feel better. Could you possibly post a letter for me? I wish to send a note to my godfather."

"Of course. There's a basket on the table in the foyer. If you place it in there, I'll make sure that it goes out."

"Thank you. I think I might look at the books in the library."

"Of course, ma'am.".

Eliza softly retreated to the library where she felt she could safely tuck herself away with her thoughts for a bit. Instead of perusing the shelves, she curled up in a large chair near one of the few windows and allowed her mind to wander.

Chapter 3

This library wasn't terribly different from the library where that fateful conversation had happened. It was a scant two weeks previously, when her godfather had convinced her to attend a small dinner party with him, now that she was in half mourning. She was still grieving, but Brandon had been so persuasive, she had never been able to tell him no. He had also promised that immediately after dinner, she could go and hide in the library, if she needed to escape the crowded drawing room.

The party had been at the Forester residence and had been planned for a month as the party that would celebrate the eldest Forester daughter's return from Europe with her new husband. Brandon had misrepresented the gathering by calling it small. Everyone was there to see Olivia and Patrick, of course, but they all seemed to equally want to express their condolences to Eliza. Brandon had helped fend off their well-intentioned words, and safely ensconced Eliza among her friends. The ladies blessedly talked about the latest fashions, and who was getting married soon, and who the eligible bachelors were. Of course, a main topic of conversation was how lovely the newly formed Johnson family were. Olivia Johnson, née Forester, and Patrick Johnson were the center of everyone's attention, and the couple floated around the party like bees to flowers. Eliza had been able to tune most of it out without being rude. The gossip and giggling flowed around her as she sat feeling cold and alone.

Her parents had been such large forces in her life, and now, within the last year, they were both gone. She was devastated. Even though she had already cried an ocean of tears, if given the slightest opening, she was afraid her eyes would drown the whole room in which she sat. So she tried not to focus on anything too much. Her eyes fell on the piano that sat in the corner of the room and she focused on it as a neutral object. She loved the piano, and played very well, so she could think of music in her mind, and drive away the scarier, more lonely thoughts. Her fingers even moved slightly in her lap, playing Mozart as her mind drifted. Amy Dudley, a well-intentioned friend, noticed the direction of her stare, and grabbed her arm with encouragement. "Oh, Lissie! You should play something for us! You play so beautifully."

Eliza protested, but she caught her godfather's encouraging smile across the room, and so she sat, looking through the music that was set on the stand already. She found a song she knew well and began to play. Sections of the room quieted as she gained an audience, but she ignored the people, focusing instead on the keys and pedals of the beautiful instrument before her. She poured all her anguish and confusion and loss into the song, playing with a passion she rarely displayed in public. When she finished, she received a polite round of applause, as she sat there staring sightlessly at the sheet music. The friend who had encouraged her to play to begin with took her arm congenially and guided her back to the group of ladies. Amy was one of Eliza's closest and oldest friends and knew how much she was hurting inside. She was determined to watch out for her friend during this trying time. They sat next to each other on the settee while Amy kept hold of Eliza's hand.

"You play so beautifully, Lissie, I wish I had your dedication to it."

"Thank you, Amy." Eliza patted Amy's hand to let her know she wasn't quite on the verge of falling apart, and the two girls smiled at each other. The conversation around them had turned to hats.

At dinner, Eliza was seated next to Vincent, Amy's

older brother, whom Eliza considered to be like a brother to herself. He teased her and kept her engaged in light conversation throughout dinner, and she was grateful to him. He had only recently returned home from studying law at Queens College, and he entertained her with stories of the antics of his classmates. Of course, he would invariably paint himself as an innocent observer, and never a co-conspirator. After dinner, Eliza realized that she was actually smiling, and maybe coming out had been a good idea, after all. As the company retired to the drawing room for after dinner drinks, she began to feel tired. The endless grief had sapped her energy.

As promised, she was able to withdraw to the library which she found to be blessedly vacant, and she settled into a wingback chair near the fireplace with a book of poetry. And that was where it had all come about.

Upon reflection, she was shocked about the events that unfolded that evening, and also not so surprised, given her circumstances. With her mother having passed away, and no living female relatives, her possibilities for introductions were greatly reduced. Her friends' mothers had to look out for their own daughters' interests first, and so it was left to her godfather to be her guardian, caretaker and, apparently, matchmaker.

When they had arrived at the party earlier, after settling Eliza among her friends, Brandon St. John had taken himself off to visit with the assembled men. Just as he had convinced Eliza to attend the dinner party, he had equally persuaded his nephew, the son of his dear sister, to do the same. Jonathan's father had passed away in a hunting accident six months previously, a scant month before Eliza's own father succumbed to a fever. Jonathan had thrown himself into his father's work to escape the sadness and loneliness.

He had come home two years previously, having completed his college studies, to work for the family shipping company at his father's behest, so taking over entirely came somewhat naturally to the young man. For the last two years, he had worked diligently, and neither he nor his father were very active socially. Edmund had gone to a certain number of functions for business reasons, to talk to other men of industry, and to perhaps meet new investors, and he had encouraged Jonathan to go with him for the same reasons. Edmund learned rather quickly that the local mothers considered Jonathan to be quite a catch. The young man was handsome, smart, reserved, and a bit of a mystery, having been out of town for the last ten years, last having been known to anyone at the age of 14. Unlike the other boys who went away to school, Jonathan hadn't come home for summer. He spent a week with his father at Christmas, but other holidays and summers, he would visit a distant aunt who lived in Vermont, whose own son had left for the wide open west, to seek adventure, leaving his widowed mother in need of some help from time to time. Help he was able to provide. So, Jonathan was, to the local female population of New York, considered quite the catch, if a bit of a mystery.

Jonathan, having no interest in romantic entanglements, spent social evenings generally ensconced in male conversation, avidly avoiding any coquettish female gazes. And desperately trying to avoid mothers of daughters. After his father's unexpected death, he had the perfect excuse to eschew public engagements, and he was loath to attend this one. He was, himself, in half mourning, which he tried to use as reason to stay home, but Brandon had twisted his arm, mentioning that the Dudleys would be there, and Vince Dudley was newly graduated from law school, and hadn't Jonathan wanted to find a lawyer versed in contracts? The entire Dudley family were lawyers, and they specialized in contracts, and if Jonathan were looking for advice, he could do a lot worse. So he had agreed, and he was in the midst of discussing a particular contract issue with both the father and son when Eliza began to play. Vincent, catching sight of his angelic blonde sister standing next to her raven-haired friend who sat at the piano, caused him to pause and pay attention to the music.

The other men stopped talking to be polite, while the girl played. She played well, and with a bit more force than was typically on display at a dinner party. But Amy stood over her like a guardian angel, daring anyone to say anything bad about her friend. At least the girl was skillful. Jonathan noticed that she was pretty, as well. She had dark curls that were pinned close to her face, and her pale neck gracefully bent over the instrument. She looked vaguely familiar. But then, so did most everyone in the room. These were all people who had been part of his childhood, in one form or another. He supposed that this girl must be the daughter of one of his parents' former friends.

At dinner, he had been seated across the table and down a few seats from Vincent and Eliza. He found himself seated next to the fair Amy Dudley, who proved to be a delightful dinner conversationalist. She split her time equally between Jonathan and the gentleman to her right, a Mr. Downing. Amy was 19, the same age as Eliza, and what only her brother knew was that there was precisely one man she had an interest in flirting with, and it happened to be a former schoolmate of Vincent's. The brother had been facilitating the passing of correspondence between his sister and his chum for almost a year now. Jonathan was saved from any attempts at flirtation, and Mr. Downing was a little disappointed by the same.

It wasn't until after dinner drinks when his uncle had cornered him in the drawing room. "I hope you're having at least a little bit of fun. The duck was exceptional, didn't you think?"

"It was wonderful, Uncle."

"There's someone I'd like you to meet, Jonathan. Well, re-meet, I suppose. You knew each other as children."

Jonathan eyed his Uncle with skepticism.

"Trust me," said the older man, as he led the younger man into the library.

There, tucked away almost hidden from view, was the pale, dark haired young lady who had played the piano. She looked up as the two men entered the room and started to rise from the wingback chair.

"Elizabeth Montgomery, may I introduce my nephew, Jonathan Stanton. Jonathan, Elizabeth is my goddaughter, the daughter of some very good friends of your late parents."

Elizabeth offered her hand demurely, and Jonathan took it, performing a perfunctory bow. "It's a pleasure to meet you," she said.

"You as well," Jonathan spoke with a reserved air, slanting a sideways look at Brandon.

"You two may not remember this, but when you were very young, you played together at Jonathan's family home. Your parents were not only old friends, your fathers were business associates. Jonathan, surely you remember Gregory Montgomery."

"Yes, of course," he said, turning to Eliza. "I'm so sorry for your loss."

"Thank you. I'm sorry for yours, as well," she returned.

"Thank you." They were both as stiff as the oak trees standing outside the house.

In truth, she did remember him from childhood. He was handsome then, too, if more outgoing than he seemed to be as an adult. Though that would hold true for most children. He had been a natural leader among his peers, and all the smaller children looked up to him.

"Well, now that you're reintroduced, and I don't want to tire either of you with idle conversation, I must admit that I have a business proposition, of sorts, for both of you." Brandon sat on the sofa opposite Eliza's wingback chair and gestured for both of them to sit, as well. As they took their seats, he continued, "Eliza, I have been keeping an eye on your father's business up to this point, and I know you're not naive about it. But it really needs a proper manager to oversee the production and delivery schedules. Manufacturing is not my forte.

"And, you may be aware of this, your father and Jonathan's father worked rather closely together at times, since Edmund's shipping company serves as an excellent distribution point for your father's textiles, bringing them to England and France. I have an idea that I want to put to you both. I won't keep you in suspense: I propose you merge the two companies."

He paused to gauge their reactions, but he maintained a hopeful and positive expression. Eliza appeared to be considering the suggestion as rational, but Jonathan was rather agape. He wasn't sure how his uncle proposed merging the companies, but he was positive it was something he wasn't going to like.

Brandon continued, "Now, hear me out. We would need to hammer out the details, but Jonathan, you already do a great deal of scheduling. All you would need to do is coordinate with the foreman at the mill, and arrange the deliveries at the docks, really. Which is something you would do, anyway. Then distribution is handled, and the foreman and manager of the mill can focus on it running smoothly. You would just need to check in quarterly to make sure everything is working properly. Gregory had hired a new foreman when...well, last year. The man is more than competent, and practically runs the place."

"What would I do?" asked Eliza. "Are you suggesting I just sell my father's company?" That idea upset her. She had enjoyed bookkeeping with her father; he had taught her how to review ledgers and track the incoming and outgoing materials and products. She had been having biweekly meetings with the foreman for the last five months, stepping in with her father gone, and it had given her something to focus on in her grief, and the numbers had soothed her. She didn't know if her godfather was aware of her role in the business, and she was becoming increasingly distraught.

"No, no, my dear, not sell. I don't mean to say that you should sell it at all," he assured her, leaning forward to pat her hand.

"Then what are you suggesting, Uncle?" Jonathan's jaw was tensing slightly.

"Well, not to be indelicate. I love both of you, dearly, and I want the best for both of you. Jonathan, you are strong, intelligent, and a natural leader. Eliza, you have a gentle strength, and while you are as sweet as a dove, you don't let anyone push you around. I think that the two of you would make a strong couple. My suggestion is that you consider marriage."

It was Eliza's turn to be aghast. She had been so enveloped in grief that while a year ago, she had been tittering behind her hand with all the other young ladies, discussing the eligible young men in town, she hadn't thought of such things since her mother had died, and her father had leaned on her for so much. Her world had developed into such a fragile, crystalline structure, and it took all her strength of mind to keep it in daily balance. She was afraid that it might shatter at any moment. Marriage was anathema to that construct.

"Now, before you say anything, either of you, let me say this. Don't decide immediately. Think it over. Talk to each other. And if you decide against it, you won't have hurt my feelings. It's a big change, and a serious commitment. My honest opinion, knowing both of you, is that you would suit each other. But you will have to determine if that's really true for yourselves. If you'll both excuse me, I must step out a moment. I'll leave you two to discuss matters." With that, Brandon rose and left the room. Any mother would have been appalled at him leaving the two unmarried young people unchaperoned, but he knew his nephew well enough to know that Eliza's virtue was in no way being threatened, and this would be the fastest way for them to reach a conclusion.

Eliza and Jonathan stared at each other, dumbstruck, not particularly knowing what to say. Jonathan broke the silence first. "The duck was very good tonight, I thought."

Eliza laughed. A genuine, heartfelt laugh because he had startled her out of her reverie, and he smiled in return.

"Yes, I thought it was quite good. The dressing on the salad was also delightful."

"It was, though between you and me," he whispered conspiratorially, "I thought the pudding was a bit lackluster."

Eliza emitted a mock gasp, bringing her hand to her lips.

"You mustn't tell the hosts I said that, of course!" his voice dripped with mock seriousness.

"No, never, you have my word." Her solemnity was just as overwrought as his had been.

The two sat in slightly less tense silence for a moment. The temporary levity and absurdity had distracted them.

Eliza giggled slightly, but tried to cover it with a cough. Jonathan studied her with a newfound sense of ease. She really was quite pretty. A little timid. Graceful. Glancing at the book still held loosely in her hand he asked, "Do you like poetry?"

"I do," she nodded. "It lets my mind escape itself somewhat. Do you enjoy it?"

"My mother did," he said. "She had a few books that have become especially dear to me."

"Which books?"

"Wee, sleeket, cowran, tim'rous beastie; O, what a panic's in thy breastie! Thou need na start awa sae hasty; Wi' bickerin brattle! I wad be laith to rin an' chase thee; Wi' murd'ring pattle!" Jonathan recited with a Scots brogue and a devilish grin.

"Burns!" Eliza cried happily. "I love Robert Burns."

"*To a Mouse* was my favorite as a child. My mother also loved Milton and Shakespeare. I learned to read, partially, by reading sonnets."

"I know a bank where the wild thyme grows; Where oxlips and the nodding violet grows; Quite over-canopied with luscious woodbine; With sweet musk roses and with eglantine; There sleeps Titania, sometime of the night; Lulled in these flowers, with dances and delight," quoted Eliza. "My mother used to read me the plays as bedtime stories."

They smiled at each other conspiratorially.

Feeling somewhat emboldened, Eliza asked, "You're in the shipping industry?"

"Yes."

"Do you travel much?"

"Honestly, no. My father did, two or three times a year, and I'll need to, but I've only been on one trip to Europe with him. It was beautiful, though. Have you ever been?"

"No. Traveling sounds lovely, though. Father always wanted to be close to the mill, in case something went wrong, so we haven't traveled much. I mean...I haven't traveled much," she stammered in confusion over the phrasing.

"I see." The conversation lulled.

"You know," Eliza confessed, "I hadn't really thought of getting married, not since my mother passed away last year. It just all became so hectic, with father, and the business, getting married seems quite foreign."

Jonathan relaxed a bit as she spoke. "Since we're speaking candidly, I must confess that I hadn't particularly thought of marrying, myself. It's just not something I have an interest in. I wish I could express that to all of the mothers circling around out there," he wryly glanced toward the door, and the murmuring voices coming from the rest of the house.

"What might you expect from marriage, if you were to get married?" Jonathan ventured to ask.

Eliza considered a moment. "I'm not sure I know how to answer that. My parents had what you might call a marriage of convenience. Which, I suppose, is what my godfather is suggesting," she paused a moment in thought. "My parents were fond of each other. They got along well and didn't fight. They were straightforward with each other. I think," and here she paused again before continuing. "I think I could be content with a marriage like theirs."

Jonathan took a moment to digest. What she had described was so unlike his own parents' marriage. But it sounded safe, and simple. Uncomplicated.

. . .

And that had been the turning point, where they both started to consider what Brandon had suggested. Once they had decided, and told Brandon their decision, it didn't seem important to wait. Neither of them wanted to make a big fuss over getting married. Now it was done. What neither of them fully anticipated was that marriage was the start of something, not the end of it.

Chapter 4

Eliza sat in the library of the Stanton house now, contemplating that fateful decision and trying to deduce what changes awaited her in life. The shadows had grown long, and it was probably near time for dinner. She ascended to her room and changed into a conservative evening dress and descended the stairs. The clock was just striking 7, and she met Mrs. Davis in the foyer.

"I was just coming to fetch you. I meant to say that dinner is at 7, but you're already dressed and ready," she beamed, leading Eliza into the dining room. Only one place was set at the big table, and Eliza looked around, slightly confused.

"Where is Mr. Stanton?" she asked.

"Mr. Stanton is in the habit of eating dinner in his office," Mrs. Davis tsked quietly. She seated Eliza at the table and fetched the serving dishes.

Eliza sat and ate in silence, feeling uncomfortable in the large dining room by herself. At home, her father had also taken to eating in his office after her mother passed, and she had begun sharing meals in the kitchen with Molly and Mrs. Grayson, the housekeeper. She couldn't bear the loneliness of her own dining room, at home. This room didn't have the same emotional baggage, so it wasn't nearly as lonely in that sense. But the room was huge. She took the opportunity to study the artwork on the walls. At least the food was delicious, an opinion which she made sure to share with Mrs. Davis. The housekeeper simply smiled at her.

After dinner, Eliza retreated to the drawing room, but alone, she struggled to entertain herself. Mrs. Davis was busy in the kitchen and she didn't want to get in the way there. She sighed. Retreating to her room, she realized she hadn't finished unpacking. She took the few personal things out of her trunk and arranged them on the shelves and in the chest. Her mauve gown had disappeared, as had her stockings, and she assumed Mrs. Davis had taken them. She retrieved a sketchbook and a pencil and struggled with where to go. Back to the library? The drawing room? The sitting room in the west wing was tempting, but she felt awkward walking past her husband's suite. She wasn't quite prepared to run into him in the hallway, yet. She sighed deeply and sat on the loveseat in her own room. She opened the book and started sketching somewhat idly. A rabbit. A little stream with a fat duck floating in it. A tree...a willow tree. She realized that she was sketching the garden from memory. It dawned on her that she lived here, now. She could enjoy the gardens any time she wanted. Glancing outside, she saw a full moon beginning to rise, and on a whim, she slipped on a shawl and went downstairs. Before she could think twice about her choice, she was out the door of the drawing room and onto the terrace. She breathed deeply in and could smell honeysuckle and lilacs that were planted close to the house. She stepped somewhat gingerly at first, in the direction of the rose garden where the roses were silently waiting to bloom. The topiaries had been freshly trimmed, and she could see other flowers that had already bloomed. She stood next to the fountain in the center of the garden and wrapped her arms around herself, feeling surprisingly happy outside in the gardens. It was exhilarating. She wanted to explore further, but the moon only offered so much light, so she stood there, breathing in the fresh air and scent of flowers.

She was surprised to find how much better she felt outside. The big house had developed an oppressive air, making her feel small and uncertain. The gardens were massive, but they felt welcoming. The flowers were friendly, at the very least. She chided herself for that thought, because Mrs. Davis had been exceptionally friendly and welcoming to her. But the housekeeper obviously had her own schedule and manner of doing things, and it wasn't her job at all to entertain Eliza. She hadn't seen her husband since they had arrived, and she had to assume that he was still tucked away in that room upstairs. She sighed, wondering what exactly she had gotten herself into.

She didn't know that she was being observed. Jonathan stood at the window of his bedroom, which overlooked the rose garden, with the drapery twitched back. He had heard the movement of someone outside, footsteps crunching softly on the gravel, and he was surprised to see his little bride outside alone. He watched to see what she would do, but she seemed frozen next to the fountain, her face upturned to the night sky. She looked serene, though. He sighed to himself. What was he supposed to do with a wife?

Chapter 5

Jonathan's immediate solution to the predicament of having a wife was simply to avoid her. He had spent two weeks studiously avoiding Elizabeth, while she wandered the house and gardens, sketched in her book, and did who knows what else. He didn't know, and he had thoroughly convinced himself that he didn't care. They occasionally saw each other in passing, but they hadn't had a conversation more substantial than a vague greeting, and they hadn't coexisted in the same room for more than a minute in that time.

Eliza, for her part, was convinced that she was slowly going crazy. At least that's how she felt. She had no idea what she was supposed to be doing, so she wandered the house like a ghost. She had even tiptoed past Jonathan's office and into the sweet little sitting room, but she had felt like an intruder there, her presence a violation of a sacred space, and so she had quickly left. She was listless. She had half-filled her sketchbook and read four books from the library, and it was only her first fortnight in the house. Surely, she would be driven fully mad by the end of the month. She knew the thread count of the tapestries in the dining room, and she had made up names for all the people in the portraits throughout the home, if their names weren't already displayed. She had learned the names that existed, and she had begun greeting some of the portraits when she passed them. They didn't respond, but this was similar enough to the interactions she had with her husband, that it seemed socially acceptable. So, she talked to the portraits without fear of reprisal.

When she had agreed to this marriage, she hadn't originally assumed that she would have to move. She thought that she could be married for the sake of a business arrangement, and stay in her own home, in her own familiar surroundings. But her godfather had convinced her that that wasn't going to work. And that while she was making the decision to get married for practical reasons, that shouldn't stop her from pursuing a marriage that was more fulfilling. She had allowed herself to tentatively think about Jonathan as a potential spouse. Someone she would spend time with and come to know. She felt certain that she could like him; that she in fact already did like him based on their limited interactions thus far. She began to assume that that feeling would naturally grow. In the brief time between deciding to get married and actually getting married, she had come to consider that it had the potential to be a real relationship between two people, even if it had started somewhat abruptly.

She had never really had a relationship with a man before. She was so young; she had only just experienced her first flirtation the previous year. It wasn't that she didn't have friends, but she was naturally quiet and reserved. The few friendships she had, she treasured dearly, and cultivated carefully. But truthfully, her mother had been her greatest friend. The two of them spent so much time together. Under her mother's tutelage, she had learned to play piano and speak French; she had learned to knit, sew, and embroider. They had spent countless hours together reading aloud. She had been such a constant in Eliza's life, and losing her by itself would have broken Eliza's heart. The fact that she had fallen ill, and Eliza had nursed her for several months, watching her slowly fade away, was devastating to the young girl. The aching loneliness that had been left inside of her was impossible to fill. She had turned to her father, and he had pulled her into his own aching breast, and the two of them had grieved together. The romance her parents had was not one for the ages, but they had cared about each other deeply. They had developed a love that was gentle and patient, undemanding but certain.

Some people may have not even recognized it as love, and per-haps that was true for Eliza at times. But had they, in life, been asked the question, they would have happily admitted to the charge of loving one's spouse. His heart was broken, as well, and the sorrow had brought him closer to his daughter.

For her to then, shortly following her mother's death, also lose her father had left her feeling like a ship lost in a stormy sea without sails or a compass. If it hadn't been for her godfather and Molly, she might have wasted away to her own death. The maid had ensured she ate and bathed. Brandon had visited often, always offering love and encouragement. He was the one who had encouraged her to directly participate in the running of the mill. He had brought her books, and spent long hours easing her out of her sadness and into rational thought. He did the impossible--he gave her hope. Hope that she still had her whole life ahead of her, and that she could find happiness. He had been the guiding beacon that brought her battered ship into a safe harbor. As she sat contemplating all of this, she prayed for his guidance to continue.

Blessedly, fate was on her side, for the hour of eleven brought a visitor. When Eliza saw her godfather enter the parlor with Mrs. Davis, she promptly burst into tears. Bran-don and the housekeeper shared worried looks as they both rushed to her side.

"My dear, what's the matter? I thought you'd be happy to see me. Are you hurt?" Brandon looked her over but didn't see anything overtly wrong.

Through tears she struggled to say, "I'm just...just...so happy," she sobbed, "to see you."

"Should I get Mr. Stanton?" asked Mrs. Davis.

"No! No, I mean," Eliza said, holding out her hand to stop the woman, "I'm fine."

She gathered her composure around her like a warm blanket. "I'm fine, really. I'm just surprised. And happy to see my godfather. I'm fine."

Mrs. Davis hesitated. "Shall I get some tea?" she offered

hesitantly.

Eliza wiped her face delicately with the linen handkerchief Brandon handed her, "Yes, please, Mrs. Davis. Please, godfather, sit."

She smiled up at him, but she was somehow even more pale than usual, and he was instantly worried about her. "So," he began, "tell me the truth. Did I make a horrible mistake, thinking you two could be happy together?"

He braced to hear the worst, but Eliza seemed to not know how to answer the question.

"My dear, he…he hasn't hurt you, has he?"

"No."

"Has he been mean to you?"

"No."

"What has you so upset? You can tell me. I'll do anything in my power to help you."

"I," she faltered, "I'm lonely," she said with deep emphasis.

"Lonely?" Brandon was confused, and only slightly less worried. His tone was curious as he asked, "Where is Jonathan now?"

Eliza looked at her hands, twisting the handkerchief slightly. "I don't know," she said softly, looking up. "Mrs. Davis says that he works long hours, so I assume he's either in his office or in his bedroom. I haven't seen him for more than a passing moment since the morning of the wedding." Her voice rose in pitch and desperation as she spoke.

Brandon silently fumed to himself. "I see. So let's start over, shall we? I received your letter, and you had some questions about your family home?"

"Oh, yes!" Eliza recovered slightly and was grateful to talk about something other than her absent husband. "I know I said that I want to keep the house, but what about the people? Mrs. Grayson and Molly and Mr. Abraham?"

"Oh, that. Yes, of course. If I remember correctly, Mr. Abraham was already living with his daughter. He still visits the house several times a week to check on the property and make sure the ladies don't need anything. Mrs. Grayson and Molly are right there still, keeping everything clean and at the ready for the moment you feel like spending some time in the city." He smiled, hoping this would put her at ease some.

"Oh, good! Very good. I was worried. I should have asked more questions earlier, I just didn't think things all the way through," she said, trailing off a bit. She appreciated the truth of that statement. She internally chided herself for being thoughtless. "But, tell me, godfather, would it be possible, I mean, might it be that Molly could come here? Mrs. Davis is so busy with the house, and I don't like to bother her, and Molly...Molly is someone I can talk to." She trailed off, not really sure what else to say.

Brandon was beginning to appreciate the depth of his godchild's loneliness. "Of course, Molly can come here. I think she'd love to live in such a big house in the country. I believe Mrs. Grayson probably has a granddaughter, or niece, who can come keep her company and help around the townhouse. Consider it done, dear. I'll bring Molly here tomorrow morning myself, assuming she's willing. I'm sure she'll be delighted." He vowed to offer the girl a raise himself, if it made the difference in her coming or not. But he was fairly certain she truly would view it as an adventure. Working for the Stanton family, like working for the Montgomery family, was a less demanding proposition than one might expect from some of the other families in the same social class. Both clans had a more relaxed relationship with their staffs.

Eliza felt relieved. She served the tea that Mrs. Davis had brought in, and a few moments later, Brandon dared to ask a delicate question. "You are upset, dear girl. Talk to me, please. Tell me what has made you so distraught?"

"I suppose," she started slowly, "I didn't know what to expect. This house is so large, and I find it somewhat intimidating. It's just so very empty. It's like ghosts live here. It feels haunted by memories and things that used to be. And I'm like a ghost myself! I'm uncertain of where I belong, and what I should be doing. I don't have a purpose, godfather. So, I just try to stay out of everyone's way," she sighed deeply. "I just don't want to inconvenience anyone."

Her godfather grew distraught to hear this. "Eliza, you are strong, and brave. You're the lady of the house, and that means you belong here. You must see this as your home. I know that sounds daunting. You've only ever known one home until now, and this is very different. But I think you may find that it's not as different as you may think. And you can have adventures, and new experiences!" He paused to reflect. "You have to allow me to speak for my sister, for a moment. She and I were very close. I loved her so much. She would have loved you. She would have wanted to welcome you into this home with smiles and open arms, as a loving mother-in-law would," he grew misty-eyed thinking of his sister. "She was such a warm soul. She wanted everyone to be happy. That would have included you. She loved this house. She decorated so much of it. Her touch is in every room. That shouldn't intimidate you, my dear. On the contrary, my hope is that you can see this house the way I see it. Which is to say, it's an expression of Margaret's spirit, and love. Love isn't static. It's not a thing that exists in a solitary, isolated state. Love is an action. The love that exists in a place grows when people inhabit the space, use it, and pass their own love into it. And that's what you need to do here. Look at the house like a diary, or a family Bible. It has all the entries up until now stored inside, but it has room for so much future, as well. You're part of the future. It is both a responsibility and a privilege. Can you see that?"

Eliza sighed. "When you put it that way, it sounds lovely. And it does help me see things in a different light entirely. It is a lovely home."

"It is. It's perfectly fine if it takes some getting used to. Just don't be afraid of it. Or of anyone in it. You're possibly not the only one who's unsure of how things are supposed to work in this situation." She glanced up at him curiously. "You think your husband isn't allowed to be somewhat hesitant? This is new for both of you. You just need to give it some time. It will work out eventually," he said with confidence.

"But, godfather, we've barely spoken to each other. Giving it some time is one thing, but don't we need to at least speak? I do believe that in time, we will grow fond of each other, but that can't happen at all if we are never in the same vicinity." Rational thought dawned like the morning sun for Eliza, and she spoke more forcefully than she had in a very long time.

"That's quite true, yes. You need to stop hiding from each other. Both of you. I do realize that I may need to bring that to his attention, as well."

"Quite," was Eliza's pert response. He smirked at her, glad to see that she was apparently feeling better.

"Why don't you invite Amy Dudley for a visit," Brandon suggested, out of the blue. "You girls played so often in these gardens as children, I'm sure it would be a treat for both of you."

"Do you think that would be acceptable?" Eliza asked hesitantly.

"Lizzie, you're the lady of the house. You're more than right to invite company over. I'm here, aren't I?" Brandon responded.

"Yes, of course."

She was saved from her own awkwardness by the housekeeper. "Will Mr. St. John be joining you for lunch, madame?"

"Yes," Eliza answered quickly. Brandon smiled.

"Why don't we dine on the terrace?" he questioned. "The weather is simply divine today."

Eliza beamed at him. "That's a wonderful idea!"

"And," he added, addressing Mrs. Davis, "please make sure Mr. Stanton joins us, as well. I'm sure he will want to see his favorite uncle." Brandon's grin was almost predatory.

Eliza and the housekeeper both looked nervous. "Tell him I insist," said Brandon with an iron smile.

"Yes, sir," she said as she retreated from the room.

After she had left, Eliza spoke up. "I'm sure Mr. Stanton is very busy. I would be surprised if he joins us for lunch."

"*Mr. Stanton* is your husband, dear girl, and I think you should get an immediate start to spending more time together. Remember, don't be afraid. He won't bite you."

Eliza blushed.

"Anyway, the boy has never been able to tell me 'no.'" Brandon's look was devilish.

Shortly, they were seated at the iron table on the terrace, chatting about the gardens, when the door opened. As Jonathan approached the table, his uncle stood and extended his hand to the younger man.

"Uncle," Jonathan shook his hand, and gave a small bow to his wife. "Elizabeth. You're both looking well today."

Brandon snorted, "You're looking pale," he said baldly.

Jonathan flushed as the men took their seats.

"Eliza and I were discussing the gardens. The roses should be beautiful this year."

"Yes" The younger man glanced at the garden vaguely.

Lunch was served in relative silence. Brandon glanced between the two seated in front of him with increasing impatience. Eliza toyed with her fork, keeping her eyes steadily down. Jonathan, when he thought no one was looking, cast furtive glances at his wife.

Clearing his throat, Brandon broke the silence. "So, it's come to my attention that I made an error, when I arranged for Eliza's move here." Eliza held her breath as he said her name. Jonathan looked up, startled. "I should have arranged for her maid to move, as well. Molly. I will rectify that immediately."

"Oh. Yes, of course. If you think that's necessary," Jonathan replied.

"I do. You know there used to be three times the staff here. I don't know what your father was thinking, cutting back so much. I'm not suggesting you hire that many people immediately, but I think you'll find a growing need as you two go on."

Jonathan flushed uncomfortably. He knew that there used to be more staff, of course. After his mother's passing, and after he had been sent away, his father had had most of the house closed up and let go of most of the staff. It had seemed to function perfectly well in this manner, that Jonathan hadn't thought to question it until now.

"Moreover," Brandon continued, glancing sideways at his goddaughter, who appeared rather uncomfortable, and had been, to this point, utterly silent. "Ahem, moreover, I brought the ledgers from the mill with me, and if you have time after lunch, I'd like to go over them with you."

Eliza looked like she wanted to interject, but decided against it. Jonathan agreed to reviewing the information after the meal.

"Good! Good. You know," he smiled, "this terrace is where the two of you met for the first time."

They both gave him an alien look. "Yes!" he continued. "Eliza, do you know who first called you Lissie?"

Eliza looked puzzled, "Why, Amy, of course. She still calls me that," she smiled slightly.

"Ah, she wasn't the first, though. Your own husband is responsible." Brandon beamed while Jonathan flushed uncomfortably.

"Uncle..." he began.

"What? It's the truth. You were five, and Eliza here was an infant. Her parents came to visit to show off their precious daughter." He smiled conspiratorially at her. "Our boy here had a slight problem making the Z sound when he was younger, so he called you Lissie. Your mother was simply delighted by it!"

Eliza smiled and glanced at Jonathan from under thick lashes. He met her gaze and couldn't help but smile back through his embarrassment. She took pity on him, saying, "I'm sure your uncle could embarrass us both if he was determined to. I've done my share of silly things in front of him." She turned her warm smile to her godfather.

"What? I wasn't trying to embarrass anyone. I thought it was sweet. No, no, no. If I wanted to embarrass someone, I'd tell you what Eliza named her dolls when she was..."

"Godfather!" Eliza interrupted, her face flaming.

"What?"

Soon all three of them had dissolved in laughter. The talk turned to simpler, impersonal topics that were therefore dreadfully dull. The weather was lovely. The food was delicious, and the gardens were beautiful. Dull topics, but safe ones.

"I didn't realize how big the property was before this week," said Eliza as she set her fork down. "Stables and pastures, and what else?" she asked with some excitement.

"There are the woods, and the lake. There's a small hunting cabin deeper into the woods, as well," explained her husband.

"Well, it sounds as though you need to give your wife a tour!" Brandon exclaimed.

"That would be wonderful!" Eliza cried, but then felt the need to modulate her enthusiasm. "If you have the time, of course. I know you're very busy."

"Nonsense." Brandon waded into the conversation before his nephew could make excuses. "You two are newlyweds! Making time for each other is part of being married. Or so I'm told, at least."

Eliza reached out to cover his hand with her own with a small smile, but didn't say anything further.

"Well," said Jonathan abruptly, removing his napkin from his lap, the plates in front of them all empty. "Should we excuse ourselves to my office, uncle? To review those ledgers?"

"Yes, yes. Eliza, you'll excuse us dear, won't you?"

"If you're going to be reviewing the mill's documents, perhaps I should be there, as well. "After all, I helped father..."

Brandon extended his hand to his goddaughter and winked at her. "Let me get Jonathan up to speed on the basics, hm? And the two of you can discuss more thoroughly later?"

Seeing his real motivations hinted at, she agreed. She felt protective of her father's company, and she didn't like feeling left out, but she understood that Brandon wanted to have a private word with his nephew, as they had talked privately before lunch. She withdrew to the parlor and the men ascended the stairs to the west wing, after Brandon had retrieved a small stack of books from the foyer.

Once in the office, Brandon swiftly turned to his nephew and gave him a piercing stare. His tone was still patient as he asked, "Is it true that lunch today is the first you've seen of your wife since your wedding?"

"No, that's not true at all," Jonathan's tone was mildly petulant. "I've seen her since then."

Brandon paused. "Has she seen you?"

"Well...define what you mean by 'seen'."

"Is that really the conversation we're having?"

"No."

His uncle waited.

"We see each other in passing from time to time. And I've seen her through my window, in the gardens," the younger man said lamely.

"Jonathan."

"What am I supposed to do? We barely know each other."

"So GET to know each other! Have meals with her, at the very least. She's a charming young woman, but my dear boy, she's being driven quite mad with loneliness!"

"Loneliness?"

"Yes! I'm sure you've heard of it. She's used to being around more people. Everyone here is so busy all the time, and you're hiding from her, and she doesn't have anyone to talk to."

"Oh," Jonathan said lamely.

"That leads most people to feel lonely. That loneliness

can become maddening when a wife, for example, is so physically close to someone who is meant to be a companion in life, her husband, but she finds that he is so guarded against her that she's afraid of offending him with her presence."

"I see." Jonathan's posture was guarded.

"She won't bite you, you know." Brandon's voice softened.

"I know that," he responded peevishly.

"So why are you avoiding her?" There was genuine curiosity in the question, rather than the condemnation one might expect.

He started to deny the assertion, but stopped. "I don't know what to say to her."

Brandon sighed. "Just start with 'hello' and see where it takes you. But, and I mean this, if you want this marriage to work, and to be pleasant, the two of you must at least see each other once in a while. Have dinner together, at least. Regularly."

"Fine."

"Fine?"

"Yes! Fine, I'll have dinner with her. Starting tonight."

"Good. She's a kind and sweet person, Jonathan, and she's been through a lot. You both have. But you both deserve to be happy, as well. That is the greatest gift of marriage. You each get to be there to inspire the other to happiness, to be happy together. To do that, you actually have to be together. It's not a chore. If it is, I've made a horrible mistake."

"I understand, Uncle."

"Do you? I know you were young, but do you remember your parents' relationship? They were each other's world. I have never seen two people so deeply in love with each other. They should be your inspiration."

"I don't want to be like my parents," Jonathan's tone was savage. "Do you know how much father suffered when mother died? How much I suffered? He couldn't live without her, not properly. I don't want to be that dependent on another person, ever. I don't want someone to be that dependent on me."

"Oh, my boy. My dear, dear boy," Brandon was sympathetic, but only to a point. "That's nonsense."

The younger man sputtered. "What?"

"Nonsense. You heard me. Your parents had a love for the ages, and do you honestly think, if they could go back and start over again, knowing how it would all end, that they would do anything at all differently?"

Jonathan looked studiously at his feet. "No."

"No. Because what they had was worth more than gold. Great love is not always perfect. And I know your father reacted badly. I'm so, so sorry for that. But you cannot throw away your own chance at happiness with another person because it might go wrong at some future point. Gather ye rosebuds, and all that. Those aren't just pretty words. It's solid life advice. Let me be clear. I'm not at all suggesting that you try to mimic your parents' relationship. That isn't possible. You must forge your own marriage, in your own way. It just helps to not be afraid of it."

"Look who's talking, Uncle! You've never married."

"But I have loved!" Brandon spoke with passion, and pain.

His nephew looked at him with a glimmer of understanding and shameful regret. "I'm sorry, Uncle. I was out of line, saying that."

"It's not your fault, you have no way of knowing how difficult.... But trust me when I say from experience: not everyone has the opportunity to seek the happiness they desire. You do. There is no guarantee that you will find it with Eliza. But there is every guarantee that if you spend your whole life hiding in your office, you will find nothing." Tears sparkled, unshed, in Brandon's eyes as his voice grew hoarse.

"Eliza is a person, Jonathan. She has feelings, and thoughts and experiences that have molded her, just the way that you do. Besides that, she's a sweet girl who is willing to make sacrifices in her own life to make others' lives easier. She deserves so much. The absolute least you can do for her is have a conversation."

"I'll stop hiding," Jonathan said softly. "I'm not promising to fall in love with her. I don't know if I'm capable of that. But we can at least be friends."

Brandon beamed at this progress. "Friendship is a wonderful foundation for a marriage, or so I'm told. You two have all of the possibilities open before you."

Jonathan paused, seeking to scale back the emotion of the conversation. "So... earlier, you were saying something about what she named her dolls...?"

Brandon laughed, a rich belly laugh. "You'll have to ask your pretty wife that yourself."

Jonathan grimaced.

The pair spent the next two hours poring over the books from the mill. The time passed quickly, but the younger man still had questions when they were done.

"You'll need to talk to your wife, in all honesty. She really had taken over most of the regular coordination after her father passed, and she was helping him run things before he fell ill. She will be a great asset to you, as you work to take this on."

"I see."

"And on that note," Brandon glanced at his pocket watch, "I really should be going. Michael will be waiting for me."

"How is Michael doing these days?"

"Oh, very good, very good. He's been doting over his orchids. I'll have to bring him with me the next time I visit. He loves the gardens here."

"Yes, please do! He's always welcome, as are you."

"Thank you, Jonathan. Oh! Before I forget, there is one more thing you should do for your wife."

"What's that?" he asked with trepidation.

"Get your piano tuned! If I know you and your father, it

hasn't been touched for years." Brandon shook his head.

"Oh, yes. Yes, of course. I shall."

"Good, good. Come see me out."

With that, the two men descended the stairs to the foyer. Brandon stepped into the parlor where Eliza sat with some needlework. "I'm off, dear."

She rose and crossed to him, kissing his cheek affectionately. "Thank you so much for coming today."

"Of course, and I'll be back tomorrow with Molly," he said with a smile. She smiled back and they both had a sense that things were much better than they had been. He bid them both goodbye and was on his way.

Husband and wife were left somewhat unexpectedly alone in the foyer.

"So..." said he, "do I get to know the names of your dolls or not?"

Eliza looked up at him in surprise, to see him grinning down at her.

Her gaze turned mischievous as she replied, "Absolutely not."

"But shouldn't husbands know things about their wives?" He was teasing her, and she found it outrageous, but also exciting.

"Not things like that. But maybe," she teased in return, "maybe I'll tell you. One day."

She smiled up at him and he smiled back down at her in return. He took a step closer to her and reached for her hand. Curious, she gave it to him, watching closely to see what he might do. Butterflies stirred in her stomach.

He cleared his throat. "I owe you an apology," he began. "I have neglected you. You deserve better than that."

She didn't know how to respond to this. Tentatively, she murmured, "Thank you."

He gave her hand a small squeeze and then stepped away, just a step, breaking contact. "I'll join you for dinner tonight," he said, and without waiting for a response he turned and headed straight to his office.

Chapter 6

It was only four in the afternoon, so she retreated to the needlework she had abandoned in the parlor. Alone with her thoughts, she pondered the last few minutes. And lunch. She thought she may in fact like her husband's company. He could make her laugh. And he was nice to look at, she had to admit. And she had felt something when he had taken her hand and teased her: excitement.

She hadn't known entirely what to expect from marriage, but the first night in the house, she had waited in bed with some trepidation. She thought he might come. She didn't know if he would knock, or just enter, but in the end, she had fallen asleep and he hadn't come. Six more nights had passed the same way, and moreover, the days had passed, and they'd barely seen each other. Now, today, she had seen him, talked with him, laughed with him, and he had held her hand. He had teased her, which might have been a step toward flirtation? She wasn't at all sure. She was sure that they were going to have dinner together. She felt unexpectedly nervous. As dinner grew closer, her unease grew.

She changed for dinner, choosing a sapphire gown that made her skin seem to glow. Her dark hair was pinned up in a simple twisted braid, with small curls at her temples. She studied her face in the mirror. Her cheeks were a little flushed. She tried to calm herself. It was just dinner. She had disliked dinner in this house, previous evenings. The food was excellent. Mrs. Davis was a wonderful cook. But the large dining room was so empty. It was so large, and being alone there put a large emphasis on her quiet solitude. And Mrs. Davis refused to hear of her eating in the kitchen. Lunch on the terrace had been a novel experience, and one she intended to repeat. But dinner on the terrace seemed a bit too unorthodox. But tonight, the dining room would be less empty. It would be less lonely.

She considered the possibilities. So far, her place had been set at the foot of the table. Would Jonathan sit at the head, with the entire length of the table between them? That seemed odd. Her family had had a smaller dining table. Family meals had been formal, but not strained. The table downstairs comfortably sat fourteen. It was intended for entertaining, something that previous generations of Stantons had done extensively. Eliza wondered how family dinners had worked with Jonathan's parents. She supposed she may gain some understanding tonight. There was nothing that would be gained by dawdling in front of the mirror. She took a deep breath and went downstairs.

Jonathan was waiting for her in the foyer. He had changed into evening dress and freshly shaved. He looked handsome. He turned when he heard her footsteps on the stairs. His breath caught when he saw her in her blue dress. It was cut lower at the neck than her day dresses, and he was distracted by the snowy skin it revealed. Before he could embarrass himself by staring, he dragged his eyes to her face. "You look lovely."

"Thank you," she replied, blushing. "You look handsome."

He gave her a slight bow and offered his arm. "Shall we?"

Her flush deepened as she took his arm, and he led her into the dining room. To her relief, she saw that two places were set opposite each other, near the head of the table.

"This is the seating arrangement my parents preferred. I hope you don't mind it."

"It's perfect." She smiled up at him as he pulled out her chair for her.

Once seated, Mrs. Davis promptly served the first

course, a green salad.

"It's wonderful to have a vegetable garden," remarked Eliza. "The salad couldn't be fresher."

"Yes. And the preserves last through the winter. It's one of the things I missed most at school."

"Did you enjoy your time at school?" Eliza asked, hoping to learn something about her husband.

"No," he replied shortly, before turning his focus to his salad.

"I'm sorry. I didn't mean to upset you." Eliza was cowed.

"No, I'm sorry. It's not…. You haven't upset me. I learned a lot at school. I had friends, some of whom I keep in touch with. But the circumstances that led to my leaving for boarding school tainted any happiness it might have held."

She wasn't entirely sure how to respond. She generally knew that his mother had taken ill and passed. She was also aware that shortly afterward he had gone away, and his father had become largely reclusive. But she had been a small child of 9 at the time. She learned that scant information later in life, from talkative friends. Or, more accurately, their mothers.

"It's good that you were able to make friends."

"Yes."

They continued to eat in silence for some time.

"I enjoyed riding," he blurted. "There were horses at the boarding school I attended. And my Aunt Charlotte had horses."

"Your Aunt Charlotte?" Eliza's curiosity was piqued.

"My father's aunt. She lives in Vermont. Her husband passed shortly after, well, shortly after I left for school. I spent most of my breaks with her, helping her around the house. She had a housekeeper, but she liked having family there. Her own son left for the Northwest Territory fifteen years ago to seek adventure."

"How exciting for him. But his poor mother. It's wonderful that you could be there for her."

"She mostly wanted company, I think."

"That's what most people want, deep down, isn't it? To not be alone."

Jonathan studied his empty plate, and was grateful that Mrs. Davis chose that moment to come take the salad plates away and serve the soup course. The couple paused their conversation until she had finished, murmuring their thanks to her.

"Is that what you want, Elizabeth? Company?" he asked a few moments later.

Eliza paused to consider. "I don't enjoy being alone, if that's what you're asking me."

"Sometimes being alone can feel like the safer option. It gives one absolute control over oneself."

They continued to eat in silence. The conversation had strayed into awkward territory, and neither was sure how to navigate forward safely. During the main course, Eliza couldn't take the silence anymore. Casting about, she asked, "Do you remember the dogs you used to have?"

He smiled at the memory, "Of course! Chance and Digger. They were wonderful dogs. My father even taught Chance to bark four times in response to the question 'what is two plus two'. They were the best. They went to live with Aunt Charlotte when I went away to school, so I got to see them quite often. Brilliant animals. Did you ever have pets as a child?"

"No. I always wanted a kitten, but my mother didn't care for animals like that."

"That's a shame. There are cats in the stables. They keep the rats away."

Eliza got excited at the mention of the stables. "Would you be willing to show me the stables sometime? if you have the time of course."

He considered for just a moment before suggesting, "Why don't we go tomorrow? It's not a terribly long walk, and you can see more of the property."

She smiled sweetly at him. "I'd enjoy that very much."

He returned her smile. They finished the remainder of the meal with lighter, friendlier conversation. She was filled with excited anticipation, while he sat there wondering what he'd gotten himself into. In point of fact, he wasn't sure what had come over him in making such a suggestion. He justified it by reminding himself that he had promised his uncle that he would work toward a friendship with Eliza, and in truth, he had enjoyed her company and conversation up to this point. So, he would take the necessary steps to spend more time together. He was amused that after all the time he'd spent feeling uncertain and even perhaps afraid, he now found himself smiling.

After dinner, the two retired to the drawing room for coffee. As the hour drew late, Jonathan excused himself, as he had more work to do before the end of the day. Eliza stood and approached him before he left the room. "Thank you, for joining me for dinner. I enjoyed our conversation," she said shyly.

He took her hand impulsively, saying, "I did, as well. May it be the first of many," he smiled and lowered his head to kiss her hand in a sweet gesture. Eliza blushed. She didn't know entirely why, but she wanted to extend their time together. She took another small step toward him, her hand still held in his.

"I... I'm looking forward to tomorrow."

He hesitantly met her gaze. "As am I," he said huskily, before clearing his throat. He took a small step back, dropping his hand. "Until then," he said before giving her a small nod, and turning and leaving the room.

In his office, Jonathan sat behind his desk and dropped his head into his hands. He sought to martial his simmering feelings. Confusion and frustration sat like twin devils on his shoulders and drove him to work well into the night.

Chapter 7

Eliza sank gently into a softly upholstered chair, feeling somewhat bereft. She brought a hand to her breast, where she could feel her heart thumping. What was this effect her husband had on her? She felt distinctly the sensation of yearning, rooted deep in her stomach. But she had no idea what exactly she desired.

She tried to put the thought from her mind, and occupied herself with her sketchbook for the remainder of the evening.

But when she retired to bed that night, she thought back to the sensations that her husband had inspired. She was surprised to find that such their small amount of time together today had felt so monumental. It had been the first time they'd had a real conversation since their wedding. And it had been a fun conversation. She had enjoyed talking to him. One day, she vowed to herself, she would stop being surprised that she actually carried feelings of fondness for her husband. But they were still so new, today was not the day to achieve such a feat. She felt an ease in talking to him that was unusual for her. It normally took her some time to warm up to a person, and when she thought about Jonathan without facing him, she was intimidated by him. But actually talking with him turned out to be quite easy, on the whole, as well as enjoyable.

She allowed herself the girlish pleasure of imagining his face. His strong jaw with the neatly trimmed beard and mustache. He had a straight nose and a strong brow underneath a smooth forehead. His hair was short and fashionable, though it could become mussed with surprising ease. When he was unsure of something, or frustrated, he would ruffle his hair, making him look more rakish. He had strong hands with smooth fingers. He cared about his appearance, clearly, as he kept his nails neat and trimmed. He had broad shoulders, which fit his tall frame well. Those shoulders tapered to a trim waist. Eliza vaguely wondered what he looked like without his shirt, and then was scandalized at herself. But her mind went back to the warmth of his lips against her hand. The small gesture had made a large impact. She felt hot and restless, lying in bed, caught up in these thoughts. She was intensely aware of how her long nightgown tangled around her legs. She pulled at it to free herself, and finally gave up and got out of bed. She was feeling warm, anyway, and thought a glass of water might help.

She wrapped her dressing gown around herself and belted it loosely, lit a candle to light her way through the darkened house, and left to seek the kitchen for a drink. She would be so happy when Molly was here, she thought to herself. Molly was in the habit of leaving a glass of water on the nightstand each night for just this purpose.

The house was indeed dark, though the moon, still on the fuller side of waning, lit patches on the floor through uncovered windows. As Eliza gained the bottom of the stairs, she noticed a dim glow coming from the library. It must be past midnight, she thought, and so she assumed a lamp must have been mistakenly left lit in the room. Thinking she would go extinguish it herself, she approached. As she neared the door, she heard footsteps coming from inside, getting closer. She entered the doorway and was abruptly met by her husband. His ascot hung loose around his neck and his jacket must be in his bedroom, or office. He looked altogether quite disheveled, and clearly startled by Eliza's presence, as she was by his. She gasped audibly, while he cursed under his breath. She was frozen by the surprise. She didn't know whether to turn and leave, or enter the room, so she stood still in the doorway.

"Eliza, is something the matter? Are you hurt?"

She noticed that when he said her name, the Z sound was a bit softer, more susurrus. A leftover, apparently, from his childhood speech patterns.

He came to her and took her hand. "I'm fine, really," she said, coming to her senses. "I came down for some water and saw the light. I thought someone might have accidentally left a lamp burning. I'm sorry to interrupt, I didn't expect anyone would still be awake."

"I'm sorry to have startled you," he offered with a small smile. "I have trouble sleeping some nights. I find reading helps."

"I see. I should leave you to it then." She was deeply aware of being dressed only in her night clothes, her dark hair falling in a soft braid down her back.

Seeing her appear like a ghost had startled him, and it felt slightly illicit to be standing here with her at midnight in the dim light, more alone than usual. But he wasn't ready for that to end, either, a thought he wasn't going to dwell on too much. The unsettled feelings he had tamed earlier reared up inside him at the sight of her.

"Can I offer you something a bit stiffer than water? If you're having trouble sleeping, a glass of sherry may help," he offered, thinking that he could use a drink himself.

Eliza was torn. Taking him up on his offer felt immoral, wrong somehow. But they were married, so it really wasn't wrong at all. She held her dressing gown a little more tightly closed, but ultimately decided, "Yes, that would be lovely."

They smiled at each other as he led her into the library, to a drinks cabinet. He gestured to a nearby sofa, for her to sit, while he poured her a small glass of sherry, and for himself, a glass of scotch. She thought he may have suggested the love-seat because he would sit next to her, but after handing her the glass, he took a seat in an adjacent chair.

"Do you often have trouble sleeping?" she asked, not quite sure what else to say.

"Yes," he answered simply. "Do you?"

"Not usually, no."

"Is there something on your mind?"

She looked at him closely to see if he was joking. In just a week, her entire life had been upended. She felt a bit like a lace parasol in a rainstorm storm must feel: unprepared, fragile, and not necessarily fit for the task at hand. He, her husband, had spent days resolutely ignoring and avoiding her, and today had been an absolute about face. He had been attentive and even sweet at times. He might well have been a totally different person. It was such a drastic change, and she was confused by it, and she didn't know what he really wanted. Although the change would be quite welcome, if it were sincere.

"I'm just still getting settled here," she said carefully.

He had the grace to look abashed. "Of course," he said.

"I hope the weather is nice tomorrow. I'm looking forward to our walk."

Jonathan smiled at his wife. "So am I. I haven't been to that part of the property in weeks. Do you ride?"

"No. There wasn't the opportunity to learn, in the city."

"That's a shame. Would you like to learn now?"

"Yes!" The thought excited Eliza. "That would be lovely!"

"Good. We'll talk to Joshua about it tomorrow. The horses need exercise, if we're going to keep them. I think Father would come down from Heaven and shoot me himself if I sold his horses."

Eliza was vaguely stunned. "I didn't realize your father cared so much for horses."

"He enjoyed hunting. He was an avid sportsman, and quite skilled with a gun. He'd take whomever he could strong-arm into going out with him and spend entire weekends out in the woods, at the cabin, shooting at things. The horses and riding were all a part of that for him."

"I see. Do you enjoy hunting, as well, then?"

"I can't stand it. I do still enjoy riding, though, on the

occasions I can make time for it. And the woods all around here have trails that are suitable for the horses."

"That sounds wonderful. Will we see the woods tomorrow?"

"A little bit. You know where the maze garden is, yes?" She nodded at him and he continued, "There's a walking path from the back of that garden through a tree line that takes you to the lake. The woods arc around one side of the lake, and the pasture and stables are on the other side, with more forest beyond, circling back around. It's really not far at all, but the tree line hides it from plain sight, if you're in the gardens."

"I see. I was too young, the last time I was here as a child, to be allowed to wander that far."

"True. I think you're old enough now, though," he said, his eyes twinkling in the low light of the gas lamps. She blushed and nodded, laughing slightly.

Eliza stifled a delicate yawn and noted, "The sherry must be doing its job. I should retire."

Jonathan rose and took the glass from her, replacing it on the sideboard. "I hope you sleep well," he said warmly.

"Thank you. You, as well," she said as she rose.

"Goodnight." She thought he might approach, do or say something more, but he stayed where he was.

"Goodnight." She turned and exited the room, heading back to her bedroom. There, she extinguished her candle, took off her dressing gown, and climbed back into bed. She was definitely tired, and she still fell asleep with thoughts of her husband's handsome face in her mind's eye.

Chapter 8

Eliza woke, feeling refreshed. The sun was shining through the thin curtains, and she was excited for what the day may hold. She didn't know what time Jonathan wanted to go for their walk, but she wanted to be ready. She put on a printed cotton day dress with short sleeves that seemed appropriate for the sunny weather. She fixed her hair simply, coiling a braid up at her crown, and curling the shorter hair around her face. Looking in the mirror, she saw something she hadn't seen for most of the year. A young, excited, fresh faced girl who seemed genuinely happy.

She paused to consider. She really was happy, which stirred some small feelings of guilt, and confusion. Yesterday had been a lovely surprise, wherein she had gotten to spend time with both her beloved godfather, and also her new husband. She really quite thought that she liked Jonathan. Besides being handsome, and obviously hardworking, he had a sense of humor, and he was enjoyable to talk to. He was also thoughtful, in his own way. What she couldn't determine at all, in spite of trying, was his opinion of her. He seemed to enjoy their conversations. And he had suggested today's excursion himself, which meant spending more time together. But was he just doing his uncle's bidding? He had changed completely since Brandon's visit, and Eliza couldn't help wondering if that had more to do with the other man's influence, rather than with herself. So perhaps her husband was making more of an effort, but did he really want to, or was it to mollify guilt his uncle had inflicted upon him? Or was this an assigned task to be accomplished? These thoughts sat like seeds of doubt in Eliza's mind, and her happiness faded slightly.

She forced herself to move past those doubts and focus on the fact that, regardless of her husband's motivations, she was destined to have a lovely day. And Molly would be here at some point, as well! She hoped that the girl would be happy about it.

Determined to have a good day, Eliza descended the stairs to the dining room. For some reason, breakfast didn't bother her the way that dinner did. Mrs. Davis set the buffet so that Eliza could come put together a plate for herself at her leisure, and Jonathan could either do the same at some point, or else Mrs. Davis could bring him one up in the late morning. It was a very informal time of day. This morning was no different.

Eliza ate breakfast and then retreated to the parlor, where she had left her needlework basket. She was in the midst of embroidering a floral border on a napkin. Her mother had taught her the gentle arts of sewing and embroidery, and she was quite good at both. Needlework was soothing to her. While she worked, she allowed her mind to wander to the events of last night.

If her husband didn't genuinely want to spend time with her, he wouldn't have offered her a drink, surely? He would have let her get her water and go back to bed immediately. Clearly her godfather could not have foreseen such a random encounter occurring, and so he would not have been able to leave instructions on how Jonathan ought to comport himself in such a situation. Eliza realized she was fretting and forced herself to stop. Today's walk would be a clue, wouldn't it? She had to admit that if he would just kiss her, it would answer a lot. Wouldn't it? Because wasn't that the real question? She enjoyed spending time with him, and he seemed to enjoy it, as well. But so far, he had really seemed to treat her more like a sister than a wife. Hadn't he? She was an only child, but that was nevertheless what it felt like.

What complicated her thoughts ever so slightly was

that her first and only kiss, which had happened last summer, had come from a man she had always considered to be like a brother, and so it had caught her quite off guard. Vincent Dudley. Her mind wandered in that direction. When she saw him recently, it had been as though that night the previous year had never happened. She didn't feel like there had really been resolution at the time, but clearly, he had come to some conclusion on his own. And that somehow added to the confusion she felt now.

Back then, before her life had turned upside down and she had lost so much in such a short time, she had existed in the oblivious bliss of being a young, pretty girl just coming out in society. She had come of age and was enjoying being part of the more adult crowds at parties. She had been at a dinner party with her parents at the Dudley home. She and Amy, who had been fast friends since they were small, were almost inseparable. Except this evening, her brother Vincent had a university chum visiting, and Amy was smitten with the young man. She was sitting next to Eliza on a loveseat in the drawing room, but she only had eyes for the dark-haired man standing across the room, talking to her brother. Amy had begged her friend to ask the boys to join them in the garden, on the pretense of getting some air. It wouldn't be inappropriate for them to all go as a small group. Eliza had readily agreed, encouraging her friend, whose target seemed to be interested in her, as well.

Proper introductions had already been made. It had been easy, therefore, to coerce the boys outside, and they quickly divided into pairs, Amy and Louis, Vincent's friend, taking the lead, with Eliza and Vincent falling behind, as default chaperones. Each pair walked arm in arm, but this hadn't stood out to Eliza, as she had walked in this way with Vincent before, as well as her father and her godfather. She didn't see anything romantic in it. As they walked, they had joked and teased, as they had done most of their lives. They purposely lagged back a bit, Eliza supposed to give Amy and her beau some private time. So it surprised her when Vince had stopped walking forward and had pulled her into the shadow of a tree.

"Is something wrong?" she had asked, concerned.

He had seemed nervous as he replied, "No. Yes. I mean," he ran his hand through his short hair. "Something is wrong. I can't go any further..."

"Are you hurt?" Eliza asked, worried. Thinking perhaps he had twisted his ankle or picked up a stone.

"No, I'm not hurt. I just can't go on hiding my feelings any further. Eliza, you must know how I feel about you. You can't be surprised."

Eliza was, in fact, surprised. She had no idea what feelings he was talking about.

"Eliza, I am a man of many flaws. I'm still in school, and it will be a few years until I establish myself. I would only be so lucky if you could find it within yourself to return my affections. Eliza, I love you."

Her eyes had widened, but she misunderstood what he was saying. "Vince, I love you, too! You scared me. I thought something had happened! You have always been a part of my life, an important one, for as long as I can remember. You and Amy are both my oldest friends! Of course I love you, just as much as I love her."

"That's not the kind of love I mean," he had responded with a small laugh. He ran his hands through his hair again, looking at her askance. Then he had stepped in, taking her hands and leaning forward. He had moved very slowly. He had given her time to back away, to stop him. She hadn't known exactly what he was going to do, until his face was so close, she couldn't help but anticipate, and then she had felt her stomach flop in a confusing way, a flush bloomed like roses in her cheeks, and then she felt his lips on hers. Delicate, sweet, and chaste. He had slipped one hand to her waist and held the kiss for a long moment. His lips had been warm and pleasant and undemanding. His hand hadn't strayed from her waist, and the other hand still grasped her hand gently. "Do you see now?

But she didn't see anything, not clearly. She had always thought of Vince as a brother, and now he was trying to tell her he saw her as much more than a sister. Or as not a sister at all. "I..." she had started to say, but then Amy and Louis, Vincent's friend, interrupted them.

"There you two are!" Amy exclaimed. "We thought we'd lost you." She cheerfully shepherded the group back toward the house, chatting happily the whole time. Eliza and Vincent hadn't had the chance to talk again, as her parents wished to leave soon after they returned from the garden. He had promised to pay a visit before he left again for his final year of school.

That visit had happened one afternoon the following week when Mr. Montgomery had been away, and Vincent had been received by Mrs. Montgomery and Eliza. The three had sat in the cheerful parlor of the townhouse and discussed trivial things. Ann, Eliza's mother, had asked after Vincent's school progress, his family's health. Mrs. Montgomery was vaguely surprised that he had visited without his sister, but she wasn't naive. She could see the way the young man looked at her daughter. She could also see that her daughter was not exactly enthusiastic to receive his attentions. Lest she be wrong in her observations, she did give the two young people a few moments alone toward the end of the visit. She excused herself from the room on a flimsy pretense. Vincent had taken advantage of the opportunity, as expected.

"Eliza," he said, "we were interrupted the other night in the garden. I hope I conveyed my feelings to you clearly."

"Vincent," she began, not quite knowing what to say. "You did. At least, I think I understood what you were saying. I care about you very deeply. I feel like I've known you my whole life."

He smiled broadly at that.

"But," she continued, "I just don't know if I feel the way you feel. I do think you are a wonderful man, please understand. I'm just, well, rather confused I suppose. I've always thought of you, well, as a brother, as you are the brother of my best friend."

His face fell, but his hopes were not dashed completely. "I'm Amy's brother, but do you think that you could see me as more than that, to you? Can I hope that, with my affections revealed, yours may in turn grow?" He was sitting on the edge of his chair, facing the loveseat where she was perched.

Eliza hesitated, bringing her hand self-consciously to her cheek. "I suppose it's possible." She looked up somewhat pitifully. "It's just such an unexpected thing, really."

Sensing that her mother would return soon, and that their time together was drawing to a close, Vincent smiled again, "Just allow me to write to you, please. And...and promise to write me back. We can take our time. I won't be finished with school for another year, and then when I'm back, we still wouldn't have to rush. I just want to know that I have a chance to try to make you happy."

Eliza smiled. "Of course you can write, and of course I'll respond!"

"Good!" He leaned back, a bit more at ease. "We'll do that, then."

At just that moment, Mrs. Montgomery had come back in, smiling to see both young people looking happy.

The following week, he was thoroughly ensconced in school, but before his first letter could arrive, Ann Montgomery had taken ill, and Eliza's life had rapidly turned upside down. His first letter went unread for a week, and then went unanswered for another two. Three weeks later, her mother on her deathbed, Eliza, while exhausted and upset, took a few brief stolen moments to write a quick note in reply. She had been so upset, and that had come across as she explained her mother's illness, not wanting to complain, but needing to share her grief. They had continued to exchange correspondence, but rarely, and as Eliza's world slowly fell apart around her, she had practically forgotten that kiss in an evening summer garden. It didn't feel real to her. He knew that it was inappropriate for him to write her love letters when she was feeling so much grief.

That night, at the Forester dinner party just a few scant weeks ago, it had been as though the event had never occurred. Vincent had teased her just as he had when they were children, and they talked of silly things. There had been no allusions to deeper feelings, the kiss, or anything other than friendship. Eliza had to admit that she was relieved by that.

She couldn't help but remember that simple kiss now, though. For the first time she questioned if she had made the right decision. She perhaps would have been wise to revisit that conversation with Vincent. But in her heart, she knew that, while she loved Vincent, his kiss had made her uneasy, more than elated. She was comfortable around him generally, but the thought of romance with made her uncomfortable. So, at the very least, it was probably best that that had quieted itself down in the interim year. Of course, her thoughts continued, that didn't mean that she had been wise to marry Jonathan.

She turned her thoughts to her husband, for what seemed like the hundredth time. If she was being truthful with herself, she had to admit that he excited her in ways that Vincent never had. Without knowing what he might feel, though, she was left with some uncertainty. His sudden attentions had just served to confuse her, rather than to reassure her of anything.

It was now mid-morning, and Jonathan chose that moment to enter the parlor, smiling brightly. He was dressed in quite a dapper fashion, his breeches disappearing into tall, polished boots, his ascot smartly tied. The military-inspired garments that were fashionable for the year fit him well. Her heart leapt a tiny bit inside her chest when she heard his voice.

"Good morning! Are you ready for our little adventure?" he asked with a smile.

Chapter 9

The previous day and evening had been challenging for Jonathan. While he didn't think he could hide from his wife forever, he had been a bit shaken by his uncle's intervention, such as it was. He wasn't entirely sure getting married had been a good idea. It had seemed to save him from the pressures of being seen as an "eligible bachelor," and the pursuit of all the single young ladies, as well as their mothers. He had begged God to save him from the mothers. And so this marriage seemed like an answer to that prayer. He was off the market. But then he found himself in possession of a wife. Just as Eliza had assumed that she could stay in her own home after the wedding, Jonathan was ill at ease with the idea of adjusting his daily life around the new presence of a woman. The fact that he found himself wanting to reschedule his days so that he may spend some amount of time with Eliza was just as disconcerting.

His parents truly had been beacons of love when they were together. They were never far from each other when his mother had still been alive. He remembered clearly the fond gazes, the loving touches, the stolen kisses when they thought they were alone. He even remembered his father pulling his giggling mother into dark corners with a wolfish grin, presumably to have a moment of togetherness. They had been silly together, laughing like children, running through the gardens. His memories of them were haloed with rosy glowing light. But then his mother had fallen ill. A fever had progressed rapidly and took her life within a few short days. His father had been distraught. The sounds he had made in his grief had been animalistic. He had destroyed the furniture in his office, on a rampage of madness, driven there by his wife's absence. Jonathan had witnessed all of this from the corners. His bright, loving parents were suddenly gone. His mother literally, his father figuratively. In his grief, his father hadn't been able to even look at the boy, who looked so much like his dearest Margaret. Jonathan had been sent away almost immediately after the funeral, allowing Edmund the freedom to wallow in his grief alone.

The indelible imprint left on Jonathan had been one of fear and revulsion. He resented being sent away, when he himself was grieving. He had wanted to be close to his father, to have the warmth of his loving embrace. Instead he was met with cold nothingness. He was sent to a school where he didn't know anyone, and was struggling with the loss of his sweet, doting mother. His Aunt Charlotte had been a godsend. The only person who kept him sane, she was a surrogate grandmother, of sorts. Nothing like his own had been, but kind in her own way. Her husband had passed just recently, and while she spoke of him with fond sadness on occasion, Jonathan was not directly presented with a different model for marriage. He was left with the wildly emotional impressions of his parents.

Thus, finding himself married, he was left blundering a bit. He absolutely wanted to avoid the tempestuous feelings his parents had felt. As wonderful as their love had seemed, it had burned too brightly. He thought in hindsight that his father had been shattered by it in the end. He had been left a broken, lonely man, a shell of his former self. But of course, there had to be some middle ground to be achieved. He certainly liked his wife well enough. They hadn't spent a mountain of time together, but the little interactions they had had were satisfyingly pleasant. He thought she was pretty. She seemed to be accomplished at certain polite things, as a lady of her standing ought to be. There was no harm and all the reasons to get to know her a bit better, surely? Lunch had been enjoyable. And while dinner had had its stiff moments, they had genuinely laughed together. She was easy to talk to. He hadn't had conversations as easy as that with a woman before.

Last night, well, maybe he had overstepped himself a little bit by inviting her to share a drink with him. She had seemed so delicate, though, and sweetly disarming. He found himself rather quickly wanting to occupy more of his time with her presence. If he was honest with himself, more than once now, he had wondered what it would be like to kiss her. He wondered how she would react to that. He tried to consider the thought rationally. They were married. It was allowed, even expected. But he was afraid of offending her, and he was still quite wary of losing any part of himself to her. Becoming friends and spending time together enjoying each other's company was just fine, but there still had to be boundaries in place. He wanted to keep his wits about him, and he was positive that he absolutely did not want to fall in love with her. That could lead to tragedy. To that end, neither did he want to lead on her affections. And thus, he was confused. He found himself thinking that the outing they had planned today would be a wonderful opportunity to define the boundaries of their relationship. They could be friends. They could spend time together. They could even seek happiness together, as his uncle had worded it. He would just stop short of falling in love with her. He spent not a little bit of time that morning trying to figure out where kissing might fall in that scheme of limitations.

And so, he had taken a little extra care with his appearance this morning. He had woken up unusually early, especially for going to sleep so late. He had puttered about in his room and then his office. He was actually excited for a simple walk, but then, he had been cooped up in his office for a solid week. That had been a bit extreme, even for him. He was also excited to see what Eliza might think of the horses and the woods. He had arranged for a picnic lunch as a surprise. He reasoned to himself that at midday, it would make absolute sense, and it wasn't necessarily a romantic gesture at all. It was a measure of pure practicality. He hoped she liked it, though. Upon reflection, he enjoyed making her happy. At least, he enjoyed making her laugh and smile. He felt unduly nervous, and was mildly aggravated by that. But he was determined to have a nice walk with his wife. He looked out the window one last time, before descending the stairs. The sky was pure blue, with just a few clouds drifting lazily overhead. A perfect day.

Chapter 10

Eliza smiled at Jonathan who was standing in the doorway of the parlor, her cheeks dimpling slightly. "Of course I'm ready. Let me just fetch my shawl."

She gathered her shawl and, upon reflection, a parasol and met Jonathan in the foyer. They exited the back of the house together, and he offered her his arm as they started toward the gardens. She smiled again as she took the proffered arm, and he smiled down at her. They walked quietly past the roses and topiaries.

As they neared the little bridge that crossed the stream, he asked lightly, "Did you sleep well last night?"

"I did, thank you for asking. And yourself?"

"Yes, our little conversation helped quite a bit, I think." They were halfway across the bridge when he stopped walking and turned to her. "It occurs to me that I need to apologize to you. My absence in the last week was inexcusably rude. I'm sorry that I abandoned you as soon as we got home after the wedding."

She digested his words, and they soothed some of the confusion she had been feeling earlier, just a bit. "Thank you for apologizing, but I fear I must point out that this is your second apology on this subject. I do understand that you're a busy man. I do not wish to make unreasonable demands on your time. I wouldn't expect you to inconvenience yourself for my sake."

He cleared his throat, feeling some shame, "Yes, I suppose I am often busy, but you deserve some of my time and attention, as my wife."

The way he put it sounded vaguely transactional, rather than personal. Eliza was rapidly reverting to confusion again, like a pendulum, she found herself swinging back and forth between clarity and bewilderment. She disliked the idea of being a chore for him to complete. But perhaps she was reading too much into his words.

"I have enjoyed the time we've spent together," she said, cautiously testing the waters somewhat.

"As do I," he said with a warm smile.

That made her feel decidedly better. "You know, I helped my father with his bookkeeping for the mill. Correspondence, as well. Perhaps I could help you with your work? And certainly the work that pertains to the mill," she offered hopefully.

The offer was pleasantly surprising for Jonathan. "Would you enjoy that?" he asked.

She gave an enthusiastic nod, "I would! I dislike being idle."

He nodded and gestured to suggest they continue walking. "It's a rather modern suggestion, but I think we could make an attempt at it, if it pleases you," he said warmly. They crossed the bridge and entered the wildflower garden, each feeling rather content in the moment.

Eliza smiled as they followed the meandering path. This garden had always been her favorite. It was more wild, with secret nooks created by cleverly placed boulders and trees and bushes, and fat clumps of flowers that drew butterflies and bees in a delightful medley of wings and buzzing. There was a small man-made pond that was home to fish and frogs. The trees were planted close to the path, so they offered much shade and a romantic canopy overhead. This was the garden of little girl fairy stories. It was still all too easy to expect a little gnome to pop his head out from behind the moss-covered rocks, or to find him fishing just beyond the roots of a tree that had grown toward the pond. Her husband studied her expression from the corner of his eye, and couldn't help but notice the sheer delight on her face.

"My mother loved this place. She loved all the gardens, but she spent the most time here. She said it was a magical place." His tone was slightly hushed and reverent as he peered up at the leafy canopy.

Eliza smiled broadly. "She was correct. This has always been my favorite, as well."

He laughed gently, without condescension. "I'm surprised you remember it so clearly. You were what, eight the last time you were here before this week?"

"Nine," she retorted with mild indignation. "Some of my most vivid childhood memories happened in these gardens, you know. In fact, Amy and I took a blood oath under that red maple by the pond, to always be best friends no matter what."

"A blood oath?" His eyebrows couldn't arch any higher than where they sat at that moment.

"We used a pin to prick our fingers," she explained.

Jonathan laughed at the mental image of the two little girls undertaking such a solemn thing. "That's adorable. Did you know, I broke my arm falling out of that very tree? When I was ten."

"No! Oh, that must have been terribly painful."

"Oh, it was. I didn't learn any lessons, though. I kept climbing trees."

It was Eliza's turn to laugh, a delicate tinkling sound that floated up to the leafy canopy. "That's what little boys are supposed to do, isn't it?"

"I suppose so," he smiled down at her. He seemed to find himself smiling a lot in her presence.

They came to the little gazebo. "I suppose this old thing could use a new coat of paint," Jonathan assessed. Eliza nodded, a vague but elusive memory tugging at her brain. But they were already moving on toward the labyrinth, past the little gazebo without stopping. "Shall we go through, or around?" he asked teasingly.

"Through, of course. Is around really an option that one might find appealing?" she answered seriously.

"I just wanted to verify your feelings on the subject," he replied with a grin.

The maze hedges were just a wee bit taller than Jonathan, and he stood over Eliza by a solid six inches. It was not the sort of maze one could get easily lost in, however, regardless that the average person could not peer over it. The path was simple and winding, bringing the traveler to the fountain at the center with ease. Short dead ends had been employed to provide space for additional planting, or the presence of a bench. The only potentially confusing part of it was that it was a square garden, with entrances on all four sides. Therefore, one could enter the garden from one side and exit it on another. The middle of the maze was a wide circular space with a large fountain marking the center. The ledge of the fountain was wide enough for someone to sit on it, though they may get splashed if the wind was blowing strongly enough. The center of the fountain was crowned with two women, standing back to back, draped in diaphanous clothing, each holding a water jug that tipped a continuous stream into the larger basin.

The couple walked leisurely, talking of inconsequential things as they went. The occasional chipmunk delighted Eliza, and Jonathan enjoyed watching her face light up when she saw one. At the center of the maze, he guided her to the path that would lead them out in the correct direction. He pointed out the paving stones that were carved to subtly suggest which path led to what, a small detail she had never noticed before. The path they had followed in featured a stone with a gazebo where it met the open courtyard. The path they proceeded to take had a horse's head inscribed at the entry to it, cleverly, in the manner of a Chess knight.

"What are on the other two?" Eliza asked curiously.

"One of them features vegetables, as that way leads back to the vegetable garden, and the garden house. The other one is a tree. It leads to the woods."

The simplicity of that answer was mildly deflating, but it helped her see how the grounds fit together. "There are a lot of woods around here," she observed.

"They ring the property," he explained. "We're fairly well secluded here, and while the gardens are extensive, and there's enough room for the horses, the rest of the property is undeveloped. I believe my grandfather may have had some ideas of farming at some point, or perhaps logging, for the number of trees. But the shipping business took off, and he never did anything with this land, other than build the house and the gardens. My father and mother further developed the gardens once they inherited."

"I didn't know that your grandfather started your family business."

"Oh, it was a whole family affair. My grandfather and his brother, my Aunt Charlotte's husband, started together with a single ship that Uncle David captained. I was able to read some of his old diaries when I stayed with her. He had some amazing exploits. It's almost no wonder their son left to seek adventures of his own. He could have easily joined one of the family ships, and explored the seas as his father did, but I suppose he wanted to chart his own course in life."

"Have you ever heard from him? He would be around your father's age, wouldn't he?"

"He would, yes. I believe he was a few years younger. He had his father's 'adventuresome spirit,' according to Aunt Charlotte. But in lieu of the ocean, he sought the wilderness," there was some wistfulness in Jonathan's voice.

"You sound as though you have an adventuresome spirit yourself," teased Eliza.

"Haven't you ever wanted to travel?" he countered.

"I suppose so. My family came from England, and I'd like to see where they were from. I've heard it's absolutely lovely there."

"It is."

"You've been?" The thought excited her.

"Once, when I was a young boy, before my mother passed away. My father and I went on one of the ships to visit his brother, my Uncle George, who lives on that side of the world. He manages the family business on that end. We got to travel a bit and see the countryside. It was beautiful."

"Oh, how wonderful! I didn't realize you had another uncle. Does he have a family?"

"Yes. He's married and they have five children. Three boys and two girls. He's a few years older than my father was. I'm the same age as Matthew, his third son. John and Luke are the oldest, twins, and Martha and Esther are the youngest. Esther was just an infant when we were there. We keep in touch through letters, but Uncle George hasn't been home here for at least two decades."

"That's incredible. You have so much family! Do you regret not being closer to them?"

"Not really," he answered thoughtfully. "They've always been so far away. When I was a very small boy, I remember George and his wife Cynthia visiting. The boys stayed in London with Cynthia's parents. But those two instances are the only times I met them, so we were never close. I wouldn't begin to know what it would be like to be closer. Do you have no other family?"

Eliza smiled ruefully. "I had a younger brother, Benjamin, but he died as an infant. My mother had a sister, Julia, who passed when she was a child. I'm all alone in the world."

Jonathan's heart tugged. "You've got me now," he said in a low voice, tucking his hand over hers where it rested in the crook of his arm. "And picture Uncle Brandon's face if he heard you say those words."

Eliza felt a surge of guilt. "True enough. He has been there for me my whole life. Like an uncle, or a second father, even." She was still trying to determine what role her husband might fill in her life, ultimately, so she delicately evaded referencing Jonathan. He didn't fail to notice, though.

He mulled the dual subjects of marriage and family over in his head as they neared the end of the maze. He didn't know precisely how they would fit into each other's lives, but it was assuredly at least as friends. When he had come back home, two years ago, he began working with his father, but they hadn't been close by any measure. He had come of age so far removed from his father, the two exchanging the odd letter or card. Beyond that, they had kept very little contact, such that they were practically strangers upon his return. Neither had seemed to mind, both keeping to themselves. They worked amicably enough; Jonathan was a swift learner, and Edmund a keen teacher. They would periodically share a meal together, but they didn't talk much on those occasions. When Brandon joined them, occasionally accompanied by Michael, the talk would be more extensive, largely prompted by their guests. Mulling this over, Jonathan realized that it wasn't going to help him determine how to live with Eliza. She clearly needed more from him than the vaguely anonymous contact he had with his father. Thus far, he enjoyed having more than that with her, now that he had had more than one opportunity to experience it.

His thoughts turned to Aunt Charlotte, who had been a grandmother to him, basically. She was his great-aunt, but she had found that to be a clumsy title, and preferred that he simply call her "Aunt". She told him stories of her husband and her son, and had made him treats and given him chores and structure. He had loved her in a way very different from the love he felt for his mother. It was a gentle love, soothing and warm in a way he hadn't needed love to be previously.

They were on the path that led through the tree line, now, in territory Eliza hadn't previously seen, so she was caught up in looking at her surroundings. She didn't notice that her husband was deep in thought. Though as she looked around, she, too, contemplated the potential unfolding of their relationship. She was already feeling easier around him. Not quite as comfortable as she had ever felt around Vincent, but she had been much closer to Vincent as a child, and he really was like family to her. And while she didn't feel tense around Jonathan, walking like this with her arm tucked into his, being close enough to smell him, and occasionally feel his breath on her forehead when he spoke or laughed, she felt vague excitement. She felt a heat in her belly that nothing else had ever caused. It wasn't an unpleasant situation, though, simply curious. As they broke through the trees on the edge of the pastureland, she gasped, bringing them both back to the present.

They were on a slight rise, the fields gently rolling around them, and the wooded hills beyond were in their full summer glory. A few more clouds had gathered in the sky, but the sun still shone brightly down on the people, as well as the horses that were grazing in the field before them. Jonathan smiled at Eliza's blatant pleasure at the sight. They slanted down toward the stable, a sturdy green painted building that fit perfectly into the picturesque landscape. A young man appeared at the door of what appeared to be living quarters adjacent to the stable section, and waved. Jonathan returned the wave, and the couple headed in that direction.

"Joshua, good morning. How are you doing today?"

"I'm doing well, and yourself, sir?" the man answered. He was a young man, perhaps 23 or 24, and he had a sunny smile set into his deeply tanned face. He was tall and well built, with darker features than her husband's.

"Very well. Elizabeth, please allow me to introduce you to Joshua Miller. Joshua, my wife." Jonathan made the introductions, gesturing between them.

Joshua nodded to Eliza, "It's a pleasure to meet you, ma'am."

"And you, Joshua."

The three of them proceeded to take a small tour of the stable and pastureland, the men both pleased to see how Eliza enjoyed everything she saw. Turning to the hired man, Jonathan said, "I'm hoping you may have time to teach Mrs. Stanton how to ride."

"It would be my honor, sir." Turning to Eliza he added, "Whenever you're ready, ma'am, you just come on out and we'll get you in the saddle."

"That would be wonderful!" she said.

They had come to the back of the stable, where a flat bit of land was set with a snowy white cloth and a picnic lunch had been set. The view was lovely, featuring the wooded hills, and the building provided some shade. Eliza gave a small gasp and glanced at her husband who smiled down at her in return. "I thought we might be hungry by the time we walked out here, so I arranged lunch for us," he explained.

She smiled sweetly at his thoughtfulness. Joshua excused himself, telling the couple that he'd be around if they needed him, but subtly assuring their privacy in the same sentence. Jonathan helped his wife sit before sitting himself. She set her shawl and parasol aside.

They enjoyed the sandwiches, fruit, and tea that had been provided. Eliza recognized Mrs. Davis's hand in the preparations and smiled at the secret-keeping. "This is very thoughtful of you, thank you."

"I'm glad you like it," Jonathan responded softly. He reached out to take her hand. "I made a mistake in the beginning, and while I know I have apologized, this, I suppose, is a gesture of my sincerity. An attempt to make things better, and show you that I intend to be more attentive to your needs and happiness."

Eliza considered this. It definitely made her feel better, and she was deeply enjoying herself. She decided on a whim to be blunt. He seemed like the sort of man who would appreciate that. "I like spending time with you," she began.

"I like spending time with you," he responded.

She smiled. "Good. Then I think we can do well together. However, I must be equally considerate of your needs and happiness. I can't in good faith ask you to do anything for me that would in turn make you unhappy or dissatisfied."

"I think I understand what you're saying," Jonathan began. He felt heartened by the sentiment. "I hope you can see this as a new beginning for us. Spending time together is enjoyable. It shouldn't be a burdensome thing between a husband and a wife, and assuredly, I don't find it to be such with you. We will find our way together." His tone rang with confidence that eased Eliza's heart.

The conversation turned to lighter things as they finished their lunch. They sat in the shade of the stable, enjoying the view for a while longer, until Jonathan, with some reluctance, said that they should probably start back to the house. Eliza agreed and they stood, bid farewell to Joshua and the horses, and started back up the hill. The sun was a bit glaring, and Eliza raised her parasol. In a gentlemanly act, Jonathan took it and held it for her as they walked. The canopy of the trees was dense enough that the parasol was unnecessary, once they reached the edge of the meadow. In fact, on their return, the bit of trees seemed to be more shadowed than they had been earlier in the day. When they emerged on the other side, they saw that more clouds had drawn in, and it was beginning to look like rain.

"I suppose you were correct about returning to the house," Eliza said, pulling close into Jonathan's side. "I hope we can get back before the rain begins."

He looked at the sky dubiously and started walking a bit faster. It truly wasn't any more expedient to go around the labyrinth than to go through it, so they retraced their steps fully, moving faster than their original leisurely pace in the other direction had been. The shadows cast by the hedges and trees seemed a touch menacing, and fat drops of water started to sprinkle from the sky. Just as they reached the other side of the hedge maze, the skies opened up. The couple made a dash to the gazebo, ducking in as thunder crashed overhead. Startled, Eliza clung to her husband, burying her head in his chest. He held her close, panting slightly from the short run. They looked up at each other, both a little sodden and disheveled, and simultaneously they burst into laughter. Feeling a bit like naughty children perhaps, they continued to laugh as the sky fell down around them.

"I promised an adventure, didn't I?" Jonathan asked before laughing again.

"You certainly did," she returned. "And you have definitely delivered."

Taking a deep breath, he said, "I've always loved the smell of the rain in summer." Glancing down at his soggy shirt he added, "Preferably from a dry spot."

She nodded in agreement. "This is a lovely place, though, to wait it out." She pulled her thin shawl around her shoulders futilely. She was slightly chilled, her thin cotton dress providing little warmth. She sat on a bench out of the wind.

Jonathan noticed her shivering and sat close to her, impulsively putting his arm around her shoulders and drawing her near. She stiffened slightly. "Let me help keep you warm," he said softly, "you'll catch a cold like this." She nodded and softened into him, turning into his warmth. He rested his head on hers and felt the cool dampness of her hair. He raised his other hand to brush the damp curls out of her face, his fingers lingering on her jaw. He felt a desire that was foreign to him.

She looked up, her dark eyes meeting his light ones. That tightness was there in her belly, and her nerves jangled. She curled her small fingers around his hand that still lightly cupped her face. His gaze glanced down to her mouth, and he leaned slightly forward. He paused, inches away, uncertain. She tilted her chin ever so slightly in his direction, which was all the acknowledgement he needed. He lowered his lips to hers, kissing her softly, tenderly.

Eliza was shocked. Jonathan's mouth was warm on hers, gentle, but the heat in her stomach was intense. She felt her face flush. Without realizing it, she kissed him back, moving her lips softly under his.

He moaned low in the back of his throat as he felt her

respond to him. He had one arm wrapped around her waist, and the other hand cradling her face. He rubbed her jaw with his thumb. His tongue traced her lower lip, and combined with his thumb's motion, he slowly encouraged her to part her lips. When she did, his tongue probed gently, caressingly. She gasped, but didn't pull away. A few hot moments later they separated.

Eliza rested her flushed cheek against his chest, half in shock, half trying to hide. Jonathan was rather surprised, as well, as that hadn't been part of the planned activities for the day. Not that he hadn't thought about it. He grinned to himself slightly. Laying his hand gently on her shoulder, he pulled back so that he could see her face. She shyly looked up to meet his gaze and saw his smile. Her lips curled up in return, blushing. The rain had steadied into a gentle downpour, but it didn't seem to be considering ceasing, at least for the moment.

"Are you cold?" asked Jonathan with care, keeping one arm locked around her waist.

She shook her head slightly, amused at the question. "No."

"Good." He wasn't entirely trying to ignore their kiss, but he thought she might appreciate some delicacy. "We can wait out the storm here, if you like. It seems like it might not stop for a while. Or we can make a run for the house. Have you a preference?"

Eliza considered, seeming to still be in a slight daze. She settled comfortably against him, leaning into his warmth, as that was, in fact, keeping her from being chilled. She laid her cool fingers on his chest, turning inward. "I think I'd rather stay here until it slows more," she said softly, glancing up at him again, "if that's acceptable."

He smiled to himself again, enjoying how her body fit so easily into his. "That's perfectly fine," he reassured her.

A scant half hour passed before the rain really seemed to let up to a light sprinkle. The young couple hadn't said much, but what was said had been inconsequential observations about the weather, the grounds, the gazebo. Jonathan took the liberty of toying with the now somewhat wild hair that fell around Eliza's face. She, on the other hand, traced the buttons of his shirt in vague circles. They were not in a rush to disentangle their embrace, but as the rain finally ceased to be anything but the drips from the trees, they started to pull away slowly, separating themselves into two distinct forms once again. At last they stood to return to the house.

This time, when she tucked her hand into the crook of his arm, he covered it with his other hand, bringing them into a more intimate pose. Eliza and Amy had walked this way a dozen times, giggling and sharing secrets, but this was somehow so much different. An intimacy that was far more exciting: perhaps some further proof that the storm, or the walk, or the day as a whole had brought a change in their relationship. Before they reached the little bridge, at a spot near the pond where the path took a sneaky turn around a large boulder, Jonathan took a sudden step off the path, upsetting Eliza's balance just enough to make her jostle into his chest. He caught her around the waist and dipped his head low. He paused just long enough to give her the opportunity to object, but she surprised him by completing the distance, bringing her lips to his in a soft kiss. He brought both arms around her in a warm embrace, holding her close, while she brought her arms up around his neck, bringing the two of them closer than they'd been while sitting down. However, they didn't linger there long. Mere moments, and then he pulled away slightly, kissing her cheek, her forehead, and the tip of her nose. He smiled down at her as they broke the embrace. Eliza was flushed bright pink, and she hurried slightly as they completed the walk back toward the house, picking up the pace marginally.

Mrs. Davis met the two of them on the terrace, holding a lap blanket that she draped over Eliza's shoulders. "I'm so happy to see that you two aren't completely drenched! Did you stay at the stable during the storm?"

"No," replied Jonathan. "We were able to make it to the

gazebo, though. We need to see to having that thing painted, Mrs. Davis."

The housekeeper nodded, mildly surprised. "Of course, sir."

"We should both get out of these damp clothes," he continued. Back at the house, the storm passed, his responsibilities and insecurities had flooded back to him. "I have some work to get done before the day is through, if you'll both excuse me."

He did offer Eliza a small smile before leaving to go back inside. She hugged the blanket to herself, and gave in to the ministrations of the housekeeper, who clucked over her.

Let me make you some hot tea," the older woman offered. "While you change clothes."

"That would be wonderful," she responded, turning toward the house.

Chapter 11

It was just striking 3 p.m. as Eliza was putting on a fresh dress. She had taken down her hair to brush it out and make sure it was dry. It was at this moment there was a knock on her door. She finished fastening her dress before opening it.

Mrs. Davis stood there, looking somewhat pleased, "Mr. St. John is here, ma'am. With a young woman named Molly."

Eliza's excitement ballooned, but she instantly realized something she had overlooked. "Oh, Mrs. Davis! I really should have mentioned this yesterday. Can we talk a moment?"

"Of course, ma'am."

Eliza led the housekeeper to the settee at the foot of the bed and encouraged her to sit. "Molly was a maid at my parents' home in the city, and well, I've honestly missed her presence. Not that there is much that I need, but this is such a large house, and well, it would be lovely if she were willing to come work here. I should have talked to you about it yesterday, though," Eliza said with concern, "do you have any concerns about that?"

The housekeeper patted Eliza's hand. "Mr. St. John brought it up with me yesterday as a possibility, and I think it's wonderful. Mary would be happy to have a younger girl to talk to during the day, and if I may say, I expect now that you and Mr. Stanton are married, you'll be more inclined to entertain. If I'm not overstepping, ma'am, when the master was a young boy, the staff was more than twice in number what it is now."

"Yes, that's what my godfather said," replied Eliza. "It

makes perfect sense. The house and the grounds are quite large," her mind wandered absently before refocusing. "If you're pleased with the arrangement, and Molly is willing, then I'm more than happy. We can talk about adding more staff later, as the need arises."

"Yes, ma'am."

"In that case, I'll be downstairs just as soon as I fix my hair," Eliza said. The housekeeper nodded and went back downstairs.

Eliza descended a few minutes later, to find Mrs. Davis and Molly chatting quietly, and her godfather looking on approvingly. He smiled at Eliza as she came down the stairs.

"Molly was too excited to come here," he said. "I think she missed you as much as you missed her."

"Oh, this is wonderful," Eliza told him before turning to Molly. "I'm so happy you're here!" she exclaimed. She clasped Molly's hands in her own and the two girls smiled at each other.

Molly was a year younger than Eliza, and while they stood the same height, where Eliza was dark, Molly was light. She had blond hair, neatly tied back, and light gray eyes. Her face was round, and she looked perpetually cheerful. "Thank you, miss!" she said happily. "I appreciate the opportunity you've given me."

"I hope you'll like it here," Eliza replied. "The house and the gardens are lovely, and I know you'll get along well with Mrs. Davis and Mary."

The housekeeper took this opportunity to take Molly's arm. "Let me show you your room, dear, and give you a tour of the house." The younger girl nodded eagerly, smiling, and the two of them walked away.

"Her things are just inside the door," said Brandon. "Shall we sit down?"

"Of course, how rude of me!" Eliza led the way into the parlor. "Would you like some tea? Please say you can stay for dinner. I'm sure Jonathan would love to see you."

Her godfather raised his eyebrows at her. "You sound like a different woman, Eliza, from how you were yesterday. I'm happy to see it, but what's happened to make you so cheerful?"

She blushed. "Jonathan and I have had the opportunity to spend some time together. In fact, I honestly can't believe it's all been just since yesterday. But it's been simply wonderful." She paused to consider the difference of her life in the house without his presence versus her life in the house with his presence. It truly was the difference of darkness and light.

"Well, I'm happy to hear it. I want nothing but for the two of you to find happiness. Unfortunately, I can't stay for dinner. I have plans already that I must keep. I'm sure you understand. Tea, though, would be lovely."

Eliza smiled and excused herself to ask Mrs. Smith to start the tea. She also ran into Mrs. Davis and Molly, mid-tour, and asked if the housekeeper wouldn't mind letting Mr. Stanton know that Mr. St. John was visiting, should he wish to come down to visit. After these small tasks, she returned to her godfather in the parlor. Mary shortly entered with the tea.

"So tell me what you two have been up to," invited Brandon.

"Well, we had dinner last night, and then today we took a lovely walk through the gardens to the stables. Jonathan had arranged for a picnic." Eliza's dimpled grin said volumes about how those activities had gone.

"That sounds lovely! Were you lucky enough to miss the storm that passed through? That was a nasty spot of rain."

"Not entirely, but we were at the gazebo near the maze when it started, so we took shelter in there." She blushed slightly.

He pretended not to notice the blush, but couldn't help but to tease her slightly. "That sounds romantic," he observed as he sipped his tea.

"And Joshua is going to teach me how to ride!" Eliza rushed to add. "I'm quite excited for that."

"Well, good! Maybe we can all go riding together some time."

"That would be lovely."

It was at this moment that Jonathan entered the room, "What would be lovely?" he asked. "Hello, uncle. What a surprise to see you back so soon."

Brandon stood and faced his nephew with a smile. "Hello, Jonathan. I was just saying that once Eliza here learns how to ride, we could all go riding some time. Just like the old days. It could be fun."

Jonathan's smile was a little hesitant. "Hm," was all he said, keeping his post just inside the door to the parlor. "I came down to say hello, but I'm sorry I can't chat. I have to catch up on some work before dinner. Will you be joining us?"

"I'm afraid not," Brandon said apologetically. "No, I have plans with Michael already,"

"Oh, well next time you'll have to both visit us together. He hasn't seen the house in ages. And the gardens are in bloom. He enjoys plants so."

"Of course, that sounds delightful. We can plan for it."

"Well, I really must get going, but it's good to see you, Uncle." Jonathan shook Brandon's hand, gave Eliza a smiling nod, and exited the room.

"He seems to be quite chipper today. It looks like you're both doing some good for each other. Shocking, really, that a man and his wife might actually find that they enjoy each other's company," he teased. In point of fact, Eliza was a little disappointed that Jonathan hadn't stayed longer to visit with their guest, but they had had a long outing already today. She smiled at Brandon. They continued to talk for another half hour or so before Brandon excused himself to leave.

Chapter 12

Eliza sat at her vanity before dinner, while an excited Molly arranged her hair. "The house is so beautiful, miss. And the gardens! I've never seen so many flowers! This is like heaven. You must be so happy here."

"I'm so glad you like it! I was very concerned you wouldn't want to come. I hope you like working with Mrs. Davis and Mary. Mr. Davis is very nice, as well. There's also a boy who helps with the gardens, and Joshua takes care of the horses."

Molly's eyes widened to the size of tea saucers. "Horses?"

"Yes! I got to see them today." Eliza turned around excitedly. "If you like, we can go together and see them soon!"

"Oh, yes, that would be wonderful, miss."

Eliza shifted forward in her seat. "I'm so glad you're here. I've missed you."

"I'm happy to be here. And d'you know, my gran lives close to here. She has a little house where she lives with my aunt and uncle. It will be nice to be able to visit them more easily."

"How lucky! I had no idea. I'm sure Mr. Davis would be more than happy to take you to them on your days off, if he's not otherwise busy." The girls smiled at each other and finished preparing Eliza for dinner. She wanted to look especially nice tonight. Molly was able to style her hair in more complex and interesting ways than she could manage on her own, and just being generally happier added a rosy glow to her face, making her look radiant. On a whim, she clasped her mother's cameo around her neck, on a delicate chain. Her gown was a deep plum, cut in the style of a Grecian goddess. It showed off her pale delicate shoulders, and draped straight down to the floor. It was simple, but its simplicity let her natural beauty shine.

She hadn't talked about her marriage with Molly, though the maid had shyly noted that her husband was quite handsome. She had not commented on how far removed Eliza's room was from Jonathan's, but that didn't stop her from wondering. But it was indisputable that the views from the room were sublime, and Molly had quite enjoyed them earlier in the afternoon.

Eliza felt more nervous now than she had on the morning of her wedding. She went down the stairs slowly. Her nerves were jangling, and she wasn't wholly certain that Jonathan would be joining her for dinner. But there he was, standing in the foyer, studying his pocket watch. He heard her on the stairs and when he turned, he was stunned by the sight before him. She looked like a goddess, practically glowing. She was beautiful.

Jonathan's stomach clenched. He was struck with a curious combination of joy and fear. Disconcerted, he made an effort to push both down as he stepped forward to meet his wife. He bowed. "You look lovely, Elizabeth."

"Thank you." She smiled.

"Shall we?" He offered her his arm, and escorted her into the dining room. Similar to the previous night, he seated her first, and then took his own seat.

Eliza's nerves stayed with her, unfortunately, and dinner was relatively quiet. Conversation was limited to murmured compliments of the food. She was distracted by her nerves, and afraid of saying something foolish. She found herself disproportionately occupied with thoughts of their afternoon escape from the rain. She was feeling physical longings that were quite new to her, and she didn't entirely know how to handle them. She had had the wild impulse, when she met him at the base of the stairs, to throw herself into her husband's arms.

Jonathan, for his part, was struggling with his unexpected feelings. He thought he liked Eliza well enough. He enjoyed talking to her. He deeply enjoyed making her smile, and laugh. However, he highly valued having some distance between them, as well. He was fine with the idea of happiness. But he didn't want anything like the emotional dependence his parents had had for each other. Therefore, any overwhelming sense of emotion was enough to make him withdraw somewhat. He had spent not a small part of the late afternoon thinking about that kiss in the gazebo.

It was his fault, in the sense that he had initiated the kiss. He didn't know what had come over him. But she had been so soft and charming. It had seemed like the right thing at the time. And she had responded to him. He had spent a small but dedicated part of the afternoon wondering if she had ever been kissed before, or if that had been her first.

His first kiss had been in those very gardens. He had been 14, and Olivia Forester had been 13, and the minx had cornered him and kissed him. He had barely known what was happening. He thought he'd learned one or two things since then, but he had never had much interest in women in that way. He was more interested in studying, in being outdoors with friends, or alone, reading. He was an avid reader, and a lot of what he'd learned about women had come from books. Or more lascivious friends. Being confronted with physical desires now confused him greatly. Granted, he was still young at the age of 24, but he was an adult, and he had thus far assumed that what he felt was normal, and that the strong urges and passions experienced by some of his comrades were childish, or overstated. He realized that up until now, he had considered having strict control over his sexual urges to be a kind of strength. And so, he identified those ambiguous feelings that were beginning to rise as a result of Eliza's presence to be a weakness. The experience of those nascent feelings was confusing to say the least. These thoughts were still consuming him at dinner. Was wanting to kiss his wife a weakness? Put that way, it seemed foolish to even think such a thing. Of course husbands and wives were meant to kiss each other. That realization made him feel better. He smiled up at Eliza and realized the meal was almost at its end. While he was looking at her, he saw that she was staring at her plate, playing with her food more than eating it. He became concerned.

"Is there something the matter?" he asked. "Not feeling poorly, are you? The rain today...you could have caught a cold."

Eliza looked up with a small smile. "I feel fine, thank you." After a pause, she added somewhat stiltedly, "Thank you for today. I enjoyed it greatly, our time together. This afternoon."

"I'm glad," he said warmly. "I had a good time, as well. I was wondering if you still had an interest in working together?"

She nodded. "Yes, I do."

"Wonderful! We can start tomorrow, if you like?"

"Yes, yes that would be acceptable."

"Good. Just meet me in my office? In the morning, whenever you like. You are," he felt embarrassed that he hadn't said this earlier, "more than welcome in my office, of course, at any time."

She blushed. She had, in point of fact, been treating his office as a sacred space that her presence would be a violation of. She felt uncomfortable just passing by the door, hence she had left the beautiful sitting room unused. "Thank you," she said, smiling at him. "I will meet you in the morning then. But the evening is still early. Would you like to adjourn to the drawing room, perhaps join me for some coffee?"

Jonathan studied her with some slight wariness, but in truth, he wanted to spend more time with her. "That sounds like an excellent idea," he said.

She smiled at him, her dimples showing, as he stood

and walked around to pull out her chair. They moved to the drawing room. Eliza was feeling brave and emboldened as they entered the cozy room. Thoughts of that afternoon in the gazebo were still swirling in her head, and she felt giddy. She paused and drew close to him, resting her hand on his shoulder. Jonathan was mildly startled, but equally pleased. Their kiss was at the forefront of his mind, as well, and he felt the blood rushing in his ears. He placed his hand over hers, and put his other hand at her waist.

"Lissie," he murmured before dropping his head to kiss her. His lips were warm and strong, moving across hers with confidence. He pulled her close, so that their bodies were pressed together, adjusting his arms so that both hands were at her waist holding her tightly against him. He could feel her soft body melting into his as her hands crept around his neck and up to his hair. Bold indeed, Eliza kissed him back, tentatively probing with her tongue this time, eager to explore. Her fingers tangled in his short silky hair. One of his hands slipped down to her hip, and she moaned softly into his mouth. Jonathan broke the kiss first; breathing raggedly, he rested his forehead against hers and created some space between them, keeping his hands high on her hips. Her hands slid to his shoulders.

Hesitantly, she asked, "Why did you stop? Was something wrong?" Her face was flushed, and she felt her body thrilling to its core.

He chuckled hoarsely. "Nothing is wrong. I just think we shouldn't get carried away."

Chastened, she took a small step back. "I see." But she didn't see, really, at all. Wasn't this sort of intimacy part of marriage? Even her parents, to whom the word "passionate" would never have been applied, though they were good people and devoted to their family, had managed to conceive twice. Eliza didn't fully understand the exact mechanics of conception, but she knew enough to know that men and women came together intimately in a way she hadn't yet experienced. That thought made her pause. She stepped fully back, breaking their embrace, and walked to a sofa, taking a seat.

"Jonathan," she began questioningly, "do you wish to have a family? Children? At some point, I mean, not necessarily immediately." It seemed like a perfectly valid question, but her voice wavered greatly. In Eliza's mind, all families contained children. It was an inseparable part of marriage. But it finally occurred to her, given Jonathan's reticence and distance, perhaps that wasn't how he envisioned marriage working.

In fact, Jonathan looked rather stunned by the question. He saw the world much the way that Eliza did, in that families consisted of parents and children. At some point in the last few weeks, he neglected to think that with marriage came the expectation of children and family. Mrs. Davis entered the room at that moment with a small knock, bearing the coffee, saving him from answering immediately. It gave him a few moments to reconcile his thoughts on the subject. Even though his parents' relationship and his mother's death had had a profound effect on his perspective of romance, he had nevertheless always pictured another generation of Stanton children playing in the gardens, climbing the trees, and exploring the woods. Such that, when Mrs. Davis had left, and he had taken a seat in a chair near Eliza's sofa, he was able to answer clearly, if slowly. "Yes. I suppose I have always expected to have children at some point."

This made Eliza feel a bit better. At least they felt similarly on the subject. She smiled and relaxed a bit.

"But," he added, "I don't think there's any rush."

She nodded, "Of course not. I just realized that it was something we hadn't really discussed before. I think it's good that we understand each other's expectations," she said the words carefully, not with hesitance so much as deliberation. There had been times in the last week when she had been loath to know her husband's expectations; afraid that he wouldn't want marriage in any traditional sense at all, afraid that he may want their union to exist on paper only. That thought had made her feel more like a hostage than a wife. The last two days had dispelled some of those fears, but he was still clearly keeping her at arm's length.

The couple didn't linger over their coffee. Jonathan wasn't in a talkative mood, and he was putting obvious distance between them, leaving Eliza feeling slightly bereft, and alone in spite of his presence. Dissatisfied, she tried to make small talk, but his responses were brief and not conducive to conversation. Shortly, she pleaded tiredness and retired to bed, leaving Jonathan to his own devices in the drawing room.

He hadn't been purposely ignoring her that evening, and when she left the room, he was sorry to have lost her company. He was occupied with the thought that he had kissed her three times, now. Each time, his agitation grew. He wrestled with the question of how to be a husband. Perhaps if he didn't enjoy Eliza's company, it would be easier to resolve. But as it was, he quite enjoyed her company. He found himself wanting more time with her, rather than less. Furthermore, he had quite enjoyed kissing her. Thrice. And he had a strong desire to enjoy more of that, as well. Being utterly out of his depth with these desires, he was left wondering if giving in to them would be failure, or success? Or somehow both.

Chapter 13

The next morning, following breakfast, Eliza stood outside Jonathan's office door, hesitating for a moment. She knocked lightly, and then entered. He sat at his desk with a ledger open in front of him, rising as he saw her. "Good morning," he said warmly. His jacket was draped on the back of his chair, and he looked quite casual. His desk was heavy dark wood, and aside from the chair he occupied behind it, there were several other chairs in the room, as well as a small table. Shelves stood tall and imposing along the walls, almost as densely spaced as the library downstairs. Though these featured a few small framed portraits, and what must be souvenirs of various Stanton travels, along with an assortment of books. The windows were open, letting in a slight breeze.

"Good morning," she said cheerfully.

"Shall we get right to it?" His tone was brisk, but friendly. "I've been going over the records for the mill, but perhaps it would be best if you explained what you know about it first."

Eliza took a seat in one of the chairs across from him, took a quick look at the book open in front of him, and the books set to the side, and launched into what she knew of her father's business. It was quite a lot. She explained everything, referencing the books as necessary. It was quite possibly the longest and easiest conversation they'd had. She felt eminently comfortable discussing the mill, and Jonathan was pleasantly surprised, and engaged.

At one point, he couldn't help but observe. "It's rather unusual for a woman in your position, with your family and standing, to know about such things as this, and to participate so heavily in her father's business dealings."

Eliza looked up at him frankly, "I suppose that's true. My mother taught me all of the things a young woman should know. In many ways, she wasn't just a mother to me. She was a teacher, and also my friend. When she passed away, my father and I started to spend more time together. One of the ways we found to do that was for him to teach me what he knew. It brought us closer. And I like numbers and mathematics. I find the logic of it to be soothing. It makes sense in a world that isn't otherwise required to make sense."

"I see," he said, subdued. "Thank you for sharing that with me," he added, before continuing with their previous discussion.

After she had explained her father's business, and he had had all his questions answered, they switched roles and he explained the shipping business to her, as she had expressed curiosity about it. They spent hours like that, talking and asking and answering questions, looking at figures and maps. Mrs. Davis brought them food at some point, but they were so deep in conversation they barely noticed. She chuckled over the two of them to herself.

Jonathan was amazed. Talking to Eliza just like this was like talking to any man about work. His fears and doubts fell away, and it all became very straightforward. The only significant difference was that his wife was animated in a way that reminded him of her femininity, and he occasionally caught himself staring at her neck or lips as she spoke, bent over the desk. Those instances were momentary, though. She was intelligent and knowledgeable, and he enjoyed conversing with her. He came quickly to an understanding of what she had meant about the logic of concrete ideas providing a reliable foundation, from which one could have a rational conversation, unburdened by the niceties or requirements of formal conversation. In this manner, they were less a man and a woman conversing, and more like two professionals. Given that they were married, there was no impropriety in the two of them being alone together. Barriers of societal manners were somewhat stripped away, unnecessary to their discussion.

For Eliza, this was the most at ease she had been in weeks. She felt solidly grounded in the mental work. There was no ephemeral nature to mathematics, at least not as pertained to running a business. Moreover, she was pleased to find that her husband didn't try to patronize her, or dismiss her. He listened, and respected her knowledge and ideas. She quite enjoyed herself, which helped her to relax. By the mid-afternoon, they were both feeling satisfied and happy with their progress. They had agreed to visit the mill two weeks hence, and spend the night in the city. Eliza drafted notes to the mill foreman and Mrs. Grayson at her family townhouse to alert them to the visit. Separately, Jonathan jotted a note to his uncle, apprising him of the progress and visit, and asking if he and Michael would like to join them for dinner at the townhouse.

Satisfied with their work for the day, they separated to prepare for dinner. In his room alone, Jonathan was thoughtful. He felt far more secure in his footing with his wife now. The last few days had allowed him to see parts of her that were more private, less formal, and he increasingly found that he enjoyed spending time with her. He saw, now, how they could easily develop a friendship, and this made him feel content. He was very much looking forward to their little trip into the city. He also found himself quite excited to share a certain surprise with her. Originally, it hadn't seemed like such an occasion to have the piano tuned. He had heard her play several weeks ago, so the suggestion from Brandon hadn't surprised him. But it had been accomplished today, and while it had originally seemed like an incidental household chore, he was now anticipating her response to the news. Smiling to himself he straightened his cravat and shrugged on his waistcoat. He checked in the glass to fix his hair, glanced at his pocket watch, and realized he was a full hour early. He sighed, settled into a comfortable chair in the corner of his room, and picked up a book.

He ended up becoming so engrossed in his book that he was five minutes late for dinner, and Eliza was already seated at the table when he entered the dining room. She seemed mildly surprised when he entered the room. "I'm sorry I'm late," he said. He paused on a whim and kissed her cheek before seating himself. "I hope you haven't been waiting long."

In truth, Eliza had dawdled at the foot of the stairs for a full five minutes waiting for him, before deciding he must be eating dinner in his office again, and had proceeded into the dining room alone. Her cheek flushed when he kissed it. "No, not at all," she lied, smiling. "I'm glad you're here."

She was wearing a dove gray gown, accessorized with simple jet jewelry and her hair was all trapped in braids that were intricately woven together in a Grecian style. Jonathan was starting to wonder if any color looked bad on his wife. "You look radiant," he told her, making her blush.

"Thank you," she murmured.

The meal was served, and their conversation this evening was much easier. They talked of their respective histories within their families' businesses, which led naturally into talk of their families, and that, in turn, led to sharing silly and poignant memories. She told him about her parents, and her unique relationships with each one of them. She told him about how the friendships she had made in childhood had stayed with her and shaped her adolescence and young adulthood. It helped that he knew most of the people she referenced, and he could picture them easily. In turn, he told her about boarding school and college, about his Aunt Charlotte, about the friends he had made in various places and the antics of young men. The incidents that were polite to share, at any rate.

They sat at the table and continued talking for a long while after the meal was finished, and it was fully dark when they retreated to the drawing room. Jonathan had forgotten his little surprise until now, but his excitement mounted as soon as they entered the room, and remembered. He caught Eliza's hands in his, smiling wide. "I have a surprise for you," he said.

"Oh?" She smiled in anticipation. The anticipation turned to slight confusion as he turned slightly and gestured at the piano grandly with one arm.

"The piano has been tuned," he announced, after she failed to react immediately to his gesture.

"Oh!" Eliza clasped her hands in delight. She was thrilled, which made her husband quite self-satisfied. He watched her cross to the instrument and lovingly lift the cover. She hesitated before touching the keys.

"Go on," he urged. "Play something."

She glanced at him as she sat down and played a chord. She smiled and began to play. Jonathan poured himself a drink and sat down to enjoy the view. His wife was skilled, but moreover, she genuinely seemed to love playing. It brought both peace and joy to her, and it made her seem to shine. When she had finished the song, he clapped and insisted she continue playing. After she had played to her contentment, he offered to pour her a drink. She accepted and sat down on the sofa where he had been sitting. He handed her the glass and retook his seat, smiling at her.

"Are you pleased with my little surprise?" he asked.

"Absolutely," she answered, smiling back at him. "Thank you."

They settled comfortably into the sofa and picked up the thread of the conversation they had been having about their childhoods.

"When did you begin playing piano?"

"My mother always wanted a daughter who could play the piano. I think she started teaching me before I could walk," quipped Eliza. "I honestly don't know how old I was. Some of my earliest memories are of sitting at the piano with my mother, while she played. She loved it so much. Did you ever play?"

"Only as much as my mother ever made me," he said, laughing lightly. "I suppose my mother wanted a son who played piano, but her son was more interested in climbing trees in the garden."

The two laughed together. "I think my mother would have fainted if she saw me try to climb a tree," she confided. "That didn't stop me from wanting to, though."

"Have you never climbed a tree? Not once?" He raised his eyebrows in shock.

"No, not ever. I think you would find that most girls haven't."

"Well, if we ever have a daughter, and she wants to climb trees, I'd let her," Jonathan declared. Eliza laughed. He thought that she might think he was joking, so he felt the need to reaffirm, "I'd teach her to do it myself!"

"I'm not arguing." Eliza put on a mock-serious face. "You'll not see me standing in your way. But on the other hand, if we have a son who likes the piano, I'm going to teach him how to play."

It was Jonathan's turn to laugh. "Of course you will." He was vaguely stunned that they were discussing future children with such ease. Three days previously, they had barely spoken five words together at once. He marveled at the rapidly changing tide of events.

The two settled into an easy, comfortable silence for a while. "I thought I might write to Amy Dudley, to let her know that we'll be in the city next week, to see if she might want to come for a visit, perhaps have dinner with us?" Eliza asked.

"That's a wonderful idea. I was going to wait and see what the response was before telling you, but I had dropped a note to Uncle Brandon already much for the same purpose."

Eliza smiled at him. "That was quite thoughtful of you. If you don't mind increasing the guest list, I'll write to Amy in the morning."

He nodded. "That's settled, then. You know, if you'd like, you could invite Amy here, to stay for a few days. I think people will expect us to start entertaining before too long, and we might as well start with people we like," he teased.

"Oh, that would be absolutely wonderful! I think she'd love it. We used to play together at your parents' summer parties. Did you know that's how we met, she and I, and became friends?"

"It doesn't surprise me, really. But all the more reason to invite her. In fact," Jonathan had a realization, "Isn't Vincent Dudley her brother? We should invite both of them. I had started to pick that man's brain at that dinner party, and I'd love the chance to talk to him further."

"Oh," said Eliza, "Of course. That's a lovely idea." She had slightly less enthusiasm for this idea, considering what had happened last summer with Vincent. But at the Forester party, he had acted like nothing was any different between them, so perhaps he had moved past it. And she was married now, so there was sure to be even less awkwardness between them, if there were any at all. She rallied and declared, "I'll write first thing in the morning."

"Good. That's settled," Jonathan glanced at his pocket watch. The hour had grown late without them realizing. "Should we retire?" he asked.

"That might be for the best," Eliza agreed, realizing the time.

They rose and he escorted her to the landing, where their ways parted. They paused with some awkwardness. He bent toward her, and she expected him to kiss her, but he only kissed her cheek. "Goodnight, Elizabeth," he murmured in her ear.

"Goodnight, Jonathan," she returned, once again feeling confusion envelop her.

He turned and ascended the stairs to the west wing. She, likewise, turned and started up the stairs to the east, but she paused two steps up and turned back. "Jonathan," she called.

He paused and turned back, coming back down to the landing, "Yes?"

"I," she stammered, unsure of precisely what she wanted to say. He approached with concern, stopping a step below her and taking her hand.

"Is something the matter?" He was concerned.

"No, I just," she paused again, before coming to a bold decision. "I want you to kiss me."

His surprise was obvious, but he smiled and leaned forward to once more brush his lips over her cheek, but she turned at the last moment so that he kissed her lips instead. He pulled back, shocked. She gazed into his eyes, daringly. "Let me escort you to your room," he said, taking her arm firmly, but gently. He knew what she wanted. At least, he thought he did.

They walked to her bedroom door and he opened it for her. Blessedly, Molly wasn't there. He followed Eliza into her room. Her heart was pounding. This was the first time he had entered her room, and she didn't know entirely what he might do. He paused just inside the door and took her hand, pulling her close. He cupped her face with his other hand, and looking into her eyes, he sighed softly. He guided the hand that he held up to wrap it around his neck, and then dropped his hand to her waist. He bent his head and kissed her waiting lips softly, delicately. He kissed her as though she was the most fragile of butterflies, but that still wasn't what she wanted, and he knew it. Gradually, step by excruciating step, he deepened the pressure of his lips, moving with deliberation. His tongue invaded her willing mouth and tangled with hers. He raised the hand that held her face up to tangle in her hair, as the hand that was at her waist lowered to her hip. Hot moments built a frantic excitement within Eliza, but then he began to draw back. The kiss grew gentle once again, and he placed soft, individual kisses on her lips, her chin, her cheeks, the tip of her nose. Putting small bits of space between their bodies. He bent his head low and rested his forehead on her shoulder, breathing deeply. He kissed the fragile space where her neck and shoulder joined before straightening, and put a full, purposeful step between them. Her hands rested lightly on his chest, while he brought both hands to her waist. With a slightly roughened voice, he said firmly, "Goodnight, Lissie. Sleep well." Softening a bit, he kissed her lips lightly again, once, "I shall see you in the morning." With that, he was gone. Out the door before she could even respond. She fell against the door, panting slightly, still feeling tight and hot and tingly all over. She raised the back of one hand to her cheek and sighed, smiling.

She got ready for bed in a blur. She stayed awake in bed with thoughts of his kiss, his warm hands on her body, chasing circles around her mind. And when she slept, she had dark and exciting dreams about a faceless man who held her close.

Chapter 14

The days followed on, and the newlyweds established a new schedule. They ate breakfast separately. Eliza still never saw Jonathan first thing in the morning, and had no idea what his morning was like. But she was accustomed to rising early, reinforced by the presence of Molly, who by old habit, brought her coffee first thing and helped her to dress and ready herself for the day. After a leisurely breakfast and turn about the topiary garden, if the weather was friendly enough for it, Eliza would meet Jonathan in his office and the two of them would work. After the first day of sharing information, it was no longer necessary for her to spend as many hours there, and with the two of them working cooperatively, Jonathan found that his hours could be shortened as well. They spent their afternoons enjoying separate pursuits, for the most part. Jonathan often stayed in his office longer, diligently reviewing information, correspondence, and numbers, or enjoying a pleasurable book quietly, while Eliza would sketch or do her needlework downstairs. The two of them would always have dinner together, and Jonathan would escort Eliza to her room afterwards, sharing hot kisses with her, but no more, before retiring to his own room.

On the third day of this new arrangement, the afternoon was especially lovely, and Eliza took the opportunity to visit the stables. She brought Molly with her for company, and because she knew the maid deeply desired to see the animals. Joshua was cleaning a saddle in front of the stable, enjoying the fine weather himself, when he saw the two ladies approach. He greeted them with a bow, and Eliza introduced him to Molly. After just a little conversation, it was decided that both ladies would start riding lessons, which could happily begin immediately. Eliza had come to rely on Molly as a companion as much as a maid. As the girl was enthralled with the horses, both of them learning to ride together seemed like a natural course to take.

They spent several hours learning about the horses generally, the stables, and getting to know the horses they would ride. The Stantons had five horses altogether, and Joshua chose the two most docile geldings for the ladies to become acquainted with. They brushed them and fed them treats, getting to know them and their temperaments before attempting to mount them. Joshua had prepared the tack for one side saddle, but another one would need to be cleaned up for the second horse, so while he demonstrated properly saddling and bridling a horse, the ladies realized that they would need to come back the following day to continue their lessons. They were full of smiles as they waved to the stable hand and the beasts and headed back to the house. They were flushed and happy upon their return.

And so, the days followed. The nicest days saw the two girls slowly learning to ride, interspersed among other activities. Eliza finally felt comfortably settled into her new life, with just one exception. She knew that Jonathan was still keeping her at arm's length, in some ways, and she was beginning to both look forward to and resent his goodnight kisses. As much as they excited her and pleased her, she was beginning to feel frustrated. She wanted more from him. She longed to beg him to stay with her for the night, but she was loath to say those words. It had scarcely been a few weeks of their improved interactions, and she was afraid of saying or doing something that would make him retreat back to a more isolated existence.

Jonathan was quite pleased with the current situation. He found his wife an excellent work partner, and he enjoyed the time they spent together in that way. He had the freedom to spend more time in his day devoted to more enjoyable pursuits, and he found himself happier than he had been in as long as he could remember. He didn't like to admit it, but he didn't enjoy living with his father. After he came back from school, his father had been different. Quiet, dour even, and remote. The older man worked quietly, and spent much of his free time out of the house, alone in the woods, walking or riding. Jonathan had offered to go riding with him several times, but the rare occasions they had actually gone had been quiet and awkward. It wasn't that his father didn't love him, and Jonathan knew that. The man just no longer knew how to express himself with ease. His heart had been broken when Margaret died, and he'd never managed to put it back together again. While Jonathan wished he'd had more time to repair the relationship he had with his father while he was alive, he was now in a position where he simply experienced less stress in his days, with his father not present. The most difficult part of his days, he acknowledged with some irony, were the late evenings with his wife. Every night, he would escort her to her bedroom. That first time had set the precedent. He would bring her into the room, kiss her goodnight, and then leave. Frustration was growing on him like moss. He expected that repetition would diminish the feelings the kisses roused in him, but the contrary seemed to be true. Every night, he seemed to feel more, want more. It was these moments that scared him. He wanted to be in control of his feelings and desires, and the control he felt now was tenuous, at best. Hence the frustration. However, on the whole, things were going quite splendidly. He assumed that he just needed to give things more time, and that in time, his emotions would cool and steady. It had barely been a month, after all, and that really wasn't long at all.

Their trip to the city was imminently approaching, and they were both looking forward to that. They had gotten confirmation that Brandon, Michael, Amy, and Vincent would be joining them for dinner that evening, and they were looking forward to a little adventure and company.

Chapter 15

The morning of their trip dawned clear and bright, and they set off early. Eliza and Jonathan were both chipper, and chatted in a friendly manner about inconsequential things. They headed straight to the mill, where they met the foreman, who greeted Eliza warmly. Introductions were completed, and the couple enjoyed a tour. Jonathan was impressed and pleased with the operation and the foreman's knowledge and professionalism. Eliza asked after the small amount of company housing, and made sure the dining hall was staying well-provisioned. She greeted several of the workers by name, and asked after the families of several others. She listened attentively, which further impressed her husband. She had clearly immersed herself into the goings-on. The three, finishing their tour, spent an additional hour or so sitting in the office discussing procedural matters and concerns. The couple made tentative plans to visit once a month, with the understanding that more regular visits could be arranged. But with all things going smoothly, and the foreman being well used to running things, once a month seemed to be all that was necessary.

Afterwards, the couple turned toward the Montgomery townhouse. Eliza was excited to see her family home again. Mrs. Grayson met them at the door and greeted them happily. They agreed heartily with her suggestion that they might wish to freshen up. Smiling, she led them upstairs to the master suite. She opened the door to reveal that the room had not only been opened up and aired out, but had been decorated with fresh flowers. Eliza smiled in delight, even while she was mildly disarmed at being presented with her mother's suite.

Observing her mistress's pleasure, Mrs. Grayson beamed. "I'll leave you two to clean up, then. I'll have lunch prepared for you when you're ready."

Before either Eliza or Jonathan could say anything, the housekeeper had quickly retreated. The two looked at each other. Eliza hadn't specified which rooms to make ready, and she was only just realizing that she may not have specified a number of rooms, either. Disconcerted, she walked to a door and opened it to find the room her father had slept in still closed up, the furniture shrouded in sheets. She left the suite and walked to another door in the corridor and saw her former bedroom in the same state. In a daze, she walked into the room and looked around, becoming mildly distraught. Jonathan had followed her, immediately understanding her concern. "It's not a problem, Elizabeth. I'll go find Mrs. Grayson and ask her to prepare a second room." He turned to go do just that, but Eliza stopped him, catching his coat sleeve.

"Wait," she said, considering the issue. "Is it really necessary? I just don't want to cause a fuss and it would be a lot of work just for one night," she trailed off feeling uncertain, and also a little embarrassed.

He turned to look at her closely. He wasn't sure she fully understood what she was suggesting. "It wouldn't make you uncomfortable? To share a bed?"

She blushed and glanced down. When he put it that way, it made her feel brazen for suggesting it, and she wondered if she had offended him, or made a mistake. "If it would bother you..." she began.

"I didn't say that it would bother me," he interrupted gently, "I asked if it would bother you."

Blushing furiously, but daring to raise her eyes to meet his, she replied, "I don't see anything wrong with a married couple sharing a bed."

"That's fine, then. That's what we shall do." With that, he turned and went back to the master bedroom. Eliza took one last turn around her old room, taking in all the furniture that was draped in white, like a room full of old ghosts, before following him.

Standing in the master bedroom, she began to question the idea of sharing the room. She noted that there was a dressing screen, though, and that made her feel better. And the closet was large. She could do this. Jonathan had taken off his waistcoat and loosened his ascot. He stood looking out the window. Eliza retrieved her brush and sat at the vanity. She began to fix her hair, and she used the cloth in the basin to gently pat her face and neck. It was early afternoon, and she was debating whether to change into a clean day dress, out of her traveling clothes, or to just wait a bit longer and change straight into her dinner clothes. She decided on the latter course of action, but at least she wanted to take off her boots, and replace them with slippers more suited to being indoors. That decision being made, she turned to face away from the vanity and bent to remove her boots. Jonathan caught her movement out of the corner of his eye and turned to watch. He didn't mean to stare, but he was enthralled by his wife's delicate fingers at work, and her fine ankle as it was revealed when the first boot came off. He quickly averted his eyes as she shifted to the other foot. He blushed a bit, and was glad the window was in front of him.

Shoes changed, Eliza suggested they go downstairs to relax in the parlor some, before dinner. Jonathan agreed, and they descended the stairs. He was thankful to be in a room that didn't have a bed in it. They enjoyed tea and light sandwiches, and then they both took the opportunity to enjoy a book for a while. It was a quiet, pleasant afternoon.

All too soon, it was time to dress for dinner. Tactfully, Jonathan excused himself a half an hour earlier than necessary to do so, such that he could be finished dressing by the time Eliza entered the bedroom to do the same. She was mildly relieved when he stepped out of the room while she was still behind the screen. She redid her hair and put on her stockings and shoes in complete privacy. She wore the plum gown again, as it was appropriate for the small party they were hosting.

She descended the stairs just as their first guests arrived, admitted and introduced by the butler, Mr. Abraham. Brandon and Michael both looked handsomely fashionable, and had brought a bottle of wine. They shook hands with Jonathan, and each kissed Eliza on the cheek. The four of them took seats in the parlor, after Mrs. Grayson had taken charge of the wine.

"Eliza, you look lovelier every time I see you," remarked Brandon. "That country air is good for you."

"Thank you," Eliza replied. Turning to Michael she said, "you really must come visit us at the house. The flowers are all blooming, and I know you'd just love it."

"Yes," Michael agreed. "I'd like that very much indeed. I don't want to impose myself on newlyweds, though. I'm sure you two are enjoying your privacy."

Everyone chuckled. "Nonsense," said Jonathan. "You might as well be one of the family. You'll always be welcome."

"Well," began Brandon, "are the two of you planning to pick back up the tradition of hosting summer parties? Not this year, of course, but perhaps by next?"

Glancing at his wife before speaking, Jonathan answered, "We haven't spoken much about it yet, but I think it's something we've both considered. It would be nice to have more life in the old place."

"Yes, it's a large house," agreed Brandon. "Definitely made for more than just one person."

Before he could make a suggestion the younger people were not quite ready to hear, Eliza piped up, "I am planning to invite a few friends to come stay for a while, soon, so that should fill it up for a little while, at least."

"That's a capital idea, my dear!" Brandon encouraged.

It was at that moment that Amy and Vincent arrived. After salutations were exchanged, Jonathan suggested, "Gentlemen, why don't we adjourn to the library for a drink, to give the ladies a chance to visit?" Eliza cast him a thankful smile, and the two groups separated.

Once Amy and Eliza were ensconced in the parlor, Amy let out the squeal she had been holding in. "Elizabeth Ann Montgomery STANTON! How on earth could you get married and not tell anybody? Not even your best friend in the whole world?" She feigned a pout.

"Oh, Amy!" Eliza was instantly contrite. "I'm so sorry! It all happened so fast!"

"It's all well, silly goose. I'll forgive you instantly as long as you tell me all about it. I want all the details. Tell me, please!" she begged.

Eliza laughed. "I'm not sure what there is to tell," she began lamely.

"Lissie! I didn't even know you were acquainted with Jonathan Stanton! He is--was--only the most eligible bachelor in all of New York! And all of a sudden, you're married to him? Lissie," her tone turned serious and low, "you weren't trying to avoid a scandal, were you? You're not...pregnant?" The last word was barely a whisper.

"No!" Eliza said with vehemence. "No. Not at all!"

"Oh, dear, I'm sorry. I'm sorry! I just had to ask. What other explanation is there?"

"It's simple, really. My godfather, Mr. St. John, is Jona-than's uncle. He suggested the match. To secure my father's business."

"Are you telling me that you married the most hand-some man in town as part of a business arrangement?"

"Well, yes," said Eliza shyly.

"No. There must be more to it than that. Tell me that it started out as a business arrangement, but then you took one look into those dark, stormy eyes--"

"His eyes are blue," Eliza interjected.

"Ah ha! So you did look into his stormy BLUE eyes, and fell instantly in love, and the two of you just couldn't bear to be apart." Amy sighed dramatically; hand raised to heart.

Eliza laughed softly. "Nothing of the sort I'm afraid. We met, we chatted, and we found each other agreeable, that's all, really."

"Agreeable! Lissie, you can't just base a marriage on whether or not you find each other agreeable." Amy was clearly offended by this idea.

"Well," conceded Eliza, "He is also quite handsome. And intelligent. And he makes me laugh."

"Well," Amy was at least slightly mollified, "that's something. But tell me more! What's it like to be married? To," she lowered her voice conspiratorially, "live with a man?"

Eliza considered the question seriously. "The Stanton house is lovely. The gardens are even prettier than I remember them being as a girl. And there are horses! Did you know that? I'm learning how to ride."

"Ooh," Amy squealed, "is *Jonathan* teaching you?"

"No. The stable hand, Joshua, is. And Molly is learning with me! Oh, yes, Molly came with me," she added with a smile.

"Well, that's wonderful, but that doesn't tell me anything at all about being married! What's it like," she paused, lowering her voice again, "to be with a man?"

"Well," Eliza hesitated, not knowing how to answer. "We work well together. Actually, in the beginning, at first, it was quite awful. But then it got better--"

"Yes," interrupted Amy, "that's how mother said it works."

Eliza looked confused for a moment. "Now, we spend a little bit of time working together each day, and we have dinner together every night, and every night, just before bed," she paused and blushed, lowering her own voice, "he kisses me."

"What do you mean, he kisses you?" Amy looked nonplussed. "You mean that he *just* kisses you? And then what?"

Eliza studied her hands. "Well, and then, he goes to his own bedroom, and I get ready to sleep."

"That's all? He doesn't do anything...*else*?"

"Well, no." Eliza lowered her head in embarrassment.

Amy looked deflated. "So you mean you and he haven't..." she trailed off, uncertain as to how to finish the sentence.

"No, we haven't."

"Well, that isn't a problem, though, isn't it? I mean, surely at some point... Anyway, mother says it's painful. I don't know if I'd want... I mean, I'm not sure if I'd want it to happen at all, myself." Eliza knew that her friend was lying to make her feel better, and it was kind.

"He says he wants children," she explained, "so I'm sure, eventually..."

"Yes, of course," Amy said comfortingly. "You don't suppose... I mean, I'm sure this couldn't be possible at all, but you don't think there's the possibility that he might, well, be interested in another woman?"

"No?" Eliza was shocked by the notion. "What would make you say such a thing?"

"Oh, forget I said anything at all," Amy rushed. "I'm sure it's nothing."

"What's nothing?" Surely her friend wouldn't have brought up this idea with no reason.

"Well, you must remember how much Olivia Forester wanted him? I mean, she practically threw herself at him. Maybe... there was some mutual interest there?"

Eliza balked. "Olivia Forester is *married*. She's Olivia Johnson now."

"Yes, true, but Patrick Johnson is twice her age, at least! We all know that she just married him for his money."

"Amy!"

"What? It's not my fault if it's true."

"Well, firstly, Olivia and Patrick are wildly in love. Everyone knows that they fell in love at first sight and couldn't wait to get married. It was the wedding of the decade, according to the society news. And even if she had been interested in Jonathan before meeting Patrick Johnson,

that doesn't mean Jonathan is interested in her. He certainly
wouldn't do anything about it, if he was, while she was married. And he's married now, too!"

"Oh, Lissie," Amy clucked. "You're so naive. But I'm sure
you're right anyway. Jonathan probably just doesn't want to
rush you. After all, you got married so quickly."

"Yes. Yes, I'm sure you're right. Anyway, let's talk about
you. How's your beau? The chum of Vincent's?" Eliza was more
than happy to change the subject.

"Oh," Amy said airily. "We broke it off."

"I'm so sorry! What happened?"

"Well, I think we just grew apart, is all. He stopped
being exciting." She shrugged carelessly. "There are plenty of
opportunities out there for me."

"Yes, there are, and you'll find the perfect one."

"I'm sure I will. Just like you did." She smiled at her
friend.

"Amy, I've been wanting to ask you. Would you like to
come stay with us for a few days this summer, in the country?
You could bring Vincent with you, and it could be just like
when we were children."

Amy beamed. "I'd positively love to! That sounds divine. I'll ask Vincent, but I'm sure he'll come. He loves you. Yes!
Thank you so much for asking."

Eliza was as thrilled as her friend. "Wonderful! It's all
settled then. Just name the day." The two girls smiled at each
other, and continued to chat about more trivial things until it
was time for dinner.

The dinner conversation was light and boisterous.
Everyone was in high spirits, and all was happiness. Eliza
couldn't help but notice that Vincent was staring at her intensely more than once throughout the meal. She seemed to
be the only one who noticed, though, and was glad for that.
The party chatted long into the evening, but at last it was time
for everyone to go home. Brandon and Michael left first, waving and promising to come visit soon. Amy and Vincent left

soon after. The only notable thing about their departure was that when Vincent took Eliza's hand, he bent low over it, and his lips pressed to the back of her hand for an *almost* indecent amount of time. But everyone, including Eliza, blamed it on the hour. They were all tired.

As Eliza and Jonathan turned to the stairs, triumphant hosts, they separately reflected on their evening. They each felt blessed to have such wonderful people in their lives. The closer they got to their bedroom, the more nerves replaced Eliza's exhaustion. She was increasingly unsure of what sharing a bed would be like. Her hands grew clammy and her breath shortened as they entered the bedroom.

Once in the room, she picked up her nightgown and dressing gown and quickly stepped behind the dressing screen. She took off the plum gown and hung it carefully on a hook with trembling hands. She slipped out of her petticoat and stays, her stockings and slippers, and found herself deeply aware of her own nakedness. She quickly slipped on her night dress and pulled her dressing gown close, belting it tightly. Taking a few deep breaths to steady her nerves, she stepped out from behind the screen to find the room empty. Jonathan had apparently stepped out and she hadn't heard the door. Curious.

She sat down at the vanity, deflated, and took her hair down, brushing it and putting it into a loose braid for sleep. She wiped her face and neck at the basin, and considered her situation. No matter how many times she glanced at the door, it failed to open. There were few choices, and she went with the most logical. She climbed into bed and under the covers, putting her dressing gown close by, so she could reach it from bed. She pulled the covers up to her nose and lay there, tense. She waited for a long time, and eventually she fell asleep. She woke at some point in the night, and tried to find her bearings. She was aware of a weight in the bed with her, and she turned to look. In the dark, she could make out the outline of her husband's shoulder and head. She could hear his deep, regular breathing. His back was to her, as he laid on his side. Realizing that he had come to bed after she had fallen asleep, without waking her, without any fuss at all, she thought that perhaps she was being silly to worry. She turned over and happily went back to sleep. She awoke again after the sun had risen and once again found herself alone in the bed. In the end, she was mildly disappointed. As she dressed for the day, she considered what Amy had said about Olivia. Jonathan had never once mentioned Olivia. But would he mention her if he was interested in her? Would he have married Eliza if he had feelings for another woman?

Olivia had gotten married the previous year. It had been a glorious wedding, well attended, with all the trimmings. She had a special gown made for the occasion, as well as a full trousseau. She had made sure everyone knew all the details, as well. She and Patrick had gone on a honeymoon to Europe and had been gone a full year. They had decided on an extended tour, and some speculated they may stay abroad indefinitely. Eliza had been surprised at the dinner party her parents had hosted; the fateful one that had led to her own engagement and marriage. The couple had reportedly enjoyed Europe immensely, and were temporarily staying with the Foresters while they looked for a new home together. Had that been just several weeks ago? She thought back to the last time she might have seen Olivia and Jonathan together, but nothing came to mind. Olivia was several years older than Eliza. The two girls knew each other, but they weren't close at all. And while Eliza knew who Jonathan was, they hadn't had a conversation as such, until her godfather introduced them. Prior to that she had barely realized that he was in attendance. She couldn't remember seeing them together at the party, but she wouldn't have noticed if she had. It was entirely possible that they had seen each other, and talked. Her hands balled up in the covers as she realized that she had no real way of knowing.

Eliza considered how very much her life had changed in the last few weeks. But she could only stay abed so long.

LISSIE

Sighing deeply, she got up and quickly bathed and dressed. Her shaking hands this morning were due to frustration, rather than fear. Downstairs, she found Jonathan sitting in the dining room, enjoying coffee while reading the paper. "Good morning," she said stiffly as she entered the room.

"Good morning. Did you sleep well?"

"I did, thank you." She crossed her arms, waited to see if he might say anything else. With his eyes firmly on the paper he didn't notice her posture, so she was met with frustrating silence. She issued an exasperated huff.

Jonathan glanced up with innocent eyes. "Is something bothering you?"

"Did you sleep well?" she asked pointedly.

He cleared his throat. "I did, thank you."

Jonathan had stayed up long enough last night reading to be sure that his wife would be asleep when he finally came to bed. He had then slept lightly all night, deeply aware of her presence next to him. He had awoken at daybreak to find that, at some point in the night, he had turned to face her. His arm had been wrapped around her waist, and she had snuggled back into his body. He had been loath to move, as the position had been delightful, but he was cautious of her reaction, should she wake in such a manner. So he had risen as quietly and carefully as possible, so as to not wake her, slipped on his clothes, and descended the stairs. He had been immensely grateful for the coffee.

Eliza's movements were rather more brusque than usual, but she didn't pursue further discussion. He was smart enough to gather that she was irate, but he was at a loss. He had done everything he could think of to make her comfortable. Afraid that anything he could say would just irritate her more, he stayed silent. After the light breakfast, quickly eaten, the two of them packed up and headed home.

117

Chapter 16

The ride home was as uneventful as the ride into the city had been, though it was more tense. Eliza did take the opportunity to tell Jonathan that Amy was thrilled about the idea of coming for a visit, and that she thought Vincent would enjoy it, as well. Otherwise, they discussed the mill and some of the more notable people there. He asked after Eliza's riding lesson progress, and she asked if he had begun reading anything of interest. The conversation felt stilted, and forced. Questions about Olivia Johnson swirled in Eliza's head, entwined with the memories of the previous evening.

Arriving at home they were both tired, if for separate reasons, and chose to go to their separate rooms to relax. Eliza desperately wanted to bathe again after all the driving, and Jonathan just as deeply wanted a nap.

Due to the nap, Jonathan was once again late for dinner. Eliza was less anxious about his absence this evening, given the events of the previous two days, and she didn't linger in the foyer waiting for him at all. Therefore, she was quite surprised when he turned up, while Mrs. Davis was serving the soup. Both ladies looked up in surprise.

"Forgive me for my tardiness," he said, as he sat down.

"It's not a problem," murmured Eliza. "I half expected you might wish to dine in your office tonight."

"No, no. Not at all. I enjoy our meals together." He flashed her a charming grin. She smiled back, cautiously.

"So," he continued, picking up a thread of conversation from earlier, "did the Dudleys say when they might be joining us here?"

Patting her lips with her napkin, Eliza replied, "Amy thought two weeks from now might suit, but she needed to confirm with Vincent. We had discussed them staying at least three days, but potentially up to a week. Again, it depends upon Vincent."

"That's understandable. But that sounds delightful. It gives us enough time to plan, and Mrs. Davis will need the time, of course, to prepare rooms and menus and such. Which you'll want to coordinate," he rushed to add.

"Yes," agreed Eliza.

"You'll certainly have an understanding of their preferences already, but the two rooms next to yours have the nicest views. Of course, the rooms on the other side of the hall get better light during the day." He was animated, attempting to excite Eliza about the impending visit. She seemed to be rather subdued this evening.

"I'm sure they'll both enjoy the garden views as much as I do," she said.

"Is there anything special you'd like to do while they're here?" A more open-ended question was sure to draw her out some.

"Nothing particular comes to mind. Though I'm sure they would both enjoy a tour of the grounds. For that matter," she realized, "I still haven't been past the stables and pastures, myself. I assume the woods would be a shady spot for a walk, this time of year."

"Shady yes, but make sure to not go alone. Joshua or I should accompany you."

"Is it unsafe?" Eliza's eyes widened.

"Well," he hedged, "it's probably perfectly fine. I played in those woods as a boy extensively. But there are wild animals, and... Well, frankly, my father died in those woods. It was determined to be a hunting accident, but his horse threw him. My father was a skilled horseman, and I'm just not sure what could have spooked his horse to that degree. It has made me consider the woods in a more cautious light, is all." He smiled to soften the darkness of his words. "I wouldn't want anything to happen to you. I would be honored to escort you through the forest."

Eliza nodded. "I understand. That would be lovely," she said, giving him a small smile before continuing her meal.

"Good. We shall do that, then. Perhaps Saturday? If the weather is agreeable."

"Perhaps," she nodded. "If the weather is pleasant."

Jonathan was perplexed at his wife's behavior. It wasn't that she seemed unhappy or distressed. She just didn't seem to be speaking as freely as he had become accustomed to. "Are you feeling unwell?" he asked cautiously.

"I'm feeling fine, why?"

"You just seem unusually quiet. I thought maybe you were tired from the trip. Or perhaps you're developing a head cold?"

Eliza felt vaguely offended. "I feel perfectly fine," she said distinctly.

"I didn't mean to offend you."

"I'm not offended," she lied.

They devolved into silence for most of the rest of the meal. After dinner was over, Eliza wanted to simply go to her room. She wasn't in the mood to dawdle in the drawing room. When Jonathan began to escort her, her initial inclination was to tell him that it was unnecessary. But she realized that such a deviation from what had become their norm would incite a conversation she wasn't prepared to have. She clenched her jaw as they ascended the stairs. When they had reached her door, and he had opened it, she spun so that she was across the threshold, but could stop him from following her.

"Upon reflection, I think I really am quite tired this evening," she offered him a small, tense smile. "I'm sure all will be well in the morning. Goodnight."

He was caught off guard, and saying "goodnight," in return was an automatic response as much as anything else. As soon as the word had been uttered, she closed the door in his face, and he was left alone in the hallway. Jonathan was mildly perplexed. Eliza was obviously upset about something, but if she wouldn't talk to him about it, he couldn't do anything to help. And she clearly didn't want to talk to him about it. With that realization, he retreated to the library for a drink with a book to keep him company.

In her room, Eliza found herself on the verge of tears, and she wasn't at all sure why. Her chest ached. She angrily kicked off her shoes, and then threw herself face down on the bed otherwise fully dressed. She screamed into her pillow until she had no air left, following the scream with deep breaths. What was wrong with her? Why was she upset? Absolutely nothing had happened. Of course, she reflected, that was perhaps part of why she was upset. She hadn't known what to expect the previous night to be like, but she hadn't expected it to be so monumentally lackluster. She had built up a certain anticipation for sharing a bed with her husband, and the actuality of it had been a complete disappointment. She wouldn't have even known he'd come to bed, had she not woken up in the night. But their arrangement at home was a clear indication that he had no interest in sharing a bed with her, so why was she so surprised? She sighed, chastising herself. Her nails dug into the bedspread, and she forced herself into a sitting position, wiping her tear stained face with her hands.

Eventually, Molly knocked and entered, bringing Eliza a glass of water, and asking if there was anything she could do to help her get ready for bed. Eliza roused herself and submitted to Molly taking the pins out of her hair and brushing it out. She moved like a poseable doll as she got undressed with help. She slipped her nightgown over her head. She thanked the maid and bid her goodnight. She laid in bed, tossing and turning. Unsurprisingly, she couldn't find sleep. Her mind wouldn't clear.

Frustrated, she got up and put on her dressing gown. She practically stomped to the door and opened it, stalking down the stairs. A dim light was coming from the library, but she ignored it, turning instead toward the drawing room. She opened the door to the terrace and swept outside, into the still summer night. Pacing toward the topiary garden, she breathed deeply of the sweet floral air. It was still unseasonably warm, even though the sun had set hours earlier. Being outside helped calm her nerves. The roses had just begun to bloom, and she could see their buds in the moonlight. Being outdoors soothed her frazzled nerves. Her pace slowed, as she enjoyed the night air on her face. She tipped her face up to the moon, much as she would to the sun, and breathed deeply.

Jonathan hadn't expected to see his wife again this evening, but there she was, before his very eyes. Standing like a moon goddess with her face upturned to the sky, he was struck by the sight. He had decided to take a meditative walk, himself, and was just coming back to the house. He couldn't miss the ghostly figure of Eliza, and he stood entranced by her for a moment. When she lowered her face and turned, he decided to make his presence known. He wasn't standing too far away, but he was obscured in the shade of a tall, columnar cedar. He cleared his throat and stepped away from the shadow.

Eliza gasped and turned on her heel, clasping her hand to her chest.

"I'm sorry. I didn't mean to startle you," Jonathan said softly as he approached.

Catching her breath, she shook her head. "No, no. I just wasn't expecting anyone else to be out here at this time of night."

"I understand. I was surprised to see you, as well. I'm glad I did, though. I was worried about you." His voice was tinged with care. He had slowly been walking toward her as they talked, approaching as cautiously as he would a wounded doe, and he now stood a mere step away. "Are you feeling any better?"

She looked searchingly into his face and sighed. She

took half a step away and hugged her arms to herself. "The night air is helping," she said truthfully.

"I'm glad." He reached out and brushed her arm with his hand. He disliked seeing her upset, and he wanted to be able to comfort her. But she seemed ambivalent towards his touch. Confusion washed over him. "Elizabeth--Lissie, did I do something to upset you?"

She looked up at him with anguished eyes. She didn't know how to explain her disappointment to him. It seemed like such a childish thing, especially in light of her tantrum earlier. She couldn't tell him that she was disappointed about the previous evening without drowning in her own embarrassment. She couldn't ask him about Olivia Johnson, because she had no idea what to ask. So she was at a loss as to how to answer his question. Frustration choked her.

Seeing what looked like tears in her eyes, and not being able to bear it, he stepped in to close the gap between them, and pulled her close. He cradled her head against his shoulder, and whispered words of reassurance, as one might do with an infant. After a moment, he pulled back slightly. "I think I may know the problem," he said. "You're upset after seeing your family home half closed up, aren't you? And sleeping in your parents' room?"

Eliza realized that he was probably at least partially correct, and nodded silently, laying her head back on his shoulder. He continued to stroke her hair and back and whisper soothing nonsense. After a short time, she straightened her neck and took half a step back, smoothing his lapel where she had laid her head. Furtively glancing up, she said, "I think I feel better now, thank you."

"Good," he said, smiling slightly. "May I escort you back to your room?"

She nodded wordlessly, and the two went back inside. He hesitated a few steps from her door, fearing a repeat of what happened earlier. He paused entirely and bent to whisper in her ear, "Lissie, may I kiss you tonight?"

Her cheeks flamed, and she was thankful for the relative darkness in the corridor. She nodded, and they continued into her room. With the door shut, Jonathan stood facing her, and took her face gently in both hands. Unlike previous evenings, he rained small, gentle kisses across her cheeks and the bridge of her nose, prompting her to giggle softly. He smiled, and then leaned down to kiss her properly. She rose onto her toes, and wrapped her arms around his neck, while his hands moved to her hips. His warm lips slanted across hers as he took the kiss deep. Unlike other nights, she was in her nightdress and dressing gown. There were no stays or petticoat between them, and she felt softer. He could feel her curves more freely, and his hands roamed the curve of her waist, learning things about her body that had previously been hidden. She gasped as his thumb grazed the sensitive underside of her breast, warmth immediately flooding between her legs. "I'm sorry," he gasped, pulling away, "I didn't mean to--" but she stopped his words with a kiss. She pressed herself firmly to him. He returned the kiss, but kept his hands firmly clamped at her waist. She began to be aware of a bulge pressing into her belly, and that was when he pulled away, placing a step between them. His breath was ragged. "We should say goodnight," he breathed out.

Flushed and hot, she wanted to continue kissing him. She wanted him to touch her again. But she was determined not to force him into doing something he didn't want to do. She forced her passions aside, and nodded in agreement. "Yes, it's late." Her own voice was less than steady.

"Goodnight," he said, his hands still firmly on her waist. He bent and kissed her one more time.

"Goodnight," she whispered. And with that, he turned, letting go of her, and quietly closed the door after exiting through it.

Chapter 17

The following morning dawned bright and clear, and omened a good day. In fact, the day followed much as any of the other days that had preceded the trip into the city. Eliza was back to her old self, all distressing thoughts seemingly dissipated, and Jonathan was pleased and content.

Finally, Saturday dawned. There were a few clouds in the sky, but it was clear enough, Jonathan whistled tunelessly to himself, upbeat about their planned woodland outing. He had risen early and presented himself at Eliza's door while she was still getting ready for the day. Molly answered the door, and he asked to speak to his wife for a moment. Molly closed the door. A long moment later, Eliza answered it, wearing her dressing gown. Her husband beamed at her, and presented her with a stack of neatly folded fabric. "Good morning!" He was quite chipper.

"Good morning. What on earth is this?" she asked, taking the fabric from him.

"Well," he explained, "if we're still going out into the woods today, a thought came to me. If you'd like, I could teach you to climb a tree!"

"Climb a--" Eliza was flabbergasted. She shook out the top piece of fabric to find that it was, in fact, a folded pair of trousers, that had been fitted with a drawstring at the waist. "Trousers?"

Jonathan's grin intensified. "If you'd like to try climbing, I thought these would make it easier. You don't have to wear them," he rushed to clarify, "but if you'd like to, it's not as though anyone will see you in them. We're going to the most secluded part of the property, after all."

Eliza looked dubiously at her husband. "I'll consider it."

"Good." With one last smile at her, he spun and walked back down the hall. She brought the trousers inside and showed them to Molly, who shrieked.

"You can't possibly be thinking of wearing those!" she cried.

"Well, he's right, it might be more sensible in the woods. I don't know if there are paths that have been cleared, or what it's like at all. If you and he are the only ones who will see me, how bad could it really be?"

"Have you ever worn anything like those before, miss?"

"Well, no. I can at least try them on to see what it's like, though." With that, she set to dressing in the garments he had provided. There were trousers, a simple shirt, vest, and a jacket. Not unlike a boy's skeleton suit, really, and she wondered if these had been his old clothes from boyhood. She decided that she needed to wear her stays, but obviously the petticoat wouldn't do. She put on a pair of drawers, because it seemed the right thing to do, and then put on the pants. They were loose without being baggy through the legs, but they did nothing to disguise the outline of her behind. She craned, trying to see herself. "That's not so bad, is it?"

Molly studied her objectively. "They fit," she decided. "And if the only one who's going to see you in them is your husband, that's not so bad. I don't think he'd want anyone else seeing you, though, that's for sure."

Eliza hm'ed to herself as she slipped on the shirt and tucked it in, and then followed with the vest and jacket. She did a little spin in front of the maid.

"I don't think you'll pass for a boy, miss. But then, that's probably just as well."

Eliza laughed, increasingly delighted by the naughtiness of wearing the trousers. She fidgeted while Molly secured her hair in a simple braid pinned around the crown of her head. Her hair was cut so that small tendrils curled around her face almost no matter what she did, as that was the fashion, and she decided that that was acceptable for today. She didn't want to look like a boy, after all. Even while wearing boy clothes, she enjoyed her femininity. Given her outfit, Molly offered to fetch her breakfast to eat in her room, to which Eliza agreed. She was practically humming with excitement, like a string pulled taut. She ate quickly, and had to refrain from running down the stairs, looking for Jonathan.

He was in the library, waiting for her to turn up. Hearing her footsteps on the stairs, he met her in the foyer. He stopped short when he saw her dressed in the trousers and jacket. Her legs were long, and the trousers couldn't conceal their shapeliness. His mouth went dry. "You look…" he began.

But she stopped him, laughing. "Don't say it! I don't want to know."

He laughed back at her. "I was going to say adorable."

"Well. I suppose that's not so bad."

"Not at all." His look was appreciative. "Are you ready to go?"

"Yes!" She was practically bouncing where she stood.

"Then let's go!" He stopped to pick up a picnic basket on the way out. Holding it up slightly he said, "this one won't be a surprise, but bringing something to eat made sense."

She smiled at his thoughtfulness. The two headed out the back door and angled toward the willow tree. She looped her arm through his casually. On the way, he gave her a rough idea of what to expect.

"There are horse trails and walking paths throughout the property, but some of them are more overgrown than others. I know the main path around the lake is clear, and the path that branches directly off the maze garden, which loops around the other side of the horse pastures, should be clear enough. The trails are loosely marked so we shouldn't get lost, and we can turn around and head back whenever you're ready to. We don't have to walk an entire trail." She nodded in understanding. "It's going to get warm, so feel free to take off the jacket. I can hold it if you'd like. And we can also pause to rest whenever you need to."

She laughed at him. "I'm not that fragile."

"I didn't mean to imply you were. It can just get tiring. In fact, I may be the one to cry uncle and need a break. You never know," he teased.

They walked in companionable silence, crossing the bridge toward the wildflower garden. "Do you have a preference for which direction we go?"

"The lake," Eliza answered decisively.

Jonathan smiled down at her. "The lake it shall be, then!"

As they drew nearer to the gazebo, they both slowed a bit, each thinking back to that rainy interlude a few weeks prior. But they continued on without stopping. Through the maze and past the thick tree line, they angled away from the stables this time, going instead towards the lake. A small section of it opened up onto the pastures, but the rest of it was surrounded by woods. Jonathan explained that a branching trail connected the woods around the lake up to the tree line they had passed through. There were small footpaths that wound throughout the forest, scribed through time by both man and beast.

The pastures lay like a cauldron surrounded on all sides by the trees. Sloping gently, but generally lower than all the area around it further out, with the lake naturally being the lowest point, and off center to the open area. At the moment, he told her, they were north and a bit east of the main house. The lake, and the small cabin that they could see across the water, were due north of the house. Jonathan guided Eliza toward the northernmost part of the pasture, where it met the lake and the woods at the same time. As they got closer, she spied a trailhead, marked with a small colored flag that had been pinned to the tree. Now that she was looking for it, it was easy to see. They unceremoniously entered the woods.

It was instantly a degree or two cooler, and the dappled shade was welcome. Insects buzzed around them, and she was immediately aware of some of the benefits of the trousers. They were almost immediately out of view of the pasture and it was like entering a different world. As much as the manicured gardens each created their own special vignette of nature, the forest was wildly resplendent with trees and moss and ferns. Birds sang loudly, and they could regularly hear the snuffling of rabbits or squirrels in the underbrush. Eliza glanced around in all directions in sheer delight, and Jonathan enjoyed watching her childlike wonder. He drew her attention to a small fallen limb in their path, and helped her step over it, before following her. With her a step ahead in crossing the log, he couldn't help but notice how the trousers suited her curves, but they were rapidly brought abreast again, and his attention turned forward. They walked with an unhurried pace, stopping here and there to catch glimpses of the sparkling water, or to spot a particular bird or chipmunk. The path was strewn with general forest debris, and Eliza made sure to watch where she stepped, cautious of her ankles. For the most part, the path was easily wide enough for them to walk arm in arm, next to each other, with the picnic basket on Jonathan's other side occasionally brushing against a fern or shrub. Once or twice, they were forced to walk single file, Eliza going first, with Jonathan following behind her. He swore to himself it was because he was better prepared to respond if she tripped over something if he was behind her, and the view was purely incidental.

Eliza was entranced. Having grown up in the city, this was her first time setting foot in a real forest, besides the thin patch of trees that separated the more formal gardens of the house from the stables. It even had a unique smell, sharp and earthy at the same time. Twigs and leaves cracked underfoot, and the random branch reached out to catch at her hair and jacket. She was definitely starting to get warm, the clothes altogether comprising more than she would typically be wearing in the summer, and she was grateful to remember that she could shed the jacket, and equally grateful that the shirt still provided sun protection for her shoulders. She was developing a fast affinity for boys' clothes. True to his word, Jonathan took the jacket from her to carry, once it was off.

They came to a small clearing on the lake, which Eliza learned was about halfway between where the trail had started, and the cabin. He asked if she would like to stop and eat here, or forge on ahead. She was too excited to think about stopping, so she asked if they could continue on. He was more than happy to oblige. They made it to the cabin as the sun was cresting past noon. Jonathan didn't have to look at his watch to know the time. He wasn't going to complain at all, but he was rather pleased to put the basket down. The small hunting cabin was almost as exciting to Eliza as the woods had been. It was a quaint looking structure, rustic but cheerfully welcoming. At its size, she expected that it was just one room, and Jonathan confirmed as much. To his astonishment, when he tried the door, he found it locked. That was unusual. But perhaps with his father's absence, Joshua had had the presence of mind to lock the door for safety reasons.

"I'm sorry we can't go in. I'll have to talk to Joshua about where the key is. But there's a table with benches outside facing the lake, and that's where I thought we could eat anyway. It's a brilliant view."

"That sounds delightful!" Eliza preferred the idea of staying outside, anyway.

The couple made their way around the house and found the table exactly as Jonathan had described. It sat in the shade of the trees, and had a picturesque view of the woods all around the lake, and the pasture where the horses grazed, with the stable in the distance. Eliza was astonished at the distance they had walked.

"And we're only about one third of the way around the lake," Jonathan said. He checked his pocket watch. "It's a quarter past one, so we may want to consider turning back for today, rather than making the full loop around."

She was shocked at the time. "I had no idea we'd been gone so long!" They had taken a meandering and relaxing path through the gardens, and had not rushed their way through the woods, so it had taken more time than it might have. He smiled at her. He had greatly enjoyed the time thus far, and was glad they hadn't rushed. They happily unpacked the lunch that Mrs. Smith had prepared. They had both built up quite an appetite on the hike thus far. "You're right," Eliza agreed after a while. "Turning back probably makes more sense for today."

"There will be more opportunities to explore," Jonathan promised. Under the table, his foot found hers, and he gently stroked the toe of his boot across her instep. She looked up in surprise and blushed. He grinned at her.

They continued eating, and when they were done, they packed up and turned back the way they had come. "I really am sorry you couldn't see inside the cabin," he said. "It's an interesting little place, though emphasis on 'little'."

"It isn't a problem." She smiled up at him shyly. "There will be a next time, right?"

"Of course! I promise."

With that, they set off. The shadows were growing long by the time they got close to the entrance. They had had a long day of adventure, and Eliza was starting to feel it in the muscles of her calves and thighs. She thought the night might feature a long soak in a tub, and she moaned a little bit thinking about that luxury. Jonathan stopped and looked at her with surprise apparent in his face.

"Erm, was that out loud?" Eliza asked in a small voice. He nodded, a smile twitching at his lips. "I was just thinking about how good a bath would feel," she explained.

"Ah! That explains it completely. A bath."

"Yes. A bath," she emphasized.

"Nothing else on your mind, then." It wasn't particularly a question, more a teasing observation.

"No, not at all. Well, actually, I was thinking that today was absolutely splendid. Did you know this was my first time really being in a forest? And I'm immensely glad you suggested the trousers. They were eminently practical." She smiled up at him, eyes wide and innocent.

"I'm glad you liked them," he said, holding in a grimace. She clearly had no understanding of how alluring she looked dressed like that. He felt it important, therefore, to add, "You probably shouldn't wear them in front of anyone else, though. Just me."

"Oh, yes, of course. I wouldn't dare. I don't even want Mrs. Davis to see me in them," she assured him. On further reflection, she thought to add, giggling, "Though Amy would probably die! She would never expect me to wear something so brazen."

Jonathan held his tongue. He didn't mind the idea of her wearing the pants in front of Amy, but the idea of her wearing them in front of another man, like Vincent, set his teeth on edge. But he didn't want to make her think he might be jealous. He wasn't jealous, he assured himself. He simply had a sense of propriety, and was protective of his wife's honor.

By the time they got back to the house, it was already six o'clock. Jonathan asked Mrs. Davis to postpone dinner by an hour and to arrange a bath for Mrs. Stanton in her room, after passing the largely empty picnic basket off to the woman. The housekeeper nodded with a smile, and Eliza thanked her husband with a small nod. They started to part ways on the stair landing, but Jonathan turned back, catching Eliza's hand. A sudden, daring whim caused him to pull her close and bring his lips crashing down on hers. While one arm wrapped firmly around her waist, the other tentatively skated lower, rounding firmly around the curve of her behind. Eliza was shocked, but also excited. She moaned softly against his lips before bringing her arms to his shoulders. Giving her one final squeeze, he released her, kissed the tip of her nose, and then spun to head to his room, leaving his dazed wife to stare after him. It took her a moment to process what had just happened, but then she turned and practically skipped to her room, where Molly was already preparing her bath.

Eliza sighed and leaned against the door, smiling. Molly turned around, "Good day, miss?"

"Oh, yes, Molly! A wonderful day!"

"Good, miss. I'll have your bath ready in a few moments."

"Thank you. That's going to feel good. We walked so much! All the way to that little cabin around the lake and back."

"Goodness! That is quite a long way. You must be sore!"

Eliza groaned in response and began stripping out of her clothes. "Yes! Though I tell you, Molly, these clothes were a genius idea. I didn't even try to climb a tree, and yet they were amazingly practical. There should be trousers for women out there."

"That would cause a scandal," observed Molly, laughing.

"Well, maybe the world could use a good scandal every now and then," teased Eliza.

When the bath was ready, she was eager to sink into it. Even just hip deep, it felt good on her aching muscles. She scrubbed well, with Molly helping to do her back. She decided to go ahead and wash her hair as well, since dinner was going to be an hour later.

After her bath, and once she had dressed for dinner, Eliza felt wonderful. Jonathan was waiting for her at the bottom of the stairs. He had clearly also bathed, and looked dashing in his breeches and starched cravat. She couldn't help but notice how his soft leather boots conformed to his calves. She caught herself staring and quickly directed her gaze up. He kissed her cheek when she reached the bottom of the stairs, smiling as he took her arm.

"You look beautiful," he said. His voice was low.

"So do you," was her unthinking reply. "I mean," she

stammered, "you look quite handsome."

He chuckled over his thanks. He seated her, his hand brushing her shoulder as he stepped away.

Eliza narrowed her gaze on her husband, as he seated himself. "We spent almost all day in the forest today, and do you know what we never did, not once?"

Jonathan looked at his wife blankly. "What?"

"I never got to climb a tree!" She broke into peals of laughter.

He laughed, deep belly laughs. "You didn't! You wore those trousers for nothing," he said as he winked at her.

"You're never getting those trousers back, husband. They're mine now! And you still must teach me to climb a tree."

He laughed even more. "I wouldn't dream of trying to take the trousers away from you, wife." He grinned on the word. "If you want to put them on again tomorrow, we can go back and climb trees."

Eliza thought of her aching legs and groaned. "Maybe next weekend. I don't think my legs could take it."

"It's settled then, next weekend." He paused thoughtfully. "Is that when the Dudleys are expected?"

"No, that's the weekend following."

"Oh, good. Well, then. Next weekend our goal shall be to conquer a tree!"

"That sounds wonderful. And perhaps we can explore the cabin more thoroughly."

"That reminds me, I need to ask after the key. To be truthful, I didn't realize there was a lock on the door to begin with. It used to always be open when I was younger. But things change. I have only been out there a small handful of times as an adult. It was more my father's retreat. Come to think of it, this was the first time I'd been out there since..." he trailed off.

"I understand," Eliza said, not wanting to make him say the words, and unable to bring herself to say them. "I'm sorry."

"No, no, it's not a problem. I'm not upset, I promise." He

smiled at her. "Just thinking."

The rest of their dinner conversation focused on lighter topics. They enjoyed teasing each other as much as they enjoyed talking of more serious things. After dinner, Eliza was yearning to play the piano. She had stretched every other muscle in her body that day, and she wanted to stretch her fingers, as well. Jonathan was more than happy to listen to her play. When the evening drew to a close, and he escorted her to her bedroom, after he had kissed her sweetly, she held him tightly to her, rather than letting go when he paused and started to pull away.

"Jonathan." her voice was husky. "Stay."

He groaned low in the back of his throat. "You don't know what you're asking."

"Show me," she whispered.

He brought one hand to her face, cupping her cheek. He rubbed his thumb across her lower lip, looking into her sweet face. He bent his head and kissed her again, long and slow. His hand tangled in her hair. But he drew back once again, this time using his hands on her waist to set her firmly away, even if it was only a space the breadth of a hand. "Not yet, sweetheart," he murmured.

"When?" she choked out, while tears pricked the back of her eyes.

He rested his forehead against hers, taking slow, measured breaths. "I don't know," he kissed her forehead. "I'm not ready yet. But I'll see you in the morning." He kissed the tip of her nose gently. "Goodnight, Lissie."

She made an inelegant noise of frustration and leaned against the hard door once he had left. She didn't understand. Then and there she resolved to stop trying to understand. She didn't feel as though she could be any clearer about what she wanted without being flatly indecent, and she thought that that shouldn't be necessary. Either her husband wanted her, or not. And the way he kissed her, the way he touched her; she brought her own fingers to her lips where his had so recently lingered. It surely suggested something of desire. But clearly not enough. He had said "not yet". Which implied a future.... Well, they were married, weren't they? They had a lot of future in front of them. She could be patient. That decision made, she readied herself for bed, and slept soundly.

Chapter 18

The next week passed in a happy blur of sameness. Eliza and Jonathan had found a daily schedule that fit them like a comfortable shoe, and they fell into it with ease. Eliza got confirmation from Amy that they would be arriving a week from Saturday, and they were too excited about their country getaway. Eliza was able to plan for that event with Mrs. Davis, Mary, and Molly. They would get the spare rooms aired out and prepared, and review meal plans and general ideas for activities. Mr. Davis popped in to say that all the berries were coming up splendidly, in full flower now, and the ladies may enjoy an afternoon helping to harvest them once they were ripe, an easy task that everyone, including Eliza, was happy to help with. She thought Amy would delight in putting on an apron and playing farm girl in this manner, as well.

Quite sadly, the following weekend brought rain and more rain. Never heavily, but steady enough to put off any further adventures in the forest. It also meant no riding for Eliza and Molly. But there was still plenty to do around the house, in addition to the work that kept Jonathan and Eliza both occupied every morning. She had endless needlework projects to keep her busy. Mrs. Davis happened to peer over her shoulder one afternoon to see that she was embroidering fine flowers on what appeared to be a napkin. Eliza noticed her observations and showed Mrs. Davis what she had been working on in total. A full tablecloth and napkin set, embroidered with pansies, roses, daffodils, and lilies. Her work was fine and delicate, and therefore time consuming. Mrs. Davis was enthralled, and delighted to learn that the tablecloth was long enough for the dining room at the Stanton home. "If I ever finish it," Eliza teased. "It will only take one or two more decades, perhaps." Mrs. Davis tsked and doted on the work the young mistress had already achieved. It would be an heirloom added to the family home, and it made the housekeeper, who had been with the house since before Jonathan had been born, misty eyed to contemplate.

Besides needlework, Eliza spent her time indoors during the rainy weather sketching and playing the piano. The entire household enjoyed having music in the house, so she played freely, whenever the urge struck her to do so. Occasionally, she and Jonathan could both be found in the library, reading separately.

The following days passed in much the same manner, but as the fateful weekend of their intended company's arrival drew closer, the couple's anticipation grew. Eliza was excited to host her friends, and Jonathan was happy to see his wife so excited. He also looked forward to having more people around the house. He had found that since Eliza had lived in the house, the entire place seemed brighter, and more alive. He would swear, if asked, that there were fewer shadows. Had he asked Mrs. Davis about this, he'd have learned that there were, in fact, fewer shadows. Having a lady in the house had inspired Mrs. Davis to rather boldly, in her mind, make the decision to open more curtains and let light into more rooms. The elder Mr. Stanton had wanted to keep many of the curtains closed, wishing to dwell in shadows physically as well as mentally. His passing hadn't been enough to make the housekeeper suggest a change, but the young master's marriage, and the presence of a new lady of the house, like a fresh spring blossom, needed the fresh air and sunshine. As no one had said anything about it, Mrs. Davis assumed she had made the right choice. And Jonathan assumed that his wife had conjured a sort of magic. Eliza, blissfully unaware, simply enjoyed having the draperies opened, and assumed that it was how the house had always been.

Chapter 19

Friday evening, Eliza was on pins and needles. She felt like a child waiting for a holiday. Jonathan remarked during dinner that she was practically humming with energy, teasing gently. He had to coax her into eating.

"I've never hosted before, unless you consider that dinner we had in the city. I'm just so nervous. I want everything to go well, and for them to have a good time here," she explained.

"That dinner went smashingly well. And these are your friends. Our friends. Of course they'll have a good time. If you did nothing but sit in the parlor all day and visit, you know that Miss Dudley would be over the moon. You have nothing at all to worry about." Jonathan was getting quite good at reassuring his wife, but it was particularly easy when there was nothing to worry about.

"You're right," she agreed. "We shall have so much fun."

"We will." He purposely included himself. He wanted to let her know that he was there for her, that they were approaching this together. He would support her in whatever ways she needed. If that happened to be taking Vincent away for a drink and a pipe in the library so the two girls could gossip, well, that was the least he could do for his pretty wife.

He sighed to himself a little, knowing more about what his pretty wife wanted from him than she did, and feeling like a heel for not giving it to her. But at least he could do this part. He could help to host properly. They had never talked about that night when she had asked him to stay with her. He thought she may be upset, even resentful of him, the following morning, but there had been nothing like that at all. She had been her sweet, cheerful self. Which made him feel all the worse. She had asked him to stay, so simply, so guilelessly. He was a fool for saying no. He was terribly afraid that he had hurt her feelings. He was still wrestling with the feelings that she inspired in him. He was waiting with growing impatience for those feelings to temper, to cool a bit, before progressing things further. That hadn't happened yet. If anything, his lust was intensifying, and that didn't suit him. He liked Eliza, very much. He yearned for it to simply be easy. He wanted to be able to bed his wife in a manner that was pleasant, devoid of burning desires and desperate yearning.

"What's on your mind?" Curiosity tinged her voice, as she brought him out of his reverie. "You're looking very serious all of a sudden."

"Hm? Oh, nothing really. I was wondering if either of the Dudleys enjoy riding, that's all." He lied, feeling his stiffness press against his breeches.

Eliza laughed lightly. "That hardly merits such an expression. Amy doesn't know how to ride, I'm quite sure, but Vincent may."

"We'll find out tomorrow." He smiled at her through gritted teeth, pushing both the lustful and self-flagellating thoughts from his mind.

"Yes, we will! Oh! I've been meaning to ask. When we were at the lake, at the cabin, there was a small dock. Has there ever been a boat?"

Jonathan thought for a moment, glad for the distraction from his internal musings. "Yes, in fact, there was a small rowboat. I wonder if it's stored in the cabin? I don't know where else it might be. That reminds me, though, Joshua said that there isn't a lock on the door at all, but that the door has started to jam a bit, in warm weather. He said it was probably just stuck, and that it simply requires a really good yank."

"Well that's interesting. It surely seemed locked when we were out there. We'll have to try again."

"If Joshua doesn't beat us to it. He said he'd ride out

there and take a look at it, if he got the time to do so."

"Perfect," sighed Eliza happily, thinking about more than just the cabin door. She was feeling quite pleased with their plans, all things considered. They finished the rest of their meal companionably, but Eliza found herself restless afterwards.

"Would you like to take a walk in the garden?" she asked.

"You don't mind that it's dark out?" The sun was setting later in the day, this far into summer, but it was still fully dark out by the time they had finished their meal and quit the dining room.

"Not if you're there to protect me," she teased.

He tweaked her nose and grumped, but he offered her his arm, which she took, and they strolled out into the dark garden. It was getting hotter. June had flown past and they were at the beginning of July. It would get hotter still. It still cooled substantially with sundown, and the gardens were pleasant, dark and fragrant. The paths through the rose garden were spread with light colored shell, and they seemed to glow gently in the evening light, making it easy to find their way.

"I'm glad to see that you're enjoying life here," Jonathan spoke out of the blue, his voice carrying on the still night air.

"I am," Eliza said warmly. "I almost can't imagine anything else, now. It's so lovely here."

"That makes me quite happy."

She snuggled his arm, smiling up at him, even though she was sure he couldn't see her. They walked on, their feet making small crunching sounds on the shell. The roses were in bloom, and the air was heady with their scent.

Unhurried, they made the full circuit of the rose garden, and when Jonathan would have turned them toward the house again, Eliza gestured toward the willow tree with a questioning murmur. Nodding, he turned in that direction instead. The path was less clear here, so they stepped a bit more carefully. He made sure to hold her firmly lest she trip in the dark. The creek babbled in its watery bed, and the willow rocked gently in the breeze above. Outlined in the thin, silvery moonlight, it was a dreamlike vision that hardly seemed real.

They crossed the bridge and wandered into the garden. Daisies and coneflowers bobbed sleepily on long stems, while sweet william and hydrangeas made dark clouds among the cedars and box shrubs. Tall grass sighed, and crickets sang. It was a peaceful evening that lulled the couple into silent meditations as they walked. The pond was home to boisterous frogs bent on making merry deep into the night. The gazebo loomed out of the dark.

Spotting it, Jonathan came out of his reverie. "We should head back, it's getting late," he murmured.

Eliza nodded slowly in agreement, and the two of them turned around to meander back to the house.

The following morning brought with it a slight sprinkling of rain that had Eliza fretting. She paced the foyer and parlor, wringing her hands. Logically, she knew that the rain wouldn't affect their plans, but the fact that something wasn't perfect caused her some stress. Mrs. Davis clucked over her distracted air, and Jonathan was wise enough to tuck himself out of the way for the most part. However, by 1 o'clock the clouds had cleared, and the Dudley carriage was pulling into the drive. Eliza and Amy embraced on the front porch, each so happy to see the other. The travelers came inside, shepherded by Mrs. Davis, amidst a hail of greetings and introductions. The housekeeper showed them to their rooms to freshen up, promising to have tea in the parlor when they were ready. Jonathan had stood back during the initial arrival, cordial, but mostly trying to stay out of the way. Eliza beamed at him, and impulsively hugged him. He hugged her back, smiling down at her indulgently.

Chapter 20

Jonathan, Eliza, Amy, and Vincent sat in the parlor. The ladies perched upon what had become Eliza's favorite love-seat, while the men each occupied a wingback chair nearby. Comfortably arranged for conversation, they discussed trivialities such as the drive, the weather, and mutual acquaintances in the city.

"Are you planning to host summer garden parties, the way your parents did?" Amy asked Jonathan excitedly.

Glancing at his wife, he replied, "Yes, we've discussed it. Not this year, of course, but next year. It's good to have people back in the house again. It's too big for one to live alone."

"It's a beautiful house," Amy sighed wistfully. "And I can't wait to see the gardens. Are they just as magical as they were when we were children?" she turned slightly to question Eliza.

"More so," Eliza promised. "Since the weather is cleared, I thought we could have dinner on the terrace tonight."

Amy clapped her hands in childlike excitement. "That sounds wonderful. Oh, Lissie, we must have as many adventures as possible while I'm here. Now that you're married, it's only a matter of time before you won't have time for little old me, anymore," she pouted.

"Nonsense," chuckled Eliza.

Vincent interjected, laughing, "My dear sister is under the illusion that everyone who gets married up and disappears in a cloud of smoke."

"Well," she said defensively, "so far, they have. Lissie

is just the last in a string of no less than three of our old mates who've gotten married and virtually disappeared. Mary Smith, Olivia Forester, and Jane Sewell have all gotten married in the last year or two, and of the three of them, I've only seen Jane and Mary once since. And Olivia not at all. The Forester dinner party doesn't count, as we barely got a word together. I'm not letting my Lissie disappear like that."

"Amy," Eliza said softly, "Jane and Mary both got pregnant right away, and now they have infants. And Olivia and her husband went to Europe. I've moved four hours away, by carriage, and you're absolutely welcome to come visit at any time. We'll be in the city at least once a month to check on the mill. I'm not disappearing, I promise. And one of these days very soon, you're going to get married yourself, and I bet we won't see you for at least a year afterwards," she teased.

Amy grasped Eliza's hand sincerely. "I didn't tell you my latest decision! I'm not getting married. Ever."

"What?" Eliza was shocked. "What do you mean you're not getting married?"

"Men aren't worth it, Lissie. No offense to the two of you," she glanced at the men, "I'm sure you're both lovely, but you," she looked to her brother, "are family, and you," glancing toward Jonathan, "are off the market. And now so am I. I'm going to become a bluestocking," she finished with relish.

"Amy, you don't care for reading," Eliza said helplessly.

"A spinster, then. Either way, I'm going to stay single and enjoy every blessed moment of it." She was devoutly sincere in her statements, though Eliza knew her well enough to have doubts.

Vincent leaned toward Jonathan and whispered loudly, "She's put out because Lucas Bradley believed her when she said she wanted to stop seeing him."

"I did want to stop seeing Lucas Bradley," Amy said.

Eliza felt lost, and Jonathan had stopped trying to follow a while ago. "Is Lucas Vincent's friend from law school?" she hazarded a guess.

"No," clarified Vincent, "that was Louis. Lucas works for our father. He's a bookkeeper."

"And he was only paying any attention to me at all because Father told him to," Amy said, clearly miffed. "So, when I found that out, of course I told him I didn't want to see him anymore. I don't want to see anyone anymore. My trust has been betrayed." Amy's voice was deeply grave, and it was odd coming from her petite, fair form. She looked remarkably like a china doll, with wheat blonde curls and milk white skin dotted with the smallest amount of freckles which she loathed. Her dress was a white cotton lawn printed with pink roses, accented with pin tucks across the bodice. All she was missing was a bonnet and some sheep to complete the appearance of feminine, angelic innocence, so hearing her swearing off men with such seriousness was incongruous to say the least.

"Well there are no men here who can torment you," Eliza said soothingly. "Just gardens and horses."

Amy lit up at the mention of the horses.

Mrs. Davis appeared then and beckoned to Jonathan, who rose and excused himself. He was gone just a few moments, and returned grinning at his wife, carrying a basket. Clearing his throat, he said, "Make that gardens, horses, and kittens!" He smiled at his wife, before placing the basket at her feet.

Inside, they all saw and also heard two mewling kittens. They weren't brand new newborns, but they were clearly juveniles. Both women gasped in delight.

"Joshua thought these two might be happier up here at the house," Jonathan explained. By way of further explanation, he added for the Dudleys' sake, "Joshua manages our stables. One of the barn cats had kittens, and one of these was the runt. He raised it by hand, and the other one is more reserved, so he says, and thought they'd make a good pair to have up at the house, where they will get more human attention."

Vincent chuffed a small laugh at that, but the women were engrossed with the little balls of noisy fluff. "I think we've lost them," he murmured to Jonathan.

Jonathan nodded. "Can I offer you something stiffer than tea?" he asked, checking the time on his pocket watch.

Vincent nodded, and the two men made quiet excuses and slipped out to the library, while the ladies were cooing over the kittens.

"Cats, in the house?" Vincent raised his eyebrows once the men were in the library.

"Oh, I'm sure they'll stay in the gardens for the most part. But Elizabeth had mentioned something about a kitten at some point in the past. The house is big and quiet, and she gets lonely from time to time," Jonathan said, by way of explanation.

The other man nodded. "Makes sense, then. So, how's business?"

"Going well, thanks. Thank you again for your help on that contract issue. It's smooth sailing for the moment." Vincent groaned at the pun, and both men laughed.

Back in the parlor, Eliza and Amy had moved to sit on the carpet to play with the kittens and chat about names. They decided the black one with the white feet would be called Boots, and the calico would be Mittens. The two would have stayed on the floor through dinner if Mrs. Davis hadn't popped in to remind them about it. The two happily bounced up the stairs, giggling like school children to get dressed.

Dinner was a merry affair on the terrace in the slanting evening light. The four continued to chat, and the kittens played nearby, stalking each other, which provided much entertainment. Amy was suitably impressed by the gardens, and the sight inspired Amy and Vincent both to reminisce about childhood. Jonathan got to hear the story of Eliza and Amy's blood oath from the other perspective, and Vincent reminded Jonathan of the games the boys used to play, and the adventures they used to have. They hadn't been close, but they were close enough in age to have been part of the same circle.

"So how many horses do you have, now? Do you get to

ride much?" Vincent asked.

"Five horses. Eliza has been learning to ride, but sadly, I don't get out there too often," answered Jonathan.

"That's a shame. If they're anything like I remember, the woods are beautiful around here."

"They are!" Eliza enthused. "We haven't taken the horses out in them, but we went for a walk around the lake two weeks ago. It was positively breathtaking. Well, part of the way around the lake. To the cabin and back."

"There's a cabin?" asked Amy, who had never seen that part of the property.

"Oh, yes!" her brother cried. "It's a little rustic thing right on the lake. I've always wanted to see it up close."

"We should go. We thought it had been locked when we went out, so I didn't get to see inside, either," shared Eliza. "But it was a lovely walk."

"Locked? I'm surprised that the door even had a lock," Vincent strained to remember.

"It doesn't." Jonathan looked abashed. "It was just stuck. It had been so long since I'd been out there, I wasn't sure if my father had added one. So," he added cheerfully, "we must absolutely go again. We could go tomorrow?"

Amy looked less than enthused about traipsing through the woods, but she was a sport, so she generally agreed with the other three, who were rather more excited about the prospect.

"We can bring a picnic," said Eliza with a bright smile. "And make a day of it. We can also see if we can find the boat."

"Boat?" Amy perked up.

"Yes, there's a dock, and Jonathan said that there was a rowboat there, at one point," she said, gesturing to her husband, "but we didn't see it when we were out there."

"I thought possibly my father hauled it into the cabin? I vaguely remember it being brought in somewhere during the winter, in case the lake might freeze. So where it may be now is a bit of a mystery."

The conversation meandered more as the foursome ate. Amy was delighted by the idea of picking berries, and she was enthusiastic to tour the rest of the gardens. Vincent was distinctly interested in seeing the stables. Jonathan and Eliza played happy hosts, and all was well and merry. When dinner was over, the four withdrew to the drawing room and Jonathan poured drinks. Amy coerced Eliza into playing piano, and the men were content to sit and watch with their Scotch in hand.

As the evening grew late, Amy was the first one to excuse herself to go to bed. A few moments later, Eliza decided she would follow. As she rose, both men stood respectfully, and she bid them goodnight. It was a break in their evening routine that neither she nor Jonathan had really planned for, but with guests, it couldn't be helped.

Eliza was also a bit more self-conscious of their marital sleeping arrangements, with other people in the house. While she knew it wasn't unheard of for couples to have separate bedrooms, it was slightly more unusual for them to be in different wings of the house. But she had to admit to herself that she had what must be considered an unconventional marriage, and she was determined to accept it for what it was. Even still, she was glad not to have their normal routine be witnessed by friends sleeping just down the hall. She tried to wonder what it would be like to an observer, to see them both enter her room, and then her husband to re-emerge mere moments later to retreat to the far side of the house. Perhaps, from that perspective, it was not particularly odd. She was unsure.

In her room, she sighed happily and reflected upon the relative successes of the day. And the kittens! She was so pleased her husband had remembered, and been so thoughtful.

A half an hour later, she was dressed for bed and sitting at her vanity, brushing her hair, when there was a knock at the door. Assuming it was Molly, she called, "Come in," without turning around. The door opened, then closed again. Eliza heard a distinctly male throat being cleared, causing her to gasp and turn, clutching the hairbrush to her chest. Jonathan stood in front of the door, looking mildly embarrassed.

"Is something the matter?" Eliza stood and reached for her dressing gown as she asked the question.

Her husband cleared his throat again and took a step forward. "Of course, everything is fine. I just, ahem, wanted to say goodnight."

Eliza gave him a low laugh. "I thought we said goodnight downstairs."

"That's not how we normally say goodnight." His observation was pointed.

She drew a deep breath. "Jonathan..."

He closed the small distance that was between them and raised his hand to brush her hair behind her ear. "You know, you rarely say my name," his voice was low, "and this is the first time I've ever seen you with your hair down."

She turned slightly so that they weren't quite facing each other, observing, "we've been married for two months now."

"Yes." He thought for a moment. "A little longer than that. Almost three months."

"Yes."

"Are you upset?"

She took another deep breath and closed her eyes for a moment. When she opened them again, she smiled softly and turned back to him. "No. You wanted to say goodnight? Properly?"

He couldn't help but be concerned. "Please, tell me what's troubling you. I can't help if I don't know what the problem is." He placed his hands on her arms, looking into her eyes beseechingly in the dim light.

She sighed. "It's just that...we've been married for almost three months and this is the first time you've seen me with my hair undressed. Doesn't that strike you as just a little odd? Are you," she hesitated, "unhappy with our marriage?"

"Of course I'm not unhappy!" he exclaimed, startled. He considered for a moment before speaking. "I just think it's a good idea to not rush anything, that's all. Elizabeth, I think you're a wonderful woman."

She softened and gave him a small smile. "I suppose I'm just being silly," she conceded.

He drew her into a warm embrace. "We're all allowed our silly moments in life," he assured her. He kissed the top of her head, and then her forehead. His eyes met hers just before he brought his lips gently to hers. He kissed her gently, as though she was precious crystal, and might break. Pulling away, he whispered, "Goodnight."

"Goodnight," she replied.

He let himself out and eased the door shut. She sighed and sat heavily down on the settee that was at the foot of the bed. She was just beginning to detangle her thoughts on what had just transpired when there was another light knock at the door.

Perplexed, she stood and opened it, quite surprised to see Vincent standing there. "Vincent! Is something the matter?"

"No, not at all, I just hoped to have a moment to talk to you. Alone." He glanced down the hall. "May I come in for a moment?"

Eliza was tired, and torn between her sense of propriety and not wanting to be rude. "Can we talk in the morning, please? It's getting rather late." Her tone was apologetic, but it was rather inappropriate for him to want to enter her room, particularly when she was dressed for bed.

"Eliza," he began, but paused. "Of course. Morning. We can talk in the morning. I shouldn't have bothered you in this way. Goodnight."

"Goodnight." She smiled softly and closed the door.

Chapter 21

Everyone awoke the following morning, excited about the day's plans. Some were more excited than others. Eliza dressed in a simple day dress, preoccupied with thoughts of her previous jaunt in the woods, with Jonathan and the trousers. She lamented not being able to wear them this time. She wondered if her husband was thinking about the same thing.

Quitting her room, she found Amy in the hallway. They shared greetings and went arm in arm to investigate breakfast. They found the men enjoying coffee in the dining room. Unhurried, the ladies ate while all four discussed the day's weather and the planned excursion. Amy's excitement was finally roused at the prospect of seeing more of the property.

After breakfast, and after acquiring their picnic lunch, the group set off. The sun was shining, and it was a warm day. The ladies walked a little ahead, bonneted heads together, while the men trailed behind. They could hear the girls taking turns pointing out garden features and exclaiming. Amy was delighted by the sight of the little bridge beneath the willow, and paused a moment to peer into the brook below. Eliza pulled her forward, promising more wonders ahead. The men were easily entertained by the women's excitement. The winding path with its little alcoves and nooks was slower to traverse with the numerous stops and pauses to admire the planting, or the presence of a bench or statue, or the pond. Jonathan was relaxed, and content to simply smile at his wife's girlish pleasures. Vincent was equally entertained, but appeared a bit more tense. Jonathan assumed the man was simply anxious to see what lay ahead.

As they approached the little pond, Vincent left the path a step or two and called to his sister to come and see some turtles, who had crawled out of the water to enjoy the sun. Amy stepped away to attend to her brother, and Eliza fell back a step, glancing at her husband who was looking at her with dancing, happy eyes. They smiled at each other, ignoring the siblings for a moment. They didn't hear the quiet words passing between the other two, assuming they were discussing the turtles. Amy shortly returned to Eliza's side, pulling her attention away from her husband once more.

The guests were dutifully enthused over the gazebo, which had just recently been repainted, and they delighted upon seeing the labyrinth. "It's just as I remembered it," Amy gasped in amazement. "I was afraid it would be smaller in reality."

She rushed forward, pulling Eliza on. "Remember all the games of make-believe we played here? We were princesses, imprisoned in the maze by a dragon, and only a handsome prince could rescue us!"

"I remember having to play the prince, once or twice," Vincent murmured dryly.

Laughing, Amy ran ahead, dashing into the maze. Jonathan and Eliza both, at this point, knew every step by heart, and moreover, had a good general understanding of how it was constructed. Jonathan had a plan view of it that had been drawn by the original gardener who built it hanging in his office, as it had hung since it had been his grandfather's office. There was no real way to get lost. There were simply four entrances, one on each side, that all led to the middle. They weren't concerned about Amy getting lost, so they didn't rush to catch up. When they reached the fountain at the center, she was there, smiling at them beneath her bonnet.

"Silly goose," chided Eliza gently, "you don't know where you're going!"

"Hurry up, then!" countered the other girl.

Once the four had left the maze, Amy was unimpressed.

"It's just trees. Where are the horses?"

"Come on," encouraged her friend, tugging her arm gently. They trod quickly through the tree line and came out upon the pastures, whereupon Amy gasped. The sun was breaking through some white fluffy clouds in an arrestingly pastoral way, making the pasture, barn, lake, and the grazing horses look like a painting.

Eliza pointed toward the lake, "See the cabin?"

Amy squinted. "We're walking all the way there? And back?"

"It's not so bad, I promise. And the forest is beautiful!"

The two girls in their long, straight cut dresses and bonnets looked picturesque themselves, against the quaint backdrop of pasture and forest. Walking a few steps behind, Jonathan made a solemn promise to himself to bring Eliza back here once their company had left, so that he could follow through on his tree climbing promise. The prospect of seeing her in the trousers once again factored into the decision only a small amount, he promised himself.

The trailhead was still clearly marked, and the woods were shady, but the air was a bit thicker this much later in the summer. The trees blocked the breeze, and Eliza was happy this time, to be wearing the light dress with only her stays and petticoat underneath. The sleeves of her dress were short, leaving her arms bare. She suspected that she would have been less comfortable in the boy clothes this time. The party stopped here and there to spot birds or rabbits or squirrels. The odd view of the lake through the trees and brush was captivating. They paused at the little clearing, but all of them wanted to wait to enjoy their picnic at the cabin. The men took turns carrying the basket. By the time they reached the small structure they were both happy to be able to set it down and not worry about it for a while. Happier still to think that it would be lighter on the way back, though neither one shared their thoughts on the subject out loud.

Once at the cabin, Vincent became slightly more animated, excited to revel in childhood memories. Amy was delighted by the rustic sight. It took both men to convince the door to open, and they all peered inside, stepping across the threshold one at a time. Jonathan opened the shutters, letting light and air into the single room. There was an obviously disused stove in the corner, with a small table and chairs, and a squat but soft looking bed peeked out from behind a painted screen. It was simple, but not plain. The walls were bare wood dotted with paintings of ducks in flight and deer caught standing in a glade on the walls. The stove was ornate, and the chairs had pretty carved backs and cushioned seats. A few pans and a pot hung from hooks near the stove and there was a small cabinet which surely contained the necessities for simple cooking and eating. Everything looked neat and orderly, though there was a light coating of dust that stood as testament to the cabin's long vacancy.

After a brief exploration of the single room, which didn't take much time, they spread their picnic lunch on the table outside, overlooking the lake. "Still no boat," Jonathan observed, as they ate. "It may be around the other side of the cabin."

After eating, they further explored, and indeed found the boat and its oars, leaning against the far side of the cabin, having been covered by a canvas tarp. The tarp bore a collection of leaves and debris, a suggestion of how long it had been in that position. The men pulled the tarp away, revealing the boat which appeared to be in good condition. "Should we see if she's seaworthy?" teased Vincent.

"Why not?" replied Jonathan, and the two of them manhandled the thing to the edge of the water. Easing it in slowly, it appeared to still be watertight.

Amy began to develop an idea. "Would it be possible to row back to the pasture, rather than to walk back through the forest?"

The other three looked at each other blankly.

"I don't see why not," Jonathan began. "There is another

dock over there. I don't know if the boat would hold four people, though." He eyed the small boat skeptically.

"I don't mind walking back," Eliza volunteered.

Amy beamed at her. "If your husband would be so kind as to row me back, I'm sure Vincent would be more than happy to walk with you?" she suggested innocently. "Or the other way around, of course. But I know how Vincent loathes rowing."

"I made the mistake of doing crew at Queens," he said miserably. "I didn't know what I was getting myself into."

Jonathan laughed, "No worries, old man. I'm happy to spare you the rowing, and your sister seems keen on taking a further break from walking. It's my pleasure to row, if you can promise to watch out for Elizabeth." He smiled warmly at his wife.

Vincent executed a small bow. "On my honor, I shall return her to you safely."

"Good, good, then it's all settled." His tone was slightly questioning as he glanced at everyone, but all assembled seemed pleased with the solution. "Are we ready to head back now?"

Chapter 22

Amid general agreement, the men helped Amy board the rowboat, and loaded the picnic basket in as well. Jonathan settled in and grabbed the paddles. Waving them off cheerily, Vincent and Eliza turned to the trail to begin the easy hike back.

After a few minutes of companionable silence, Vincent broached the subject he had wanted to discuss the previous evening. "Eliza, when I came to your room last night, I wanted the opportunity to talk privately, just the two of us."

"I see. We have that chance now." Her tone was gently curious. "What's troubling you?"

"I suppose I wanted to express my confusion," he said, then paused.

"Confusion?" she prompted.

"Yes. Last year, I thought, well, I thought that we had an understanding. I mean, I know the past year hasn't gone to anyone's plans. Given everything you were going through, I thought it would be indelicate and boorish to pursue any romantic overtures. I was under the impression, though, that when I got back home, we would have the ability to talk further. That I might have the opportunity to court you properly, the way you must know that you deserve. And then, it seems like overnight, you were married. You have to understand, please, that I'm concerned for you. For your happiness. Forgive me if this is none of my business, but Eliza, were you in trouble? Were you forced to marry?"

She flushed, and was happy that they were walking, so she didn't have to look directly at him as he spoke. "I wasn't forced, no," she murmured.

"Then can you please explain it to me? I'm confused beyond reason. I didn't think you even knew Stanton."

Eliza sighed. "My godfather is his uncle. He suggested the match, and upon consideration, we both agreed that it made sense." She paused a short while to compose her thoughts. "Vincent, I appreciate your tact and understanding in the previous year. I suppose I misunderstood matters, and thought perhaps your interests had shifted. My godfather made the suggestion because my father's business needed clear leadership, and my father and Jonathan's father had a close working relationship. He made it seem as though consolidation was logical."

Vincent was aghast. "Eliza, you're 19 years old! You've got your entire life in front of you. Not to mention, you're from a good family, with good connections. You got married for the sake of a business arrangement?"

"Vincent, please don't use that tone of voice. I'm not a child."

"You're not a child, no. You're a young woman, and you deserve so much more. Don't you see that?" Passion gripped his words, and he gestured grandly as he spoke.

"I'm sure I don't know what you're referring to, Vincent," she said primly. "I'm happy here. Jonathan is very kind and we get along with each other very well. I have everything I could possibly want!"

"What about love?" His voice was anguished.

She paused walking, and hesitantly looked at him for the first time since they had begun their discussion. He took advantage of the opportunity, and gently took her by the shoulders.

"Eliza," his voice was hoarse as he spoke, "I still love you." His eyes fell to her lips.

Before he could do or say anything else, Eliza reminded him gently, "Vincent, I'm married."

He dragged his gaze back to hers, sighing frustratedly.

"But don't you want more? From life? From marriage? More than just a business arrangement and complacency?"

She turned away from his grasp and began walking again. "I don't know what you mean."

Struggling for discretion, he spoke carefully. "Eliza, your bedroom is in an entirely different wing of the house from his. You know that if you and he haven't...that is, if you have only existed together as, say, a brother and sister might, since you've been married, you could file for an annulment."

She gasped at the suggestion, affronted.

"I don't mean to offend," he rushed to add. "I'm not saying you should do that. I just..." He ran his hand through his short-cropped hair. "I want you to know that you have options. More options than you may realize. You never had a proper courtship. You can't have, there wasn't time. You deserve someone who will idolize you. Someone who sees you as their queen, who would retrieve the moon for you if you asked it of him. Stanton just doesn't seem the type for that. All I'm saying is that you could still have that. I'm offering that to you."

"I... I don't know what to say, Vincent. This is entirely unexpected." Spots danced in front of Eliza's eyes, and she felt flushed.

"I understand. I do. You must be as confused as I was," he laughed somewhat harshly. He took gentle possession of her hand and placed it in the crook of his arm. "Please, take some time and consider, really think about what I'm saying. You deserve a more fulfilling life, and I'm offering it to you. We could get a house in the city near my parents and Amy. She would be delighted to have you as a sister! I can take care of you, Eliza. And I want to."

"I need to think," she breathed, feeling overly warm.

"Of course," he said soothingly. "Take all the time you need. I'm here for you, always."

"Thank you," she answered softly.

They continued on in relative silence, though he kept

possession of her hand as they walked. She was grateful when further conversation was of a lighter variety, back to the topics of wildlife and the beauty surrounding them.

"Vincent?" Eliza, after having some time with her thoughts, had considered something she felt important. "What about your parents? They couldn't possibly be happy if you were to choose someone who had previously been married."

"Is that what you're worried about? Eliza, my parents love you like a daughter already. If you were to have your marriage annulled, they would accept you without question," he spoke with assurance.

"You haven't already spoken to anyone about this, have you?" she asked curiously, anxiety washing over her in waves.

"No." His answer came slowly. "I may have mentioned it as a hypothetical to my father, in the sense of one lawyer speaking to another lawyer, about the idea of annulment generally. But he would have no way of knowing I meant you."

"You're positive of that? And Amy doesn't know anything about it?"

"Well, Amy knows that I have feelings for you. But I can't help that. She knew last year. It wasn't exactly a secret then."

"I see. I just don't want anyone to have expectations, I suppose. I really do need some time to consider things. You understand, surely?"

"Yes, yes of course. No one expects anything of you. I just want you to be happy. That's all Amy wants, too."

Eliza nodded, and was wordlessly grateful to see the end of the trail ahead. They exited the forest and turned to see Jonathan helping Amy disembark the rowboat. The pair had clearly not rushed, anticipating the walk would take longer than the rowing. The four converged again.

"You look flushed," Jonathan noted to his wife. "Are you feeling unwell?"

She smiled wanly. "I think it's just the heat. It's worse

now than it was the last time we came here."

Amy looked at her friend worriedly. "Oh dear. Would you like to sit down a moment?"

"No, no." Eliza waved off the worries with a smile. "Let's get back to the house."

With that, they turned and made their way back the way they had come, the girls once again linked arm in arm, leading the men like shepherdesses.

"How was the boat?" asked Eliza.

"Oh, it was delightful," Amy grinned. "I was able to tell your husband all about our childhood antics, too. I kept him quite entertained."

"She did, at that," Jonathan piped up from behind them.

"Oh, goodness," Eliza said, feigning concern, "should I be worried?"

"I don't think so," Amy said virtuously. "I think we were perfect children. What could we have possibly done that would be embarrassing?"

Vincent snorted and Amy shot him a dirty look over her shoulder.

Eliza laughed, feeling easier now that they were all together again. Once they had arrived at the house, she excused herself to the others, desiring to bathe and perhaps take a small nap. They were all feeling delightfully worn out, and this proposition sounded equally good to everyone. They decided to reconvene at dinner time.

Alone in her room, Eliza considered the conversation she and Vincent had had. She felt chilled from the shock. She had no expectation at all that he might still have feelings for her, and she couldn't help but acknowledge that her feelings for him hadn't changed. Of course she loved him, but that couldn't possibly be the sort of love that could sustain a marriage. But then she considered the relationship she had with her husband. She ruefully had to acknowledge that while she and Jonathan had an amiable relationship, he did not love her. Her feelings for him felt increasingly complicated. She put it all from her mind as she bathed using the basin and cloth that sat on her vanity. She had stripped out of her clothes and stood naked, enjoying the delicious feeling of the cleansing cloth on her skin. As she ran the cloth down one leg, she allowed her mind to drift to Vincent. She pictured his face in her mind. He was attractive enough, and a good age. He was intelligent and kind. But thinking of him left her entirely unmoved. Switching legs and switching men, her mind wandered to Jonathan. Instantly, her body felt electrified. She allowed herself to imagine that it was his hands stroking her body with the wet cloth, and she immediately became flushed and felt a heat curl up in her belly, a purring kitten of desire. Driving those thoughts away, as she switched to a dry towel, she had to admit that those feelings hadn't always been there, for Jonathan. They had grown with time, as well as with his kisses. If she was being fair, she thought, she had to allow that the same sorts of feelings could possibly grow for Vincent. And Jonathan held himself back, aloof. Vincent clearly had no interest in doing that. He wanted her, all of her, and that was an attractive notion.

But she reminded herself that she had made vows before God and friends. She and Jonathan had forged a happy existence together, and there was clearly room for it to grow. There was promise in her future with him. It wasn't clear, though, what that future would look like. Even if certain things changed, and progressed, would he always be distant? Would he perpetually keep her at arm's length, emotionally? The thought of that possibility weighed heavily upon her heart. It physically hurt her to consider it. She sat down on her bed heavily, mind over-full. She felt guilty and foolish to even consider what Vincent had said. But hadn't he been right about some things? She was still young. Her 20th birthday was at the end of this month. Did Jonathan even know that? She had a vague thought that his own birthday was some time in the winter, but she was horrified to realize she didn't know precisely when. Surely that was odd, and an ill portent. She felt nauseated, and was glad to be sitting. She couldn't help but wonder if she had made a horrific mistake. She climbed under the covers, still naked as the day she was born, and cried herself to sleep, not knowing quite what else to do.

She was awoken some time later by a soft knock on her door. "Miss?" Molly said softly. Eliza was relieved it wasn't anyone else.

"Yes," she croaked; her voice hoarse from crying.

"Are you feeling poorly, miss? Can I get you anything? You don't sound well."

"Some water, please, Molly. That would be wonderful."

"Yes, miss." The maid turned and departed, shutting the door softly. That provided Eliza the time to get up and put on stays and a petticoat, at least, and her dressing gown.

Molly returned and handed her a glass of water, assessing her appearance. "Should I get Mr. Stanton?" she asked doubtfully. "Or Miss Dudley?"

"No, no, thank you. Molly, you have been as close or closer a friend to me as Miss Dudley for the last two years. May I confide in you?"

"Of course, miss!" Molly was pleased that Eliza considered her a friend. The two had become quite close, it was true, since she had begun working for the Montgomery family.

Eliza gestured, and both girls sat on the settee. "Oh, Molly. I don't know what I'm doing. It's possible I've made a very serious mistake."

The blonde girl smiled sympathetically, but waited patiently for Eliza to elaborate.

"Vincent, Mr. Dudley, says that he's in love with me. He wants me to get an annulment from Mr. Stanton, and marry him instead," Eliza said in a rush.

Molly was stunned. Even if she had wanted to say something in response to that, she wouldn't have known where to begin.

"Please don't breathe a word of this to anyone, Molly. He's giving me time to think it over. I just...I don't know what to think! I love Vincent like a brother. It's frankly odd to consider marrying him. But when I married Mr. Stanton, we barely knew each other at all, and he still.... He.... I don't wish to be indelicate," she said gingerly. "But you know that we don't sleep in the same room. We've never, that is to say, he and I have never..." she groped for the right words. "We haven't consummated our marriage." She hung her head in shame.

"I don't know what to expect from a future here, with him. He says that he wants children, so that has certain implications. But he's just so distant. And it hurts." Her voice was anguished, choked by unshed tears.

"Do you love him, miss?" Molly asked carefully.

"I don't know," sobbed Eliza. "I mean, I like him. I enjoy being around him. I enjoy talking to him. He...excites me. But is that love? God, I would give anything for my mother to be alive right now. She didn't prepare me for any of this." Eliza was on the verge of hysterics, and Molly quickly retrieved the glass of water, encouraging her to drink, and patted her arm consolingly.

"Thank you," Eliza sighed. "I'm just at a loss. It doesn't feel like either decision is the right one right now. Jonathan keeps me at arm's length, and I don't know how to get closer to him, or if he even wants that. And Vincent...Vincent is a good friend. I don't know if I could bring myself to see him as more than that. Does that make any sense at all?"

She was met with an earnest nod. "It does, yes. May I make an observation?"

"Of course, yes. Please do."

"Well, I've noticed the way Mr. Stanton looks at you. He may not say it with words, and he may be bad at showing it, but I think he feels something for you. I don't want to say what those feelings might be, but maybe it's worth talking to him?"

Eliza took a deep, steadying breath. "Yes, you're probably right. Definitely right. I should talk to him. Oh, what time is it? Do I have time before dinner?"

"It's a quarter past 6, miss. If you get dressed quickly,

you could speak to him before dinner, I'm sure. But mightn't you want to wait a bit? To figure out what you want to say?"

"That would make some sense, but if I wait, I'll turn coward," Eliza felt determined in the moment, but knew the feeling wouldn't last. "Quickly, help me get dressed, please."

"Yes, miss." The two got to work. Eliza, being dressed and ready for dinner in under 15 minutes, stood outside her husband's bedroom door with her heart in her throat just as the clock in the foyer struck the half hour.

She knocked lightly on Jonathan's door, wishing he would answer, and wishing he wouldn't in the same heartbeat. He opened the door. He was dressed but for his jacket, and he was clearly surprised to find his wife standing before him.

"Elizabeth? Is something the matter? Are you feeling ill?" He looked his pretty wife over. She was dressed for dinner, but she seemed distraught. "Here, come in. Come in."

This was the first time she had entered his room, and that realization unsettled her. She had no idea what she intended to say. She looked around, buying time. The room's walls were covered in a pale blue damask wallpaper. The bed was a four poster that stood against one wall. Much like her room, there was a small sofa at the foot of it. It was a large room, and there was a small seating area at the other end, with two plush chairs and a small table, facing a fireplace. Shelves flanked the fireplace. There was other furniture, but her eyes refused to settle on the fine details anymore. She looked at her husband, afraid she might cry again.

"Sit down," he urged, guiding her to the loveseat. "Tell me what's the matter. Please?"

"I," she began, then paused. "I need to know how you feel about me," she blurted.

Jonathan looked surprised. Sensing his wife's distress, he gently took her hand in his. "I care about you, Elizabeth. I must hope that my actions express that to you. I enjoy your company; I like spending time with you. You make the house, and my life, brighter and happier." He smiled at her. "I think you're kind, and beautiful, and intelligent. But please, tell me, why are you upset? Have I done something?"

"No." She glanced away. "Yes. I mean to say, you haven't done anything, but I think that that's part of the problem. Not that there's necessarily a problem. I just find myself confused." She sighed and glanced back up at him. His words had made her feel lighter, better. But there was still something that she couldn't put her finger on.

"I'm confused, as well," Jonathan admitted. "I know that when we got married, we weren't very well acquainted. It seemed like the wisest course, and still does, I believe, for us to take time to get to know each other before we get closer." He struggled to express himself.

"You mean to say that you believe keeping a certain kind of distance between us while we, as you say, get to know each other, better allows us to do that? To get to know each other?"

"Yes." He smiled at her.

She took a deep breath, unwilling to bluntly tell him that that made no sense, she decided to confront another issue instead. "Every night, you escort me to my room and kiss me."

"Yes," he hesitated. "Does that bother you? Should I stop?"

"I just find it perplexing," she confessed. "I enjoy it. You seem to enjoy it. But you never seem to want more than that." She stared into his eyes boldly, daring him to respond.

"I do enjoy it," he leaned close conspiratorially, oblivious to her point. "I look forward to it every night. When it comes to more...I want both of us to be clear headed about the steps that we take."

She nodded, even though she didn't understand what he was saying. She felt entirely clear headed about what she wanted.

He rubbed her hand gently, soothingly. "Shall we go down to dinner?" he asked softly.

She smiled slightly and nodded, his obtuseness grating

her sensibilities beyond reason. She didn't feel as though she'd gotten a sensible answer to any question she had posed. Her mother had succeeded too well in teaching her daughter to put polite manners above all else. Eliza felt hamstrung in the conversation. She wanted to scream at him that he was wrong, that he wasn't making sense. But she restrained those impulses. She balled her hands into tight fists at her sides, vowing to revisit the conversation when they had more time.

He rose and offered his hand. She unclenched one fist in order to take it and stood. "Jonathan." She paused, another question coming to mind. "Why is my room so far away from yours?"

He arched an eyebrow. "I thought I had told you. Your room has the best view of the gardens. I thought you would like that. Would you prefer to move to a different room?"

"No, not at all. I was just curious. That was thoughtful of you." Her tone was indifferent, but he failed to notice.

They met the others downstairs, and enjoyed a lovely dinner. Everyone was relatively quiet after the day's exertions, and they were all eager to go to bed shortly after dinner had finished. There was no lingering over drinks that evening.

That night, when Jonathan escorted her to her room, he remained for a longer period of time. Instead of standing near the door and staying there, he urged her to sit with him. They held hands as their knees touched.

Knowing that she felt frustrations that she was too shy to mention, he moved one hand to her knee, grazing her leg softly. She glanced down at his hand, questioningly. "I'm worried about you," he said. "I want you to be happy."

With that, he leaned forward and kissed her. The different position was interesting. While there was less contact between their bodies, she was hyper aware of the contact they had. His hand shifted slightly to grip her thigh, while his other hand cradled her head. She tentatively reached a hand to touch his knee, and her other hand went naturally to his back. His tongue invaded her mouth and stroked gently, insistently.

He brought the hand cradling her head down to her back, while his other hand shifted caressingly over her thigh, while her hand unconsciously shifted to his leg as well. Feeling her delicate fingers on his inner thigh, through his thin breeches, he broke the kiss, breathing heavily. He caught her hand in his, and smiled at her. She smiled back, feeling somewhat dazed. He placed a small, chaste kiss on her lips, and then stood. He bent and raised her hands to his lips, kissing her fingers gently. "Goodnight, Lissie," he whispered.

"Goodnight," she whispered back. Then he was gone.

Laying in bed that night, Eliza's frustrations calcified into anger; she beat her pillow with tightly clenched fists. She worked out her frustrations in this manner until she was spent, and exhausted. The conversation with her husband had provided little clarity as to her current deliberations. For that matter, the cuddling, the way he had touched her, had only emphasized that she had two imperfect choices in front of her. She was so upset by this evening's interlude, she considered telling him that she had changed her mind. She didn't want him to kiss her at all if he was going to torment her in this way. Sleep enveloped these restless thoughts.

Chapter 23

My Dearest Jonathan,

It's been so long since we last spoke, but I must hope that I still hold a place in your heart, just as you hold one in mine...

I am delighted to inform you that Mr. Johnson has purchased the former Southland estate, and we took residence this past week. We are neighbors, now! I hope this news brings you joy, for you must know that I am overjoyed that we are once again so close to each other...

I have longed to be close to you...

I beg for you to visit soon, as you are always welcome.

Yours, Always,
Olivia Johnson

That was the substance of the lengthy letter Jonathan received mid-morning the following day, delivered by messenger. Those were the lines that jumped out at him from pages of polite nonsense about Europe and their shared acquaintance. He was eternally grateful that he had been in his office and Mrs. Davis had delivered it to him herself. Moreover, contrary to their usual custom, Eliza had tarried in the parlor after breakfast to visit with their guests. He hastily shoved the letter in his desk drawer, lamenting that it was warm enough that lighting a fire in the fireplace would be excruciating, and cause questions from the others. He considered tearing it to little pieces, but he wanted to burn it, later, and it would be easier to burn whole.

Clearly Olivia hadn't heard of his marriage, or so he

hoped. He wondered if her marriage was that unfulfilling. He couldn't fathom what else might cause her to write such a personal letter. His own dear Elizabeth would be brought to tears by it, if she were to read it, he was quite sure. What on earth was he supposed to do now? He had been so sure he'd be free of Olivia's attentions once she was married. That appeared to have only been a temporary reprieve. He needed to let her know that he was now married, and absolutely not interested.

. . .

The summer Jonathan had been fourteen, at one of the several parties his parents hosted each season, Olivia had caught his eye. She had been pretty, and her height, even at thirteen, made her stand out among the other girls. They had known each other for as long as each of them could remember, but this was the first time Jonathan had noticed her as a man notices a woman. He and the other boys had occasion to talk quietly amongst themselves, and most of them agreed that Olivia was one of the prettier girls they knew.

The boys had been playing with a ball that got away from them, and Olivia had been the person who returned it. She handed it to Jonathan, keeping her eyes down, but looking up at him through her lashes. "Here you go," she said softly.

"Thank you." He bowed cheekily and grinned at her.

She smiled back and lifted a hand to play with a loose lock of her hair. He thought that her posture was strange. They were the same height, but it looked like she was ducking her head a bit. Perhaps she was self-conscious about her height, he reasoned.

Not knowing precisely what else to say, she bobbed a small, awkward curtsey and said, "Enjoy your game! Win for me."

He chuckled, thinking that it wasn't really the kind of game a person could win, as the boys were just kicking the ball around, but he decided to be a sport, "Of course, my lady." With that, he grinned his cheerful boyish grin and rejoined his mates.

Later that afternoon, she was sitting underneath a tree with a book, looking as pretty as a picture. No other girls were around, which was rather curious. Jonathan was running to find a friend who had wandered away into the gardens, and he all but tripped over Olivia. He stumbled a bit, but didn't lose his footing. "Sorry about that," he said, bending down to make sure she was uninjured.

She shifted and looked up at him, her dark eyes a severe contrast to her pale skin. "I'm fine," she assured him. "Are you hurt?"

"No, I'm fine," he grinned at her.

"Good. I would never forgive myself if I hurt you." Her voice was soft, and she fluttered her eyelashes as she spoke.

"Is there something in your eye?" he asked, concerned.

"No," she answered abruptly, red creeping into her cheeks. "I'm perfectly fine."

"Okay, then. I'll be off. Be careful!" And just like that, he bounded deeper into the gardens.

As the shadows grew longer, someone proposed a game of hide and seek, something that all the children could play together. Once the Seeker had been chosen and blindfolded, the rest of the assembled group scattered in all directions. The only rule was that they had to stay within the gardens. They couldn't go in the house, and they couldn't go into the woods.

Jonathan was one of several who chose to cross the little bridge and enter the gardens there. A few ran toward the kitchen gardens, and the smallest children either hid among the roses and topiaries, or tagged along with older siblings. The energy of youth, and familiarity with the grounds and paths brought Jonathan swiftly to the hedge maze. He looked around furtively. He wouldn't be the only one to hide in there, but it was a good spot, nonetheless. You could enter the maze, but then exit on one of the other sides, and still be technically in the gardens. So it was one way to avoid the Seeker, and run back to home base.

Jonathan paused in the center of the maze to catch his

breath. He would be safe there for a little while. He kicked his feet idly as he meandered around the fountain, forcing himself not to whistle, which would give away his location. He was only mildly startled when he saw a flash of white on the path. He sighed in relief as he said, "Oh, it's just you."

"Just me?" Olivia asked, adopting an offended expression. "Were you hoping I was somebody else?"

Jonathan reddened, chagrined. "No, no, that's not what I meant. I just meant you're not Tom, that's all." He offered her an apologetic smile.

"Well," she said in a high, clipped tone, "I suppose that's okay, then." She swished her skirt with her hand as she walked forward. Jonathan noticed that she seemed to be swinging her hips out as she walked, and he thought to ask her if she'd been injured. Before he could get the words out, though, she was standing in front of him.

She was standing very close. He could feel the hem of her dress brush against his pant legs. She seemed nervous. She was ducking her head again, and looking up at him from downcast eyes. He kind of ducked his own head a little bit, to try to see her better, and before he knew what was happening, she had pressed her lips against his.

Almost as soon as his brain registered that he was having his first kiss, she stepped back. Like a scared rabbit, she turned and fled, without another word. He just watched her go, both stunned and confused.

Jonathan, once again, found himself alone by the fountain. The kiss had been brief, and in hindsight, he was struggling to determine if Olivia's lips had somehow been hard. They had felt rather wooden, which was strange. Overall, the kiss had left him let down. It hadn't been what he had expected. But then, he had vaguely expected that he would initiate his first kiss, rather than the girl. Since Olivia had run off without a word, he was left to assume that she had been disappointed as well. He shrugged it off, and went back to plotting how to return to home base, in the game.

. . .

He sighed. He thought he'd made it clear that he wasn't interested in the past. He had flirted with her, yes. He had found her pretty and, well, he had been fourteen. Pretty and interested in him in return had been his only real criteria for a girl at the time. But that had been almost 10 years ago! He had gone away and had all but forgotten about her. He came home and she had clearly not forgotten about him. She and her mother both had been on him like vipers. They drove him to avoid the city and any society parties or events like the plague. She hadn't taken the hint. He had tried to gently let her know that he wasn't interested, and when she'd finally gotten married, a wedding invitation he had happily ignored, he thought that she'd finally gotten the point. He vaguely wondered if Eliza had attended that wedding.

Maybe he was reading too much into the letter. He pulled it out and reread it. He was positive that it was indecent. He was entirely sure his wife should never read it. He considered his options. He knew that if he ignored it for too long, he could expect Olivia Johnson to simply knock on his door one day, in the spirit of a neighborly visit. He had to respond. He had to make it very clear that he was married. And he had to tell Eliza something on the subject. He considered for a moment, remembering that Amy Dudley had just mentioned Olivia the other evening. The visiting siblings would provide the perfect buffer.

His steps held clear purpose as he approached the parlor from which he could hear sweet laughter emanating. He paused long enough to fix a cheerful smile on his face. If he entered the room looking concerned, that wouldn't go over well.

"Jonathan!" Eliza saw him first, and smiled at him as he entered. He saw that they had brought the kittens inside again, and were enjoying watching them play on the carpet. Someone had given them an apple, which they were rolling around.

He returned the smile warmly. "I'm not interrupting anything, am I?"

"Not at all, is there something going on?" she asked.

"In fact," he paused to include Amy in his grin, "our Miss Dudley seems to be a touch clairvoyant."

Amy looked confused but pleased.

"You were just decrying the absence of the Johnsons from your life, and I've recently learned that they've taken up residence at the former Southland estate. They're our new neighbors!" His cheerfulness felt a touch forced to himself, but no one else seemed to notice it.

"That's wonderful news!" cried Amy, and Eliza agreed with a smile.

"We must have them around soon," his wife commented.

Winking in Amy's direction, Jonathan was ready with a response that would delight everyone present. "Why don't we invite them over while the Dudleys are still with us, this week, so that we can make a little party of it?"

The two women were delighted, and just slightly shocked that he had been the one to propose such an idea. But they enthusiastically agreed.

"Oh!" Eliza interjected, "how would you feel about also inviting your Uncle Brandon, and Michael? We did say we'd have them out soon, and that would round out our party nicely."

That idea pleased Jonathan greatly, and he smiled warmly at his wife. "That sounds splendid! I do need to do a few more things before I can join you for the rest of the day, but why don't you decide on a date and we can get the invitations out this afternoon?"

"Wonderful!" responded Eliza happily. Jonathan left the three of them to discuss the details, which they did animatedly. Eliza called Mrs. Davis and Mrs. Smith in to confer, as well.

The Dudleys were set to stay through Wednesday, but

as it was now Monday, they decided to stay a few days longer, to facilitate the get-together. Friday was decided upon for the event, and both brother and sister were delighted to extend their stay. A menu was decided with the help of the cook and housekeeper, and plans were set.

The two girls intended to help Mr. Davis pick berries that day, and so had dressed simply for the occasion. Vincent declined to join them, choosing instead to walk down to the stables. Giggling, the girls each picked up a basket from the kitchen and headed to the kitchen garden, tying their bonnets in place as they went. Before they left the house, Mrs. Smith lent each a snowy apron, just in case the berries would stain. Amy was thrilled to be playing farmgirl for the day, a quaint jaunt that was surely going to be less wearying than the walk through the forest had been. She had rather rapidly decided that she was not suited to country life, and that while a visit was delightful, she wondered how her friend was getting along with it full time. As it was one of the few times they'd had alone so far, she took this opportunity to delicately ask about just that.

"It's lovely here, Lissie, but don't you find it lonely at times? Or dull?" The two had approached a row of blackberry bushes, per Mr. Davis's directions, and were carefully picking around thorns, immediately glad to have the aprons.

"Not at all!" Eliza was shocked by her friend's question, though she knew it was innocent enough. "Perhaps it was a little lonely in the beginning, while we all got accustomed to one another. But everyone here is lovely, and I don't think I've felt lonely in ages. And I have quite a lot to keep me occupied. Between the gardens and the horses and Jonathan, I don't think I could ever find it dull." She happily ignored the first week she had been there, and focused on the subsequent time instead.

"Well, I suppose that's good. You don't miss the city at all, then?" Amy still couldn't understand how her friend, who had grown up with the theater and restaurants and shopping, could so easily settle into a provincial life.

Eliza considered the new question for a moment. "Of course I miss it. It was my first home. But that's why we kept the townhouse," she said reasonably, "so that we can have both experiences."

"How often do you plan to go back, then? You must visit when you do!"

Eliza laughed at her friend. "We'll be in the city at least once a month, to check on the mill, and of course we'll visit. Or you could visit us. I'll be sure to write to let you know when we'll be there."

"Yes, that last dinner was quite lovely. Your godfather is such a charming man! As is his friend. I'm glad that they'll be joining us again."

"I am, too," she smiled warmly. "They're practically the only family Jonathan or I have left. I love them dearly."

"You seem different, Lissie, from when we last saw each other in the city," Amy observed. "Have things...changed, between you and your husband?"

"A little bit," Eliza answered.

"Are you happier?"

"I am. I really am. And I think he is, too."

They worked in silence for a few moments when Amy started up on a slightly new subject. "Don't you think it's a bit of a coincidence, Olivia and Patrick Johnson moving in next door, when we were just talking about them?"

Eliza considered for a moment. "Well, it's a small world, as they say. Though, to be honest, I don't even know where exactly the Southland estate is. I take Jonathan's word for it that it's next door, but 'next door' here means something a bit different than it does in the city."

Amy laughed at the truth of that. The Stanton estate was quite secluded. "I have to wonder if they've even heard the news that you're married, though. They haven't been back for very long, and everything happened so quickly."

"That's true. Jonathan said that he received news, but

he didn't say how he found out. I suppose one of them wrote to him? It's not like he's likely to run into someone in the street."

"I wonder if Olivia wrote to him," Amy said idly.

"It's entirely possible. What are you thinking?"

"Oh, nothing really. It's just unlikely that it was Mr. Johnson. I don't believe he really knows the Stantons. Of course, I could always be wrong," she hedged.

"It would make more sense for it to have been Olivia," Eliza conceded. "She and Jonathan have known each other since childhood. Just like you and I," she said, smiling brightly at her friend.

"And Vincent," Amy was quick to add.

"And Vincent, yes. We all go back, don't we? It's funny that we're here in this place now, given that it's where we all met," she mused.

"This isn't where we met," Amy countered indignantly. "We met at the tea shop down the street from your house when my mother and your mother were both there with us, and my mother asked your mother where she had found your jacket, because she thought it was very pretty."

"Your memory is astounding." Eliza was stunned.

Amy smirked at her. "Then they found out that our fathers knew each other incidentally through some club or other, and they decided that we should be friends."

"How old were we? Five? How on earth do you remember any of that?"

"Well I don't remember it, precisely," Amy allowed. "Mother told me how it had all happened."

Understanding dawned on Eliza. "That makes so much more sense." She paused. "How is your mother, by the way? I feel like I haven't seen her in ages."

"You haven't. She wasn't at the Forester party last spring, because she had taken ill with a slight cough. She's better now, of course. Oh, she would be delighted to see you! The next time you're in town, you really need to come by ours, for a visit."

"I shall," agreed Eliza. "That would be lovely. Your mother was always kind to me."

"She thought you were a good influence," confided her friend. "You were always the responsible one."

"Shush now, you're a perfectly lovely person, and your mother knows that."

"Oh, she knows I'm lovely, and loud, and that I know what makes me happy in life. What I want for my future. I won't settle for anything less. She calls me childish, and says that I'll feel differently when I'm older. I'm an adult!" she whined. "I do know what I want."

"Well, what is it?" her friend asked soothingly.

Amy looked up seriously, meeting Eliza's gaze frankly. "I want passion and authenticity. I want someone who craves adventure and has a burning fiery soul who can excite me."

"And that wasn't Lucas Bradley?" Eliza asked gently.

Amy sighed and turned back to the berries. They had pretty well picked through the blackberry bushes, so they turned to the blueberries. Thankfully, those had no thorns. "I really thought Lucas was different," she said dejectedly. "He was so funny, and I thought that he had passion, but it turns out I was fooling myself. He was just trying to please me to please my father."

"What does your father have to do with it?" Eliza was confused.

"Lucas works for papa. And papa has this silly notion that now that I'm of age, he needs to marry me off to someone, and because he found Lucas acceptable, he told him to court me! Can you imagine? Having a man be instructed to court you!"

Eliza averted her gaze, fiddling with her basket.

"Oh, I'm sorry, Lissie. I didn't mean that as offense. I mean, in a way, I suppose Mr. Stanton was told to court you," Amy rushed her speech awkwardly, deeply apologetic.

"It's nothing to worry about, Amy. Please go on. I can't believe your father would actually do such a thing! That's quite shocking. Are you sure you didn't misunderstand?" Eliza sought to reassure her friend that she hadn't been offended.

"That's precisely what *Mr. Bradley* said. Lucas," she explained softly. "I misunderstood things, that's actually what he tried to tell me. I told him that he was insane, if he thought I would settle for a man my father set me up with. I want passion, Eliza! I want a man to pursue me. I don't want to be put up like some prize horse at auction, for the man my father chooses for me."

Eliza was torn. "Didn't you say that you really liked Lucas, though? Mr. Bradley?" she asked tentatively.

"I liked who I thought he was. I thought he was bold and courageous. I mean," she chuckled, "pursuing the boss's daughter, after all. Isn't that a rather daring thing to do?" Her face turned stormy. "But it's not the same at all if the boss told him to do it! That makes me no better than an assignment to complete. And that's exactly what I told both my father and *Mr. Bradley*."

"What did your father say?"

"He said the exact same thing Lucas did! That I misunderstood. That he only wanted what was best for me, what would make me happy. He even called me 'his little princess'. Well. I suppose princesses get traded in marriage all the time, don't they? For land or horses or whatever," she sniffed. "My family aren't royalists."

Eliza stifled a laugh. It was 1807, after all. Not that there weren't still royalists here or there, but it seemed a silly distinction to Eliza, since they hadn't even been born prior to the war. But Amy's family had been proud of their role in the war, such as it had been, and she had been instilled with that pride from her birth.

"So you want someone passionate, who isn't afraid to hide his feelings for you," Eliza summarized her friend's feelings.

"Yes. Precisely!" Amy was pleased that her friend understood her.

"How do you know," Eliza questioned cautiously, "what someone feels for you?"

"Why, they have to tell you. Or better yet," she answered with relish, "demonstrate their feelings. Flowers are a classic display of affection. Or chocolates." She gasped, "Or kittens! Oh, Eliza, has Jonathan come around? Are you two in love?"

Eliza laughed ironically. "I don't know. I don't think so. The kittens were sweet, though. He has turned out to be a surprisingly thoughtful man. And he makes me feel things." She trailed off vaguely.

"What kinds of things?" Amy prompted enthusiastically.

'Well," she hedged, "excited? So, so excited."

"Excited is good!" Amy crowed, but then paused. "But, well, are you fulfilled? Is it what you want marriage to be?"

"Not precisely. I'm frustrated, as much as anything else." She blew an exasperated breath.

"Do you think it will get better?"

"I hope so. It's gotten better so far. Who's to say it won't keep getting better?" She tried to put on a hopeful air, but her friend saw through her.

"Lissie...I haven't wanted to bring this up, because I really just want you to be happy, but...what about Vincent?" Amy's voice was gentle.

"What about Vincent?" Eliza avoided meeting her friend's gaze.

"Well...I know that he has feelings for you."

"But I'm already married."

Amy set her basket down, turned to her friend, and took her basket from her, setting it on the ground next to hers. She took her friend's hands earnestly. "Lissie," she said frankly, "I don't know everything that's in Vincent's head, but I know that he loves you, and he would accept you no matter what. I'll only say this once, and then I won't bring it up again, but I would be absolutely in heaven for you to really and truly be my sister! So, whatever else may or may not be, just know that you have a whole family who would accept you with open arms, if you wanted it."

Tears sprang to Eliza's eyes, and Amy embraced her. "Oh, dear, I didn't mean to make you cry! I'm sorry! I just want you to be happy. And, well...do you think that you might have, possibly, made a mistake?"

"I don't know!" sobbed Eliza, shaking into Amy's thin shoulders.

Amy made soothing noises and patted Eliza's back, guiding her to a nearby bench so they could sit. Her friend obviously needed a good cry, and she sat through it all with her, murmuring nonsense words of peace.

Some time later, the tears dried up, and the sniffles stopped. Eliza wiped her face with the hem of the apron she wore. "Thank you." She smiled at Amy. "I think I just needed a good cry."

"I understand. You've been through a lot. I'm sorry if I made it harder for you."

"No, no, you really didn't. I'm just so torn. But things have been so pleasant with Jonathan lately. I really like him," deep feelings tinged her voice.

"So, just take your time, then. It seems like you're happy here. Really happy."

"I am," she breathed out.

"Good." Amy hugged her. "That's all that matters right now. Let's keep picking berries, shall we?"

Eliza nodded and the two returned to their baskets and the bushes. By the end of their outing, their arms were sore, and they had picked so many berries! But that was the plan, for the following day, Mrs. Smith would make preserves. The garden house had an outdoor kitchen attached to it that was perfect for canning. The housekeeper was delighted by what the girls had accomplished, and insisted that they rest in the parlor while she made them some lemonade. The girls washed up quickly, and were met in the parlor with lemonade as well as cucumber sandwiches and some cold chicken. The girls were famished, and they sat down to eat.

Once they'd had a few bites, Amy offered, "Would you like my thoroughly unbiased, unrequested opinion on what you should do?"

"Yes" Eliza's answer was emphatic.

Amy giggled. "Well, I think that you should just enjoy yourself."

"What?" She was dumbfounded by that advice.

"Think about it. You want to be happy, right? You're trying to decide your whole future, yes?" Amy was being quite rational.

"Well, yes, I suppose so," Eliza conceded.

"So, just be yourself. You have the opportunity to be around both men right now, take it. See who makes you happiest. See who makes you feel the most zing."

"Zing?" Eliza asked.

"Zing! You know, that fluttery feeling you get in your stomach, and your face flushes, and you feel like you might be ill? Oh, Lissie, please tell me you've felt that sort of thing before!" Amy implored.

"Yes," Eliza answered hesitantly, "Yes, I have."

"Good. So just spend some time with each of them, separately, and see which one you like best." She considered a moment. "And maybe see if Olivia is anything to be concerned about."

Eliza considered the advice. It did make sense, if in a somewhat mercenary sense. But she was left with a question. "So who did you feel a 'zing' with, then?"

Amy faltered. "Well...Lucas Bradley. Maybe 'zing' isn't a good criteria for making that sort of choice," she admitted wryly.

"Maybe Lucas Bradley is worth further consideration?"

"We're not talking about me right now," Amy said primly, smirking at Eliza. Eliza smirked back, and the two dissolved into giggles.

Chapter 24

Dinner that evening was abuzz with discussion of the dinner party at the end of the week. Invitations had been drafted, inviting both Mr. and Mrs. Patrick Johnson, as well as Mr. Brandon St. John and Mr. Michael Crowley to join the Stantons and the younger Dudleys for dinner Friday evening, at the Stanton residence, dinner to be served at 7 p.m. Both Jonathan and Eliza, for their own separate reasons, made sure the wording included the phrasing "Mr. and Mrs. Jonathan Stanton." It would delight Brandon to see it that way, and it would provide a forewarning to Mrs. Johnson, if she had any ideas in mind about Mr. Stanton's availability. Of course, this was not discussed by anyone explicitly.

The girls regaled the men with their adventures in berry picking, omitting their discussion topics, for the most part. They all laughed over the stories of the kitten antics. Everyone had seen them do something different, and all of it had to be shared. Boots was the more adventurous of the pair, and had enjoyed attacking the apple that Vincent had given them to play with. Eliza had had to rescue Boots from the draperies, which he had managed to partially climb. Amy had gotten Mittens to eat a tiny piece of chicken from her fingers. Jonathan surprised everyone with the tale of how, finding himself alone in the library while the rest of the group had been occupied outdoors, Mittens had grown tired, and curled up to sleep using Jonathan's left foot as a pillow for her little head.

Vincent had spent a large part of the day talking to Joshua. It rapidly became apparent that both of those men had an avid interest in horse breeding, and had found much to talk about on the subject. Two of the horses that Joshua had care of were Morgans, and he was enthusiastic about their attributes. Vincent had been thrilled to find such a knowledgeable horseman to talk to, and the two men had a plan to ride the following day.

They spent the evening after dinner merrily playing whist in the drawing room, enjoying each other's company with sherry for the ladies and brandy for the gentlemen. Throughout the evening, and particularly during the game, which happened to pair Eliza with Vincent, and Amy with Jonathan, Eliza endeavored to achieve two things, per her friend's earlier suggestion. Her first goal was to be herself, which was harder to do when one was thinking of it as an objective than one might think. Her second goal was to enjoy the company of both men present, and discern if either of them proved to be more desirable than the other.

She was shocked later that evening when she was left with the realization that she had failed spectacularly at both objectives. Thinking back over dinner and the card game as the evening drew to a close, she reflected on all the things that had gone wrong. She had stammered, dropped her fork three times, and nearly spilled her wine. She couldn't keep her hands from fluttering like nervous butterflies. She second guessed every word that escaped her lips, and had somehow found herself being alternately more and also less talkative. Even Amy had not so delicately nudged her with her slippered foot under the card table, giving her a questioning look. Thankfully, neither of the men seemed to notice anything amiss.

After the game had ended, Amy took Eliza's arm, suggesting they stroll around the room some, while the men discussed horses. Once they were relatively away, where they could speak privately, Amy whispered, "what is wrong with you? Are you feeling unwell? You're acting very strangely this evening."

Eliza blushed. "I'm just trying to be myself," she hissed back.

Amy stifled a giggle. "You're being exactly the opposite of yourself, Lissie."

"What do you mean? I've been trying so hard, all night." She glanced at the two men and blushed again. "I suppose I just don't exactly know what it means to be myself. How can I be anything but myself? How is that even possible?"

Eliza was typically the friend more prone to quiet reflection, and demure disposition. Amy, however, had developed a more shrewd side, tinged with cynicism. "My dear, as women, we have the pleasure of being whomever we want to be on a whim. We can be bold and flirtatious," she said as she struck a pose which made Eliza giggle, "or we can be shy and sweet." She turned half away and hid part of her face beneath her hand, as though it were a fan, batting her eyes. "Or we can be cruel and vicious, but I recommend only using that one when it's strictly warranted. And all of that is just a kind of play acting, like we used to do when we were little girls. Half the world, at any given time, is just play acting, pretending to be something because it helps them get what they want. Men do it, as well. They act one way, and then all of a sudden, they're different, and not what they had seemed."

Eliza began to think her friend was no longer talking about her dilemma and was perhaps thinking of a different man, one not in this room. Amy continued, her diaphanous white skirt swishing delicately at her feet as they walked. "Take my brother, for example." Eliza's ears perked up. "He seems, for all the world, to be a gentle man without a care in the world, right? Undemanding, thoroughly unbothered, yes?"

Eliza nodded, considering what she knew of Vincent. "But he can turn that off in an instant," Amy revealed. "He's a lawyer now, remember? He can be shrewd, sharp, and persuasive, at the drop of a hat. He told me that that's actually become a tactic to succeed at work. He lulls people into believing that he isn't going to put up a fight, and then he can later throw them off their guard."

Eliza was shocked. That was utterly unlike the Vincent Eliza knew, a fact which begged her to ask, "So which one is the real man? Is he truly that vicious, or is that just an act to succeed at work?"

"Well," Amy's response was slow and measured, "I think the real Vincent is somewhere in the middle. He's always been like that, and I've known him my whole life. He's not vicious, at all, but he's quite cunning. He's always been smarter than people are inclined to give him credit for, upon first meeting him, and he knows how to use that to his advantage. So I suppose what I meant, when I gave you that advice earlier, was that you shouldn't pretend around either one of them." She glanced where the men sat, playing another card game. "Relax. But don't think about relaxing, because then you won't do it."

Eliza sighed, considering her friend's words. "I may spend some time in Jonathan's office tomorrow morning," Amy looked confused, but Eliza explained, "We work together. I think being in that setting, having something to occupy my mind, other than him, would help clear my mind a bit."

Her friend was skeptical, but at that moment, Vincent asked, "What are you ladies whispering about? Should we be worried?"

"You should always be worried, brother," was the response.

Everyone laughed. Shortly after, they all retired to bed. About a half an hour after they had quit the drawing room, and Jonathan and Eliza had said goodnight privately, Eliza was in her nightgown sketching quietly before bed. She was startled by a knock at her door. Rising, she donned her dressing gown and opened the door. "Vincent!" she said, surprised, "Is something the matter?"

"I was hoping we could talk again," he said, somewhat

sheepishly.

"This really isn't appropriate," she answered, glancing furtively down the hall.

"Just a moment, please. I've barely gotten to see you today," he pleaded with her, taking a small step toward her and the door, so that his foot was crossing the threshold.

Holding her dressing gown closer, she backed further away, which he took as an invitation. Stammering and blushing furiously as he pursued her retreating steps, she insisted, "Just for a moment. You really shouldn't be here."

"I just wanted to ask if you had an opportunity to think about what we discussed yesterday," he didn't waste time getting to his point.

Eliza huffed a laugh. "I've thought of little else."

He smiled hopefully and took another step forward, cupping her shoulders in his hands as he said, "Dare I hope?"

"Vincent," she said, hesitating. She twisted half out of his grasp before continuing, "I've been thinking, but I haven't made any decisions. It's a lot to consider."

Boldly, he moved one hand to gently caress her face, since in spite of her words, she hadn't moved completely away from him. She turned her face into his hand slightly. His voice was low as he said, "I understand. I don't wish to rush you." He gently kissed her forehead, his lips lingering. She covered the hand that still cupped her cheek with her own small palm, curing her fingers around his. She drew it away from her face, giving his hand a small squeeze as she did.

"You should go."

"Eliza..." He drew her name out long, as he stared longingly at her mouth. That was when she stepped back, increasing the space between them.

"Goodnight, Vincent," was her gentle, but firm, reply.

He exhaled through his nose, obviously frustrated, but not vicious. "Goodnight. I look forward to the time when we can say goodnight and it doesn't mean I have to leave your room," he said boldly, but quickly left before she could respond.

She exhaled a sigh of relief after the door was shut again. She sat down at her vanity, nervously fiddling with her brush and comb. On the one hand, that entire scene had been wildly inappropriate. She abruptly stood and began pacing. On the other hand, it gave her a rare opportunity to gauge her experience with Vincent directly against similar experiences with Jonathan. Her steps faltered and her face flamed as she thought of her husband. How would he react, knowing that another man had been in her bedroom, so late at night? With her not fully dressed? She realized that she didn't actually know. She bit her thumbnail in consternation. She was fairly certain that he wouldn't be happy about it. That it would be read as a betrayal. And, she admitted to herself, it had been a betrayal. That thought left her queasy, as guilt washed over her.

She sat down again, this time on the settee. On the one hand, her skin had burned at his touch tonight. She still felt the jitters in her stomach, and her legs were weak. She couldn't tell, though, if the excitement stirred in her had been from him alone, or from the illicit nature of his nighttime visit.

She considered both men honestly, and had to admit to herself that if her husband would be more expressive, or have more obvious feelings for her, it would be an easy choice to make. She toyed with her hair as her thoughts began to calm. She had to wonder if she could settle for having her feelings and desires go unrequited, if it meant she could be with Jonathan. That seemed a vast demand on her 19-year-old heart. At least in view of a man who was offering her more than that. But wouldn't that potentially result in the opposite happening? She would be living with someone who felt things for her that she couldn't reciprocate. She was also fairly certain that knowing Vincent's feelings toward her, she would inevitably feel a lifetime of guilt and failed expectation if she never felt the same toward him. She sighed, because she wasn't positive that she wouldn't be able to reciprocate those feelings. She might, in time. But if that was the case, was it possibly also the case that Jonathan's feelings could grow with time? Hadn't he basically said that precise thing? But she considered the guilt that she felt when Vincent expressed his feelings to her. She didn't want her husband to feel that same guilt. Though, she didn't love Jonathan, did she? So it wasn't precisely the same.

Eliza stood and paced around the bed. She took her dressing gown off, setting it to the side, but then she just as quickly picked it back up again. She balled the fabric up in her hands and continued walking aimlessly.

What did she feel for her husband? She liked him; increasingly day by day, she liked him. She respected his mind and his abilities. He was thoughtful, which was also increasingly apparent. The entire problem was that that also described how she felt about Vincent. Except there was something different between them that she couldn't quit pinpoint. She enjoyed spending time with both of them, but there was something that felt more special about being with Jonathan. She began to wonder if perhaps that was love? Romantic love was something she hadn't experienced before. It hadn't been something her mother had talked about with her. She had always pictured it as being some wildly sweeping emotion, which left one breathless and joyful. She felt that way when he kissed her. She paused, pressing her fingers to her lips. But was that simply lust? When he pulled away from her, it made her chest ache. Confusion swarmed her head like bees. If this was love, she wasn't particularly fond of it. But it was magnetic. Her circling thoughts came back, over and over, to Jonathan. His laugh, his kisses, his warm hands held her entranced. She went to sleep, with the wish that she could have more confidence about her feelings.

Chapter 25

Tuesday morning dawned, and the daylight drove away the demons that had plagued Eliza the night before. She was happy to once again follow what had become her typical schedule for the day. She ate breakfast alone, and then joined Jonathan in the office for some time. She was nervous about seeing him, but he seemed quite happy to see her. The two of them fell easily into their familiar routine of reviewing and responding to correspondence, reviewing ledgers, and bantering lightly. This snippet of time helped to lull Eliza into an easiness of mind that she had not felt the previous evening.

"You're in a good mood," her husband observed. "It's very nice to have your friends with us, and I'm happy to see that you're enjoying yourself so much."

"I am." She smiled at him, "I'm glad you seem to be enjoying it, as well. Next week is when we're planning to go back into the city to meet with Mr. Sylvester at the mill. Amy has suggested that we visit her at home when we're there, so that we can visit with her parents. I haven't seen them in so long."

"Of course, that sounds wonderful. If you'd like, we can plan to stay an extra day or two," he offered.

"That might be nice. Perhaps we could attend the theater while we're there?" she suggested. Amy had put the thought of such things in her head the previous day.

Jonathan seemed somewhat surprised by the suggestion, though not put off. "I didn't know you enjoyed the theater. Of course we can plan for it, if it makes you happy."

His tone made Eliza curious. "Do you dislike it?"

"No, that's not what I meant to imply at all. It would

make me happy to go," he assured her. "I suppose I have less familiarity with it than you do. I'm struggling to think if I've attended a theater production since, well, since my mother was alive."

"Goodness!" Eliza was shocked. "Then we must plan to go."

They smiled at each other amiably. A few moments later, Eliza had a realization that made her a little uncomfortable. "I shall write to Mrs. Grayson today, to let her know to expect us," she began. "This time, I'll ask her to prepare two rooms for us," she said tentatively.

Without looking up, Jonathan nodded his head, murmuring, "Good, good. Thank you."

Eliza sighed and continued what she had been doing. She didn't know what she had expected him to say, or why she thought he might argue with that. He clearly had a strong preference for separate rooms, and that wasn't going to change just because they were in a different house. But she had to admit to herself that she was disappointed.

She sought to quell her rising frustration. Her parents had happily slept in separate rooms. But she knew that her father had at least occasionally spent the night in her mother's room, and vice versa. She was beginning to have a distinct idea of what a husband and wife might do behind a private door for some period of time. Why, oh why was her husband so averse to sharing that with her?

"Is something wrong with the numbers?" Jonathan's voice startled her out of her reverie.

"No, why?"

"You've been sighing over that ledger for easily the last ten minutes," he told her.

Eliza blushed, and focused on the ledger before her. She hadn't even realized which one was in front of her, before he'd asked his question.

"Why don't you go find Miss Dudley, and get some sunshine? I know her brother was planning to go for a ride today.

Unless she went with him, she may be looking for company,"
he suggested, thinking perhaps that his wife was unhappy
being up here with him, rather than spending time with her
friends.

She pushed the frustration and thoughts of bedrooms
away. "Amy said yesterday that she wanted to sleep in today,
take a warm bath, and be altogether decadently lazy, after the
last two days of activity. I'm enjoying my time here with you,
unless you've tired of me," she teased.

"Of course not. You enrich any room you occupy, and
I'm glad of your company. I just don't want you to feel as
though you're missing out on something better."

She found a vague irony in his words, given the
thoughts that had been running through her mind the last few
days. "I'm quite happy to be here. There is one thing, though."
She closed the ledger gingerly, and looked Jonathan in the eye.

"Yes? What is it?"

"I think," she began, blood rushing to her head with the
nerves, "perhaps we should alter our nighttime routine." She
blushed scarlet as the words rushed from her mouth.

Jonathan's eyebrows raised, and he dropped the pen
he'd been holding. "Have I done something to upset you?" he
asked carefully.

She glanced away, tracing her fingertips along the spine
of the book in front of her. "I'm just," she paused, unable to
force the word "frustrated" past her lips. She continued, "I'm
concerned about appearances. With the Dudleys right down
the hall," she glanced up, nervously licking her lips, "I would
like to avoid any appearance of things being strange between
us." She reviewed the sentence she had just spoken over in her
mind. She knew she was rambling, and she tugged at a loose
curl of hair subconsciously.

He considered her words carefully. "Do you think there
is something strange about me escorting you to your bedroom at night?"

She demurred. "I," she stammered, "it's just very intimate." Her hand fluttered graspingly at her neck. "I don't know what others might think." She stopped grasping for words and fell silent.

She was obviously distressed, and Jonathan wondered if he had upset her the other night. He thought perhaps the intimacy distressed her, which would certainly explain this suggestion. "Of course," he said, "if it would be preferable to you for us to omit that...intimacy, we certainly can. I do not wish to do anything that would cause you distress, you must know that."

"Of course." Her lashes fluttered as she cast her eyes back towards the closed ledger in front of her. "Thank you for understanding."

They continued on in silence, until it really was time for Eliza to rouse herself from the books and find Amy. They were planning to explore the gardens more thoroughly today. They had walked through, but most usually with purpose. This was an opportunity to poke and explore and just enjoy the beauty of it all. On a whim, before leaving the office, Eliza approached Jonathan where he sat at his desk and pertly kissed his cheek. He smiled at her, and wished for her to have fun with her friend.

Amy was only just descending the stairs when Eliza emerged from the office, and the two women greeted each other and proceeded directly to the gardens. Walking arm and arm, Eliza asked how her friend had enjoyed her quiet morning.

"It was lovely!" Amy enthused. "I slept in late, and then Molly brought me breakfast in bed, which was so sweet and decadent, and then she fixed me a bath and oh, it was all just lovely. Just what I needed, and now this is beautiful. And your morning? Did you enjoy your work?" She wrinkled her nose a little on the word "work". She wasn't fond of math, and the thought of work in general as being an enjoyable pastime was anathema to her. For her, to relax meant to do exactly what she had done this morning. But she knew that her friend found relaxation in productive activity.

"It was relaxing, for the most part," Eliza said cautiously. "I really *like* Jonathan," she added with special emphasis.

Amy gasped, "So have you made your decision already?"

"Can you keep a secret?" Eliza asked in a low voice. She glanced around furtively, verifying that no one was nearby. She waited for her friend to nod. "Vincent came to my room last night--"

"That scoundrel!" Amy was furious with her brother.

"He was only there for a moment," reassured Eliza. "But we spoke briefly. And he...embraced me, after a fashion. But it was in a way he would have embraced you," she was quick to add, blushing furiously. "I have to say that it was scandalous, but only because it happened in my bedroom. Had we been in the parlor it would have been strange, but not illicit. And I have to admit that it gave me the opportunity to compare him more directly to Jonathan. Oh, that sounds horribly callous!"

"It's practical," soothed Amy. "Though I am well and truly shocked that my brother would go to a woman's room at night in that way! What kind of woman does he think you are?"

"Well, that aside," Eliza said, trying to push thoughts of the incident away, "though it was wildly inappropriate, I think I'm just more confused than ever. I don't love Vincent the way he loves me, but Jonathan doesn't love me the way--"

"The way what?" asked Amy gently.

Eliza glanced down at the floor, twisting her hands together. "The way a man should love his wife," she ended lamely.

"As much as I would dearly love you to be my sister," Amy hugged Eliza's arm to her before continuing, "I just want you to be happy. You don't have to make a decision today. You can take your time."

Eliza sniffled a bit. "That's what Vincent keeps saying. And poor Jonathan doesn't know anything about any of this, and I feel so guilty!"

"Oh, dear." Amy looped her arm around her friend's shoulders. "Let's put it from our minds for a while. Just don't think of it, and let your mind be easy."

Eliza nodded.

The two continued their walk, shifting their conversation to lighter subjects. They had made a complete circuit of the rose garden, admiring the topiaries and the roses, and had moved toward the small bridge underneath the willow tree. That section of the grounds provided so much to see and explore, the girls stayed busy for hours. As they were returning to the house, their conversation turned to Friday.

"I'm not sure what to wear," Amy fretted. "I brought evening dresses, of course, but I want to look nice. What are you planning to wear?"

"I don't know yet. I have a plum silk that's lovely, but it's a simple cut." She pondered the question for a moment. "Jonathan seems particularly fond of my dove gray gown, and it's fashionable."

"Oh! If you wear dove, I can wear my pale pink, and we'll look so pretty together!" Amy had always liked to plan their outfits as pairs, thinking about the two of them as two halves of a perfect whole.

They entered the drawing room, and immediately heard feminine laughter from somewhere nearby. The girls looked at each other in surprise, as that hadn't sounded like any of the women who worked in the house. They entered the foyer, and determined that the voices, now plural, were coming from the parlor. They were both stunned, upon entering the parlor, to see Jonathan entertaining Patrick and Olivia Johnson.

Seeing the ladies at the door, Jonathan and Patrick both stood. Olivia stayed seated, looking regal in a cream poplin dress, with her hair piled high in a riot of falling curls. "Ladies!" Mr. Johnson said warmly, "Please, forgive us for coming by without notice. Mrs. Stanton, I presume." He approached Eliza with a twinkling smile, and she offered him her hand. They had met previously, prior to his marriage, and certainly prior to hers, and he was also acquainted with Amy. He kissed her hand delicately, before turning to Amy. "Miss Dudley, I hope you're doing well. When we got your gracious dinner invitation and learned that Stanton here had gotten himself married, we just had to see if you were available for a less formal visit, to allow us to congratulate the happy couple right away."

"Thank you, Mr. Johnson," Eliza replied graciously, as they all took seats, "I apologize that we weren't here to greet you when you arrived. Olivia, you're looking quite well."

"It's perfectly fine," she replied, smiling broadly, "Mr. Stanton has been a perfect host in your absence. And Amy, dear, it's such a surprise to find you here, as well! You must be enjoying the fresh country air."

Amy gave Olivia a small, tight smile that was bordering on being a grimace.

"Olivia," Eliza drew her attention, "Amy was just the other day remarking how much your presence had been missed in the last year. Have you enjoyed touring Europe?"

Olivia returned the smile with delight, having been given a bit of a stage. "That's precisely what we were just talking about with Mr. Stanton." She smiled at Jonathan, a toothy grin. "Europe was absolutely divine, you simply must go. And not just to England, but the entire continent. We went to France, Germany, and Spain, and each was just more picturesque than the last. The castles in France and Germany are to die for. And the Spanish are so quaint and delightful." She continued to talk at length about all of the places they had visited, the people they had met, and the food they had eaten. Her husband occasionally interjected with a detail, but for the most part, he seemed content to sit back and let his wife do the talking. The other three occasionally exclaimed or made a brief comment, but Olivia was a skilled speaker, and her speech about their travels was obviously well-rehearsed. She seemed to pay special attention to Jonathan, and at times appeared to be speaking directly to him, in particular. Amy and Eliza exchanged a look more than once over this habit. It was just subtle enough to not be appallingly rude, but obvious enough to be noticeable, at least to the other women present.

Amy had done a slight disservice to Patrick Johnson, by referring to him as old. He was older than the rest assembled, that was true, but he was surely not past the age of forty, and that was hardly ancient. His dark brown hair was starting to lighten just at the temples in a dashing way. He was tall and broad shouldered, tapering to a narrow waist. His dark eyes twinkled. He and Olivia, who was herself tall and fair-skinned, with her dark hair and eyes, made a lovely matched set. Olivia was three years older than Eliza and Amy, at twenty-two, but that slight advantage of age, combined with the several inches of height between her and them, had always tended to make the two younger girls feel quite small. Whether that was a result of, or a cause of Olivia's natural bent toward leadership, the woman nevertheless exuded a strength and confidence that had always been magnetic.

By the time the Johnsons took their leave, they had expressed a warm wish that the Stantons and the Dudleys should pay them a visit whenever they might wish.

Over dinner, when the visit was discussed generally, Vincent was only slightly sorry to have missed the couple. He wasn't particularly close to either of the Johnsons, and he had greatly enjoyed his ride. He seemed to be taking to country life easily. Jonathan even jokingly offered to see if there was any nearby property for sale, should Vincent have an interest in moving upstate himself. Vincent laughingly declined. He was a city boy, at heart. Much like his sister, he found the country charming and wonderful to visit, but he wouldn't want to live there.

That night, as Eliza readied herself for bed, she was

thankful to have no inappropriate visitors, and went to bed peacefully. She had put the question of leaving Jonathan from her mind, and was happier for having done so. She prayed Vincent would not push the issue further, which perhaps would have been an indication of her feelings on the subject, if she had been thinking more clearly. For the moment, though, she was too flustered any time she tried to think about the men, and it was easier to ignore it. The question of whether or not she would allow Jonathan to kiss her again was moot. If he came to her door that night, it was after she was asleep.

Throughout Wednesday and Thursday, Vincent was polite and attentive to Eliza, without being unseemly, which pleased her. The two of them, along with Amy and Joshua, took a short ride Wednesday during the day, and Eliza was pleased to display the skills she had developed. The siblings were duly impressed. Amy didn't ride, but she was delighted to mount a horse and have Joshua lead it slowly around the pasture, much as one might do for a child.

The ladies spent more time in the kitchen garden, picking berries. It was a very large garden, comprising beds for root vegetables, lettuces, peppers, and tomatoes, several fruit trees and the berry bushes. In addition to the blackberries and blueberries, there were also raspberries, and some few beds of strawberries. There were squashes and gourds, and set off to one side was a dovecote, filled with chirping birds. The garden house contained a potting area within a small greenhouse, as well as the Davis family's living quarters, and the outdoor kitchen. Closest to the main house lay small beds with fragrant herbs. Separated from the rest of the grounds by a leafy hedge, the garden felt like its own little world. It was just as much a delight to experience as the rest of the grounds.

As the days passed, so did the nights, and each night Jonathan bid Eliza goodnight in the drawing room, with words only. Thursday night he found that his feet brought him to Eliza's bedroom door, late, after everyone else had gone to bed. His feet had acted of their own accord, without his brain's interference, and he caught himself just as he prepared to knock. She had asked him not to do this sort of thing, and he would respect her wishes. He missed those moments alone, though. He longed for the feel of her soft body and her warm lips. He groaned, lowered his hand away from the door, and walked back to his own room, sighing in frustration.

Jonathan was unaware that Eliza lay in bed at that very moment, restlessly fighting with the covers. She squeezed her eyes closed and wished that a knock might sound at her door. She fell asleep and dreamed of a man coming to her in the night, kissing her where she lay in her bed. The dream man climbed into bed with her, and touched her in darkly erotic ways. She woke in the middle of the night with her nightgown twisted up around her thighs. She felt hot and breathless, and she sat up, panting. She took a cool sip of water from the glass nearby, her mind grasping at the dim memories of the dream. It faded quickly, as dreams often do, and she laid back down to resume her sleep.

Chapter 26

Friday dawned bright and clear. The girls were all a-twitter with delight over the upcoming evening. Eliza's dream was all but forgotten, and she was looking forward to the dinner party. The small number of guests were all set to attend, and they were excited about the little party. It seemed quite a fitting way to cap the weeklong visit of the Dudleys. Mrs. Davis, Mary, and Molly had all paid special attention to cleaning, dusting, and polishing, so that everything shined. Eliza and Amy took special pleasure in cutting and arranging flowers from the garden. Mrs. Davis had shown them how certain beds were planted especially for cutting, such that stems could be cut without causing the gardens to lose their beauty. Mrs. Smith and Mary had been busy in the kitchen for the previous two days, and the entire house smelled delightful.

Vincent hadn't approached Eliza privately again, though the stress of anticipation weighed on her. She fully expected Vincent to approach her again, and when he did, she had no idea how she might respond. If she thought about it at all, her mind circled back to that endless loop of feelings chasing after feelings, forever unresolved. It was wont to drive her mad, so she simply ignored it and hoped that clarity would come to her eventually. In the meantime, she had devoted her attention to avoiding any situation which would leave them alone together.

Guests arrived precisely on time, and gaiety reigned supreme. Throughout dinner, conversation was boisterous and happy. Eliza was seated between Brandon and Michael, and couldn't be happier about it. Amy filled out their side. Across the table, Vincent sat next to Olivia, with Jonathan and Patrick on the other side of Olivia, with Patrick facing Amy. The arrangement was intimate and cozy, taking up most of the center of the big table, and leaving the ends empty.

As Eliza bent closer to catch what her godfather was saying during the main course, Olivia delicately leaned close to Vincent and whispered, "If you keep looking at her like that, she's going to think you've mistaken her for the dessert course."

Vincent drew his eyes away from Eliza as he choked a bit. "Excuse me?"

"I don't mean to be rude, I just thought you would appreciate knowing that you're being a bit overt in your...appreciation of our hostess," she continued in a whisper.

He considered denying it, but feeling as though he'd been caught red handed, he tacitly acknowledged his sin with a chuckle, "Being a bit obvious, was I?"

"Indeed," Olivia confirmed. But if her assumption had been correct, she considered, it might be to her own advantage. "If I may be frankly candid with you, though," she confided, "I wish I had the same vantage point with our host," and she gestured discreetly at Jonathan. Her travels abroad had certainly had an effect on Mrs. Johnson's sense of propriety.

Vincent uttered a surprised, scandalized, "Oh!" He was careful to keep his voice low.

"Perhaps at some point we can do each other a favor," Olivia said obscurely.

"Perhaps," he replied, not fully taking her meaning, yet.

Dinner ended happily, and the party all retired to the drawing room. Smaller groups immediately formed consisting of conversations and talk of a card game starting. Jonathan happily poured drinks, and Eliza was ensconced in a conversation with Amy and Michael.

It was a small thing that seemed inconsequential to Jonathan when Olivia asked him to show her the library some time later, while everyone else was otherwise occupied.

. . .

"Oh, Jonathan!"

Those were the words Eliza heard as she approached the library, looking to see if perhaps that's where her husband had taken himself off to. Not one to be bold, she didn't march into the room. Instead, she peered gingerly past the partially open door. The sight of her husband and Olivia Johnson locked in a passionate embrace made her heart break. She raised her hand to her mouth to stifle a gasp, and she quickly moved back out into the hallway, out of sight. Eyes streaming, she ran up to her room, suddenly grateful that it was far from any of the rooms her husband regularly inhabited. She was in shock. She locked her door and stood, breathing heavily, trying to make herself calm down. They still had a house full of guests, and she must compose herself, even if she felt like something very large had been placed upon her chest.

She took just a few moments in front of her vanity to blot her face and steady her breathing. It hurt so much, but she had experience at hiding pain and sadness. With one last deep breath, she stood and left the room. In the drawing room, Jonathan and Olivia weren't to be seen, and Eliza assumed they were still in the library. She shuddered. Amy made her way to her friend, seeing her looking pale.

"Eliza, is something the matter?"

Eliza gave her friend a smile. "It's fine. Though, you know that concern that you had about my husband and a certain old friend?"

Amy understood the thinly veiled reference and nodded.

"Well." Eliza's smile was tight and forced and her eyes were glassy. "it turns out that you were right."

"Oh, Lissie!" Amy was immediately wrought with an array of emotions. None of them were good. "Where are they? What happened?" she hissed.

"It doesn't matter," sighed Eliza, dejectedly. She was still wrestling internally with the wrenching pain coursing through her chest.

At that moment, Jonathan appeared in the doorway. He looked as though he was going to approach his wife, but Eliza and Amy turned away to discourage him. He was caught and pulled into a conversation by his uncle, saving the girls from an uncomfortable encounter.

"That's it, Lissie," Amy said decisively. "We're leaving tomorrow morning, and you're coming with us. You can stay with our family for a few days, or we can bring you to your house, but either way, we're getting you out of here."

Eliza sighed and nodded. "Yes. Yes, I want to leave. We were supposed to go into the city next week, anyway. I can just tell him I've decided to go alone."

"Are you going to confront him about...?"

"No," she said decisively. "I can't. I don't know what I would say. I don't want to see him. I just need some time away."

"Yes, and you shall have it." Amy was instantly protective.

The rest of the evening passed in a blur. Blessedly, Olivia and Patrick left almost immediately after she came back into the room, which was a few minutes after Jonathan. Brandon and Michael left at some point, with a hail of kisses, handshakes, and well wishes. Shortly after that, Eliza pleaded a headache and went up to her room by herself. Molly happened to be there, which Eliza was thankful for.

She hurriedly explained to the maid that she would be leaving for the city in the morning, and asked that she please pack her things. She also informed Molly that she would send for her shortly, to join her in the city.

"Are you planning to stay for an extended time, miss?" The maid was shocked.

Eliza hesitated. "Possibly. I haven't decided anything yet."

"Yes, miss. I'll pack your things right away. Will Mr. Stanton be joining you, miss?"

"No." Eliza's voice was harsher than she had intended. "I'm sorry. I mean to say that he will not. I... want to continue my company with the Dudleys, and Mr. Stanton has work to do here. He can't be troubled by my wants."

"Yes, miss," Molly replied hesitantly, having the distinct feeling that there was more being said than what had been said aloud. But she knew it wasn't her place to ask questions.

"Thank you, Molly."

"Of course, miss."

With that, Eliza sat down with her stationery. She wrote two letters. One was to Jonathan, explaining that she wanted to spend a little more time with the Dudleys, and so she would be returning to the city with them. She added that she could handle the mill visit on her own, and so he should stay here and save the trip. She didn't mention when she would be back.

The second letter she would have delivered tomorrow after they arrived at the Dudley residence, to alert Mrs. Grayson to the slight change of plans. It would just be Eliza arriving for an unspecified, but extended period of time, starting a few days earlier than originally planned.

She didn't want to go directly to her house; she wanted to spend a few days with the Dudleys as Amy had offered, surrounding herself with normalcy, and a family she was comfortable with. But she wanted the option to go home when she desired it.

After feeling satisfied with her letters, she undressed with Molly's help and climbed into bed. When a quiet knock sounded at her door, she ignored it and pretended to be asleep already, leaving the knock unanswered.

The following day, the traveling party left relatively early with no fanfare. Eliza explained that she'd be returning to the city with the Dudleys in the briefest of ways to Mrs. Davis, and left the letter for Jonathan in the woman's care. And then they were on their way. Mrs. Davis thought it was a little odd, but wasn't greatly troubled, and she carried the letter to Mr. Stanton's office.

Jonathan was saddened at his wife's decision, but he understood that she wanted to see her friends more. He sat at his desk, studying her brief letter, feeling both surprised and disappointed that she had chosen a letter to convey the news, rather than saying goodbye in person. He traced her signature gently with his fingertip, thinking that he hadn't gotten nearly as much time with her in the last few days, and he missed her instantly. He had also hoped that her presence this morning might help to erase the unsettling experience with Mrs. Johnson the previous evening. He shuddered, thinking about it again. He had it in the back of his head that he might still go to the city as planned, and meet Eliza as a bit of a surprise, but the planned trip wasn't until later in the week, which would give her the time she desired with her friends.

Meanwhile, Vincent was unaware of anything other than that Eliza was going to come home with them, and stay for a few days. He was quite happy with what he saw as another opportunity to perhaps sway her feelings. He thought back to the strange little conversation he'd had with Olivia Johnson at dinner and wondered if this was somehow part of the "favor". Eliza looked rather tired, more like the wan creature she had been at the Forester's dinner party back in the spring, rather than the bright, happy girl she'd been during the previous week. Any time he started any kind of conversation, however, his sister shot daggers at him with her eyes. She looked like a blonde angel of vengeance, hovering over Eliza delicately, daring him or anyone to come too close. Clearly something had happened to one or both of them, and Vincent was smart enough to avoid his sister's wrath. He sought to maintain a pleasant silence, therefore, for the rest of the trip.

Chapter 27

Mr. and Mrs. Dudley were more than happy to have Eliza return with their children, and they doted on her as though she were one of their own. They had the room next to Amy's prepared immediately, and insisted the travelers all rest, upon arriving home. Amy practically dragged Eliza up to her own room, while the guest room was being aired. In the privacy of the bedroom, behind the closed door, the girls sat on the bed.

"Now Lissie, tell me everything. Let it all out," Amy immediately demanded.

Eliza looked at her friend, distraught. "Well, last night after dinner, you know that we were all chatting, and Jonathan was at the drinks cabinet. After the card game, my godfather wanted a drink, but Jonathan had gone. He was missing for several minutes, when I thought I might go look for him. I went to the library," she paused, choking on a sob, "and I saw him kissing Olivia Johnson!" she wailed, covering her face with her hands.

Amy embraced her, offering her a handkerchief. "That absolute beast. Right in your own home with you in the other room! Did they see you?"

Eliza dabbed at her eyes. "No, I don't think so. I ran away immediately. Oh, Amy! It hurts so much! How could he? I thought...I mean, I know he doesn't love me, but how could he marry me and then...?"

"He's scum," Amy said assuredly. "He's worse than scum. If anything, it's better that you found out now. I'm so, so sorry, darling. You deserve so much better than this. And that,

that *harlot* is married! Her poor husband!"

Eliza just cried, in a way she hadn't allowed herself to do yet. She sobbed on the bed while Amy patted her back, making soothing sounds, interspersed with the small number of curses she knew spat in the direction of *that man*, as she was currently referring to Jonathan. After Eliza had calmed down a bit, she looked at her friend with serious eyes.

"I just don't want anyone to know. It's so deeply embarrassing," she choked, feeling her face flame just thinking about it.

Amy nodded, understanding. "You're just visiting your dear friends who love you. And if you go back to your townhouse, well, it's your family home, isn't it? It's where you grew up. You're entitled to visit. The country gets so dreary. No one will fault you for wanting to be in the city for a time. No one. It will all be just fine. I promise. No one shall know a thing that you don't wish them to."

"Thank you." Eliza gave her a weepy smile. "You're the best friend a girl could have."

"We need a distraction," Amy said decisively. "We'll go to the theater, and we'll go *shopping*. You haven't been shopping in ages. And we can get tea at the tea house where we first met! Oh! That would be delightful. Mama would love to come with us for that."

"That sounds wonderful. I think I'd like that. But for right now, I think I just want to cry some more."

"Absolutely not," Amy insisted. "I will not let you wallow in pain over what some *man* did. You're better than that." Eliza stared at her friend with wide eyes, stunned. "We're going to wash your hair, and wash your face, and get you out of these dusty clothes, and then we're going to play games and tell stories, just like we used to when we were little."

"I don't know," Eliza began.

"I do," Amy said, cutting her off. "If you do nothing but lay in bed and cry all day, you're going to be all puffy and have a headache in the morning. It will just make you miserable.

You've been wandering around that big old house for months now, with no entertainment but what you made yourself. I'm going to remind you what having your best friend by your side is really like."

Eliza's gloom cleared, and she nodded hesitantly. "I'd like that, yes."

That evening, Amy pleaded a headache on Eliza's behalf, and asked her maid to bring up a plate of food for her friend. The following morning, she insisted Eliza join the family for breakfast, and attempt to put the nastiness behind her. Thus started the campaign of distraction.

Amy's mother, Lydia Dudley, truly was a delightful woman, and she loved having the two girls in the house. She demanded to know all about her children's visit with the Stantons, and waxed long about the fun they had all had at the house years previously. She was jubilant at the idea of Eliza staying with them for a few days, and eagerly agreed that the theater and shopping would be wonderful diversions for the girls. The normalcy and maternal cluckings were soothing to Eliza's raw sensibilities. Vincent joined the ladies in the afternoon and lamented that work would keep him from enjoying their company more often, now that they were home.

Surprise came home with Mr. Jacob Dudley Monday evening, in the form of Lucas Bradley. He had brought his employee home for dinner, or so he said, and he beamed at his family. Lydia gave her husband a stern look, but welcomed the young Mr. Bradley graciously. He was introduced to Eliza, who thought the man was charming. Vincent arrived home shortly after his father and guest, knowing what the scheme had been, and eager to avoid any tantrum his sister might have. Amy, for her part, greeted her father warmly, and Mr. Bradley with cold formality. She then simply informed her mother that she had suddenly acquired quite a vicious headache, and she would be unable to attend dinner this evening. She hoped Mr. Bradley would accept her apologies. She heard her father mutter, "Amelia," tinged with frustration, but ignored him.

Overall, the assembled company tacitly agreed that that could have gone much worse. Dinner was lovely, and Eliza found Lucas to be intelligent and witty, as well as handsome. She could understand what her friend had seen in the man. After the meal had ended, she didn't tarry long in company, excusing herself to check on her friend.

Unsurprisingly, Amy was stewing in her bedroom, sitting at her vanity angrily brushing her hair. Eliza had knocked lightly, but knowing her friend was unlikely to admit an anonymous visitor, she had cracked the door and announced herself. Once in the room, Eliza took the brush away, and began to gently braid her friend's hair, lest she do damage to it in her frustration.

"How could he?" Amy cried. "How could father ambush me like that? What was he thinking? Bringing *that man* into this house. He couldn't have done that last week, when I wasn't here?"

"I think your presence might have been part of why he did it," observed Eliza.

"It's mean," declared Amy. "It's just mean and spiteful. He knows that I'm not interested in any man he wants to try to sell me to, like I'm some calf at auction. Is it going to be like this from now on? Is he just going to start a parade of eligible young men through the house?"

"Is it possible that he thinks Mr. Bradley might be special?" Eliza asked sincerely.

"Oh, of course Mr. Bradley is special. Special in the lengths he went to in order to deceive me! Ugh. I can't believe he would dare to show his face to me. He knows what I think of him."

"I'm sorry, dear. Why don't we go out tomorrow? Like we had talked about. I think we both need a distraction, now," Eliza suggested.

"Yes. Yes, absolutely. And father is going to buy me a new hat." Her tone was spiteful, but also hurt.

Chapter 28

Meanwhile, at home, Jonathan was blissfully unaware that his wife had witnessed anything untoward, that she was currently wildly upset with him, and also that she had, for all intents and purposes, left him. He continued about his days as he always had, though feeling distinctly lonely in her absence.

He was surprised, Tuesday afternoon, when Olivia Johnson called on him, without her husband. He considered having Mrs. Davis tell her that he was busy, but thought that this might be the right time to settle things, finally. He met her in the parlor, and made sure he sat in a wingback chair, after she had seated herself on the loveseat.

"I'm sorry Mrs. Stanton isn't here to greet you," Jonathan began. "You're looking well."

"I'm here to see you, Jonathan, not her," Olivia said eagerly. "I happen to know your wife left the estate, so it seemed an opportunity for us to speak candidly. Oh, Jonathan--"

Jonathan was affronted by her frankness. He held up his hand to pause her speaking to ask, "What do you mean, you know that my wife *left*?"

Olivia sighed. Her voice was high pitched, and clipped as she said, "My mother happened to see Amy and Eliza both, along with Mrs. Dudley, at a tea shop on Sunday. My mother arrived for a visit this morning, and mentioned it."

"I see. Yes, we had plans to go to town this week already, and Eliza decided to leave a few days early to see the Dudleys a bit more. I believe she also wanted to visit with Mrs. Dudley. I fail to see any significance in that." Jonathan's tone was much easier. He was unperturbed by his wife's decisions.

"Well that's why I'm here, isn't it?" She leaned forward suggestively. "You were appalled when I kissed you at the party on Saturday, but don't you see? Your wife isn't as sweet and innocent as you think her to be, either. And that's what I came here to say. Darling, it's perfectly natural for two people to pursue what they want in life, and marriage doesn't have to be a stumbling block to that. I assume that if you know that your wife is no better than I am, and willing to pursue men outside of your marriage, you'll see my suggested arrangement in a different light." Confidence rang in her tone, and she preened a bit, smoothing her skirts around her in a regal pose.

Jonathan was incensed. "You would dare to equate your *suggestion* that you and I pursue a romantic relationship with each other while we're each married to other people, to my wife visiting with friends? Mrs. Johnson, I agreed to see you today to tell you in no uncertain terms that I have no interest in being with you, nor have I ever." He stood to emphasize what he said, his voice growing in volume and vigor. "And I resent your assertions against my wife. She is merely visiting old friends, and absolutely would not, as you say, pursue other men."

Olivia sniffed in the face of his rage, remaining poised. "Vincent Dudley has had eyes for *your wife* for years now, and you're blind if you don't see that. Do you think that she went to the city to visit little Amy, or her mother? How convenient it is that her bedroom is right down the hall from tall, strapping, handsome Vincent's," she said with icy venom.

"That's insane!" railed Jonathan. He took a moment to calm himself, forcing thoughts of Eliza and the Dudleys from his mind. He paced away a few steps before turning to add, "What I need you to understand, Mrs. Johnson," he enunciated her name carefully, "is that even if I were an unmarried man, with no prospects, I would still not want to be with you. I'm sorry to be as blunt as that, but it appears to be necessary."

Olivia stood with a huff. "I have never been so insulted

in my life. See if I'll still accept you in my bed after your wife has divorced you."

With that she stood and flounced out of the house. Jonathan was dumbfounded. The woman was stark raving mad. First, she had cornered him in the library and kissed him, making her illicit proposal, and now accused his own wife of making him a cuckold. It was unbelievable. He stalked back to his office, livid, but he couldn't calm himself enough to work. He roughly pulled Olivia's letter from its hiding spot and crumpled it in his hand. Uncrumpling it, he tore it to shreds. Still not satisfied, he threw it in the fireplace and threw a lit match in after it. He stomped back downstairs. He rapidly found that every room in the house reminded him of Eliza. The kittens, who were playing in front of the fireplace in the drawing room, reminded him of Eliza. The gardens, when he walked outside, instantly brought his wife to mind. The only room that didn't immediately remind him of her was the library, and that room brought back awful memories of Olivia. The impertinent witch. The idea that Eliza might divorce him was painful. Not just ludicrous, but unfathomable. Hearing those words had brought a pain to his chest that was quite foreign.

Giving in to temptation, he mounted the stairs to the east wing of the house. He paused outside Eliza's bedroom door, preparing himself as he would to enter a sacred space. When he opened the door, he was astonished to find it so different. He could feel her absence acutely, and he struggled to pinpoint why. He slowly picked out all the differences between now and when he had last been in here, with her, Thursday evening. He first noticed that her brush and comb were missing from the vanity. Well, that made sense. She would have brought those with her. But he began to realize that many of her things were gone. Not just her clothes and toiletries, but little keepsakes and things that wouldn't be necessary for even a week-long stay in the city. He sat down heavily on the loveseat to consider. Had Olivia been telling the truth? Had Eliza actually left him, left their marriage? His chest deeply hurt now, and he brought his hand up, pressing on his sternum to try and relieve the pain. What was happening to him?

She couldn't possibly have left for good. Why would she do that? She truly seemed happy here. She seemed to like him well enough. Unless it was true that Vincent had lured her away. She had known him for years, and he had been a constant fixture in her life, so it would make sense for her to find comfort and reassurance with him. Jonathan had a mental image of the two of them embracing and it made him want to break something.

He had already planned to go to the city the following day to surprise her, so it wasn't a big change for him to decide to leave a day earlier. He quickly packed his bag and asked Mr. Davis to make ready the carriage. He fumed and debated with himself during the entire drive, going back and forth in his mind about the reason for his wife's actions. Surely Olivia had been lying. But he reflected back upon the previous week, considering all the times Eliza and Vincent had been in the same room. He was likely to drive himself mad trying to discern in hindsight if there had been any special glances or touches between them.

Arriving at the townhouse, finally, Mrs. Grayson was quite surprised. She was no longer expecting Mr. Stanton's arrival at all, and now here he was, without Mrs. Stanton. For his part, Jonathan was surprised to find his wife not in residence. He deposited his bags, and then asked Mr. Davis to proceed directly to the Dudley residence.

"I need to see my wife." Jonathan's voice was loud and insistent. He pushed past the butler who had opened the door and heard Eliza's sweet laughter coming from the room immediately to his left. As he approached, he saw her, perched on the edge of a deep sofa, and he saw a man's hand on her shoulder. He entered the room bellowing, "Unhand my wife, sir!"

Eliza looked up with a gasp at the sound of her husband's voice. "Jonathan!"

Vincent's grip tightened protectively on her shoulder, and Jonathan belatedly saw Amy as well as Mr. and Mrs. Dudley sitting nearby. "Forgive me for barging in, Mr. Dudley, Mrs. Dudley, Miss Dudley." Jonathan nodded in their general direction, his tone stiff and his words carefully enunciated. "I need to speak with Eliza."

Crimson faced, she stood, murmuring, "Please excuse us," as she quickly crossed and took her husband's arm, leading him back into the foyer. Amy's mouth made a perfect O as they left the room.

Eliza shuffled Jonathan into a nearby sitting room and slowly closed the door, mortified and confused. She turned to face him just as slowly and deliberately. "What is the meaning of this?"

"I'm sorry." His voice didn't sound remorseful, so much as reproachful. "Did you think I was just going to sit back and let you leave? You're my wife, or have you forgotten?" He was hurting, and the pain made him defensive.

"Excuse me? Shall we discuss infidelity in our marriage?" she countered. "I haven't done anything to be ashamed of. You knew where I was going, and with whom. I left you a letter."

"But you weren't planning to come back, were you?" he shouted. "I know all about Dudley's affections. You left me!" He didn't hesitate to make the allegation, having seen Dudley's hand on his wife in the parlor. The anguish in his voice tore at Eliza's heart, but she stiffened, thinking about what she had seen the night of the dinner party.

"I hadn't decided yet!" she blurted in frustration.

"What?" His disbelief was clearly apparent.

"I was yours; I was never going to leave you. But you didn't want just me, did you? You didn't want me at all!" She looked up at him accusingly, unshed tears sparkling in her eyes. Her voice turned low and dangerous as she said, "I saw you Friday night. You talk about me leaving you, like I'm the one betraying our vows, like you've already betrayed them, haven't you?" She bit back tears.

Jonathan stifled a curse. That damnable woman! He needed to explain, but he was loath to do it in the Dudleys' sitting room. "We clearly need to talk some things over, and I don't think it's the proper thing to do it here. We can go to the townhouse." He was angry, and his words were sharper than he intended them to be.

"I don't want to go anywhere with you," she responded harshly.

"I'm still your husband," he said indignantly, hurt.

She snorted in an unladylike fashion. "A husband who has no interest in his wife's bed."

"Elizabeth!" His face flamed, turning dark. "But then, you have someone else interested in your bed, don't you?"

Eliza flushed deeply. "*I* haven't been unfaithful to you," she said with emphasis, her voice low.

Restraining his emotions, Jonathan said precisely, "Let's go somewhere we can talk this over more freely."

Eliza spun on her heel, refusing to respond to him directly. They returned to the parlor, both embarrassed, both angry. Eliza spoke for both of them, saying softly, "Please forgive me for leaving so suddenly, but I think it's best if we return to my home."

Vincent rose, ready to argue, "Eliza, you don't have to go with him."

"I know that." Her voice broke slightly as she spoke. "I need to go."

"Eliza, I love you!" Vincent's voice was impassioned as he explosively exclaimed the words. He reached out to her; his actions surprising everyone in the room.

Sighing, she took several deliberate steps toward him. "Vincent...I love you," she said quietly, and Jonathan felt his chest spasm as she said the words, thinking he'd lost her for good, without getting to explain things, "but I don't love you the way you deserve to be loved by a woman."

Jonathan felt waves of relief wash over him, but Vincent wasn't done.

"Do you love him?" he asked hoarsely.

Eliza paused a long moment, before answering quietly, "That doesn't matter."

Her husband's heart was doing somersaults, and he wasn't sure he was breathing anymore, but he reached his hand out to her. She went to him but didn't take his hand. They left without any further words being spoken. The short carriage ride was also silent.

When they arrived back at the Montgomery home, Mrs. Grayson was confused but delighted to see both of them. Eliza greeted her warmly, and explained that the two of them would be upstairs until dinner time, if their rooms were ready? They were, both of them, since Jonathan had already been at the townhouse earlier in the day. It was late in the afternoon, as the two of them climbed the stairs. They entered the master bedroom, as there was the seating area there. Neither of them felt much like sitting, but it was the most private place for the discussion that they needed to have.

Chapter 29

Once the door was closed, Eliza turned to Jonathan. "You were going to explain things?" she asked archly.

He looked at his wife and let all the feelings of the last few days wash over him at once. He had missed her. He had wanted her. He had felt her presence, followed sharply by her absence. She had become a part of his life, and one he treasured. He was only just realizing the truth of that. He was also deeply aware that they were in a bedroom. His eyes darkened. "You seem to be under the impression that I'm not interested in you, as a woman."

She stared at him blankly. That wasn't what she expected him to lead with, and it confused her. He was looking at her in a way he hadn't before, at least not that she'd noticed. His normally clear blue eyes had turned stormy, and he wasn't just looking at her eyes. He was looking at her body, appreciatively. She blushed as she realized he was so openly ogling her, and it distracted her for a moment.

He approached her, slowly. When they had entered the room, she had walked toward the little table, stopping near a chair, but not sitting, while he had stayed closer to the middle of the room. He practically stalked her, the way the kittens stalked each other in the grass, but seemingly much more dangerous. "You're a beautiful woman," he breathed. He reached her and raised his hand gently to her face. She flinched slightly at his touch. "So innocent, so sweet. Do you know how much I enjoy kissing you each night before bed?"

She shivered. This was absolutely not the conversation she had planned to have. She stayed still, waiting to see what he might say next, or what he might do.

He had never been aggressive with her. But at that moment, he was feeling not just days, but months and years of frustration and loneliness come to a head inside him. He continued, his voice so low it was practically a purr, "I haven't wanted to rush you. I haven't wanted to scare you. But you haven't been afraid, have you? You like it when I kiss you, when I touch you."

He ran his thumb over her lower lip, and brought his other hand to her waist, his fingers splayed. She took a shuddering breath, and in fact, did feel somewhat fearful, but also excited. She tried to force herself to look away, to not respond to his touch, but she was powerless against it.

"I didn't get to say goodnight to you on Friday," he whispered before he brought his lips down to hers, surprisingly gentle. He raised his head slightly to say, "or Saturday," before kissing her again, moving his lips softly over hers. "Or Sunday," he nudged her lips with his tongue, tracing her bottom lip, begging her to open to him. She resisted. "Or Monday," and this time he kissed her insistently, forceful but not unpleasant, and she opened her lips to him reluctantly. His tongue invaded her mouth, thrusting gently against her own. Her traitorous hands, previously at her sides, slipped up to his shoulders where she gripped him tightly, torn between pulling him closer and pushing him away.

His own hand slipped lower, over her backside, and she thrilled inside, having flashbacks to that day she had worn the trousers. His other hand came to her waist, and pulled her close, so that her full length was pressed against him. She felt the familiar heat growing in her belly, and there was a dampness between her thighs. A tear fell down her cheek as he continued to kiss her, and he felt it on his lips, where they met hers. He drew back and saw that she was softly crying. He kissed her tears away, kissing her eyes and cheeks. "Please don't cry," he murmured, continuing to kiss her. His mouth trailed down to her throat and chest. The new sensation caused her breath to catch, and she was distracted from her tears. "Lissie," his voice was hoarse, "I want you. I know you want me, too."

He pressed his hips against her, and she felt a stiff bulge against her belly, causing warmth to flood between her legs. Breathing heavily, she whispered, "yes." One, simple word. It was true. As much as he had hurt her, he had spent far longer teasing her, exciting her, and denying her. She thought seriously that she may never have this opportunity again, all things considered. She was going to take it while she could.

Her consent thrilled Jonathan. He wasn't thinking clearly at all, but he knew what he wanted, and his wife wanted it as well. He would prove that she was wrong about at least one thing. He removed his jacket and loosened his cravat, kissing her all the while. He forced himself to pull away as he gently and delicately unfastened her dress, slipping it off, leaving her standing in stays and a petticoat. He guided her to the nearby chair, and urged her to sit with a gentle hand on her shoulder, kissing her sweetly at the same time. He bent and lovingly removed her shoes, raising her foot so that he could kiss her ankle. She shivered. He slowly ran his hands up her leg, fingers grazing lightly, enticingly. He found the top of her stocking and, releasing the clips holding it, slowly pulled it down, and off, his hands embracing her bare leg as it was revealed. She whimpered slightly before he repeated the action on her other leg. He was deeply aroused, but forced himself to move slowly.

He stood and removed his own ascot and shirt, revealing a fit chest and flat stomach. Eliza's eyes were drawn to his shoulders and biceps. She hadn't expected him to be as muscular as he was. This was her first time seeing a naked man. He reached out to her and drew her from the chair, kissing her again. With so much less clothing between them, she could feel the heat of his skin, and though she was hesitant at first, she brought her hands to his shoulders, wrapping them around his neck. He kept enough room between them that he could bring his hands up to loosen her stays, pausing in their kiss just long enough to pull them up over her head. She willingly acquiesced to this, which left her standing in a thin, sleeveless chemise that reached to her low calf. He held her at arm's length, breathing deeply, and drinking in the sight of her. Reluctantly, his hands left her to unfasten his own breeches, quickly removing them. Frustrated with his clothing, he pulled his stockings off unceremoniously. His braies hung low on his hips and didn't conceal much. Eliza stood still, uncertain.

Jonathan came to her. He kissed the tip of her nose before bending to grasp the hem of her chemise. He pulled it up slowly, his hands grazing the sides of her legs, her hips, and her waist as he moved up. When it was removed, she stood naked before him, self-conscious and anxious. Unexpectedly, he lifted her up in his arms gently, kissing her and forcing himself to keep his eyes on her face. He gently laid her down on the bed, and removed his braies before joining her. This was utterly unlike the last time they had been in this bed, but he was reminded of waking that time, which seemed eons ago. He laughed softly to himself, to which she looked puzzled and hurt.

He quickly explained, in a soft voice, "Do you remember the last time we slept in this bed?" She nodded. "Would it surprise you to know that when I woke up, my arm was around you, and you had snuggled up, pressing your perfect little bottom into me?"

She blushed, "No!"

"Yes!" he laughed and brought his lips to hers. He kissed her languorously. As he did, his hand explored her body. His fingers grazed her shoulder, to her collarbone, he traced straight down, between her breasts, over her belly, before flattening his palm on her flat stomach. She felt the heat of his hand as he moved it back up, over her ribs, and finally cupping her full, soft breast. She moaned against his lips, and her legs twitched unconsciously. He chuckled against her lips as he kneaded her, running his finger over and around her taut nipple. He bent his head and kissed it, and then kissed it again, opening his mouth to swirl his tongue around the small bud. Her hand tangled in his hair. He moved to her other breast, giving it the same attention. His lips moved lower, kissing a line down her stomach. She whimpered, drawing him back up to her lips. He paused, hovering above her, searching her face. He kissed her gently again, softly. His hand lowered to her hip, before drawing his fingertips down to her thigh. With painful slowness, his hand approached her burning center, which had begun to ache. His fingers grazed the soft thatch of hair between her legs, and she shuddered. He lifted his head so he could watch her face as he touched her most intimate place, his fingers sliding easily over her, finding her slick and hot. Her eyes widened and she gasped, arching her back off the bed a bit at the sensations that rocked her. Blindly she reached for him and brought him back to her, kissing him deeply. He groaned as he teased between her legs, letting his fingers slip and circle. He dipped his fingers lower, but held back some. He knew that she was a virgin, and he wanted her to feel as good as possible before entering her, and possibly causing her pain. He teased the small bud between her thighs relentlessly, thrusting his tongue into her mouth the same way he longed to thrust into other parts of her body. Her thighs rose rhythmically to his hand, and he felt her small nails biting into his shoulder blades where she grasped his back. His hardness bulged against her thigh. She came suddenly, feeling her body break in waves of intense pleasure, and as she moaned into his mouth, he slipped a single finger inside of her. She cried out and convulsed at the new sensation, pulling at him.

He thrust with his finger at first, accustoming her to the feeling, exciting her in a new way, simultaneously learning the feel of her most private place. He pulled away slightly and repositioned himself between her legs, leaning down to kiss her, whispering, "This may hurt a bit." He hesitated a moment before adding, "You can still say no."

She hooked an arm around his neck and kissed him passionately, whispering, "Don't stop," harshly in his ear.

He gasped as he entered her. He moved slowly, watching her eyes widen again as she made gasping sounds of shock. He saw the pinch of pain in her face and paused, cradling her gently, reaching down to massage her breasts with one hand, arousing her once again, before continuing, filling her with his length. He paused, allowing her to become accustomed to having him inside her before he began to move deliberately, unhurried. He bent his head and kissed her tenderly. She responded to his thrusts with her own rhythmic rocking, her hands exploring his back and shoulders. She felt the waves cresting inside again, building to that ecstatic breaking point, as he quickened his thrusting. They came together, crying out roughly.

Spent, he lowered himself gently, careful to shift his weight to the side of her. He kissed her sweetly, her lips, cheeks, and nose, before cuddling her close. She panted, staring at the canopy over the bed, not moving. She started to pull away, but he whispered, "Wait." He disentangled himself and rose, crossing to the wash basin. He picked up a cloth and, with his back turned to her, used it himself. He picked up a clean cloth and dampened it, returning to the bed. Gently, tenderly, he cleaned Eliza. Gently rubbing her arms, legs, and belly with the cloth. When he gently reached between her legs, grazing her sensitive spot with the cloth, she moaned slightly. The cloth was tinged with red when he lifted it again. He returned it to the basin, before rejoining her in bed. This was her first opportunity to truly see him completely naked. She had felt him earlier, but she hadn't gotten to see him. She was less shocked than she might have been, given what they had just done, but she was nevertheless fascinated. That, combined with the reeling sensations she was still feeling, distracted her from being furious. His fingers trailing lazily over her naked body, sending sparks and shocks through her nerve endings was also a lovely distraction. But she forced herself away, slightly.

Seeing her pull back, Jonathan spoke. "Eliza," he said, reaching for her hand, "I want all of you. And only you."

Tears came to her eyes. She turned away so he wouldn't see her cry. "I'm sorry for what you saw." He didn't know how much, or how little she had seen, but he hoped she had seen that he had rapidly pushed Olivia away. "I never wished to hurt you."

She sobbed, upon hearing that, and it broke Jonathan's heart. He tried to pull her close, but she shied away from him. Sighing, he told her, "I'll give you some space. But I'll be close by, you need only say my name and I'll be by your side."

She buried her face in the bed, but nodded, wishing for him to leave. Once the door closed, presumably after he had retrieved his clothes and at least partially dressed, she allowed herself to cry fully. She eventually cried herself to sleep.

Chapter 30

Eliza didn't awaken until the following morning. She felt stiff, and her face was swollen from crying. She realized that at some point, someone had come in and covered her with a blanket, and her face flamed, because she was still thoroughly naked underneath. She covered her face with her hands and breathed deeply, beginning to untangle her thoughts from sleep. Shortly after she woke, there was a knock at her door. Still naked, and not having her dressing gown with her, she called from the bed, "Who is it?"

The door cracked slightly, and she heard Mrs. Grayson's voice. "It's just me, dear." The woman entered the room bearing a tray. "Mr. Stanton asked me to bring you breakfast in bed. Such a thoughtful man." She smiled unconcernedly as she approached the bed with the tray. Seeing Eliza's bare shoulders peeking out from the blanket, she tactfully glanced away, adding, "There's a dressing gown in the closet. Let me fetch it for you."

She set the tray down and retrieved the dressing gown, one that had belonged to Eliza's mother, and brought it to Eliza. She placed the tray in easy reach, adding, "I'll come back up for the tray in a little while. Don't rush, dear. Take your time." With another cheery smile, she had gone.

Eliza was in a daze, her mind addled. Mrs. Grayson's cheerfulness was a harsh contrast to all of the emotions that had filled Eliza in the last several days. She had been angry, upset, hurt, betrayed, confused, and at best, numb. Amy had known what she was feeling, and had been sensitive to it, acting as a shield between Eliza and the rest of the world. Now, with her friend across town, she felt cold and alone. All of that didn't even take into consideration the previous evening, which she was still processing. She was in disbelief over what they had done. She had been a willing participant, but that didn't alleviate the shock.

She forced herself to take deep breaths and focus on the present. She slipped the dressing gown on, and situated the tray before her. She forced away thoughts of her husband and his "thoughtfulness." She had slept through dinner the previous evening, so she was ravenous. She ate methodically, until she was sated, and then she contemplated what she should do. She didn't want to see anyone, most especially her husband, until she'd had a chance to sort her thoughts. But her things were still at the Dudley house. She considered putting the dress she had worn the previous day back on. Her frustration mounted, as she still had some clothes in the house, but they were in her room, which is presumably where Jonathan had slept. He might still be in there. That further aggravated her, as she thought of him sleeping in her room, that which had been her place of solitude and contemplation for her whole life. She pushed that thought away, scolding herself, reminding herself that it was childish. When Mrs. Grayson returned for the tray, Eliza had the opportunity to inquire as to where Jonathan was. Learning that he was in the parlor, reading, reassured her. She informed the housekeeper that she was feeling unwell, and was likely to stay upstairs all day. The housekeeper nodded understandingly, and departed.

Once she was sure no one was upstairs, Eliza slipped furtively out the bedroom door and down the hall. She entered her former bedroom like a burglar might, cautiously, keenly aware of any sounds that might happen. She pulled several things from the closet quickly, rooted briefly through the chest of drawers, and returned to the master bedroom with a small armful of fabric, as well as a partially used sketchbook and pencil. The clothing left at the house was older, but still fit. It wasn't in the colors and styles of half-mourning, which she should still be wearing, but as she wasn't planning to see anyone today, she didn't care. She quickly dressed, donning a pale blue day dress. She settled into one of the chairs with her sketchbook and stared at it blankly.

She finally allowed her mind to wander to thoughts of yesterday. She had been shocked when Jonathan had barged into the Dudley's parlor. And embarrassed. And, she had to admit, slightly excited. She had never seen him so worked up before, so impassioned, so hurt. But wasn't it her right to be the one feeling hurt? He's the one who had kissed another woman. What had he expected her to do? Well, she reasoned, he hadn't expected her to know. That wasn't a comforting thought. If anything, it just made her more mad. But he had had the audacity to be mad at her, at Vincent. All Vincent had done was touch her shoulder. They had been laughing! Hysterically so, as Amy had just told a rollicking good story. It hadn't been anything inappropriate at all. And yet Jonathan had been angry. Then he had accused her of leaving him, and gotten angry about that. And hurt. She was confused. He was acting for all the world as thought she had wronged him. She had to admit that Vincent had made a rather scandalous proposal to her, but she hadn't acted on it.

After they had arrived at the townhouse…. What had that been? She momentarily got wrapped up in the memories of how he had made her feel, and had to admit that, at least in some ways, it had been amazing. She finally experienced what her body had been longing for since their first kiss. He had denied her for so long. Her thoughts turned dark rapidly. He had been with her, but had he been thinking about Olivia? If he had done that with her, what had he done with that other woman? Obviously, there hadn't been the time or privacy Friday night, but it was now Wednesday, and Jonathan had been alone at home since Saturday. Who's to say that Olivia hadn't paid an illicit visit? Eliza flushed, angry at just the thought of it. She forced herself back to reality. She didn't know what had happened in the last four days. She did know that her husband had made sweet, gentle love to her, and told her that he wanted her, and only her. He had apologized for hurting her. The memories of those recent events softened her somewhat, and inspired a quiet longing. But he hadn't apologized for kissing Olivia, she reminded herself. He had been sorry that she'd witnessed it, but never did he say that it shouldn't have happened at all. What did that mean? She sat pondering his intentions for a long time.

She willfully forced herself to stop thinking about him, and to turn her thoughts inward, focusing on what she wanted. She considered the many turns her life had taken over the last year. She deeply wished her mother were here. But then, if her mother were here, her life would be altogether quite different, wouldn't it? She dragged her mind back from that jagged path of thought. She simply wished that she had someone to talk to. Someone who cared about her, who had a bit more life experience in life and love than Amy had. She pondered a moment and her thoughts came to her godfather. Of course! She could always talk to Brandon. She was considering how she might meet with him when Mrs. Grayson once again knocked at the door, this time bearing some tea, and letting her know that Mr. Stanton had gone to the mill to meet with the foreman. Eliza flushed to belatedly remember that it was Wednesday, and she had planned to go to that meeting. But Jonathan's absence left her with the perfect opportunity. It was still early enough in the afternoon that she could pay a visit to her godfather, and she asked Mrs. Grayson to summon a carriage for this purpose.

Shortly, after making herself presentable for visiting, she was on her way uptown to where Brandon St. John lived. Blessedly, he was at home and both surprised and delighted to see his goddaughter again, so soon. He met her in the parlor with a kiss on the cheek, but quickly deduced from her bloodless complexion that something was the matter.

"Eliza, my dear, it's such a wonderful surprise to see you. Is something the matter?" he asked cautiously.

<pre>226</pre>

"Oh, godfather, I barely know where to begin," she wailed, immediately losing the composure that had been thinly gathered around her.

Brandon felt a distinct amount of panic. "Where is Jonathan? Is he hurt? Are you hurt?" He looked her up and down. She looked distraught, but not injured.

"Friday night, at the party," Eliza began, her eyes misting at the memory, "I... I saw him...Jonathan...*kissing* Olivia Johnson in the library." She sobbed, and Brandon handed her a handkerchief in a daze. She continued, "so I left Saturday morning and came to town with Amy and Vincent Dudley, since they were heading back already, and I've been staying with them, because I told Amy so she knows, but no one else does, and it just *hurts* so badly."

She paused a moment to blot her eyes and breathe. "And then yesterday Jonathan stormed into the Dudley residence, demanding I leave with him, and yelling at poor Vincent, acting as though *I* had been the one to be unfaithful! Can you imagine it?"

Eliza was indignant, and Brandon could not, in fact, imagine such circumstances as she had described. Delicately, trying to piece things together, he asked, "Did Jonathan have a reason to think that Vincent Dudley may have a certain affection for you?" Brandon wasn't blind. He and Michael had both noticed the silent attention Vincent had paid to Eliza during the dinner party, subtle though he had been about it.

Eliza blushed. "Vincent *does* have...certain feelings for me. He's talked to me about it himself. And then, oh," she buried her face in her hands, "yesterday Vincent declared that he loved me in front of Jonathan, Amy, *and* his poor parents. But," she rushed to add, "I told him that I do not reciprocate his feelings. I tried to be as gentle as possible, but I did tell him. Oh, I feel so bad for him."

"Well, let's focus on you for the moment. Can you tell me exactly what happened Friday night? I can't imagine Jonathan would ever do such a monumentally callous thing.

Olivia's husband was right there, as well!"

She sniffed, forcing herself to calm down. "It was after the card game ended, and I couldn't find Jonathan. I assumed he had stepped out for a moment, but when he didn't return immediately, I went to look for him. I was standing outside the library when I heard her...I heard her say, 'oh, Jonathan,' and then I looked for just a moment into the room, and they were kissing! Just like that! I didn't pause to watch; I ran immediately up to my room to compose myself. It just...it hurt *so much*. I've never felt anything like that ever before. I thought my chest was going to break open. It was though someone had hit me, beaten me. How could it hurt so much?" She peered pathetically up at him with her tearstained face.

He patted her hand sympathetically. "My dear, you're in love with him. The more you feel for a person, the more betrayal hurts. I'm so, so sorry Eliza." He paused a moment before continuing carefully, "I do have to wonder if there's more to it than that. Jonathan has never whispered a word of interest in Mrs. Johnson, and I'm struggling to believe that he is that cruel and careless."

"I don't know," she replied miserably, shaking her head. She didn't want to tell her godfather about what had happened after the two of them had returned to the townhouse, but as if on cue, he asked the question.

"What happened after Jonathan found you at the Dudley residence?"

"He accused me of leaving him for Vincent, which was outrageous. I told him that I had seen him Friday evening, with Olivia, and that I hadn't decided yet, if I wanted to leave or not. But I'm not leaving him *for* Vincent. I'm leaving him, maybe, because he's unfaithful! Which is entirely within my right to do," she answered resolutely.

"Did he explain? Or apologize?" Brandon was curious.

She hesitated. "In a fashion," she said at last. "He apologized for what I saw, but not for having done the thing."

"Is that splitting hairs?" Brandon wondered aloud

mildly.

"He didn't explain at all! I don't know what happened other than that they kissed, but that's enough, frankly, for him to apologize for it having happened." Eliza felt wretched. "I don't know. I just know that he hurt me terribly, and I don't know how to trust him now." She considered and slowly, tactfully, added, "it doesn't help matters that his affections towards me have always been rather lukewarm. That's not the right word," she said, searching in her mind for how to put it, "not lukewarm, necessarily, but distant."

"Had been?"

She blushed. "Well, he stormed into the Dudley residence yesterday and practically dragged me across town with some apparent passion. He decided that he cared about me after he thought I had left him."

Brandon shifted uncomfortably and brought his hand to his forehead, as though he was developing a headache. "I see."

She was silent.

He sighed and patted her hand again. "How do you feel now?"

"Confused," she answered simply.

He bit out a laugh. "I imagine that's an understatement."

"I spent some time this morning just thinking about what I want."

"That's good!" He encouraged her. "What did you determine?"

She sighed, rueful. "If you had asked me before Friday evening, my answer would have been simple. I wanted exactly what I had. To be where I was, with Jonathan. I have come to love it there. And," she wavered, "I suppose I had come to have certain feelings for him."

She couldn't bring herself to say that she loved Jonathan. Given the circumstances, Brandon couldn't blame her. He deeply wanted to talk to his nephew. And possibly punch him in the nose. "Now you find yourself less sure about what you want?" he guessed.

"Precisely. I already knew that he doesn't...reciprocate those certain feelings...which I have. I think I had accepted that. But feelings or not, I deserve a husband who is true, don't I? I certainly wouldn't have looked outside our marriage for...anything." She blushed, remembering the visit Vincent had paid her in the evening last week. But nothing had happened, she assured herself. She had done nothing wrong, and she wouldn't have. And kissing someone other than one's spouse was surely wrong.

"I know you wouldn't," Brandon soothed. He had been rolling this story around in his head and just had to wonder, "Is it possible that there's more to what happened Friday night?"

"If there's more, I certainly don't want to hear about it," Eliza said primly.

"That's not what I meant, dear," he said gently. "I just wonder if perhaps the kiss had not been Jonathan's idea? Olivia Johnson has always been a little, how shall I put it, aggressive? She gets it from her mother."

Eliza paused. "I hadn't considered that. But then why wouldn't he have stopped her?" she reasoned.

Brandon shrugged helplessly. "I think you need to know Jonathan's side of the story, before you can really decide what you want to do."

She covered her face with her hands, "I don't know if I can bear to hear him talk about it."

"I understand. Inflicting pain on yourself is unnatural, and no matter what he has to say, it is sure to hurt. But," he offered, "isn't it better to know for sure, to understand his thoughts and motivations, before you make a decision that could have irreparable consequences?"

"What you say makes sense, but I'm just not ready to hear it. I need to steel myself further." She hugged her arms to herself.

At that moment, Michael walked into the parlor. "Oh!

I didn't realize we had company. Eliza, dear, how are you? Are you feeling well?"

He realized belatedly that she was obviously upset. "Should I leave you two to your privacy?"

"No, no, Michael, not at all," Eliza rushed to assure him. "I needed to talk to my godfather about something, but I think a lighter conversation topic would be timely."

"Of course, dear, it's good to see you again so soon. Has Brandon offered you anything to drink yet? Tea, perhaps," he continued lightly, ceding to the request to lighten the mood.

Brandon looked chagrined. "I have entirely forgotten my manners, let me rectify that immediately." He stood to request tea to be served, leaving Eliza to Michael's care.

"It feels as though we barely spoke Friday," Eliza offered, folding the handkerchief into her sleeve while straightening her posture. "How have you been, really?"

"Oh, you know me, I've been wonderful. I was delighted to see the gardens thriving so! You must love having ready access to the grounds at the estate. It's like a fairy land."

"It is, indeed," she said as she relaxed in the familiar company, "and they just keep getting more beautiful as the summer progresses. Even the kitchen garden is lovely. That isn't one I visited as a child."

"Mrs. Davis has allowed me to sneak some herbs from the garden from time to time," he confided. "I finally just took some cuttings at one point, and started my own little herb garden on a windowsill. It's delightful." He smiled brightly.

"I understand you've been learning how to ride! Are you enjoying that?" he hazarded a bit of a guess at a safe topic.

She rewarded him with a smile. "I have! Joshua is an excellent teacher, and I have quite enjoyed learning, and being close to the horses. The woods are absolutely lovely, as well. How are your orchids progressing?"

"Quite well!" Brandon returned as the two chatted, and was shortly followed by the housekeeper with a tray of tea and small sandwiches.

Conversation stayed light as the three drank and nibbled at the sandwiches. Of course, Brandon had been part of Eliza's life since her infancy, and he had been regularly there with her and for her, as a close uncle would be. As an extension, so too had Michael been there. The two men had known each other since school, and they had moved in together after they had graduated, and begun their adult lives. They were closer than any other two men Eliza knew, and at this point, they fit together like perfectly cut puzzle pieces. Best friends, and closest confidantes. There was no question that the two confirmed bachelors would happily grow old together. Each insisted the other was the best and only regular company he needed or wanted in life. The handsome men had separately frustrated women and their mothers for more than a decade, rebuffing every advance. Now, they still had to occasionally fend off the affections of a comely widow. But each did so with such charm and humor that they were beloved in spite of their efforts to remain single. Not for the first time, Eliza noticed that the two men bore genuine affection for one another. She sighed wistfully, thinking that they were and always had been, somewhat shockingly, a better example of what she might want from a relationship than her parents had been. She reminded herself that her parents had been good and loving people, but they had never been very expressive. Prim, proper, and staid were all words that applied to her parents, at least when they were in front of other people. Brandon and Michael shared warm looks and small private jokes, and occasionally when one would touch the other's shoulder or arm, it struck Eliza as incongruously intimate. But setting aside that they were two friends, they lived together, they clearly had a certain affection for one another, and they worked well as a unit, each one had strengths that complemented the other's weaknesses.

She was drawn inexorably to considering herself and Jonathan in this way. They had certainly stumbled a bit in the beginning, but hadn't they come to learn how to work together, in more than the most literal sense? Didn't they complement each other? Or was she deluding herself? Had he been putting on an act this whole time? Had he just been trying to please her, to placate her? Sensing that her thoughts had turned stormy, Brandon smoothly pulled her back into their conversation.

Eliza was grateful to have two such wonderful, loving people she could lean on. She loved them both dearly, and by the time for her impromptu visit to draw to a close, she felt better, lighter, if for no other reason than the delightful distraction. The two implored her to stay for dinner, but she declined. She didn't particularly want to go home, with Jonathan there, but she didn't want to impose any longer. They sent her home in their own carriage.

When she arrived, Mrs. Grayson informed her that her things had arrived from the Dudley residence, and Miss Dudley had sent along a short note, as well. Eliza was happy to hear this, and heartened that the family had taken the step unasked. She immediately went upstairs to read Amy's note. She blessedly avoided any chance meetings with her husband. She didn't know where he was, or if he'd even returned to the house, but she wasn't as bothered by that as she might have been before her outing. Before ascending the stairs, Eliza informed Mrs. Grayson that she would prefer to dine in her room this evening.

Dear Eliza,

I hope you're well, given the excitement of yesterday. Please know that you are welcome to return to stay with us at any time, should you find that preferable. Our family continues to love you as one of our own. I should like to visit you tomorrow and see with my own eyes that you are well. I see no reason why we shouldn't pursue our happy diversions, and it would be pleasant, if you are agreeable, to go shopping together. The fresh air and a new hat are sure to help your sensibilities. With deepest friendship, I wait impatiently to see you tomorrow at the hour of one o'clock.

    Always,
    Amy Dudley

She smiled. Her friend's love for hats rivaled her love for Eliza. In a pinch, Eliza was sure that she would win, but that may actually depend on the exact hat in question. Going out and about with her friend would be delightful. She was also wryly amused by Amy's use of the word "excitement" to describe her husband's scandalous behavior. She was still rather mortified, and couldn't tell if she was happy that it had happened in front of friends she was so close to, or if she'd prefer if they'd been closer to strangers. She decided that neither was what one might consider to be good, and she really wished it hadn't happened at all. She sighed and settled in with a book, at a loss for what else to do, and tired of her own circling thoughts.

She read until a small knock announced Mrs. Grayson with dinner. Eliza smiled as the door opened, but her face fell immediately, as she saw Jonathan behind the housekeeper. She noticed that there was food for two on the tray that was set upon the small table, and she found that she wasn't confused so much as annoyed. She thought that surely, her request would clearly indicate to all that she wished to dine alone. Jonathan's words belied that assumption.

"Mrs. Grayson informed me that you wished to dine up here this evening," he said, grinning wolfishly, "and I think that's an excellent idea, my dear."

She was uncomfortable, but didn't want to argue with him in front of the innocent housekeeper, who was utterly unaware that there was trouble between the couple. She stayed silent until the kind woman had left the room and closed the door behind her. She turned to Jonathan, coldly informing him, "I had intended to dine alone this evening."

"I know that," he replied bluntly. "But I thought we should have dinner together, since we're both here."

She briefly considered telling him that she was no longer hungry, but she suspected that he would still sit there and eat, in front of her, whether she ate or not. He seemed insistent on sharing her company. She sat and placed a napkin in her lap.

His tone shifted to a softer, more beguiling tenor "Elizabeth…"

"Why do you call me that?" she snapped at him.

He was surprised. "That's your name. Elizabeth."

"Everyone who is close enough to call me by my first name calls me Eliza. Why do you insist on such contrived formality?"

Jonathan reddened. "I also call you 'Lissie'," he said defensively.

"That's part of why the formality is false," she informed him bluntly, narrowing her eyes.

He shifted uncomfortably. This is not what he had anticipated talking about this evening. "You remember that embarrassing story my uncle told you, about how I called you Lissie as a small child, because of a speech deficiency?" She nodded. He sighed deeply. "Sometimes when I'm tired, or nervous, or for no real reason at all, the deficiency becomes apparent, even in my adulthood. It's something I was tortured for at school, so I'm very cautious of it. It's simply easier and safer for me to say Elizabeth, rather than Eliza. There's a subtle difference between the two, but if you've never had a problem like mine, you might not even notice it."

She was vaguely stunned. She hadn't considered that it would be a reason so mundane as that. He had said her name more than once, including just now, and she supposed she heard what he was talking about, but it wouldn't have occurred to her to consider it a problem, or something to be embarrassed about it.

"Would you prefer I call you something else?" he asked earnestly.

"No." She was still taken a little aback, and embarrassed for having made such a big deal over such an inconsequential thing. "I suppose it doesn't matter. It was just a curiosity."

He nodded. He had been thoroughly diverted from what he had originally been planning to say to her. They ate in silence for some time. "Things are running smoothly at the mill," he said eventually. "You would be pleased."

"I am, thank you. And thank you for going. I had intended to do that myself," she answered shortly.

"You're welcome. Mr. Sylvester sent his well wishes."

She nodded in acknowledgement.

"You weren't here when I returned," he mentioned, vaguely questioning.

"I went to visit my godfather," she replied.

Jonathan perked up. "How is he doing? Was Michael about, as well?"

She gave him a cold stare, as it dawned on Jonathan that she had gone there because she was upset with him, and had perhaps wanted to discuss the matter with the people who were as close to family as she had in the world. He reddened.

"They're both doing well." She wasn't giving him a lot to build off of, conversationally, and she knew it. It was her petty vengeance for his having forced his presence on her.

"That's good. I should perhaps pay my own visit while we're here," he said tentatively.

She glared at him. "How long are you planning to stay?" she asked cautiously.

"That depends," he drawled. "How long are you planning to stay?"

She huffed. "I haven't decided yet."

"Then neither have I." He smiled devilishly. "I see your things arrived from the Dudley residence," he remarked.

"Yes," she said. In a suddenly benevolent spirit, she informed him, "Amy is coming to visit tomorrow, and we're planning to go out for a bit."

"Thank you for letting me know," he said sincerely.

Grimness edged into his voice as he added, "I may take the opportunity to pay Uncle Brandon a visit."

She simply nodded. As the end of the meal drew close, she expected him to leave and go downstairs or to his own bedroom. She was surprised when Mrs. Grayson came to retrieve the dishes and tray, and he stayed.

"Do you have plans for the evening?" she asked pointedly, standing and walking toward the window, deliberately putting her back to him.

"How kind of you to ask. I intend to spend the evening with you," he answered with a smile.

"No." Her reply was succinct, and her posture remained unchanged.

He sighed. He had hoped the events of the previous day would have helped matters between them. He thought he had done all he could to show her that he wanted her, not anyone else. He cursed Olivia in his mind for the umpteenth time. It finally occurred to him that Eliza didn't know that he'd put a final nail in that coffin.

Clearing his throat, he began, "Elizabeth, I want you to know that Oli...Mrs. Johnson came to the house on Tuesday, before I came here."

Eliza stiffened, shocked that she had correctly guessed that the woman would visit; she was too stunned to reply.

"She knew that you weren't at the house," Jonathan continued candidly.

Eliza rounded on him, incensed. "That...that *woman* knew that I wasn't home? So she came to see you and continue your illicit liaison from Friday evening? How thoughtful," she sneered bitingly, "for her to have the grace to not fall to your seduction with your wife in residence."

Jonathan was stunned, once again. He almost didn't know how to respond to that. Almost. "My seduction? My what? You think that I invited her over? Or that *I* kissed *her*?" His heart was breaking to pieces in his chest. "How could you think such a thing of me?"

"I saw you! Or are you forgetting that?" she fired back.

"You saw...what exactly did you see?" His curiosity fought the pain in his chest.

"I saw you kissing her! Why must you make me relive it? Are you truly that cruel?" She was on the verge of tears again, and hated herself for it. She didn't want him to see her cry.

"You must have seen just a flash," he told her defensively, "because *she* kissed *me*, which took me by surprise, but I immediately removed myself from her embrace, and told her to stop." He ran his hand through his hair. "Moreover, when she came to the house on Tuesday, alleging that you were the one having an illicit affair..."

"She what?" Eliza roared.

"She suggested that you and Vincent Dudley had a shared affection." He was unaware of the rage brewing within his wife.

"That viper!" She was livid. She focused on Jonathan, suddenly hurt. "And you believed her?"

She couldn't hold the tears back anymore. She was hurt all over again thinking that her husband would believe such absolute garbage about her. Where on earth had Olivia gotten an idea like that? Eliza's head was buzzing angrily, and she staggered to a chair, sitting heavily. She was clearly forgetting that, while she didn't have any such feelings for Vincent, Vincent had made his feelings quite transparent.

He came to her and knelt down in front of her chair. She flinched away from his touch when he reached for her hand. He offered her his handkerchief, which she reluctantly took, blotting her eyes. She was surprised she had any tears left to cry, but they kept coming.

"I didn't believe her," he said gently, "until I saw you with Dudley in that parlor. And then all the doubts came crowding in. The man did declare his feelings for you in front of a fairly large audience, including his parents."

She laughed wryly, conceding, "I knew he had feelings

for me. But they've always been unreciprocated. You didn't have faith in me," she chided him.

He desperately wanted to take her hand, but the chance that she might pull away again was too much for him to bear. "I know that, now. I'm sorry that I ever doubted you, even for a moment."

When she stayed quiet, he realized that there was still more he needed to say. "You must believe me, please, when I tell you that the same holds true for myself and Olivia Johnson. She made her inclination known, and I rejected her. I'm disgusted that she would do that to her husband, angry that she would ask me to do that to you, and yesterday, I told her in no uncertain words that even if neither of us were married, I still wouldn't want her. Please Lissie," he broke down and reached for her hand gingerly, "please tell me you believe what I'm telling you."

She looked down at him, her face tragic, "I... I believe you."

"Thank you," he cried, throwing his arms around her waist, and burying his face in her breast. After a moment, she stroked his hair gently, and leaned her head down to rest on his, sighing deeply.

"I'm still deeply upset," she said quietly.

"I understand," he returned hoarsely. "I think I am, as well."

Chapter 31

They embraced quietly, storms still raging within. After a few long moments, he stood and gently pulled her to her feet. With both hands, he delicately cupped her face, brushing a stray lock of dark hair behind her ear. With unbearable slowness, allowing her the opportunity to pull away if she wanted to, he brought his lips to hers. He kissed her gently, sweetly. He kept the kiss chaste. She responded by bringing her hands to his waist and stepping in to close the small distance between them. She found the kiss to be soothing, which is how Jonathan intended it.

He pulled away with a wan smile. "I have a suggestion," he said.

"What might that be?" she asked hesitantly.

"Something we haven't really done before," he replied. "At least, not when we've both been aware of it."

She grew confused, but willingly allowed herself to be led to the bed. He nudged her to sit, and then knelt to remove her shoes. He didn't follow the same sensuous process of undressing her as he had done the previous day, though. He simply removed her shoes, smiling up at her sweetly. He then walked around to the other side of the bed, removing his jacket and ascot, and sitting to remove his own shoes. He stopped there, though, both of them remaining fully dressed. He lay down and rolled to his side to face her, patting the bed beside him. She lay down, scooting close, resting her head on his outstretched arm. She had snuggled with her mother in a similar fashion, to read bedtime stories. He cradled her gently in his strong arms, and she was vaguely surprised at how comfortable it felt, and how well their bodies fitted together. Inch by inch, she felt her body relax, her muscles released, and she felt at least somewhat at ease for the first time in days. She sighed. He traced the lines of her face with a fingertip, softly exploring. Every now and then, he dropped a small kiss on her face, but for the most part, he just held her quietly.

After some time, he whispered gently, "Do you feel a little better now?"

She nodded shyly, having turned on her side to face him. "A little."

Their pose was so close and intimate, with their legs tangled together, and her hand rested lightly on his chest. He caressed her cheek. "You are the woman I want, Elizabeth. I told you last night, I want all of you, and only you. And I will happily spend the rest of my life showing you the truth of that."

It was the most absolutely romantic thing he, or anyone for that matter, had ever said to her, and it brought a different kind of tears to her eyes. He saw that and felt immediate panic.

"Please don't cry!" he begged her, "I didn't intend to make you sad."

"I'm not sad," she argued damply, "I'm happy. I promise."

He kissed her tearstained face, teasing gently, "You have an odd way of showing it."

She giggled. He smiled at her small laugh and kissed her face more energetically, raining small kisses over her cheeks and nose and lips until she was laughing sincerely. She stopped him by holding his face with one hand and kissing him enthusiastically. Her kiss made his heart sing with happiness. He didn't stop to question those feelings. He was just enjoying the feeling of her lips and hands on him. When they parted, they both wore happy smiles.

He debated the question he wanted to ask for a few long moments before couching it by saying, "you can say no to this, and I'll understand, but may I sleep in here tonight? With you?"

Eliza didn't reply swiftly. His nerves grew into beasts that clawed at him. Finally, quietly, she said, "Yes." The beasts grew wings and lifted off and away. He kissed her again.

Eventually, they both rose to make ready for bed. He left the room as his things were still in her old bedroom. That gave her the time to undress, bathe, and don a clean night-gown. She was brushing her dark hair when he entered, wearing a dressing gown over a white night shirt. Her nerves had begun to build and rise within her, delicate butterfly wings in her stomach, as she was unsure what his intentions were, beyond sleep. Seeing him in proper sleep clothes was new, and different, and she forced herself to stop staring. She couldn't help but notice, though, that his calves were nicely muscular. She blushed delicately as she turned back to the glass.

She brushed her hair longer than was necessary, but she was nervous. Finally, she rose. Turning, she saw that he was propped up in bed with a book, his robe discarded nearby. She approached the other side of the bed and slowly removed her dressing gown, suddenly somewhat shy. She got in bed next to him, not knowing quite what to do with herself.

Luckily, he seemed to understand. He partially closed his book, keeping a finger between the pages. "Are you ready for sleep, my dear?"

She blushed at the endearment and nodded shyly. He kissed her forehead and rolled to his side in order to turn his lamp down, then off, setting the book down in the same move. She did the same, following his lead. She lay stiffly on her back, holding the blanket to her chin. He once again shifted in order to snuggle her close, and found her in that posture. He bit back a laugh and asked, "Are you uncomfortable?"

"No," was her wavering response.

He laughed a low, gentle laugh, snaking his arm over her belly and tugging her close. "Relax," he whispered in her ear.

She wasn't sure what he wanted: if he wanted to go directly to sleep, or if he had other ideas. The truth, which she would only learn if she asked, and she was disinclined to ask such a question directly, was that Jonathan didn't have a plan, per se. He was making each decision as they came. He just knew that he wanted to be close to Eliza. He ran his fingers up the side of her ribs, where they had come to rest when he put his arm across her. It became immediately apparent that this spot, for her, was ticklish. She giggled and squirmed. The squirming brought her closer to him, and also caused her to relax, at least in a fashion. He tickled her again. She squealed and rolled on her side, facing him in the darkness.

"Don't make me respond in kind," she threatened.

"I'd like to see you try," he taunted, his fingers moving down to her hip.

Revenge in mind, she poked his ribs gently. Too gently, he didn't budge, except to find her most sensitive spots. Her fingers danced over his belly, and he yielded, laughing. She laughed in delight, snuggling close to him. He cuddled her close, promising a truce.

He rubbed her back lightly, kissing the top of her head. She made a sound like a happy kitten. His hand moved lower and he massaged her backside. Her sounds turned to a soft moan, and she flexed her hips against him. He sought her lips in the darkness and kissed her. She opened her mouth, inviting him to deepen the kiss.

She came to realize that regardless of what he may have had in mind when he asked if they could sleep together, she wanted this. She wanted him to touch her. More than that, she wanted what she hadn't gotten to do the previous evening. She wanted to touch him. To that end, she tentatively, carefully, began exploring his body with her hands. She touched his broad shoulders, running her hand down his arm where it lay around her. She slid to his chest, feeling the firm muscles and the springy hair under his shirt. That fascinated her, and she wanted to touch skin. She whimpered slightly into his kiss. As if that had been enough to convey what she wanted, he shifted away enough to tug the shirt off, over his head. He came back to her, greedy for her touch. She combed her fingers lightly through the dusting of hair on his chest, following it down his belly. She hesitated more as she drifted lower. She found it a safer proposition to explore around, rather than down, drawing her palm up over his hip and across his wide back. He distracted her lips with his own, kissing her deeply. His hand slowly, but steadily, drew the hem of her nightgown up. She felt it rise up her calf, to her thigh. When it was high enough for him to reach under, he did. He began to mirror the way she was touching him. She learned soon that if she touched his back, he touched her back. She drew her fingers over his shoulder blade, he did the same to her. Teasingly, she traced her fingers down his spine, fanning her fingers over his butt and he did the same to her. She traced the curve and moaned as he did the same.

Pulling away slightly, she moved to push at his shoulder, urging him to lay on his back. He laughed, but acquiesced to her apparent wishes. She came up on one arm, bent over him in the dark. He could barely make out her outline, but he could feel her hands on him, on his belly, his thighs. Her touch was light, hesitant. He leaned close to her and said softly, "it's okay."

He couldn't see that she was biting her lip, but he felt when she pressed those sweet, full lips to his, kissing him as he had kissed her. He felt her fingers bravely touch and explore the length of his shaft. It was standing erect, and he shuddered as she gently stroked him. He tried to stay still. He knew she wanted to discover him, and he didn't want to scare or deter her. But eventually, he couldn't stay still longer. He reached for the hem of her nightgown and pulled it off of her, flipping their positions so that she was on her back and he was over her. She giggled slightly as he did, taking his turn to touch her as she had touched him. A vague memory of an illicit story from a friend sparked inspiration within him, and he didn't limit his exploration to just his hands. His mouth joined the foray, kissing down her body. He drew one nipple into his mouth and suckled gently, tugging with his lips. She gasped. Simultaneously, his hand played at her hip, stroking lightly. He turned his attention to her other breast, showering it with the same hot attentions. He gently kissed her breast one last time, before moving lower, kissing her belly. He shifted lower, gently spreading her legs. Her breath quickened, as she began to suspect his plan. He shifted between her legs, lifting one of them, encouraging her to bend her knee so that her most intimate place was right there, before him. He kissed the inside of her thigh sweetly. Simultaneously, his hand slipped down to the thatch of curls between her legs, and then lower. He touched her gently, using his fingers to spread her slightly, and then she felt his mouth there. She squirmed a bit in shock, but he held her still. He licked and kissed her, running his tongue up and down and then back up, finding the tight bundle of nerves and circling it, kissing it, and sucking it. She twitched under his ministrations, shocks running through her body, making her convulse. He flicked his tongue a few times followed by a more thorough lick, using his finger to massage below his tongue. He slipped that finger inside her and she bucked her hips into him. He smiled to himself and continued. He heard her soft whisper saying, "please," and grinned. He moved up, his hips between her legs.

"Do you want me inside you?" His voice was rough and soft.

"Yes!" she cried, "oh, yes! Please."

He didn't make her wait any longer. He thrust into her. This time he didn't have to worry about any pain he might cause her, and she was wet for him. The suddenness was unexpected, and she cried out in pleasure. He pulled almost all the way out and thrust again, hearing her soft cry again. Knowing that he brought her pleasure thrilled him. He reached out and picked up his pillow. He urged her to lift her hips slightly, and he placed the pillow under her, coming up to his knees. This allowed him to thrust deeper into her, which, they rapidly learned, they both enjoyed. He alternated between moving slowly, and then rapidly thrusting. He reached down between them and touched her as he moved deep inside of her. She cried out, over and over, and he felt her climax around him, tensing rhythmically. He came shortly after, pounding into her with vigor. Afterwards, they lay tangled together, kissing and caressing lightly.

Pressed against him she began to say, "I..."

"You what?" He whispered into her ear.

She had realized the words she was about to say and had stopped herself. She quickly covered with, "I love how you can make me feel." It wasn't a lie.

He nuzzled her neck. "I love that I can make you feel that good. I love how you make me feel, as well."

She smiled, but not as brightly as before. She had almost told him that she loved him. She wasn't at all sure how he would respond to that declaration, and she didn't want to potentially mar what they had just shared. For the moment, she was content knowing that they shared something special with each other. He pulled her close to him under the covers, cradling her in his arms, and they both fell asleep smiling softly, tangled in each other's limbs.

The next morning, she awoke in his arms with memories of the previous night making her blush. As she stirred, she felt his lips press against her ear. "Good morning," he whispered.

"Good morning." She glanced at him over her shoulder. He smiled at her.

"It's still early," he observed.

She glanced toward the curtained window, seeing the dawn light filtering in, and nodded.

His hand, previously resting lightly on her stomach, drifted lower. "Can I persuade my lovely wife to stay in bed just a bit longer?" He grinned impishly at her shocked expression. "What? We're allowed," he assured her before shifting to kiss her.

Any resistance she might have had melted away with his kiss and she gave in, returning the kiss and allowing her own hands to roam. They had fun, lightheartedly teasing and touching until they were both panting and desperate to be connected. He proceeded to make love to her slowly, continuing to tease and prolong, kissing her as he slowly moved within her. It wasn't until she was almost screaming in need that he pounded into her, bringing them both to sweet release. They cuddled close afterwards, whispering sweet words accompanying small touches. They both felt like naughty children, and realized that this was an integral part of being newlyweds. She longed to ask him why they had waited so long to indulge in this special intimacy, but she bit her lip, remaining quiet. She leaned forward and dropped a small kiss on his chest instead. Reluctantly, they parted and rose, bathed, and dressed, trading glances that for her were shy and furtive; for him, bold and appreciative. They came together often to share small kisses and cuddles.

Chapter 32

Once again, Eliza felt like her world had made a dramatic shift practically overnight. She was still upset, and had the nagging sense that not everything had been fully settled. But she finally felt like she and her husband were on the same side, and shared the same goals. They resumed something more like their usual habits with one another, but they were suddenly, subtly more affectionate. Each of them found excuses to touch the other's hand, or shoulder, and occasionally steal a chaste kiss.

Amy arrived promptly at one, and Eliza and Jonathan both greeted her in the parlor. Amy eyed him warily, and he soon excused himself, to let the ladies enjoy each other's company in privacy. He dropped a loving kiss on his wife's forehead before leaving. Eliza's smile at the kiss confounded her friend. As soon as he was out of earshot, Amy bolted to her friend's side, demanding that she be told everything that had happened.

Eliza blushed and laughed. "We have had some time to...talk, in the last few days, and come to a certain understanding."

"Understanding?!" Amy cried. "Lissie, he *kissed* another woman! What did he have to say for himself? And then the way he barged in and made a scene!"

"I really am sorry for that." Eliza ducked her head, avoiding her friend's gaze. "He was upset. He thought I was leaving him for Vincent. Let me start from the beginning, that will be easiest." She paused to take a deep breath. "Olivia apparently kissed him, unexpectedly. He didn't want her to, and he pushed her away and made it clear that he wasn't interested in her."

"Oh, her poor husband!" Amy exclaimed.

The two girls paused to pity Patrick Johnson, who surely didn't deserve such a wife, before Eliza continued, "Anyway, I only saw the briefest moment of it, and didn't see his reaction. And then, after I had left to come here with you, that *woman* went to Jonathan and suggested to him that I had left him for Vincent! I don't know where she could have gotten such an idea…"

"Well," hedged her friend, "Vincent was paying quite a bit of attention to you at the party. She might have just made a guess?"

Eliza flushed. "I… I hadn't realized he was being so obvious. But regardless, Vincent didn't help matters when he declared his feelings for me the other day. Oh, your poor parents! Are they terribly upset with me?"

"Mostly confused, I think. Though Mama gave Vince quite the talking to, for acting like that with a married woman. She was mostly scandalized by her own son, I believe. Which frankly, I'm not upset by. Let them focus their attention on him for a bit. But anyway, we're talking about you. Your husband seemed more…affectionate than usual."

Eliza reddened again. "We have taken some wonderful steps forward in our relationship in the past few days," she said tactfully.

Amy eyed her friend shrewdly, and then squealed, clasping her hands. "Oh, Lissie, that's wonderful! So the two of you really are better now, then?"

"Yes, quite," but she hesitated a bit.

"What's wrong?" Amy asked, confused.

"I just…I don't know! I almost, the other night," she paused, stammering, "I almost told him that I loved him," she confessed wretchedly.

Deeply perplexed, Amy asked, "isn't that a good thing?"

"I don't know. I don't think those are words that he

longs to hear," she confided. "And I don't think he feels that way about me."

"Oh, Lissie. Just give it some time. I'm sure he can't help but to fall in love with you. You're a wonderful person." Amy hugged her with those words, and shortly after decided that the two needed to go on their shopping expedition. Shopping was a wonderful distraction, and her friend clearly needed one of those, if not for the originally expected reasons.

Chapter 33

Brandon St. John was surprised to find his nephew on his doorstep. He was welcoming, though his tone was cautious. "Jonathan! I had hoped to see you sooner rather than later. You must have read my mind. Come in, come in."

"Hello, Uncle. I'm glad you have time for me. Frankly, I assumed after Elizabeth's visit yesterday, it was my turn to see you."

"I see," Brandon said, darkening slightly. "So you've talked to each other, then?"

The younger man smiled hopefully, as they both sat, "Yes, we did. I'm quite happy to say that we talked at length, about many things, and have come to a resolution on some of the most notable issues."

"Oh?"

"Yes. I think we're both still a little sore, but we are surely more content with matters as they stand now."

"Jonathan, I know you have had a less than perfect time in life, up to this point, but you must know that most people would strive for being more than merely 'content' in life, yes?" His words were gentle, yet pointed.

Jonathan avoided his uncle's gaze, wringing his hands slightly. "Yes, of course I do. I'm just hesitant to overstate things. I believe that Lissie is still muddling through some thoughts, just as I am. I daresay we're both as happy as we can be, which really is quite a lot, but that it will take some time for the hurt to subside. We came so close to losing each other."

Brandon beamed at his nephew. "That is one of the most emotionally mature things I think I've ever heard you say. You were upset, then, at the thought of losing her?"

"Of course I was!" Jonathan was indignant, his eyes flashed as he looked back up. "I..." he paused, suddenly stricken.

"What's the matter, my boy?"

"Uncle, I... I care about her, deeply. It hurt so much when I thought she'd left me. And then when I saw Dudley with his hands on her!" His visage grew dark and shadowed, "I wanted nothing so much as to knock the man out and snatch her to me and never let go..."

"How do you think she felt, then, seeing you and Olivia Johnson in an intimate embrace?"

Jonathan flushed with that understanding. "She knows, now, that Olivia Johnson means nothing to me. And Olivia knows it, too."

"Good," interrupted Brandon.

"But that's not the point I'm trying to get at, Uncle. I care about Lissie. I find her to be charming and intelligent and beautiful. She's graceful, talented at so many things, she has a wonderful sense of humor, she's kind. I admire her. I'm happier and more at ease when I'm close to her. She has bewitched me! I think...I think I'm in love with her." His face was a mask of dismayed horror.

"Most men are happy to learn that they are in love with their wives," Brandon observed dryly.

"But what if I lose her? I came so close to that already, and all over stupid misunderstandings!" He was beginning to hyperventilate.

"Okay, calm down. Everything will be just fine."

"How can you know that? It wasn't fine for my parents! What if..." his eyes glazed over with terror.

Brandon stood and poured a stiff shot of bourbon. He handed it to Jonathan, ordering him to drink. He knelt down in front of his only nephew. "Jonathan... your mother loved you so deeply. I so wish she was still with us. But we can't change the past. We can only direct the future. It is your greatest gift in life to do that. You love your wife. You've already lost your heart to her, and it won't serve you or her for you to sink into denial about it. The best thing you can do now is to love her deeply. Show her, every day, what she means to you. You know that things won't be perfect, and that's the test of real love. Loving someone when things are happy is easy. Keeping love strong through strife, and arguments, and loss, that's the real test. I have faith in you, my boy. And your wife, as well. You can do this."

Jonathan paused, taking all of that in. The bourbon was helping things a bit. He looked up with renewed tragedy awash in his voice as he said, "What if she doesn't love me back?"

Brandon heroically hid his smile, answering seriously, "That's a chance we always take with love. But talking to her is a helpful step."

"Talking to her," he repeated.

"Yes," Brandon answered dryly, "it's a bit late for this, really, but you might even try wooing her."

"Wooing her?" Jonathan's ability to think beyond the last few words Brandon said was almost endearing, but not quite.

"Yes, woo her. You know, as a young man would do for a young lady he found himself attracted to. Court her? All of those things that people your age do." Brandon felt moment-arily guilty as he realized he had rushed the two young people right past this stage of getting to know one another, when he had skipped straight to suggesting marriage. But then some-thing else occurred to him. "You realize that her birthday is approaching?"

"Her birthday?" Jonathan was momentarily confused.

"Yes," his uncle explained patiently, "her 20th birthday is August 1st. That should give you a little time to plan some-thing."

"Plan something." He was clearly in a daze, but he snapped out of it enough to worry anew. "What sort of thing would she like? Should I plan a party? Or something smaller. What kind of present should I get her?" He stood and began pacing the room.

"Breathe. Take a breath. Then let it out. Now take another one. That's better. You know her. You've gotten to know her. You've seen what makes her happy, and what makes her upset, or unhappy. You can do this. This is only the first of what I promise will be many, many opportunities."

Jonathan nodded dumbly. Just at that moment, Michael entered the room.

"Jonathan! How wonderful to see you. Your sweet wife was just here yesterday. Brandon," he chided, "you really must let me know when we have guests. Especially such delightful guests."

"You're absolutely correct," Brandon conceded. "I do apologize. We were just discussing Eliza's birthday! Our Jonathan here is having some anxiety over what to do for her." He had decided to be benevolent to his nephew. Michael would happily regale him with ideas.

Chapter 34

Jonathan arrived back at the townhouse to find that Eliza and Amy were still out. Mrs. Grayson met him in the foyer, and he beamed at her. "Just the woman I wanted to see!" he exclaimed.

She blushed and tittered. He continued on, "Eliza's birthday is next month, and I'm hoping you can share with me some of her favorite things to eat. I want to plan a small dinner party to surprise her! Would you be willing to plan the menu? With all her favorites, I'll have a guest list ready by tomorrow. If you'd be willing to come stay a few days in the country, secretly, that would be an extra surprise for her! Mrs. Smith would appreciate your help and company, I'm sure."

The housekeeper was delighted by the enthusiasm the young gentleman had for Eliza, of whom she was quite protective, and she agreed immediately. The young mistress needed a purely happy occasion in her life. She proceeded to the kitchen.

Jonathan took himself to the library to consider the conversation he'd had with his uncle, and then Michael. He felt elated and anxious in equal measure. He had spent his entire life striving to not give any woman the impression that he might be interested in a romantic entanglement. He considered things his various friends had said on the subject. Many of them had written letters to the women who held their interest. They took walks, and visited, always with a chaperone. He wryly admitted that he and Eliza had skipped several steps. But he realized that they visited and took walks regularly, when they were at home. And those things had really gone splendidly well, and resulted in the deepening friendship between them. So perhaps he was already doing the right thing, in order to win her heart? He wondered how he could take advantage of being in the city with her. They had previously talked of going to the theater. That gave him some ideas!

The girls returned to the townhouse, laden with packages and laughing to themselves. Eliza was vaguely stunned when Jonathan offered to escort Amy home, when she was ready to depart. Amy was surprised, but accepted his offer. The three visited briefly, but given the hour, she needed to be on her way soon. Jonathan called a carriage and helped the driver load the parcels into it, before helping her in.

When the two had rowed across the lake, the previous week, they had made easy and light conversation. Amy had wanted to try to understand this man who had married her dear friend. Now, she had more of a mind to give him a good talking to. She was more refined than that, and settled for sitting stiffly next to him, with her arms crossed.

He wanted to talk, though. "Miss Dudley," he began formally, "I must beg your forgiveness, both for barging into your home the other day, as well as for the hurt I caused to your friend, which I know must have brought you hurt as well. I want to assure you, as I've assured Elizabeth, that Olivia Johnson means absolutely nothing to me, and she will not have the opportunity to act so distastefully again. I promise you that I will do my utmost to make my wife happy."

This small, impassioned speech surprised Amy, but it made her glad to hear. She relaxed an iota and turned to Jonathan, saying, "I'm heartened to hear you say that. Eliza is very dear to me, and my family. We want nothing but the best for her." Her tone suggested that she wasn't altogether sure Jonathan was what would be best for her friend.

"And," she added, "I'm sorry for the scene my brother caused. He means well, truly. But he shouldn't have made a declaration like that to a married woman, most especially in front of her husband."

"It's understandable," Jonathan chuckled grimly. "I suppose, we all want what's best for Lissie, and we all think we are the answer to making her happy."

She stared up at him. "Well, I suppose that might be one way of looking at it," she agreed hesitantly.

"So," Jonathan said hopefully, "might we work together, then?"

Amy was shocked, but after a moment, quite pleased. "Have you an idea in mind?"

"In fact, her birthday is next month, and I'd like to plan a small surprise party for her. You're her dearest friend. Would you be inclined to help with a guest list? We'll host it at the estate, and I'm open to any suggestions you may have to make it wonderful for her."

She squealed in delight. She absolutely loved parties! "Yes, yes, a million times, yes! Oh, we shall make it an occasion for her to remember. I'll put together a guest list tonight! Mother will be thrilled to help me."

"Just remember," he said conspiratorially, "keep it a surprise for Elizabeth."

They grinned at each other in complicity. Amy was delighted when she departed the carriage. Jonathan begged just a moment with her parents, to apologize for his boorish behavior again. They graciously accepted, and he was on his way home to his beloved. He was unaccountably nervous.

That evening, over dinner, he waffled between some shyness and giddiness. Eliza asked him what was wrong, but he brushed it off, embarrassed, as an accumulation of nerves over several days of interesting events. She laughed at his description of their ups and downs, and sought to settle him. She was, herself, a little on edge but not nearly to the same degree.

When he brought up the idea of going to the theater and dining out the following evening, she was delighted. She asked if they might go home the following day, and hearing her refer to the estate as home made his heart sing. They finished the evening much as they would at home. He even cajoled her into playing piano for him. The only real difference is that when they retired, he didn't leave her to sleep alone.

He had found that he enjoyed sleeping with her. Hearing her breathing in the dark, feeling her soft, warm body pressing against his, he slept better with her there. She found much the same. She wouldn't know it, but she smiled in her sleep as he pulled her close, wrapping his arms around her and snuggling in. Eliza enjoyed waking up as much as she enjoyed sleeping. Jonathan gently kissed her good morning, and they slowly greeted the day together.

Chapter 35

Meanwhile, upstate, Olivia Johnson and her mother sat in what had become the Johnsons' parlor mid-morning.

"Are you going for another ride today, dear?" Mrs. Forester asked politely.

"I'm planning to," she answered idly.

Her mother smiled warmly, "I'm glad the country air seems to be suiting you, dear. It's good that you're getting out so often. Do you have any plans for the garden?"

"Oh, I think the garden is simply delightful," Olivia enthused, examining her nails. "Simply delightful."

Mrs. Forester was vaguely confused. The Southland Estate gardens hadn't been cared for in quite some time, as the former owner had passed away the previous year, and he had let the grounds go for some time before that. "If you enjoy the wild look, I suppose they do have a rustic kind of charm," she conceded, before smiling brightly. "As long as you're happy, dear, that's what matters."

Olivia's face turned vaguely vicious. "I'm happy, Mother. I have almost everything I could want. Would you like some tea? Or sherry?"

"It's a bit early for sherry, dear, but tea sounds lovely," she tried not to be scandalized.

"Oh, Mother," Olivia sighed deeply. "In Paris, fashionable women have wine with breakfast. It's not shocking at all." She sighed again. "But I'll go request tea."

Mrs. Forester tactfully disregarded the sneer that came with the word "tea". "Thank you, dear."

The older woman contemplated her daughter's temperament since her return from overseas. As a child, Olivia had always been headstrong and bold. While her mother had worked to instill temperance and restraint, those lessons had only been learned so well. She had an obstinate streak that endured. When she was younger, she had had every hallmark of being spoiled, and Mrs. Forester had to admit her own complicity in that. As their oldest daughter, leading her siblings by several years, Mrs. Forester and her husband had given the young girl just about anything she wanted, that was within reason. Their means meant that many, many desires were considered reasonable. Surely, at least some of what she had been given would be considered quite normal for any girl of her class. Music lessons and dance lessons, riding lessons and tutoring in French. But she had also begged for a pony of her own, and a phaeton; she didn't want to learn ballet, only social dancing. She hounded her French teacher to teach her obscene phrases, as well as polite conversational French. Above all, she despised being told no. As it was, that was rarely inclined to happen, so her childhood was relatively peaceful.

She had managed to grow into a young woman who was well socialized, and could converse on all the polite topics of the day. It had to be admitted that she could also converse with the bawdiest of boys and men, in the lowest taverns. She liked adventure, and the hint of danger. The one thing she had been consistently denied was a pet. They had gotten her a kitten when she was 9, after she requested one, but she hadn't cared for the thing at all. One day, Mrs. Forester heard Olivia crying and rushed in to find the poor girl with bleeding hands, and the kitten limp, against a wall. Upon asking what had happened, she learned that the kitten had unaccountably clawed the girl badly, and she had reacted on impulse, throwing it across the room away from her. Somehow, the girl had thrown with enough force that the poor animal broke its back, and died. Olivia had nevertheless insisted on staging a macabre funeral service for the little ball of fluff, as it was laid to rest in the small flower bed in front of the house. She wore a facsimile of mourning clothes for a week, before her mother insisted that she stop. After that, there were no more pets. Luckily, none of her siblings thought to ask for one.

She had turned into a strikingly beautiful young woman, undeniably tall, and her height only served to emphasize the willful streak she maintained. In some ways, it made her a natural leader, mostly because she refused to follow others. She particularly seemed to enjoy ordering her two younger brothers around, as a general would lead a little army. In other ways, her need to have command over others belied a certain childishness of manner that her mother found slightly unfortunate, though she would never express that to anyone but perhaps her husband. And as her husband would undoubtedly point out in retort, that sort of attitude was found to be quite entrancing to certain gentlemen. He had to fend off many suitors once his daughter came of age.

Both of her parents knew that Olivia had been pining for Jonathan Stanton ever since the boy left, after his mother's unfortunate departure from the earth. She had been ecstatic upon the boy's return, well into his manhood. She hadn't taken his relative avoidance of social activities as a personal slight; rather, she saw it as a challenge. The more she sought to pursue Jonathan, the more overt her brazen charm became, incidentally attracting the attention of several other men who were less reticent than the Stanton boy. She had acknowledged several of the more attractive men, inviting their acquaintance. What her parents didn't know is that she saw those boys as fresh meat on whom she could hone her skills of flirtation and coy wit. She had sought to learn a few other things from these men, in quiet, dark corners of parties or gardens, where they could slip the eye of a chaperone. It had been one such indiscretion that had led directly to her marriage to Patrick Johnson.

Of course, absolutely no one but the four of them were aware of the reasons surrounding the engagement and subsequent marriage. To the rest of society and their social class, it was merely a love match, romantic in every sense, and touted to be the wedding of the season. Her parents were also not to be aware of the fact that Olivia was keenly aware of Jonathan Stanton's absence at her wedding. She read into that non-appearance an unspoken regret on the man's part, that his one true love was to marry another. Because naturally, that's what she was. His first love, and therefore his only love.

They had known each other as long as they'd been aware, being within a year of each other's age, and part of the same circle, by extension from their parents. At the tender age of 13, he had caught her nascent romantic eye, and she would forevermore be convinced that they were soulmates. At the age of 13, he was just beginning to discover his own manliness, and she watched from afar, developing feelings that were new and wondrous to her. What began as fascination grew into a caring, and then what Olivia came to identify as fierce and passionate love. The summer before he left, she had been daring enough to follow him into the labyrinth on his parents' property, during a game the children were playing. She had come upon him, blessedly alone, at the fountain and attempted her first formless and rudimentary experiment in flirtation. She had been so giddy and bold, she had even kissed him, before running away, hoping in her burgeoning romantic fantasies that he might chase her and kiss her more. He hadn't, but that didn't faze her indomitable spirit. She convinced herself that he had merely been overwhelmed with her sophisticated coquetry, and too stunned to react.

So naturally, when her wedding was announced, she proudly declared her love for her fiancé, hoping to inspire jealousy in the object of her real desires. For his part, her new husband was painfully aware of the fact that she was putting on a charade for others, even if he didn't know exactly who, due to how she treated him privately. In a bid to win her affections for himself, he had whisked her away overseas, for a grand adventuresome tour. Her mother had thought that such a romantic gesture, unaware of the underlying causes. She was thrilled that her daughter had found a man who was willing to give her the exciting life that she craved.

Clearly, Mrs. Forester had come to know, Olivia had indulged in excess while on their tour. She wanted to experience everything, as her husband put it, indulgently. They had climbed everything worth climbing, toured museums and castles, eaten in quaint pubs and fine restaurants. They had walked on the shores of Brighton, Valencia, and Cannes, collecting sand and shells at each. They had seen opera and theater, listened to symphonies and street musicians. Mrs. Forester had listened in rapt attention to all the details. She thought that it was lovely that the couple had taken the time to have a restorative stay in Bath. When they had come home, Olivia seemed just a little bit older, more mature. She still had a willful streak. But her mother had been pleased when the couple had decided to move permanently upstate. Like the Stantons, Patrick's job offered him the flexibility to do so, as long as he was willing to travel somewhat, which he was, particularly since the idea of living in the genteel country seemed to make his wife so happy.

Mrs. Forester was also delighted to see that Mr. and Mrs. Johnson had seemed to come to an understanding of marriage that worked for them both. She was a bit distraught that Patrick spent so very much time in the city, while Olivia spent so much time at the estate. But for her part, Olivia seemed delighted by the arrangement. She didn't even seem to particularly care that her mother had come to visit, to keep her company. She still spent large amounts of the day either out, riding, or else in her private sitting room alone. She hadn't banned her mother from the room, but she clearly enjoyed some solitude. Satisfied that her daughter wasn't suffering or feeling any sense of abandonment, Mrs. Forester was going to be glad to return to her own home and husband at the end of the week.

She had already decided that she would report to him their daughter's newfound love of the outdoors, and her delight in French cooking. The couple had been lucky enough to find a cook who had immigrated from France directly, who could cook all the things Olivia had come to enjoy. She would likely omit the preference their daughter had acquired for drinking at all hours of the day. She would also definitely fail to mention the abuse she witnessed being heaped upon the servants. Why, just that morning, she had seen Olivia slap her maid across the face, for failing to do Olivia's hair exactly as she had requested. She had gently suggested to her daughter that that was perhaps not the best way in which to treat those who worked for her, but Olivia had turned red in the face and screamed at her mother that she knew what she was doing, and that she shouldn't be questioned. Mrs. Forester had been quite cowed, and even momentarily frightened by the rage that made Olivia's eyes grow wide and glassy. Her entire face had contorted out of its normally pretty shape, making her ugly and disfigured looking. Mrs. Forester had subsequently spent breakfast and the rest of the morning attempting to soothe and placate her daughter, who had blessedly gone back to her regal, composed self moments after screaming.

Overall, Mrs. Forester decided to be happy for her daughter, now that she had seemed to have gotten over her enchantment with Jonathan Stanton. She hadn't even mentioned the man in quite some time. Instead, she spoke about her husband in such loving terms, calling him her love, her darling, and her one and only, and she had mentioned more than once this week how she longed for him to come home to her. Her mother saw that as clear marital success, and that was enough to satisfy her that her daughter would be happy.

Chapter 36

Friday dawned a little overcast, and Eliza was worried about the drive home, but Jonathan was unfazed. The roads they would take were practically still new, and if it rained at all, they'd have cover, and it would be a blessed break from the heat. She took heart from his assurance, and they started on their way home, bidding goodbye to Mrs. Grayson and her niece, who had taken Molly's position at the house, which was now mostly keeping Mrs. Grayson company.

Unlike other trips the couple had taken, this time they sat close to each other in the carriage, holding hands and occasionally stealing a kiss. Without the forced distance Jonathan had previously imposed on them, he was finding himself to be more inclined to little displays of affection than he would have guessed himself to be. He discovered that he wanted to touch Eliza often, to kiss her. She seemed completely welcoming to this treatment, so he was in no way dissuaded from it. He was still a little hesitant, but it was like a floodgate had opened within him, and the cold and remote shell he had crafted around himself over the previous ten years had cracked and washed away. He felt more free than he had since before his sweet mother had died, and he felt that he had his own precious wife to thank for it. As well as the metaphorical kick in the pants he had received from his uncle, he considered wryly. Which reminded him, he needed to make sure Amy included Brandon and Michael in her guest list. Surely she would, though.

The drive had never seemed so fast before, and they were home before they knew it. Mrs. Davis greeted them warmly at the door, proclaiming how they had been missed. "The house is far too quiet, now, without you," she teased. "We'll need to teach Molly to play the piano if there will be more trips in the future."

Jonathan and Eliza both laughed, and then asked how things had fared in their absence. The only thing of note Mrs. Davis had to inform them, "Mrs. Johnson paid a visit the last two days, even though I told her that you were both out of town, and I didn't know when you would return. I'll be surprised if she doesn't come today as well."

Eliza's heart tightened at that news, and Jonathan looked grim. "If she comes again, at all," he instructed, "please tell her that we're indisposed, and unable to see visitors."

Without further explanations being forthcoming, Mrs. Davis nodded in understanding. "Also," he added, "Mrs. Stanton will be moving into my room. Could you and Molly please see that her things are relocated this afternoon?"

Eliza blushed, and Mrs. Davis did her best to hide a small smile as she agreed to do as he asked.

"Thank you," Jonathan smiled once more, his mood instantly lightening. "I think we both want to get washed up after the drive."

With that, he surprised Eliza by taking her hand and guiding her upstairs, somewhat enthusiastically. When she was sure they were out of earshot, Mrs. Davis laughed at the two lovebirds, who had obviously had quite an illuminating experience in the city.

And it was the truth, later, when Olivia Johnson came to call, and Mrs. Davis told her that Mr. Stanton was indisposed, and unable to see visitors today. This news seemed to make Mrs. Johnson unaccountably happy, because it indicated to her that her Jonathan was finally home. As she had inquired about Mr. Stanton's availability specifically, Mrs. Davis omitted any mention of Mrs. Stanton's presence, or the fact that she was equally indisposed. As the woman had quickly turned and departed, the housekeeper didn't think too much of it.

Upstairs, Mr. and Mrs. Stanton had both washed the dust of the road from themselves, and were talking quietly.

"If you'd like to change anything in here, the wall color, or the artwork, you're welcome to." Jonathan wanted to make sure his wife felt like the bedroom was equally hers.

"I like this room," she assured him with a soft, flirtatious smile. "I can think of one or two things that will make me like it more. But they have nothing to do with the furniture."

"Oh?" he raised an eyebrow.

She came to him and placed her hand gently on his chest, where his shirt hung open. "Yes," she whispered, looking up at him through her thick lashes.

He groaned slightly, feeling his manhood twitch, and he covered her hand with his own. "I may have an idea of what you mean. Shall we see if we can make you more...comfortable...in this room?"

"Yes, please," she murmured just before he kissed her. She was only wearing her chemise, while he was in his breeches and open shirt. He surprised her by bending slightly and lifting her up in his arms. He carried her to the bed, and laid her gently down, kissing her deeply. Her black hair spilled over the snowy pillow, the contrast drawing attention to her rosy pink skin. She giggled as he straightened to shed his remaining clothing, before joining her on the bed.

"Is this what my wife had in mind?" he asked, nipping lightly at her shoulder.

"Mm, something like this, yes," she replied, kissing him. The two of them came together in the bed, marking it as theirs, consecrating it to their union. For the first time, she dared to lower her head, placing small kisses on the head of his shaft, before tentatively licking the length. He encouraged her to try putting it in her mouth entirely, and she did, sucking on it gently. She was surprised by how it excited her. It seemed to excite him, too, as soon enough he pulled her up and pushed her back down on the bed, gently, wasting little time before sliding into her and riding her until they were both fulfilled and happy. They lay tangled together, afterwards, panting slightly.

She turned into him, placing her head on his shoulder, and making gentle circles on his chest with her fingers. "This is perfect," she said softly, smiling up at him.

He grinned back at her wolfishly. "Good. You're mine."

"Always." Her smile widened in response.

The rest of their afternoon was lazy in the best of ways. Dinner was wonderful, and they sat making moon eyes at each other across the table. Mrs. Davis was highly entertained by the two, without either of them realizing it. Molly had rapidly realized that there had been a happy resolution to her mistress's worries, and she, too, peeked at the couple from behind the dining room door, delighted with this current turn of events.

The couple was dismayed to hear that their neighbor had attempted to visit, yet again, though neither one was particularly surprised.

Hesitantly, Eliza asked her husband, "I thought you had told her that you weren't interested in her company before you came to the city?"

"I did!" Jonathan was flabbergasted and annoyed. "I promise you, I was neither subtle nor tactful when I told her that I did not want her, and that even were I unmarried, I still wouldn't want her. I don't know what could possibly be in her head."

She sighed heavily. "Perhaps, if she comes tomorrow, we should see her? Both of us. To find out what she wants?"

Jonathan groaned in frustration, but he stood and came around the table. He knelt next to Eliza, taking her hand in both of his. "We can do that, if it would make you feel better. But I want to promise you something. I will never again be in that woman's company alone. If I have to enlist Mrs. Davis to chaperone, I will do that. But moreover," he said as he rose again, "I think it's approaching time I had a conversation with

Mr. Johnson."

"Oh, goodness. Do you intend to tell him what happened? What if he should blame you for his wife's indecency?" Eliza fretted.

"I don't intend to go into the illicit details unless it's necessary, but if she insists on harassing us further, after she has been made aware that she is unwelcome, I know of little else to do but than to bring it to the attention of her husband." His tone turned teasing. "I certainly know that I'd want to know what my wife was getting herself up to, if she was doing something foolish."

Eliza laughed, a small, tight laugh. "Hopefully I never find myself in the strange predicament Mrs. Johnson has put herself into. Oh, I shouldn't judge the poor woman. Who knows what she's thinking, really?"

"I certainly don't know, but I do believe you're right. It's time we found out, and it's also time that we present a united front. You are my better half, and I want the world to know it." He smiled tenderly.

She felt warmed by his sweet words. The man was so damnably easy to love. She had to cautiously marshal her feelings. The continued presence of Olivia was a thorn in her side, after all that had occurred, but her husband's sweet promises and his consideration of Eliza's feelings helped mollify her discontent.

Chapter 37

At the Southland Estate (it was destined to be referred to that for eternity, regardless of the current residents) Olivia was delighted that Jonathan was apparently home. He was so close to her now! She assumed, naturally, that he was indisposed because he had found the truth of what she had said earlier in the week. His wife had left him for another man, and now he had to make a perfunctory show of being upset, lest anyone inclined to gossip might assert that she had cause to leave him, and that he had earned such a callous act. But soon, no doubt, he would be eager to find Olivia's comforting arms. She vowed to be ready for him.

Mrs. Forester had left for the city that morning, thanking her daughter for being such a kind hostess, and kissing her cheek. Olivia had, in return, handed her a potted plant from the garden. She told her mother that it was basil, but Mrs. Forester was fairly certain it was a small poison sumac plant. She was careful not to touch the leaves, and as soon as the coach was far enough away from the house, she had disposed of the plant carefully, along the side of the road. She shook her head over her daughter's naiveté, and chuckled to herself. It was, nevertheless, a very pretty pot, as soon as she had thoroughly washed it back home. She would keep the pot as a sweet souvenir of her time with her eldest daughter.

She thought that next time she visited, she should try harder to cajole her youngest child, Olivia's sister Flora, to join her on the journey. She thought how much Flora, at the sweet age of 16, would love the wildness of the country estate, and it had often saddened her that the two sisters hadn't been closer. Olivia had always seemed mildly jealous of the attention Flora got as an infant, and often appeared to try to compete with the baby. After one disastrous attempt by the older sister to bathe the younger, wherein Flora came far too close to drowning for anyone's comfort, their parents stopped trying to force any amicability, and simply made sure Olivia didn't feel ignored. Now that both girls were mostly grown, Mrs. Forester thought it was high time they spend some more time together. Surely, they were bound to get along better now.

Back at the house, Olivia was relishing the knowledge that her beloved was home, and had already quite forgotten her mother's visit. She found her mother increasingly tiresome, with her admonitions of proper behavior. She just didn't seem to understand that Olivia was a grown woman, and was no longer in need of her silly suggestions on how to comport oneself. For once, she found herself wishing that her brothers or sister were around, to take the brunt of the maternal ministrations. She had hated having siblings growing up. She didn't understand why she hadn't been enough for her parents. They had to go and have more children, which unfairly took attention away from her. She felt that, as the firstborn, she should have the first right of refusal to all things, and be given special treatment. Luckily, as the younger children grew up, the boys came to adore their older sister, and she basked in their affections. They happily shared their treats and desserts with her, in an effort to win her attention and love. They let her boss them around and treat them like her own little footmen, and they happily followed her like puppy dogs. She quite missed that. Thomas and Jeffrey had been better than any servant she'd had since, for the adoration they showered upon her. She vaguely considered that perhaps she should get a footman or two. Houseboys who were young and malleable, whom she could impress with her resplendent airs.

She had found that her own brothers had regrettably grown too much in her absence. They were no longer interested in fawning at her feet. Instead Thomas had become engrossed in his course at university, and was in love with his books, and young Jeffrey had developed a roaming eye and a keen interest in flirtation. Olivia thought she could be proud of that, at least, but it left her feeling rather bereft. She didn't flourish as well when there weren't at least several people willing to devote their attentions to her.

But now, she didn't need anyone's attention. She had her love to focus on, and the fewer people around, the more she could do that. She longed to be closer to him, still. But her unfortunate husband would be arriving home that very same afternoon, and while he wouldn't bother with her much, he would expect her to be available.

She despised him, and he despised her, and it made them a perfectly matched set. He had been a scoundrel when they met. A ladies' man, more than willing to engage her flirtations and respond in kind. She was enjoying having a little fun with an older man, and he had offered to teach her the best ways to please a man. Thus, they had been caught in flagrante delicto, and subsequently forced to marry. Neither was pleased with it, but Patrick had had a rich, full life, thus far, of entertaining himself with various women, and he wasn't extremely perturbed by the thought of settling down, especially with a woman so young and wild. He thought that Olivia would be a wonderful, abiding little wife, with whom he could have any number of adventures, both erotic and otherwise. However, he had been swiftly disappointed when this engaging and daring young woman had turned into an unsightly hellcat. She didn't want to be married to him, and she let him know it. At the time, he decided to view this as a challenge, one he approached with vigor and creativity. And he had thought that things were better, by the time they returned home. He was thrilled when his wife seemed excited about the prospect of moving out of the city. He was surprised that she would like to do such a thing, given how vivacious and outgoing she was, but he was happy to indulge her. She was insistent that he purchase the Southland estate, which he willingly did.

That's when things had gone downhill rapidly. It had been a mere few weeks, but already, he was dedicated to the idea of spending his weeks in town. He had begun to indulge his illicit dalliances again there, with his wife far removed from him, and he was happier and more settled just having a weekend wife, as he had come to think of Olivia. This was the first full week he'd spent in the city, after having been there for just two days the previous week. He came home happy and relaxed, much to his wife's aggravation. From the moment he stepped through the door, she alternated between nagging him and leaving him alone. He preferred the latter treatment to the former. He tried to see a way in which her nagging could be thoughtful, or caring, and he supposed some of it was. But some of it was simply his wife being a harpy. He resolved to spend the following week in the city, as well. When he told her this, she simply shrugged her shoulders, and said that that would be a pleasant circumstance for both of them. He was past the point of being wounded by her indifference, so he settled on contentment. He intermittently tried to be sweet to her, to touch or kiss her. Sometimes she submitted, but other times she flinched away.

He was genuinely saddened by that. Of course, when they first met, but even in Europe, she had occasionally been a wild thing in bed, happily engaging in sordid encounters. He was fairly certain her claws had left permanent scars on his back. He had brought her to screaming climaxes that had disrupted their neighbors, which they both found delightful on every level. But here, at this point in time, she barely tolerated his attentions. He had found that if he got them both blazingly drunk, it could sometimes be like it had been in Europe, and on principle he vowed to make sure they both drank heavily at dinner.

He kept her occupied throughout the weekend. Drunk and occupied. At one point, he even literally tied her to the bedposts, before having his way with her. She pretended to fight it, but he had the evidence of how wet he made her, and her pleas of freedom were a shallow echo of her screams of pleasure. And so, Mr. and Mrs. Johnson had a darkly delightful weekend, which left them both exhausted and spent.

Olivia truly didn't mind it when he was forceful with her. Sometimes she provoked him just to get that kind of response out of him. What she didn't like was when he touched her in soft, mewling ways. Gentleness was not attractive to her. Monday morning, when she was able to wave him off for an entire week, she reflected that she had truly conflicting feelings for him. Love and hate, if love meant only in the erotic sense. She sighed, and sat down to plan her next move. She had given Jonathan the weekend to grieve the loss of his wife, even though the loss was only metaphorical. Surely if she visited him today, he would be willing to see her. She put on her most low-cut day dress that was still appropriate, and had her maid style her hair in a fetching manner. She clasped a necklace around her neck that had sapphire drops from the chain, with a lavaliere style pendant in the shape of a lily, set with a tiny diamond. It was sure to draw attention to her bosom, which was her goal.

Chapter 38

Jonathan and Eliza had been delighted to have their weekend unmarred by neighbors. They took the opportunity to take long walks in the gardens, he helped her pick berries for Mrs. Davis, and they even went for a ride in the woods together. Eliza had become an acceptable horsewoman in the span of a few months. She wasn't prepared to do any racing, but she could mount, walk, and even canter, as well as dismount. She was still willing to accept her husband's help with mounting and dismounting, mostly because it involved his hands on her hips, and being very close to him. They continued to act like giggling children around each other, to the perpetual delight of all the staff. Mr. Davis had caught them canoodling under the cherry tree, and Joshua had tactfully backed out of the barn after striding in to be met by the two of them embracing. His face had stayed red until after they had departed on their ride.

Monday morning found them happily enjoying their usual habits and schedule. They had quit work for the day and enjoyed a light lunch. They were sitting in the parlor contemplating another walk in the gardens when Mrs. Davis informed them that Mrs. Johnson was there to see Mr. Stanton.

Eliza's stomach twisted itself up with those words, and sharply fell when Mrs. Davis specified only her husband. But Jonathan clasped her hand and gave it a reassuring squeeze. "Please show Mrs. Johnson in," he said. "We'll greet her here. And please bring some lemonade."

Mrs. Davis nodded and exited. Returning shortly with Mrs. Johnson. Olivia looked like a snow queen in her white muslin dress, short puffed sleeves with delicate ruffles accented her graceful arms, and the relatively low square cut neck was quite becoming. Eliza felt a bit stuffy in her mauve cotton, with its simple lines and while it wasn't cut very high, she was wearing a pin tucked chemisette that covered her chest with gauzy white with a sweet ruffle at the neck. Olivia looked momentarily shaken when she entered the room, but she quickly gathered her composure. She had clearly not been expecting to see Eliza.

Jonathan stood as she approached them. They had been seated on a small loveseat, and Jonathan gestured to a nearby chair for Olivia. "Mrs. Johnson," was all he said, somewhat tersely.

"Jonathan...Eliza, how good to see you both home," she said cordially. "I hope you had a nice trip to the city."

"We did," replied Jonathan, seating himself again, and reaching to take his wife's hand, making their position as a couple very clear. "We were able to talk some things through, and then had a wonderful time, didn't we, darling?"

Eliza was mildly surprised at the endearment, but she liked it, even if he was using it for Olivia's sake. "Yes, it was lovely. Almost like a little honeymoon," she added shyly. The two smiled at each other, which enraged Olivia.

She worked to keep her emotions in check as she thought quickly about what to do now. "That's wonderful!" She smiled widely as she spoke, "Simply wonderful. Look, I'd really like to be frank with you both. I want to...apologize...for my behavior last week. I must claim exhaustion, and, well, my husband hasn't been paying me the attention I'd like him to. You see, I thought if I could make him jealous... But of course, that was absolutely wrong of me. I'm terribly sorry. Please, may we still be friends?" Her tone was pointedly pathetic, and she worked to put on her most angelic face, clasping her hands together in front of her pleadingly.

Jonathan and Eliza were equally nonplussed. Neither of them trusted Olivia at this point, and neither were inclined to accept her apology, but to refuse would be ungracious. Olivia knew that, and was counting on it. Hesitantly, Jonathan answered her, maintaining a certain level of formality, "We appreciate your apology, Mrs. Johnson. I do think that it would be best in the future, that should you visit, your husband should accompany you. We do enjoy the company of you both, after all. And if I may be so bold to say," he glanced at his wife with a small smile, "it is the sort of activity that can draw a man closer to his wife."

Olivia was greatly miffed by that response, as well as the attention the man was lavishing on Eliza. She was offended, even, that he could look at mousy little Eliza Montgomery in that way, and ignore herself. But she knew that she couldn't convey that sentiment to either of them. Instead, she murmured ingratiatingly, "Of course. I shan't take up any more of your time today. Thank you for allowing me to speak to you...both."

The farewells were more polite than prolonged, and the couple was glad to see Olivia go so easily. They had both expected her to make a spectacle. After she had gone, they both sighed and eyed each other. Eliza had barely uttered a word during the short visit. She was livid that the woman would walk in here so brazenly, after the way she had acted. Clearly, Olivia had not expected her to be in residence, and Eliza took personal offense to all of it.

She broke the silence first. "Thank you for not directly accepting her apology. I would have made a fool of myself if you had, I believe."

He put his arm around his wife comfortingly. "I had no intention of accepting any apology she made. 'Appreciation' will suffice. And let me make perfectly clear, I don't want her in this house at all, ever again. But as they are our direct neighbors, it just doesn't feel right to ask her to never come here again. Particularly since I really believe she would ignore a request like that. What I told her last week seems to have not sunk in at all, and I must deeply apologize to you for that.

I hope you know that I would never seek to hurt you, and I know that her presence must be a slight. My real hope is that if she must visit with her husband in attendance, she will be more likely to stay home. Or find another neighbor to torment." He strove to inject levity to that last sentence, and almost succeeded. It was increasingly exhausting dealing with this woman.

Sighing again, he turned to his wife, "Would it help you to know my entire acquaintance with Olivia? I don't wish to upset you, but it might soothe your nerves. And frankly, it's something I'd like to discuss because I am altogether perplexed by her actions here lately, given the limited prior acquaintance that we have."

Timidly, Eliza agreed, with the caveat that she might stop the discussion at any point. He agreed before continuing. "It's simple really. I suppose we first made each other's acquaintance when we were quite small. Similar to you and me, really. And to be perfectly honest, similar to you and me, I had a vague awareness of who she was, but we weren't what I would term friends. She was just often there, in the background. She's only one year younger than I am, so she was perhaps closer to my periphery, but truly, we barely spoke five words together before I was thirteen. I vaguely remember that we spoke once or twice, inconsequentially. The way that children do. When I was fourteen, that summer she found me alone in the labyrinth garden. She talked for a bit. In hindsight, she might have been trying to flirt with me. And then she kissed me, rather out of the blue, and then she ran away. At the time I honestly thought it might have been on a dare from one of her friends. Or one of my friends," he added wryly, but he had pulled her close to him as he talked. "It was the simplest peck, but it was a kiss, and that was practically the last event of the season. I promise you, I didn't see her again until a few years ago. When I came back, she did seem rather interested in renewing our acquaintance. Her mother was quite...involved in her daughter's interests. But I did my best to tactfully make it clear to both of them that I was not interested in Olivia romantically. In all honesty, I find her to be somewhat abrasive and her boldness is arrogant. Those are not traits I find attractive in a woman." Turning in to his little wife, he cuddled her closer. "I like women who are soft and sweet and confident, who don't feel the need to always be better than other people. Someone who has the ability to inspire others' confidence and make the people around her happier."

"Where do you expect to find such a creature as that?" teased Eliza, giggling.

"Oh, my dear, I've already found her." he kissed her temple. "And I'm keeping her." He hugged her close, causing her to giggle happily.

"Regarding Olivia, I thought her marrying Johnson would be the end of it. I have never sought out her company, nor, to the best of my knowledge, given her reason to suspect my interest might lie with her. So her most recent behavior is both shocking and distressing. Most especially because she has caused pain to my sweetheart." Again, he kissed her temple.

Bravely, Eliza dared to look up and tell him, "I like it when you call me things like that."

"Like what," he teased, "my darling, and my sweetheart?" He kissed the tip of her nose. "Then I must call you those things more often. They make me happy to say, and if they make you happy to hear, that must mean that I need to say them as often as possible. My darling."

With that he kissed her deeply, forgetting Olivia Forester Johnson completely, and wrapping himself in the cocoon of his own wife's arms. Those words had stopped scaring him a while ago, but now they brought honest joy to his heart. His wife.

Chapter 39

Olivia was absolutely furious. She had spent the entire weekend imagining being able to comfort Jonathan, holding him to her soft, womanly bosom, and running her fingers through his silky hair. She had to reconcile within herself the knowledge that he had spent that same amount of time apparently cuddling with his wife. The thought of those words brought a sneer to her lips, and enraged her so much that she threw a china vase across the room, where it shattered on the empty hearth. One of the maids came rushing at the sound of the crash, and Olivia screamed at her to clean the mess up.

And now, probably at the whimpering behest of the drab, dull Eliza, she, Olivia, had been asked to not visit without her husband present. As though she needed a chaperone. She thought darkly that her husband was the one who needed a chaperone. He was probably in the company of a different lady each night he was in the city. Of the two of them, he was the unfaithful one. Not for lack of her trying, of course. This was all his fault, she consoled herself with that knowledge.

Once they had been in Europe for just the shortest amount of time, she had all but forgotten Jonathan Stanton. He had paled in comparison to the exciting experiences Patrick exposed her to. The places they went had been beautiful. The people, the food, the art, the music, had all titillated her. All of that plus what he exposed her to in the bedroom was enough to enrapture her, and steal all of her attention. She could so easily have been his. She would have been the riotously fun and engaging partner he thought she would be, enjoying a full life of adventure and debauchery.

But there had been one night, at a sinfully decadent party in Paris, where Patrick had gotten gloriously drunk. Olivia had been chatting with a friend, and had yet to catch up to his particular state of drunkenness. They had both been flirting outrageously with another couple, when Patrick started talking about previous conquests. By itself, that had never been a cause for concern, for his wife. In fact, she sometimes insisted he give her the unreserved details of other sexual exploits while they were in the act themselves. It worked for her. It worked for both of them. Which probably helped to explain why he was indulging in that manner of tale at that time, and in that company. But he had let slip a name, attached to an outrageous claim. At first, Olivia thought she must have been mistaken, and she ignored it. But it had nagged at her, such that later, she asked him to clarify. And so, she learned that she had heard correctly. She was aghast. Dismayed. Patrick was befuddled. The incident had happened years ago. Of course, the claim he had made hadn't been purely true. He had fudged some details for the sake of bravado. Olivia had been nothing more than a child at the time. He tried to explain all of that to her, rationally, but it didn't matter. Every word out of his mouth seemed to drive her further and further over a precipice, until she was gone from the world everyone else inhabited. She became wild and animalistic. She had thrown things, destroyed their hotel suite. She had called him foul names, and refused to touch him or sleep in the same bed. He had found her one night standing over him holding a knife. It was a steak knife, but it still could have killed him. He began sleeping in a separate, locked room. He called a doctor, who gave her laudanum to calm her and dull the raging pain she claimed to feel. She stayed mostly drugged for a week. When she sobered up, she was once again in a white-hot temper. This time, he found her sitting next to the wash basin holding a knife to her own wrists. He wrestled the knife away, an altercation that left him, not her, bleeding. He again called a doctor. The doctor, once again, prescribed strong sedatives, and also treated Patrick's wounds. The doctor also recommended the couple retreat to a quieter place where the lady might recuperate, and find peace. He suggested two options, based on the fact that the couple was American. One was a sanitarium in northern London. The other was a genteel hotel in Bath. Patrick strongly considered both options. He still didn't know why this particular woman had this extreme effect on his wife, and he hoped that they could get past this, once she calmed down. He opted for Bath. He found them separate rooms that were rather distant from one another. He left her, still highly medicated in one of them. He made sure to remove all sharp items from the room before leaving her. He also left a letter, explaining that he wanted to give her as much time as she needed to soothe herself, and when she was ready, he would be happy to meet with her. They could talk, or not, it was entirely up to her. He gave her his room number, and assured her that all her needs would be taken care of, and she was free to do as she pleased, but to please, please, not attempt to harm herself.

The poor fool. He was still convinced that they could have a happy life of hedonism together. But in a manner of speaking, the plan worked. It took weeks. At first, she refused to leave the room. She didn't want to see him. But then she began to calm herself. She began to think. Like a weathervane, her thoughts turned once again, toward Jonathan Stanton. At that point, more than ever, Jonathan was on her mind. And there he stayed, but she forced herself to put on a good show for Patrick. She wouldn't let him know her thoughts. She wouldn't make him aware of her schemes. But she wanted revenge on Patrick for Jonathan's sake. She wanted to be there for Jonathan. This became her sole focus in life.

In order to return to New York, she had to convince Patrick that she was better. She had to convince him that she was happy and unbothered, and that she was at the very least content in their marriage. And she had done a stellar job of it. He was so intent on making her happy, he was putty in her hands.

It had ended up being easier than she had expected it to be, to convince him to buy the property upstate. The fool had actually thought that she would be more at ease living outside of the city. He obviously still hadn't realized that it was simply a means to an end. It brought her ever closer to Jonathan. Her Jonathan. She needed to be there for him. He just didn't know it yet.

She sat down in her sitting room to devise a new plan. The sitting room was mostly unremarkable. It had burgundy wallpaper above walnut wainscot, a brass chandelier hung in the center of the room, in an ornate plaster ceiling. The draperies and carpet both featured forest green and burgundy. The furniture was, like the rest of the room, on the darker, more bold side of design, but generally speaking, it was unremarkable, with one exception. On the wall opposite the small fireplace, in a place of prominence, was a curio cabinet that was quite precious to Olivia. On the surface, the contents looked like randomly assorted bits and bobs. The kinds of things a crow might pick up over its travels. A dried flower, a pinecone, a few acorns, a few rocks, but also a small lock of hair, a handkerchief, and a crudely drawn portrait of a boy. These things were all reminders of Jonathan, and time the two of them had spent together. Little childhood treasures of those parties all those summers ago that she had lovingly saved were on display for her to enjoy. She did enjoy them, greatly. She often came in here just to sit in front of this case, and think back on those fond memories. It was almost as though every time she did, the memories became more refined, more solid in her mind. It seemed almost like magic, and she found herself spending more and more time with them, meditating on the joyous summer days and young love, bringing her ever closer to her beloved.

Love then had been innocent and pure. Untainted by the world and grown up cares or problems. It had been so much simpler then. It had all gone and changed, in the blink of an eye. She found herself increasingly furious, and forced

JENNIFER LEE

herself to regain composure. She breathed deeply and focused once again on those objects, those memories. A plan would come to her, it always did. She was smart. She had confidence in her own enduring abilities. She was destined to be with Jonathan, and fate would undoubtedly aid her.

Chapter 40

Jonathan and Eliza found themselves ever deeper in the rosy glow of their newfound closeness. Even as they grew closer together, they separately found themselves biting back nerves and words. If only Brandon St. John could see them, he'd laugh the whole day long. He wasn't the only person who knew the two young people were in love. Anyone who saw them together for just a few minutes could deduce the facts plainly. But they were both terrified to share their feelings with the other, lest they not be returned. Oh, yes, Brandon could have happily died laughing over the poor dears.

One afternoon, a few days before Eliza's birthday, Jonathan woke his beloved with a gentle nudge. "Good morning, dearest. I have a proposal for you."

Eliza turned to him sleepily, grinning. "I already accepted your proposal, or had you forgotten? I don't think we would find ourselves here if I hadn't."

"You little minx!" He laughed before tickling her in retribution. She laughed, but fought back, and the two enjoyed a few moments of gentle play before returning to seriousness-- or a vague facsimile of seriousness, at least, one that was still quite silly.

"As I was saying," he panted slightly, "I have a suggestion for something we might do today."

"Oh," said Eliza archly, as though that hadn't been clear from the beginning. "And what might that entail, dear sir?"

He cuddled her close and whispered in her ear, "How would my sweet wife like to learn how to climb a tree?"

"Finally!" Eliza squealed. "I was convinced you had forgotten that promise."

"You wound me, darling." He clutched a hand to his heart dramatically. "I could never disappoint you in that way. A Stanton man keeps his word."

"Well, good," she grinned back, "because I think today is the perfect day to learn how to climb a tree. I won't bother with the jacket this time, though. It's too awfully hot for it."

He laughed at her again, "You can leave the vest off, as well, if you like. I mean, I wouldn't argue if you wanted to leave the shirt off, as well, but you might scandalize Molly."

She giggled. "We can't have that." He shook his head in solemn agreement.

The two of them were in no real rush as they made ready for the day. Jonathan greatly enjoyed watching his wife dress, more than usual given the trousers, and she teased him about it greatly. They ate a quick breakfast and then left the house, arm in arm, all smiles. Eliza had, in fact, omitted both the jacket and the vest, and had rolled up the white cotton sleeves of the shirt, and styled it in a way she found a bit more flattering to her womanly form. Molly had helped her braid her hair and bind it up, out of the way.

Molly was quite delighted to watch the sometimes childlike antics of Mr. and Mrs. Stanton, and found inspiration for her own future romantic prospects in their obvious devotion to one another. During her time at the estate, Molly had grown greatly. She had always been quick, and in her private time, she worked to imitate the polite manners and diction of Eliza. The fact that Eliza had encouraged her to take riding lessons with her had been a wonderful boon, as Molly loved horses. It was highly unconventional for a maid to take part in such activities, but in true testament to the small friendship that had bloomed between the girls over the last few years, they had begun to take rides together, without Joshua always there to guide them, and in truth it was safer for one to ride accompanied, rather than alone. In fact, Eliza's husband insisted upon it, out of concern for her. She watched now, from an upper window, as the pair wandered deeper into the gardens.

Molly was in on the little surprise party that Jonathan was planning, and this outing had been somewhat of a ruse to distract Eliza so that Molly, Mary, Mrs. Smith and Mrs. Davis could confer privately over the planning, with no chance that they might be interrupted. The event was so close, now. The invitations had been sent out, with the help of Miss Dudley, and they were expecting a small crowd of Eliza's closest friends. Mrs. Grayson had been in touch with the menu suggestions, and Mr. Davis would discreetly go into town to fetch her in a few days. Then the women would start in earnest on the preparations for the meal. In the meantime, the three female servants at the estate had relatively few details to really discuss, but they wanted some time to openly titter about the sweet gesture their Mr. Stanton was making for his lovely bride. They all wanted to make sure that the event was perfect for the pair. At the moment, the biggest question on their minds was how to hide Mrs. Grayson's presence from Eliza's discovery.

They had prepared one of the disused servant's rooms, and strove to make it a cheery place for their guest. Fresh linens had been washed, and were drying as the ladies spoke, and Molly, as the expert on the housekeeper from the city, was an important influence on the small steps taken for the woman's comfort. She was delighted at the prospect of seeing her friend again, and excited for her to see the lush kitchen garden that was under Mrs. Davis' purview. She assured the Stanton housekeeper that the other woman would be as awed over the beauty and abundance as she had been. Mrs. Davis had made a note to send some of the preserves and dried herbs from the garden back to town as a gesture of thanks for the help.

While the ladies huddled in the kitchen talking and giggling, Jonathan and Eliza had entered the garden maze, and turned toward the entrance to the woods. Jonathan assured her that the trees here would be nicely developed, and good for climbing, without having to walk all the way down past the stables. She was happy to do whatever he suggested, and they soon found themselves in the woods that bordered the other side of the property. Jonathan showed her the nice, wide track that connected the stables most directly to the carriage house, and the drive. She was stunned by the presence of the feature, even though it made sense. It was delightful to find that there were still aspects of the property that were new to her.

They found a tree that had a low fork in it, and strong, well-spaced branches. Jonathan demonstrated first, placing his foot in the fork, and then using his arms and legs both to climb a few feet off the ground, up into the branches. It was the easiest approach to climbing, that didn't require any shimmying up trunks, or brute strength. He showed her where to put her feet, and how to hold the branches in order to pull herself up.

Eliza stepped up as he had demonstrated. Jonathan stood on the ground next to her, with his hand on her back to steady her. "Have you got it?" he asked.

"Yes," she replied as she climbed up two more branches. Her feet were even with his chest, and she reached further up into the tree to find a new handhold.

"Don't go too high," he warned.

"Afraid I'll fall?" she asked in a teasing voice.

"Yes." His answer was blunt.

She twisted so that she could look down at him while clinging to the branch in front of her. "Jonathan...is that the only thing you're afraid of?"

He stepped back, surprised. "What do you mean?"

She twisted further, so she could look at him. "I mean," she paused and took a deep breath. "We've been through so much already, when we've only been married for such a short time. Do you ever worry that something else is going to happen to come between us?"

Concern shadowed his eyes as he replied, "Are you worried that that could happen? Nothing will ever come between us again, I promise you." He stepped back to her and placed his hand on her calf.

She shifted once more in an attempt to see him better, and as she did so, her foot slipped. She lost her grip on the branch above her and she began to fall. Jonathan reached up and wrapped both arms around his wife's waist as she fell. He managed to control the fall as they both landed on the ground. He lay on his back with her clasped to his chest, both of them panting.

"Are you hurt?" he asked.

"I don't think so, are you?" She was in better shape, given that she had landed on top of him.

"No." They both shifted so that they could sit up. He tested his muscles and movements. "I'm fine."

"Good," she said, smiling at him. Her face was flushed with exhilaration and mild embarrassment. "I'm sorry I fell. I lost my footing."

He moved a strand of hair away from her face, caressing her cheek in the movement. He sighed as he spoke, "I'm sorry it took so much time for us to sort things out. Maybe, if we had..." he paused, thinking about how much time he had spent keeping her at arm's length. "I made mistakes. But I hope that you trust me when I tell you that I will always be here for you. I will always catch you when you fall."

He availed himself of the privacy they had in the woods and embraced her, kissing her deeply. They took full advantage of the seclusion, not returning to the house until well into the afternoon, flushed and happy with their exertions.

Chapter 41

Olivia spent increasing amounts of time in her sitting room. The generally dark colors and dim light gave her comfort, as did her collected treasures. On the rare occasions she left her room, she fully left the house as often as not. She hadn't lied to her mother. She did greatly enjoy riding, and she rode every day. She would saddle her horse and take off into the woods that bordered her property, and explore the paths. That she might have been looking for something perhaps didn't fully occur to her, and so of course, she wouldn't have mentioned it to her mother.

It was just the beginning of August, and rather hot out. She began taking her rides early in the morning or in the later afternoon, to avoid the noonday sun and heat. The trails on the Southland property were rather overgrown, and not as fit for a horse as they had once been. However, woman and horse persevered, picking their way through the underbrush and low hanging branches. Some of the paths they took may have not even been paths originally. In some areas, it was difficult to tell what was path and what was forest floor. She found that low hanging branches were wont to pull at her, and she had learned that wearing a man's skullcap, with her hair tucked up in it, helped.

One day, while she was riding and sulking about not being able to visit the Stanton residence directly, she was stunned to come across the small cabin on the lake. She had never been this close to it as a child, but she nevertheless quickly realized that this was the cabin on the Stanton property. She was overjoyed, and her heart leapt in her chest. As though this had been a goal she didn't know she had, but having achieved it, she was overcome with feelings of success. This was clearly fate, working to bring her ever closer to her Jonathan.

She dedicated the rest of that day exploring the cabin and its surroundings. She stared longingly toward the barn. She investigated the meager contents of the cabin, and spent some time laying on the small bed, thrilling that she was in a bed that had been occupied by Jonathan, because naturally he would have stayed in the cabin at least once. She cuddled the pillow and blankets, and indulged in thinking that at any moment, Jonathan could come upon her, thinking how surprised he might be. He might pretend to be cross with her, but then he would see that fate was drawing the two of them together, and he would embrace her. She dozed off late in the afternoon, smiling thinking about that possibility. She had vivid dreams of her childhood. Visions of Jonathan, his parents, and her parents floated in her mind. Unexpectedly, the horrible image of Patrick came into the picture. He was lurid and drunk, flirting heavily with every woman in the dream, including the less defined women, who floated hazy and dim in the background. When he came to Olivia, he tried to kiss her, his mouth open and his tongue long and disgusting. He forced it between her lips, defiling her mouth and ravaging her body with his hands. Her sleeping body twisted, and she moaned in distress.

She woke suddenly, gasping for air. Her stomach clenched and she thought she may vomit. She draped herself half off the bed, bracing her hands on the floor in a dramatic posture. From that unique angle, she happened to spy the corner of a book that had been tucked under the bed. Curious, and thankful for a distraction from the awful nightmare, she pulled the book out. It appeared to be a handwritten journal. Opening it, she deduced that it must belong to Jonathan's father, Edmund Stanton. Seeing that the sun was sitting low on the horizon, Olivia made an impulsive decision to take the journal with her. She re-mounted her horse, and turned toward home.

She stayed up all that night, and spent part of the next several days reading the innermost thoughts of Edmund Stanton. The first few pages of the book had been lighthearted love letters to his wife, Margaret, for the most part. Olivia felt pangs of sadness as she read the sweet words, knowing what was to come for the lovesick couple. And then, like a punch to the stomach, it happened.

> I am so stricken with grief; I know not if I can even go on. That woman whom I loved so deeply, for whom I would have given my very life, has betrayed me. Even now, as she lay ill, I cannot bring myself to set my eyes upon her. The very thought of her sickens me. God help me for my thoughts, but should she leave this world, I do not know that I would shed a tear for her loss. She tells me that she can't live without me, but surely that isn't true for how else could she have participated in that most sacred act with this cretinous cur. How could my darling, beloved Maggie betray me in such a heinous way. That villainous scum *P.J.* shall regret his actions to his dying day. May I never see the wretch again in this lifetime...

It went on in this fashion, until...

> It is done. My dearest Margaret should be dancing among the angels now, but for her torments upon me in life, I do expect that she is suffering the torments of demons in hell. And my heart is no lighter for that knowledge. The boy must also be gone from me now. I cannot bear to set eyes upon him for he does naught but bring to mind his mother. It nauseates me to see him. I shall pray to God that he never finds a woman as unwholesome and immoral as his mother. But that he should devote his life to solemnity and soberness, shielding his heart from this wretched, traitorous thing we call 'love'...

The pages were filled with grief, anger, and vindictive vitriol. It fueled Olivia's own twisted soul. While Edmund never mentioned the man who had desecrated his wife by name, the initials P.J. were thinly veiled enough for Olivia to see through. The more she read, the more vindicated she became in her perception that her own perfidious spouse was a villain of the highest order. Edmund's savage anger galvanized Olivia's feelings, turning her hatred into an acrimonious acid that ate away at her sanity and composure. She had pieced together the events easily enough. Patrick had seduced Margaret, and had copulated with her, even as she lay ill with a summer fever. His claim that he had mated with a woman "on her deathbed" had been overstated, as he had said. But when Margaret tearfully confessed her crimes to her own husband, incapable of hiding her unfaithfulness to the man whom she did love so greatly, Edmund had forsaken her. He refused to see her, and in her despair over his rejection, her illness had turned for the worst, and she was gone. Died of a broken heart as much as from the fever. In his continued distress over his wife's infidelity, he had sent his son away, alone. Ripping him from his home, as well as from Olivia's love.

Olivia had not known all the details of what had happened between Edmund and Margaret, but she had known enough about their marriage to admire them. She looked up to them, as many did, as inspiration for what a husband and wife could be to each other. They were so amazingly in love, and they shone brightly in the dim shadows of reality. Of course, their holy union had brought forth her own dear Jonathan. The fact that Patrick could have come between them, seduced the sweet and charming Margaret away, had been an act of such perverted profanity that stunned Olivia, even now. He had defiled the greatest relationship in all of history, and Margaret's death had torn her Jonathan away from her. Now she knew more of the sordid story, she understood exactly how directly Patrick's contemptible behavior had affected Jonathan's life, and hers by extension. Eventually, she found where Jonathan had returned.

> The boy is back. I invited this torment upon myself, but the boy needs to learn the business. I still can't look at him without feeling disgust. At least he seems to have no real interest in the fairer sex. I shall endeavor to encourage within his heart a rightful distrust and a rejection of the considerable lie that is love. Love leads only to betrayal. At the very least, might I save the boy the kind of pain I have felt in life....

There were only a few sporadic entries after that one. The final entry shed no additional light on anything important, and she knew that the man had died when his horse threw him in the forest, smashing his head upon a rock, or so her parents whispered. Oh, her poor Jonathan! He had spent the last ten years of his life not knowing the love of parents. Her mind turned back, dark and twisted, on her own husband. She rapidly determined that he could not be suffered to live this life any further. For the pain and heartbreak he had caused, he must die. She was determined, but also fairly certain that that putrid man was in the city still. Upon learning that she had until tomorrow to see his return, she became anxious and impatient. It made her skin crawl to contemplate spending any further time in the house. Her husband's house. She no longer wanted to sleep in the bed that she had shared with him. The following day was Friday, and he would be home again. She only had to wait one night, and the solution was immediately clear. She would ride out this afternoon and spend the night in the cabin. The following day, she could easily return and dispatch with her husband, and then she would be able to go to Jonathan and tell him how she had triumphed. How she had removed the villainous thorn who had disrupted their lives so many years ago. Surely then, with that success, she would finally convince him that they were meant to be together. She was willing to kill for his sake, wasn't that one of the greatest themes of classic tales of love, after all?

She gathered up some simple food, and called for her horse to be saddled. She instructed the staff to not expect her return that evening, for she would be away visiting. The final thing she brought with her, after consideration, was a sharp knife from the kitchen. When she returned the following day, she wanted to be immediately prepared. She could do this, she assured herself. It would be little more than killing a mean cat.

Chapter 42

Friday dawned bright and beautiful. Jonathan was mightily pleased that the day of Eliza's birthday complied with his plans for perfection. As she came awake in his arms, he smiled at her and kissed her cheek. "Good morning, beautiful one. And happy birthday," he whispered into her ear.

She grinned in delight. "How did you know?!"

"A little bird mentioned something to me," he teased.

"A little bird? Might that be a 6' tall bird who has impeccable taste, and a penchant for fresh strawberries, and freshly clotted cream, of the acquaintance of a dashing man named Michael?" She teased him right back.

"Possibly a bird very much like that," he said, kissing the tip of her nose. "I think you should get dressed."

"Well that is quite unlike you to say these past few weeks." She pressed herself against him suggestively. "Are you sure that's what you really want?"

He kissed her sweetly, but then got up himself, walking to his closet. "Trust me!" He grinned at her. "You'll want to get up this morning. I have many, many devious plans for you today, and believe me, we'll get to that particular one later."

Curious and delighted, she bounced out of bed and got dressed. They descended the stairs and she was stunned that the house had been seemingly transformed overnight. Flowers and silk pennants decorated the foyer, the dining room, and the parlor. Fresh candles had been set out everywhere, and most stunningly, at the foot of the stairs stood Mrs. Davis, Mary, Molly, Mr. Davis, and Mrs. Grayson with her niece. She was beyond shocked to see the dear housekeeper who had known her since childhood standing there, and happy tears sprang to her eyes. She rushed to embrace the woman, and express her surprise. Jonathan couldn't be more pleased at his wife's reaction.

"These are the happy elves who have managed this transformation, my darling. Do you like it?"

Turning back to him, she embraced him with all her might. "Oh, it's beautiful! Absolutely beautiful!" Turning back to the staff, she said, "You are all so wonderful. Thank you so much for making this such a special day. I couldn't be more surprised!"

Jonathan hid a secret smile, for there were surprises yet to come. "Mrs. Grayson has shared with us all the secrets of your preferences, dear, and I have asked her to make plenty. I thought that it would be a wonderful start to the day if we could all share in a celebratory meal together." He held up his hand to wave off the shock of the staff. "I know, I know, it's not something my father would have ever suggested, but you all mean so much to my darling wife, and I would like for you to be able to share in her joyous day, assuming she would like that."

Eliza once again became misty eyed. Jonathan didn't know how many meals she had shared with Mrs. Grayson, Molly, and Mr. Abraham after her mother's death, and then after her father's passing. They had become so much her family, this was possibly the greatest gift Jonathan could have given her, and he didn't even know. "It would make me the happiest girl in the world," she choked out.

The assembled company sat down congenially at the dining table, where the food had been laid out. They all talked and laughed delightedly. Eliza tried to insist that everyone take the day off, and enjoy some relaxation, but puzzlingly, the staff insisted on resuming their work. Mrs. Grayson particularly enthused to Eliza about the gardens, and said that she was greatly enjoying talking to Mrs. Davis. Jonathan smiled, telling his wife that he planned to keep her busy today, as well, with a winking smile.

He suggested she find her bonnet, and then led her into the garden. After they had left the house, he told her that he wanted to show her two things. They walked arm in arm, while she enthused about the wonderful surprises of the morning. His lips had curved into permanent happiness.

They walked unhurriedly toward the gazebo, and she found that that was their first destination. Taking her hand in both of his, as they stepped into the gazebo, he said, "I wanted to revisit the scene of our first kiss. The first step that we took on our journey to where we find ourselves now." Taking a deep, shuddering breath, he continued, "I thought it might be a fitting place for the next step we take." He paused, looking fiercely nervous, and reached out so that he could hold both of her hands. Eliza was entirely perplexed, and growing increasingly nervous herself.

"Elizabeth, my darling, we have learned so much about each other in the last few weeks and months. You are kind, intelligent, beautiful, thoughtful, and sweet. You are more than I ever knew to want in a woman, and I can only hope that I might one day be worthy of your love." He paused apprehensively. "Because I must confess that I love you, deeply."

He held his breath, afraid of what her response might be. He hadn't planned to make a declaration on this day, lest it upset her. But she had shone so brightly this morning at breakfast, she had been like a beacon calling to him, he could no longer deny his feelings for her. He could no longer let his fear guide his decisions.

A tear escaped out of the corner of Eliza's eye, and traced down her cheek, she pulled her hands out of Jonathan's grasp and flung herself at him, embracing him tightly. "Oh, my dearest, dearest Jonathan. I love you."

He clasped his arms around her, and the two babbled between laughing and happy tears, each heaping praise on the other, and each confessing that their feelings had been long held. They kissed and embraced for long minutes, pledging their hearts to each other in ways that made their wedding vows pale in comparison.

After long moments, Jonathan laughed, saying, "Perhaps I should have ended our walk here. I think my other surprise may fail to match the elation of this moment."

"If it's something we do together, then it shall be perfect." Eliza laid her head on his chest, sighing happily.

Stealing one more kiss, he took her hand and led her towards her second surprise. He turned toward the vegetable garden, from the maze. She couldn't begin to guess what he wanted to share with her.

They were in the woods, and he was leading her off the path. She guessed that they were moving in the general direction of the lake, but well south of it, still. Her suspicion was confirmed when she saw a glimpse of the water off to their right. It took almost no time, until they came upon a small stream. "This is the brook that we crossed to get into the gardens," he explained. "It feeds into the lake. I had a suspicion you hadn't found this place, yet."

She shook her head mutely, as they followed the stream a little bit, angling back toward the house. "There's another bridge that crosses it, for the path that leads to the kitchen gardens. There's a small drop off at that part of the property."

All of a sudden, they came across that drop off, which revealed a small waterfall. "Oh!" Eliza exclaimed. She was enchanted by the simple beauty of it. He peered at her smiling face and was delighted at her happiness. They stayed for a time, enjoying the gentle rushing of the water. Jonathan snuck a discreet look at his pocket watch. He had timed it perfectly! He had fully intended to enjoy the day with his wife, but he was also tasked with keeping her out of the house until 4 p.m. It was quarter past three now, which left them the perfect amount of time to wander leisurely back to the house.

Chapter 43

Olivia had spent a fitful night in the cabin. She thought that she would sleep well, with the lake air coming in through the windows, and far away from anything that may remind her of her vile husband. But the cabin now assailed her with thoughts of Edmund and his grief which had been clouded by sour acrimony. She could taste it in her mouth. It enveloped her in the suffocating darkness of the night, and kept her from finding restful sleep. She had lifelike nightmares wherein sometimes she was herself, and sometimes she was Margaret. Always, she was pursued and harassed by Patrick. Always she gave in to him, reluctant, but compelled. And always, eventually, Jonathan was torn away from her loving arms. She awoke with Patrick's ghoulishly laughing grin in her mind's eye.

She lit a lamp to dispel the shadows cast by the pre-dawn light inside the cabin, hugging her arms to her body protectively. She huddled in the bed, afraid to go back to sleep, afraid of what terrors more sleep might bring. She shivered, but she wasn't cold. Nervous excitement coursed through her body. She fingered the knife, feeling a vague sense of arousal. She thought that she might actually enjoy killing her husband. She would be setting herself free, and vindicating Edmund. And Margaret, she supposed. She had to assume that Patrick had seduced the poor woman. She had been unwell, and perhaps she was out of her mind when he approached her. Olivia sought to justify the past and forgive that other woman, thinking that it was even possible that Patrick had pretended to be Edmund, like Zeus had pretended to be Alcmene's husband in order to seduce her. That must be it, Olivia decided.

Margaret had been a victim. Another one of the victims Patrick left in his wake of destruction.

It would all end this day, Olivia vowed. She would make this meager sacrificial offering in the names of Margaret and Edmund Stanton. She made it with the hope that she might finally prove that she was the one who loved Jonathan the most. That she deserved him. That she was destined to be with him. Not that little bitch Eliza. If Olivia had to kill her, as well, to prove her love, she would. She made that decision easily enough. The thought made her giddy. She giggled to herself. Thinking of the deed she had planned today made her uneasy, but this unplanned idea delighted her, and gave her energy. She didn't feel tired any longer, from the lack of sleep. She forced herself to be calm. She had a plan in place, and it wouldn't do to deviate from that plan. Once she had taken care of Patrick, she would have all the time in the world to manage Eliza. She would let the jubilant anticipation of that event inspire her this day.

Patrick wouldn't be home until later in the afternoon, and while the emotions stirred by the little cabin weren't conducive to sleep, they seemed to feed her waking energy. The longer she was awake, the more she was able to meditate on and marshal her wild thoughts. She knew that she must be focused for what was to come. She kept the oil lamp lit, because she found that staring into the small flame was a good point to fixate on for her meditations. Any time she found her mind wandering away into idle wonderings, she would shift her concentration to the flame. She stared into it, and centered her mind on the things that mattered. The hatred for Patrick that she shared with Edmund. The vile debasement he had visited upon her, and also Margaret, ultimately ripping that man and woman away from each other. Jonathan, who had been equally ripped from her. Jonathan, her one true love, her fated soulmate.

She hadn't meant to fall asleep, at all, but her exhaustion must have overcome her, and she dozed off into a dreamless slumber. She came awake again suddenly, disoriented. She flailed her arms, and accidentally knocked the lamp. The delicate glass bowl broke and ignited, creating a liquid fire that spread across the floor. She screamed, disproportionately afraid due to her sleep addled brain. She didn't know how to extinguish the flames, and so she panicked. She grabbed her knife and ran out of the cabin. The sun was still high in the sky, and she was thankful that it wasn't too late. She staggered in the blinding light of day. Olivia looked back toward the cabin and saw the fire spreading. Her horse was still tied up nearby, grazing. She clumsily untied him, but he smelled the growing smoke, and was nervous. She tried to comfort him, but she was giddy and manic. The horse reared away from her, and once he was freed, he bolted off, into the woods. Olivia screamed in rage. Her hair was getting into her eyes, and it irritated her, exacerbating her fury. She spun around, disoriented by the increasing smoke, her damnable hair, and the excruciatingly bright sun. Screaming in her frustration, she ran into the woods.

Chapter 44

Mr. Davis was merry. So far, the day had been perfect for everyone. The mistress was as pleased as she could be, and her delight had spread to all those who had the joy of being in her presence. The guests should be arriving for the party shortly, and Mr. Stanton should be arriving with Mrs. Stanton at any moment. Never one for crowds of people, and feeling comfortable with his place outdoors, Mr. Davis was cheerfully trimming the hedges in the gardens, making sure everything would be impeccable for the fine guests to enjoy. He was whistling to himself when he happened to look up and see a thin stream of smoke slither up beyond the trees.

Worried, he dashed off toward the stables. He was an older man, but years of working with his hands and on his feet had made him spry. He could run, though it still took some time to make his way to the top of the hill that overlooked the stables. He was relieved to see the stables standing perfect and cheerful, lit by the afternoon sun. He could, from a distance, see Joshua appear at the stable door. If there was no fire in sight, not even a trash fire, so where was the smoke coming from? From his vantage point, Mr. Davis could only see the closest edge of the lake, but he looked in that direction, and saw the smoke still emerging steadily from the trees. He took a few more long strides, just as he saw Joshua start to cross toward the lake, and that was when he saw the little hunting cabin blazing. Flames were spewing from the windows and licking at the eaves, and smoke was increasingly vigorous, reaching up into the sky. Mr. Davis gasped, and then gasped again as he saw what looked like a ghost, but must surely be a woman, stumble out from the forest. She wore a white dress, and he could see dark hair streaming down her back, but there was no way he could see who she was. She stumbled toward Joshua, and the two seemed to embrace for a moment. From this distance, he didn't expect to hear anything the two said, but he heard Joshua cry out, and then fall to his knees. The woman looked down at him for a moment, screamed a high-pitched scream, and then turned and ran back into the woods.

Mr. Davis immediately took off toward the downed man. By the time the older man got there, Joshua had pulled himself into a seated position, clamping his hand to his blood-stained shoulder, which was clearly badly wounded. "What happened?" Mr. Davis gasped.

"Some blazing lunatic came ripping out of the forest. When she sees me, she screams out, 'Patrick, you miserable stain, I will end you!' and then she charges at me with a knife. I guess I'm lucky she had bad aim, or I dodged enough for her to miss my heart, but she got me in the shoulder." He lifted his hand to inspect the growing bloodstain underneath before clapping it back down. "Then she pulls back and looks at me, says, 'you're not Patrick!' and then she screams, and then she runs away again. Ow, but this bloody hurts." Joshua's reply was a bit rambling, but thankfully it was coherent. He had lost some blood, and it still seemed to be oozing out, if the grow-ing stain was any indication, but he was still lucid.

Mr. Davis helped the boy up, "Dear, oh dear, this is dreadful. I wonder if the creature also set the cabin ablaze? Let's get you inside and get a look at that. You probably need a doctor."

The two men walked together, the injured man leaning slightly on his friend. Once inside the living quarters, which were thankfully bright and clean, if not overly spacious, Mr. Davis carefully cut Joshua's shirt away from the wound. "I'll have Mrs. Davis mend this right back up for you. It'll be good as new," he promised.

The stab wound was small, but deep. Finding a clean

cloth, Mr. Davis encouraged Joshua to keep pressure on it. It would cause the lad too much pain to try to mount a horse, let alone ride all the way up to the big house. The groundskeeper decided his only course of action was to leave Joshua alone and fetch help. He gave assurances that he would be quick as could be, and get help.

He quickly saddled and mounted a horse, sure that the time spent on the saddling would be more than made up by riding, rather than running. He was in excellent condition, but he'd already run quite a bit this day, and he may yet have more work ahead of him. He rode up the wide path that led to the carriage house, as it was the most expeditious route. Carriages lined the drive, and Mr. Davis cursed to himself. Clearly it was after four o'clock already, and the guests had begun to arrive! Well, there was nothing to help it. He must get assistance immediately. He ran into the house, calling for Jonathan and his wife the moment his foot hit the entryway. "Mr. Stanton! Mr. Stanton! Elsie!" Jonathan and Eliza were just emerging from their bedroom, having had the big surprise moment when they returned from their walk. They had just changed into their formal clothes.

They immediately saw the distress written on Mr. Davis' face, and their hearts froze. Something was clearly wrong. Eliza had been over the moon at the sight of all her friends, and those closest to her. Her elation was instantly dashed. Mrs. Davis joined them in the foyer, having heard her husband calling her name.

"Fire," Mr. Davis gasped. "The hunting cabin is on fire, and some crazed madwoman stabbed Joshua."

"What?" exclaimed Jonathan and Eliza in unison. Jonathan's voice was a roar, while Eliza's was barely a whisper.

Mr. Davis wheezed slightly from his exertions. "Someone has set fire to the little cabin," he repeated, "probably the same lunatic who came out of the woods screaming about someone named Patrick, that she was going to kill him. Well, she must have thought our Joshua was her man, because she lunged herself at him, and then stabbed him. I don't think it's fatal, but he's bleeding pretty badly, sir. I came quick as I could to get help."

The rest of the company had crowded into the foyer, having heard the servant's story clearly from the parlor, where they had been cheerfully waiting for the happy couple to re-join them.

"Mr. Davis, thank you. What happened to the woman?" It was the last critical piece of information Jonathan needed in order to devise a plan of action.

"From what Joshua said, she seemed to figure out that it wasn't Patrick she had stabbed, and ran back into the forest, sir, screaming like a banshee. I could hear her from all the way up on the hill."

Jonathan gathered his wits quickly and began to give orders. "Do you have a horse ready?" At a nod from the older man, he continued, "Good. Hurry and go fetch the doctor. Mrs. Davis, Molly, please go see to Joshua while we wait for the doctor. Bring the gin from the drawing room, and any medical supplies in the house. Please, hurry!" The ladies immediately set about their tasks, and Mr. Davis was already outside. Turning to the assembled company, he added, "Men, anyone who's willing, please come with me to check on the fire. The cabin probably isn't salvageable, but we need to make sure the forest doesn't catch and spread."

Brandon St. John stepped forward and spoke quietly, "Perhaps you should let me lead the others down to the lake. You may find it prudent to see if Patrick Johnson is in residence."

Jonathan saw the wisdom in his uncle's suggestion and nodded curtly. Finally, he turned to Eliza, who so recently had been so happy. "I'm so sorry, my love, but I must go. I'll return as soon as I possibly can. I love you."

'I love you," she responded with passion, nodding. Of course he must go. This was all outrageous. And clearly Patrick may yet be in danger. She was overwhelmed, but forced herself to be strong. Amy was at her side in an instant, and soon, as the other men filtered out and away toward the lake, and her sweet husband had departed in kind, the other women circled around her and they all urged her to move into the parlor. Someone found the sherry, and most of the women joined in having a small drink to settle their nerves. They had all been shaken by the news. Amy, for her part, was torn between wanting to be there for her friend, and wanting to join the men and servants who were heading rapidly in the direction of the lake and stables. But her fiercest loyalty lay with Eliza. Anyway, her mother, who was in attendance for the party, would surely protest. And so, all the ladies stayed in place, waiting for news or the doctor.

. . .

Brandon led the men to the most straightforward path, the one that cut from the kitchen garden across and to the hill at the top of the stables. It wasn't long before they came in sight of the cabin, and they were just slightly behind the two ladies who were rushing themselves to the quarters adjacent to the stable. The horses grazed in the fields nearby, unfazed. The men quick marched through the forest, making good time, but Jonathan's prediction had proved true. The building was clearly unsalvageable. But luckily for all, the surrounding trees seemed to be relatively untouched. A few low hanging leaves had succumbed to the heat, and looked rather wilted, but the fire hadn't spread, and no embers had flown. They took remedial steps to ensure that the fire would die down on its own.

. . .

Elsie Davis and Molly entered the quarters one after the other, calling out to Joshua that they were there. Molly gasped, covering her mouth in horror, at the bloody sight before them, but Mrs. Davis had clearly seen some wounds in her day. She marched up to the young man, told him to take a swig of the gin, and let her see his wound. "My husband has gone in search of the doctor, but it might be some time until they arrive. We should get you cleaned up. Molly? Here, help me cut the rest of his shirt away. The doctor will want it done anyway, and it'll be easier to clean him that way."

Molly flushed with crimson embarrassment at the amount of Joshua's tanned chest and shoulder that was already on display, but she put that aside, and did as Mrs. Davis had instructed. Joshua eyed her as she moved, his eyes growing dark, but he didn't say a word. Merely nodded in agreement. "That's good, dear. Now go fetch us some fresh water."

She did as she was told, and while she was briefly out of earshot the housekeeper whispered, "Don't toy with her, young man. She's a good and gentle girl."

Joshua looked hurt. "I would never. She's a delight. I happen to quite enjoy her company, is all."

"Well you see to it that that's all. If you want to visit her up at the house, I'll chaperone you myself, properly, but she won't be traipsing down here all on her own. There'll be no unsupervised 'company' in this household."

"You wound me, Mrs. Davis. Aren't I wounded enough for one day, already?" he teased. He had known Mrs. Davis for seven years now. He had come to the Stantons as a callow youth, and he'd grown into manhood under her watchful eye. She had begun to love him as a son, even though she didn't see him as much these days. She was terribly upset that he was injured, and teasing him about Molly was a good distraction for them both.

The young girl re-entered the cabin with the water, and Mrs. Davis warned the man that what needed to be done might hurt. She soaped up the cloth and gently washed at the bloody shoulder. Molly stood awkwardly watching, standing stiffly at attention in case her help was needed.

Mrs. Davis glanced in her direction. "Talk to him," she ordered. "Distract him from what I'm doing."

"Yes, ma'am," she stuttered, before launching into a somewhat, but not entirely, awkward conversation with the young man. The young, attractive man, she thought to herself.

. . .

Jonathan was able to borrow a phaeton from friends who had come from their country home. The light conveyance whisked him swiftly toward the Southland estate. He simultaneously prayed that Patrick would be in and that he wouldn't. He wished with all his might that he would not see Olivia. He was almost positive that she had been the wild woman who had stabbed Joshua. Who else could it have been? But why had she been at the cabin? And what possessed her to light it on fire? He was beyond perplexed, and anxious to get answers. He was equally anxious to be done with both Patrick and Olivia Johnson, for good.

Arriving at the estate, he pounded on the front door. He stopped short of screaming for Patrick. The door was answered by a solemn looking butler. "Is Mr. Johnson available?" Jonathan forced himself to be polite and sedate.

"Mr. Johnson has just arrived home from being away, sir. I don't think he's available to see visitors at the moment."

"Could you please tell him that Mr. Jonathan Stanton needs to see him immediately. It's about Mrs. Johnson. It's an urgent matter."

As Mrs. Johnson still had not returned to the estate, the butler was rather inclined to do as Jonathan asked, and admitted him to the foyer, with a request that he wait there. Jonathan paced the foyer anxiously.

Appearing at the top of the stairs, Patrick spoke with apparent surprise, "Jonathan, old boy, what a surprise to see you here. James said something about Olivia. Is she with you?"

"No, no she's not. Patrick..." Jonathan hesitated, not sure how to explain why he was there without causing immediate offense. "You know the old hunting cabin on the lake of my property?"

"Yes, I do."

"Well, someone set fire to it today. It was an old building, and to my knowledge no one was in it, thank God. But then, well, the strangest thing occurred. My stable man noticed the fire, but before he could respond, a woman came stumbling out of the forest. Apparently, she was screaming rather incoherently about someone named Patrick. She thought Joshua must be this Patrick fellow and she, well, she stabbed him. He's alive," Jonathan rushed to add, as Patrick's jaw dropped. "But he's badly wounded. And of course, you're the only Patrick anywhere near here, so I wondered if, possibly, the woman could be...someone you know?" He hedged, not wanting to so precisely point his finger at Patrick's wife.

"I need to sit down," Patrick exhaled. The color had drained from his face, and he was clearly distraught. He led Jonathan to the parlor, and without asking, poured two glasses of whiskey. Handing one to the other man, he downed his in one go, and then poured himself another. Two more shots and he was prepared to sit down and nurse one. "Olivia has been gone from the house since last night. There was an incident when we were in Paris where she seemed to lose her senses. It was as though she was a different woman, and she couldn't be reasoned with. She," he paused, searching for tact, "did things that suggested that she might want to hurt me. She did other things that suggested that she might want to hurt herself. But..." He buried his face in his hands, awkwardly because he was still holding his whiskey glass. "I thought things had gotten better! She took six weeks alone to sort through her thoughts, and to recuperate. When we reunited, I thought that she was back to her old self. She seemed so happy and light. And she was so excited about the prospect of moving to the country. I thought we were past all of that."

"Patrick, it's hard for me to tell you this, and I don't want to give you the wrong impression, but Mrs. Johnson, your wife, kissed me the night of the dinner party Eliza and I hosted, a few weeks ago," Jonathan was hesitant, and braced for every response but the one he got.

Patrick Johnson laughed. It was cynical laughter, but laughter, nonetheless. "That doesn't surprise me," he answered, "she's a woman who knows what she wants, and pursues it."

"You're not upset?" Jonathan was baffled.

"Upset? No. You would need to understand the relationship my wife and I have, but that is not the manner of thing that I find upsetting. Did she do aught else? Out of curiosity," he explained.

"Well..." Jonathan weighed his words carefully, "the following week, she paid me a visit wherein she suggested a more intimate dalliance between us. And she further suggested that Eliza might have left me for the Dudley boy."

"And did she?" Patrick asked mildly.

"Did she what?" he asked blankly.

"Did your wife leave you for the Dudley boy? Vincent, right?" he elaborated.

"No!" Jonathan was indignant. "No, she didn't." Returning to the more immediate topic at hand, "Patrick, do you think it might have been Olivia in the forest?"

The man shrugged noncommittally. "It's within the realm of possibility."

"Whoever it was has been described as a raving madwoman." Jonathan's tone was full of warning. "She intends to kill you, I do believe."

"She'd like to try," he answered smugly.

Just then, they heard a bang followed by a crash, and jumped up from their seats. Rushing into the foyer, they saw Olivia. Or a specter of Olivia. Her dress was torn and dirty, her hair was tangled and matted in places, falling down her back and in her face messily. Her eyes bloodshot, the sockets were sunken and shadowed. She had small scratches that oozed drops of blood where thorns must have grabbed at her arms. Small bits of forest debris clung to her hair and her hem. Her height just exacerbated the crazed look. In heels, she stood eye to eye with Jonathan, and only a few inches shy of Patrick. But now, she was half crouched in an offensive stance, arms bent and raised slightly, right hand gripping the now dirty knife in front of her.

Jonathan gasped, covering his mouth with his hand in shocked disgust. He fell back at the sight of the woman. Patrick adopted a vaguely menacing stance, a deranged grin appearing on his face. "Hello there, wife," he said testily. "You look as though you've had a rough day."

"I'll show you rough," she said, and she lunged at him, raising her weapon. He stood still, poised as though to accept her into a bear hug. Jonathan saw what she was doing and rushed to push her away, as Patrick appeared disinclined to try to stop her.

Olivia faltered a bit, missing her husband entirely, but grazing the length of Jonathan's right arm with the sharp little knife. He hissed and pulled back, cradling his injured arm. "Olivia!" he gasped.

She shrieked in horror. "What have I done? Oh, my beloved Jonathan, what have I done?" she wailed.

He stared at her in dazed wonder. She continued, regaining her stance with the knife, "I have to save you from this monster! We must be free of his vile, reprehensible presence forever. And then," she turned to Jonathan, madness making her eyes glassy and unfixed, "we can be together my love, just as fate has decreed. You and me, for eternity." Her voice had turned into a disturbing singsong, and she began circling Patrick, as a predator would circle his prey.

Patrick adopted a hurt expression, but stayed wary of the woman. "You don't want me anymore, my darling?" He was taunting her. "You didn't seem to find me vile and disgusting a few weekends ago."

"Pig. Despicable scoundrel. You'll pay for what you've done! You've ruined my life! You made Jonathan go away, and you'll pay for that!" Her voice wavered, hoarse and witchy, but she softened into a sickly, girlish soprano when she talked about Jonathan.

"Olivia, you must stop. This is insanity!" Jonathan tried valiantly.

"You'll see, my dearest," she said, as she turned her attention back to him. "I have to do this. It's for us. I'm doing it for us, so we can be together!"

Jonathan groaned, "Olivia, I'm a happily married man!"

Her rage found him and loosed itself. "NO!" she screamed, "You can't be happy with her! That's not how it's supposed to work. You're supposed to be mine. All mine. You were always supposed to be mine, until this buffoon made you go away." Her attention swung back to Patrick, who had begun to circle her in kind, taking on the role of the predator.

"Olivia," Jonathan was still attempting to reason with her, which at least served to amuse Patrick, "My mother died, that's why my father sent me away. It was grief. It had nothing to do with Patrick, and nothing to do with you."

"Oh, my poor dear." Olivia was using the revolting saccharine voice again. "That's just what you think." Her voice turned sinister and climbed in pitch as she spoke. "They lied to you. They've always been lying to you, the whole time!"

She cackled menacingly. Patrick determined that this would be a prudent time to intervene. Coming at her from the side, he tackled Olivia to the ground, knocking the knife out of her hand. She screamed and kicked at him, but he held her in place.

Jonathan sighed in relief, putting pressure on his wounded arm. The cut thankfully wasn't too deep, but he was glad that there was already a doctor on the way to his house. He was not in nearly as much need as Joshua probably was, but he'd appreciate the doctor's opinion, at least.

Patrick was snarling at the butler to fetch some rope and help him restrain Olivia. The two of them were still struggling on the floor. She was, at that precise moment, trying in vain to bite him. She turned her pleading eyes to Jonathan once more, "Please, help me, he's hurting me," she cried, switching to be the innocent victim in an instant. Both men were stunned at how her face shifted from its ugly mask of hate into the visage of a tearstained beauty who was being abused. Jonathan was terrified.

Thankfully, the butler returned with the rope expediently. He and Patrick managed to restrain Olivia with it, while she flung curses at them both, instantly reverting back to the murderous hellcat she had been moments previously.

Tactfully, Patrick put his hand to Jonathan's shoulder and gently but insistently walked him to the door. "Don't worry about Olivia showing up again," he said from the front porch. "There's a nice sanitarium in the city that will take good care of her."

Jonathan nodded numbly and stepped up into the sporty little phaeton. "Take care of her," was all he could think to say.

"I will," Patrick assured him. "I will," he repeated as he turned to walk back into his house.

Chapter 45

Jonathan arrived back at the house before anyone else had returned. He rushed in to find the ladies all sitting mostly silent in the parlor. Eliza dashed to him when she saw him. "Oh, my love, what happened? Tell us everything!"

The other ladies agreed with a chorus of "yes". He had left the whiskey untouched at the Johnson house, and he asked Amy to please be a dear and pour him a drink, and in exchange he would share his tale. She was quick to hand him a glass of his favorite bourbon. Eliza refused to let go of his arm, until she noticed the blood on it.

"You're bleeding!" she cried.

"A shallow cut, nothing serious. I'll have the doctor look at it after he's finished with Joshua. Is he here yet, by the way?" The bleeding had pretty much stopped by the time Jonathan had arrived home, and he was currently unconcerned about his wound. That didn't mean his wife would be the same, though.

"Not yet. Let me get you a towel. Come take your shirt off first, and let me clean you up, and then you will tell us what happened." Her voice was firm and brooked no argument. The other ladies understood, but hated having to wait any longer. Eliza marched her husband upstairs where he stripped his now torn coat and shirt, allowing her to wash the wound and put a temporary bandage on it. It was a long gash, running eight inches along the length of his forearm. But as he had suspected, it had clotted up nicely, being shallow enough. It was still oozing in a spot here or there, and he may yet have a faint scar from the encounter. Once he had put on a fresh shirt and jacket, and she had given him a very sound, almost punishing, kiss while clasping him close to her, they returned to the parlor.

He told the story of what happened with accuracy, only omitting the parts about Olivia's indecent behavior toward Jonathan. There was no reason that needed to enter the local gossip mill, and it would have embarrassed his wife. The gathered assembly was suitably impressed with the heroism of the two men in the tale, and they were satisfied that Patrick's wife had been restrained and would receive help. Conversation burst out in low murmurs, and everyone spoke at once.

"Wait until Mrs. Forester heard about the incident!"

"And setting the little cabin on fire!" It was still uncertain as to why or how that had happened.

"Surely that was an accident!"

"How can you be so sure? She wanted to kill her husband! Setting fire surely can't be out of the question."

"How do we know she was even at the cabin?" Whoever spoke sounded accusing.

"She was in the woods!"

"And who else would have started the fire?"

"Maybe it was an act of God."

"There was no storm. Fires don't just start on their own." Murmurs of agreement followed.

"Maybe it was a vagrant?" Some ladies were intent on absolving Olivia.

"Maybe Olivia was meeting someone there?"

"Maybe she had a lover…"

"Oh, don't say that!"

Jonathan personally found this unlikely, because for all the world, it seemed like Olivia blamed Patrick for her misery, and had played the victimized role of someone seeking revenge for having been wronged. In telling his story, he had also downplayed the apparent obsession Olivia had with himself, not wanting to seem boastful, and not wanting to further hurt his wife.

The other ladies continued to chatter and speak over one another, making conjectures and bemoaning the violence. Eliza was taking the story in stride, but she was clearly upset. She was frustrated and feeling helpless for having to stay home while others, including even Molly, had gone to do something productive. She was furious that Olivia had stabbed Joshua, and then the woman had further fought with Patrick and Jonathan. She thought the woman shameless and insane. She knew that there must be more to the story, but she didn't press her husband in front of their company.

The doctor arrived with Mr. Davis. He had already been given the briefest description of why he was needed, and Jonathan wasted no time directing him to the stables, though he did request that the doctor come and look at his own wound when he was finished with Joshua. Mr. Davis led the doctor back out. They were both on horseback, for the sake of speed, so they were able to ride right down to the stables. They found Joshua being well entertained and cared for by Mrs. Davis and Molly. The three had eased into a happy conversation together, and were even smiling when the other men entered. The doctor shooed everyone away to examine the boy's wound.

As they stepped out, they saw the men come out of the forest, looking a bit worse for wear. That was the housekeeper's cue to duck her head back inside and ask if their assistance might be needed, for there may be a need for them at the big house, with everyone heading back now. The doctor assured her that he would manage just fine, but that it might be best if Joshua spent the next few nights up at the main house, while he recovered. His mobility would be slightly hampered for a few days, at least. She nodded readily at that, and then shepherded Molly away, leaving her husband to help get the young man up to the house, when it was time.

The ladies arrived at the house shortly after the men. They all smelled of smoke, and had ash stains on their clothes, but they were upbeat, especially upon hearing that Olivia had been safely restrained, and wouldn't be showing up brandishing a knife any time soon. In the wake of that, they felt triumphant, having done solid work with their hands, to avoid the spread of the fire. The servants rushed to prepare wash basins for the men to clean up, which they slowly did. Some of them wanted to wear their stains for as long as possible, as badges of honor, but most were quick to clean up. Those who weren't were encouraged by the ladies to do so.

And so, after quite an unexpected and distasteful surprise, Eliza's birthday celebration was once again underway. After the adventures they had all had, all assembled were eager to eat, drink, and celebrate, for there was so much to be celebrated. They enjoyed the party well into the evening, punctuating it with music and dancing. Jonathan's arm was declared not to need stitches by the doctor, who had been invited to join the festivities. Mr. Davis and Joshua were similarly celebrated as heroes of the day, and Joshua bashfully made sure that Mrs. Davis and Molly received their due credit from all for their efforts in helping him.

After desserts had been eaten, many drinks poured, and many laughs had been shared, the company slowly departed. Brandon and Michael were the last to leave. Brandon embraced both Jonathan and Eliza, holding each one close. "You both must know how utterly elated I am that you have found love with each other. I know that it took some time, but you truly deserve each other, and you, together, are a pure joy to be near."

Michael, normally the quieter one of the pair, cleared his throat to speak, "Love is an action. It's something that you do for the people you care about most in the world. In doing so, you cannot purposefully hurt them. You may accidentally hurt them, but then you seek to make it better. The two of you have love, and together, with it, you may conquer anything."

The two men left shortly after that, and Eliza and Jonathan were left alone once more. He turned to her, his smile tinged with sadness, "I'm sorry your birthday was ruined."

"What on earth do you mean?" she replied. "My birthday was absolutely perfect. I have no doubt that I will remember this day for the rest of my life." She leaned up and kissed him gently. "Do not misjudge me, husband, I do not mean to say that every event of the day is one I would wish for, and certainly some I never wish to repeat. However, this is a day we will remember for the rest of our lives."

In lieu of another answer, he dipped his head and kissed his wife thoroughly. He followed through by lifting her gently, and carrying her to their bedroom. He laid her upon their bed, covering her in his sweet kisses, and proceeded to demonstrate his love in a more thorough, and exhilarating, fashion.

Chapter 46 - Epilogue

A year later, Jonathan and Eliza Stanton once again celebrated her birthday with a gathering of friends. This year, there was an additional guest in attendance. Margaret Ann Stanton had been born four months previously, and already had her mother's dark curls and charming smile. The parents beamed their pleasure with their baby girl, and all their guests cooed and smiled at her. She was a happy baby, and was already being treated like American royalty. Her mother was devoted to her, but her father worshipped her. He also routinely promised to give her many, many siblings to play with, when Eliza wasn't around to overhear.

The events of the previous year felt like a dream to all. The charred remains of the hunting cabin had been thoroughly razed, and the Stantons talked of building another building on the site, but were in no rush to achieve such a thing.

Olivia and Patrick Johnson had both disappeared from next door, and they were not missed by anyone. They hadn't moved back downtown, either. Nor anywhere in New York that anyone was aware of. It was supposed that she had been committed to the sanitarium in the city, while he had left for Boston, or perhaps Virginia, or maybe even returned to Europe, to escape the gossip. There were those who considered it a possibility that they had left town together, though (given her apparently murderous tendencies toward him) that seemed less likely. There were perhaps even one or two cynical people who thought that Olivia's outburst had been a coldly calculated ploy for attention, and she hadn't really been mad at all. Mrs. Johnson's wildly scandalous breakdown had been the talk of society for a few weeks, at least, until people tired of it, and when there was nothing new to say on the subject, the gossip moved on to more current salacious topics. The wheels of society churned on.

Just as Patrick and Olivia had disappeared, so had Edmund's journal. Jonathan had never known of its existence, and therefore never knew its contents. Given that said contents would have greatly upset him, one is left to hope that the journal was burned to a cinder. In fact, it's entirely possible that Olivia had brought it with her to the cabin that fateful August evening, and it had burned with all the rest. But as no one knew to ask her, the location of the journal remains a mystery.

The entire family and household were content and happy. Most especially happy were Jonathan and Eliza, who loved each other each day as if the love was at once new and bright, and also comfortable and timeless. She thrilled at his touch, and her smile warmed his soul. They were lovers for the ages, and enjoyed the feelings that poets and musicians canonize in poetry and songs. There was to be no doubt that they would survive life together, all of the highs and the very lows of it, because they had each other.

Made in the USA
Coppell, TX
02 April 2022

75925259R00184